# THE ADVENTURES OF
# BARRY & JOE

# THE ADVENTURES OF
# BARRY & JOE

## OBAMA AND BIDEN'S BROMANTIC BATTLE FOR THE SOUL OF AMERICA

## ADAM REID

DEY ST.

*An Imprint of* WILLIAM MORROW

FOR NELL, THEO, AND WYLIE.
FOR ALL MY FELLOW TIME TRAVELERS
ARRIVING IN THIS MOMENT.
AND FOR THE REAL BARACK OBAMA AND
JOE BIDEN, WHO SURELY DESERVE BETTER.
I CAN ONLY IMAGINE HOW AWKWARD IT
MUST FEEL TO BE DRAWN NAKED SO MANY
TIMES IN A SINGLE PUBLICATION.

# TABLE OF ALTERNATE REALITIES

# DEEP FAKE

# NOTE BY

# JOE BIDEN

A FORGERY MADE
USING THE INTERNET AND
ADOBE PHOTOSHOP

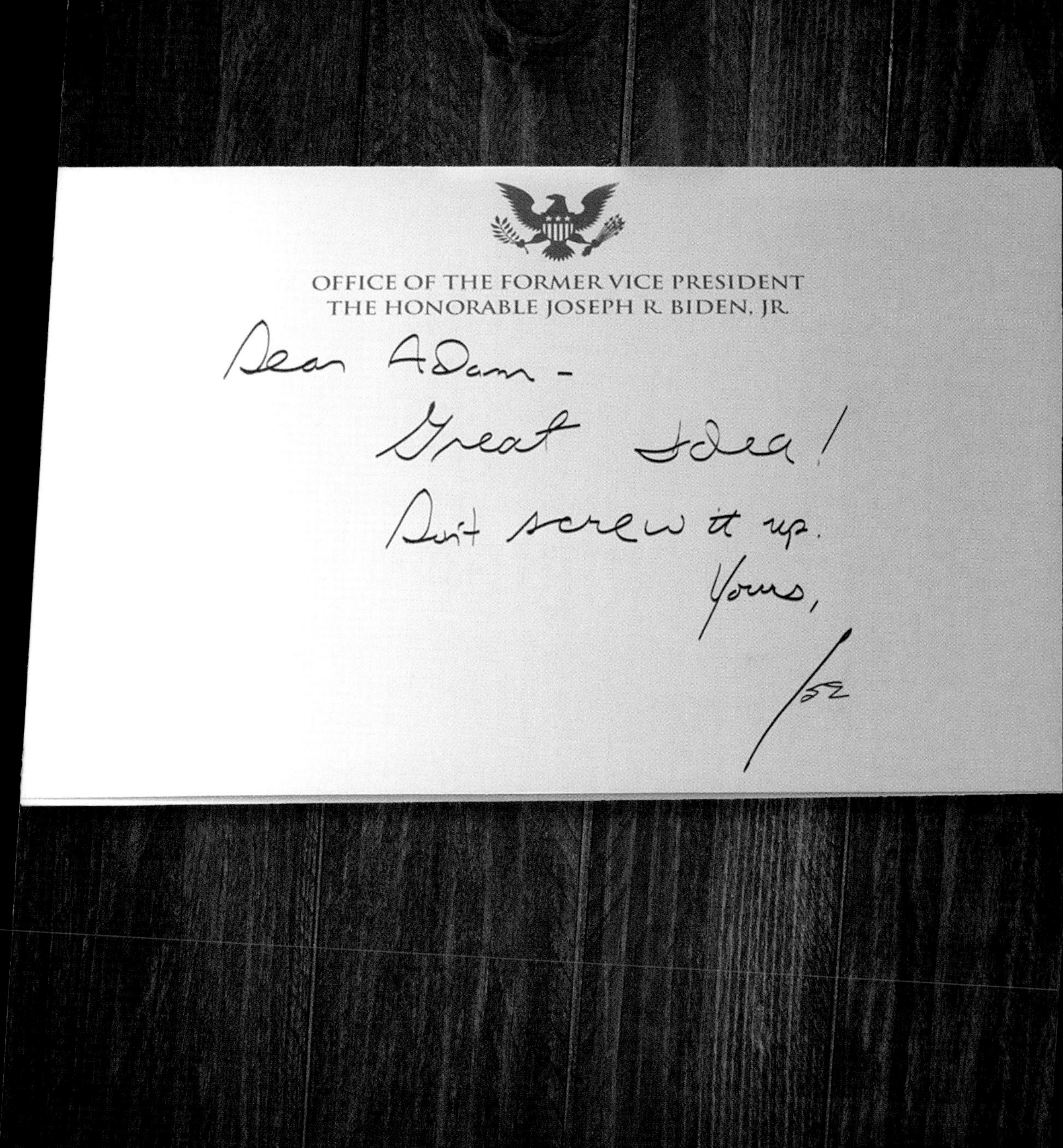
OFFICE OF THE FORMER VICE PRESIDENT
THE HONORABLE JOSEPH R. BIDEN, JR.

Dear Adam -

Great Idea!

Don't screw it up.

Yours,

Joe

# NO TIME LIKE THE PRESENT

PRETENTIOUS TEMPORAL
ANECDOTES FROM
THE AUTHOR

I t's 1989 and I'm twelve years old.

My parents are fighting, and I want to be in any other reality than the one I'm in.

I flip the giant metal television remote in my hands like a Benihana chef. This trick has become my superpower. I enjoy the weight of the remote as it leaves my thumb, twirls in the air fully twice, and then smacks back into my palm again. I do this a hundred times in a row.

*Quantum Leap* finally comes on the television. I love this show.

# YO HO

The Pirates of the Caribbean ride at Disneyland was the last attraction designed by Walt Disney. He died three months before it opened in 1967.

I have been acutely aware of time for as far back as I can remember. As early as six, I knew that in a blink I would be forty and yet still very much myself. I was wistful about it even then.

The first real-world wormhole I discovered was inside the Pirates of the Caribbean ride. No joke. Growing up in San Diego, I was very lucky that once every year or two I would end up at Disneyland. Long before there were any movies, Pirates of the Caribbean was just a cool pirate ride.

Wormholes like this one are personal. What's required are conditions that never change. You need a place you can always come back to. What makes the Pirates of the Caribbean ride ideal is that for the better part of my life, until animatronic Johnny Depp arrived, it has remained exactly the same.

Whenever I ride it, the same thing happens. I finally make it to the front of the line and into a boat. The air is damp and a sense memory all its own. The smell is something I wish I could bottle. The adventure starts slow, as the boat ride begins in the bayou at night, and I can hear the slow twang of a banjo being plucked and see the lifelike fireflies floating above the water. The beginning of this ride is the most magical to me, for it is precisely when I arrive into this self-contained continuum, with all the versions of ME that have come here before and all the versions of myself that will return later.

"FLASH!" I say to myself. And I'm in the wormhole. It's so reliable. We splash down the first fall and the merry pirate song begins. All the time and living and growing I've done in between visits vanishes in a blink and there is only me, at every age, here in my personal pirate continuum. I am that little boy saying hello to my future selves. We all ride together in the boat. And for fifteen minutes, since Pirates of the Caribbean is a beautifully long ride, we all hold hands and existentially freak out together. It breaks my heart every time.

The little boy says hello to the middle-aged me, and here I am on the other side, startled to hear him so clearly. This temporal effect is something that I have long been obsessed with. Can time truly bend to connect our younger and older selves? Can that connection change the trajectory of our lives?

# HOPE ON A STICK

It's November 4, 2008, and I'm thirty-one years old.

I'm madly in love. I've been married for exactly one month and a day. Nell and I have just come back from our honeymoon in Hawaii. I'm doing my flipping-the-plastic-TV-remote-and-catching-it thing. The news is on. It's been on all year.

There is something in the air. And then it happens. The hair on my neck stands up and goose bumps shoot down my arm. It feels like a miracle. Barack Obama has won the presidency.

I'm prouder to be an American than I ever thought possible.

# THE PENDULUM

This orange clown.

It's November 9, 2016, and I wake up early to find our worst election fears have been realized overnight. When Nell and I went to bed it was looking grim. The *New York Times*'s front page on my phone is a haymaker. The reality star has been elected president.

I'm thirty-nine years old and father to two little boys named Theo and Wylie. I wish I wasn't about to get on an airplane and leave my family for

Chicago. It is early enough that both boys are still sleeping. I don't wake them, even though I want to. I kiss Nell goodbye.

I'm emotionally hungover. I get into a cab and head for the airport. New York City looks like a morgue. Everyone is walking down the street in slow motion. The sun is out, but it feels like the cloudiest, gloomiest day of the year.

How did this happen?

If only we could go back and set things right.

The morning after Trump is elected, I have a crazy idea, inspired, no doubt, by a childhood spent in front of the television trying to escape reality. I jot it down in the Notes app on my phone at the airport.

# STRANGE DAYS

If you're like me, you're more than a bit concerned about the fate of our country, our planet, and humanity itself. I know we need all-new heroes to step in and stand up for what's right, but I can't help but intensely miss Barack Obama and Joe Biden.

I'd been holding back from developing *The Adventures of Barry & Joe* out of fear that it was too weird, too deeply silly, too pathetically nostalgic, too ridiculous to be a thing. But then the reality of Trump happened; he was sworn into office and everything he has said and done since then has turned our fears into reality. This is an actual nightmare, and not just an overblown reaction. But this book isn't about the villains. As America finds itself confronting the darkest aspects of its own history, *The Adventures of Barry & Joe* is about working together to save the future.

*The Adventures of Barry & Joe* is my attempt to combine the things I loved growing up with the themes I care about most right now. It also turns Joe Biden into a robot dog and Obama into Rambama at one point. So, you know, there's a little something for everyone.

So come with me! Take my hand! Let us escape together into the kind of brotherly love, integrity, and humanity that has become all too rare these days. I promise to return your mind in *mostly* the same condition that I found it, though maybe a click less clear about quantum mechanics.

THE PAST,
LIKE THE FUTURE,
IS INDEFINITE AND EXISTS
ONLY AS A SPECTRUM
OF POSSIBILITIES.

–STEPHEN HAWKING

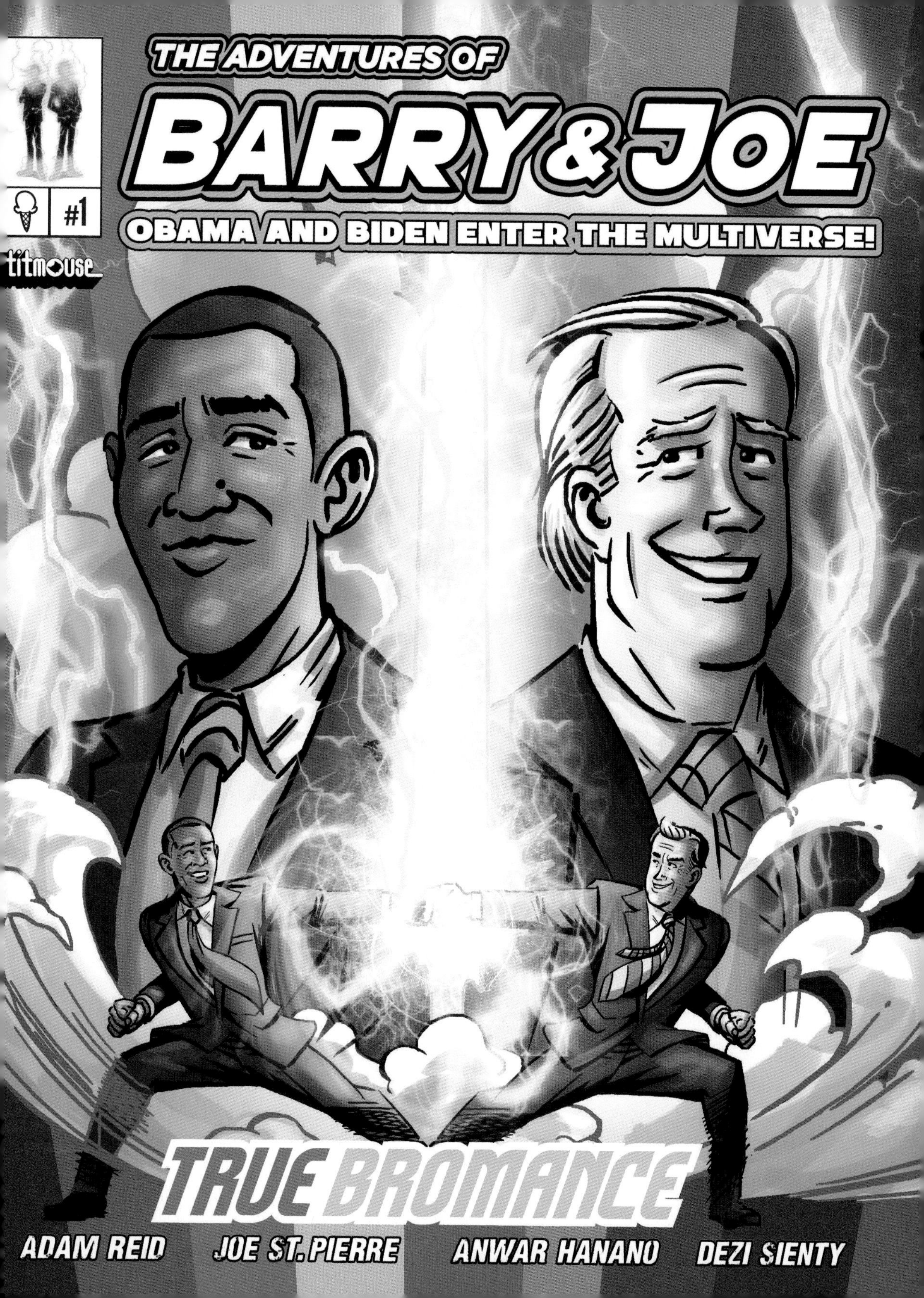
THE ADVENTURES OF
BARRY & JOE
#1
titmouse
OBAMA AND BIDEN ENTER THE MULTIVERSE!
TRUE BROMANCE
ADAM REID
JOE ST. PIERRE
ANWAR HANANO
DEZI SIENTY

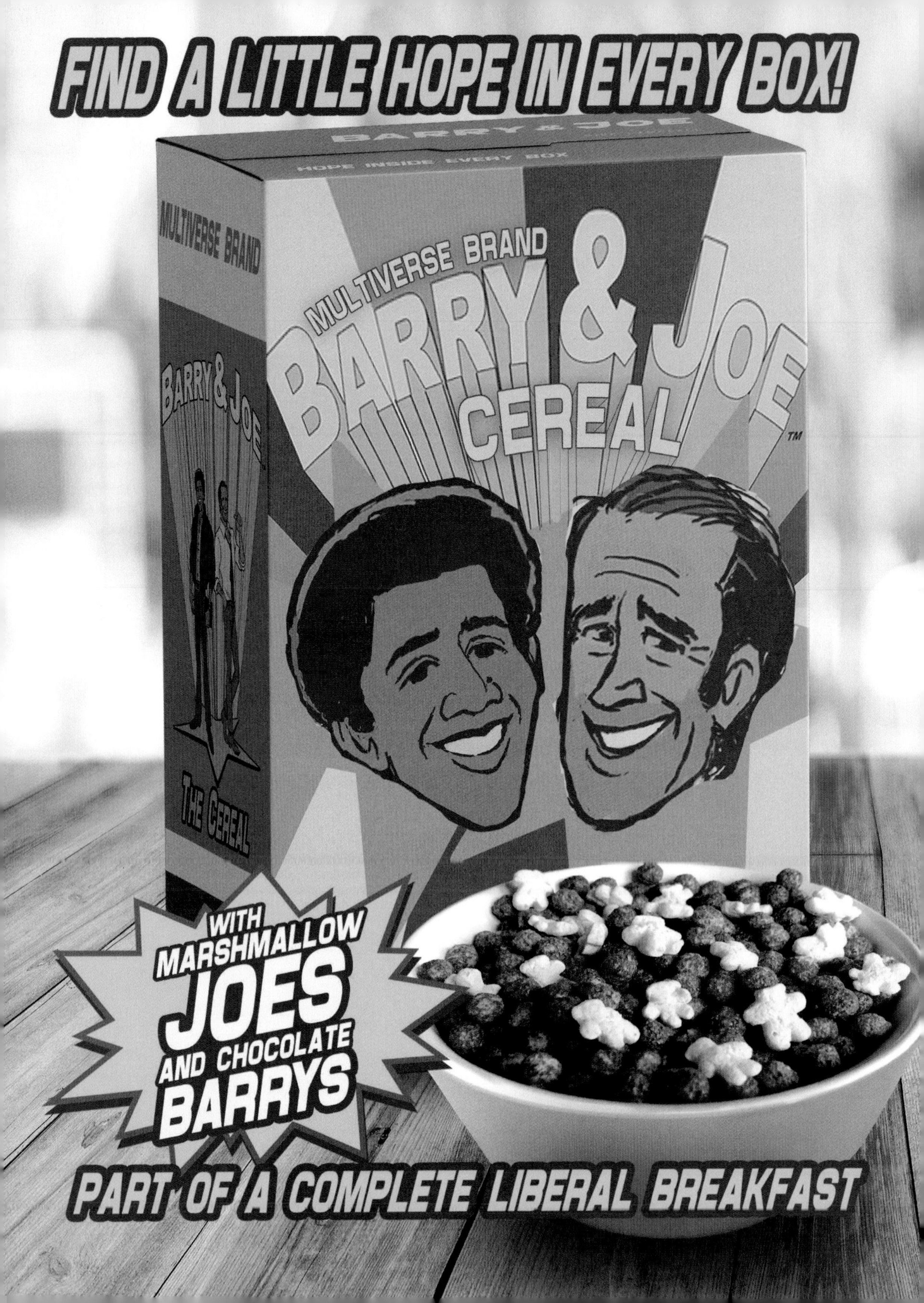

FIND A LITTLE HOPE IN EVERY BOX!
BARRY & JOE
HOPE INSIDE EVERY BOX
MULTIVERSE BRAND
MULTIVERSE BRAND
BARRY & JOE
CEREAL
TM
BARRY & JOE
THE CEREAL
WITH MARSHMALLOW JOES AND CHOCOLATE BARRYS
PART OF A COMPLETE LIBERAL BREAKFAST

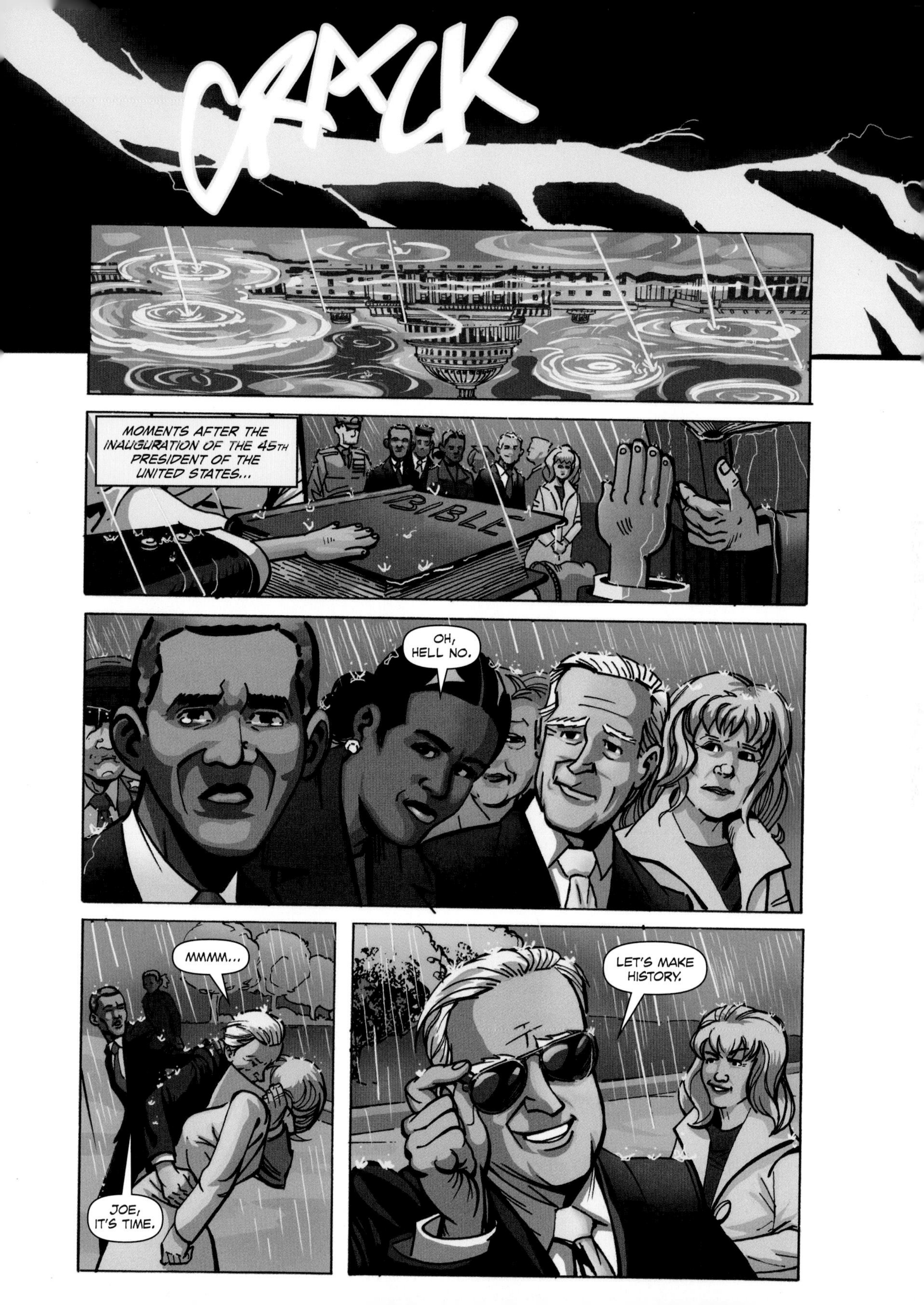
CRACK
MOMENTS AFTER THE INAUGURATION OF THE 45TH PRESIDENT OF THE UNITED STATES...
BIBLE
OH, HELL NO.
MMMM...
JOE, IT'S TIME.
LET'S MAKE HISTORY.

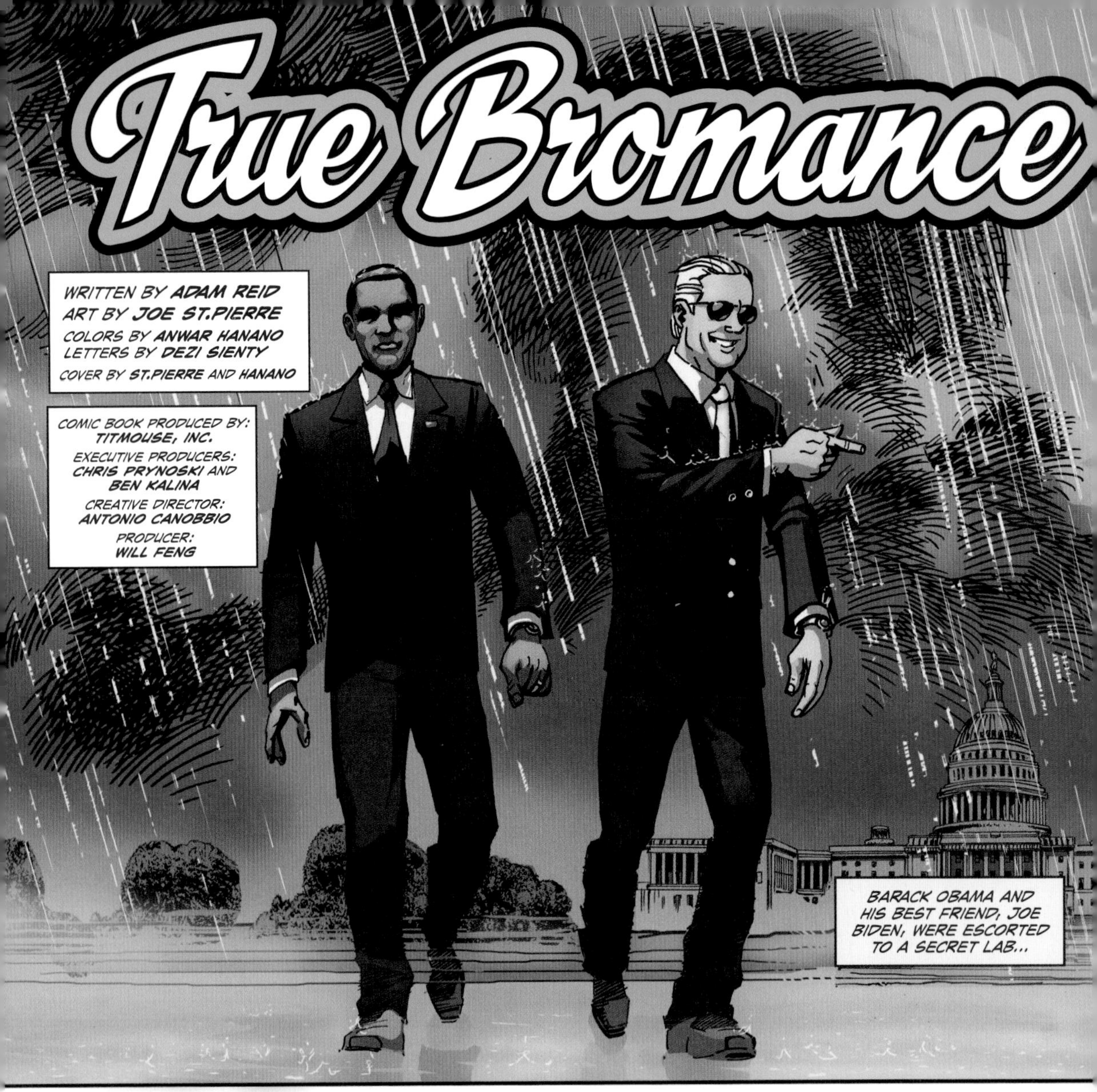
True Bromance
WRITTEN BY ADAM REID
ART BY JOE ST.PIERRE
COLORS BY ANWAR HANANO
LETTERS BY DEZI SIENTY
COVER BY ST.PIERRE AND HANANO
COMIC BOOK PRODUCED BY: TITMOUSE, INC.
EXECUTIVE PRODUCERS: CHRIS PRYNOSKI AND BEN KALINA
CREATIVE DIRECTOR: ANTONIO CANOBBIO
PRODUCER: WILL FENG
BARACK OBAMA AND HIS BEST FRIEND, JOE BIDEN, WERE ESCORTED TO A SECRET LAB...

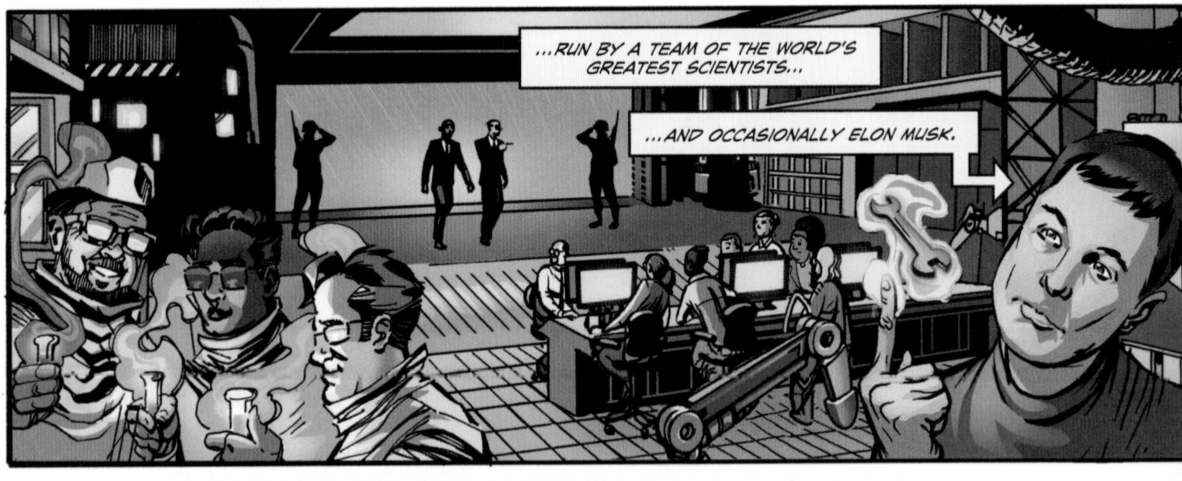
...RUN BY A TEAM OF THE WORLD'S GREATEST SCIENTISTS...
...AND OCCASIONALLY ELON MUSK.

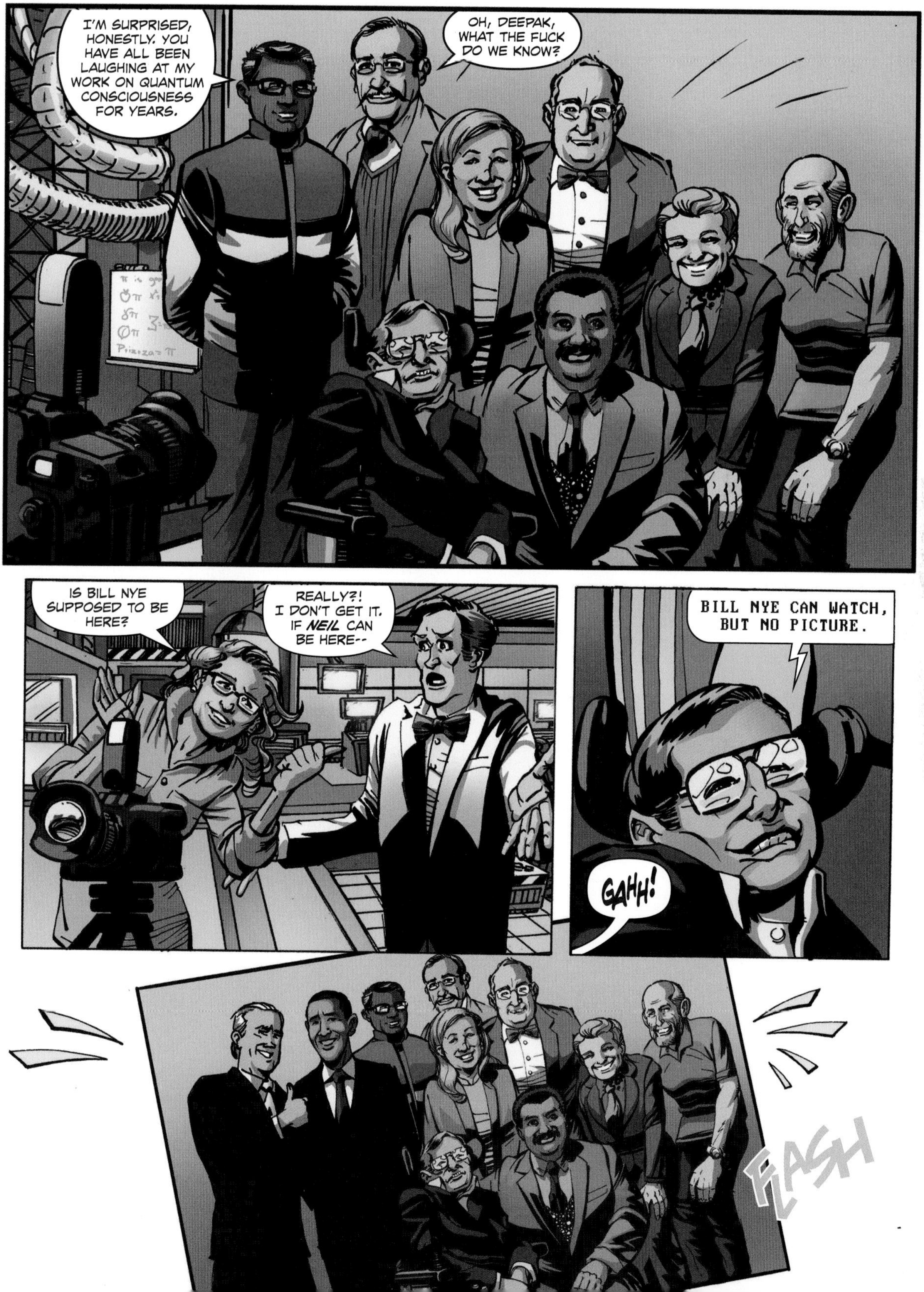
I'M SURPRISED, HONESTLY. YOU HAVE ALL BEEN LAUGHING AT MY WORK ON QUANTUM CONSCIOUSNESS FOR YEARS.
OH, DEEPAK, WHAT THE FUCK DO WE KNOW?
IS BILL NYE SUPPOSED TO BE HERE?
REALLY?! I DON'T GET IT. IF NEIL CAN BE HERE--
BILL NYE CAN WATCH, BUT NO PICTURE.
GAHH!
FLASH

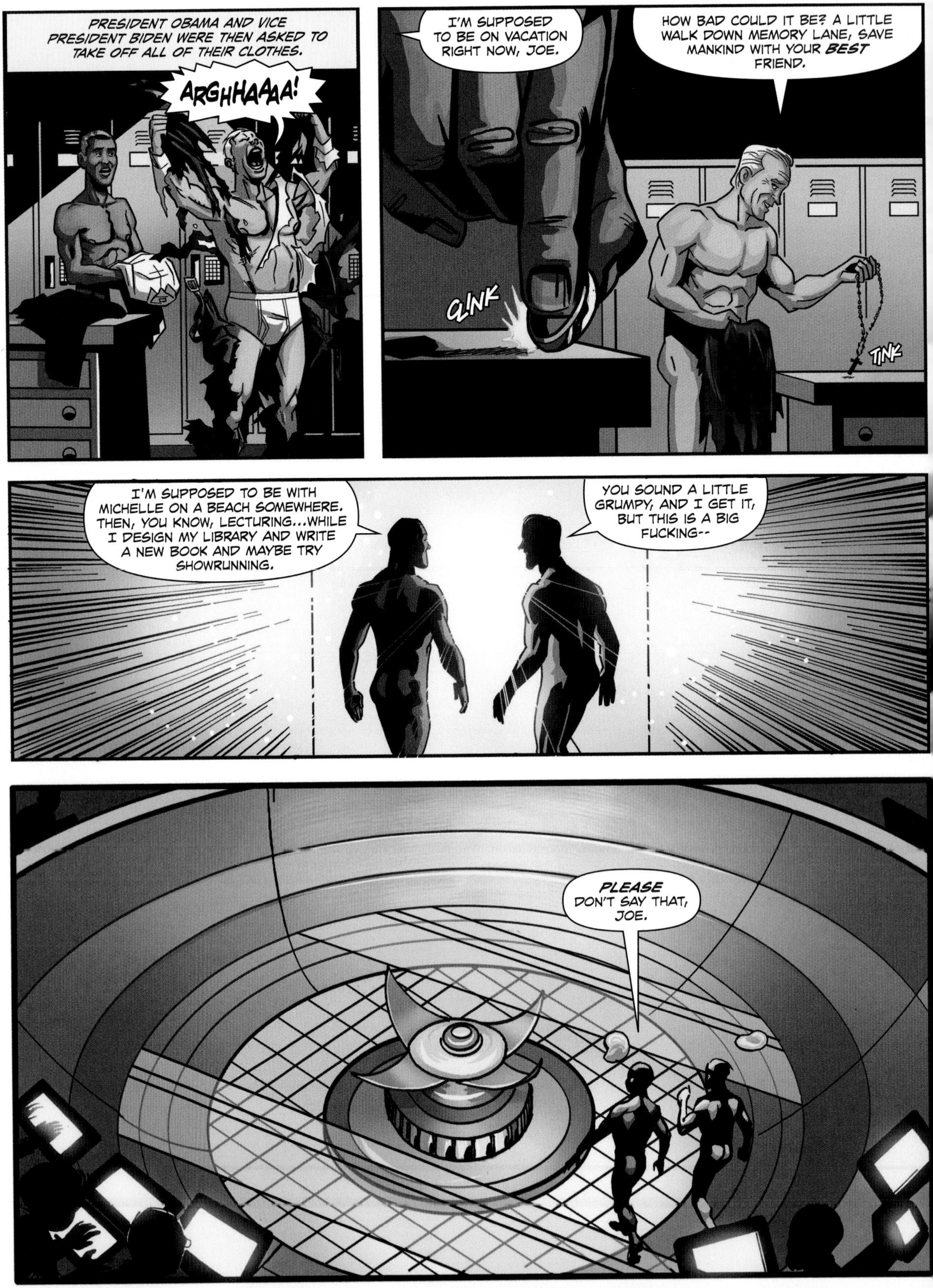
PRESIDENT OBAMA AND VICE PRESIDENT BIDEN WERE THEN ASKED TO TAKE OFF ALL OF THEIR CLOTHES.
ARGHHAAAA!
I'M SUPPOSED TO BE ON VACATION RIGHT NOW, JOE.
HOW BAD COULD IT BE? A LITTLE WALK DOWN MEMORY LANE, SAVE MANKIND WITH YOUR BEST FRIEND.
CLINK
TINK
I'M SUPPOSED TO BE WITH MICHELLE ON A BEACH SOMEWHERE. THEN, YOU KNOW, LECTURING...WHILE I DESIGN MY LIBRARY AND WRITE A NEW BOOK AND MAYBE TRY SHOWRUNNING.
YOU SOUND A LITTLE GRUMPY, AND I GET IT, BUT THIS IS A BIG FUCKING--
PLEASE DON'T SAY THAT, JOE.

SORRY IT'S COLD. THE RECOHERENCE ENGINE IS TEMPERATURE SENSITIVE.

BONG

SYSTEM CHECK. A.I. ROLE CALL. SIRI?

HERE.

I AM ALSO HERE, NEIL.

IBM'S WATSON?

ALEXA, ORDER MORE FRESCA AND PLAY "ALSO SPRACH ZARATHUSTRA."

OKAY!

BEFORE WE POTENTIALLY TEAR THE UNIVERSE A NEW ONE, I'D LIKE TO SAY A SHORT PRAYER.

JOE--

SUPER SHORT, I GOT THIS.

FOR THE FIRST TIME...IN THE HISTORY OF THE PLANET, A SPECIES HAS THE TECHNOLOGY...TO PREVENT ITS OWN EXTINCTION.

THE HUMAN THIRST FOR EXCELLENCE, KNOWLEDGE, EVERY STEP UP THE LADDER OF SCIENCE, EVERY ADVENTUROUS REACH INTO SPACE...

...ALL OF OUR COMBINED MODERN TECHNOLOGIES AND IMAGINATIONS--

JOE, THAT SPEECH IS FROM *ARMAGEDDON*.

*DAMMIT!* I THOUGHT IT FELT FAMILIAR.

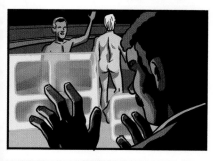

HUMMMMMMMM!

CLICK

WHIRRRRR

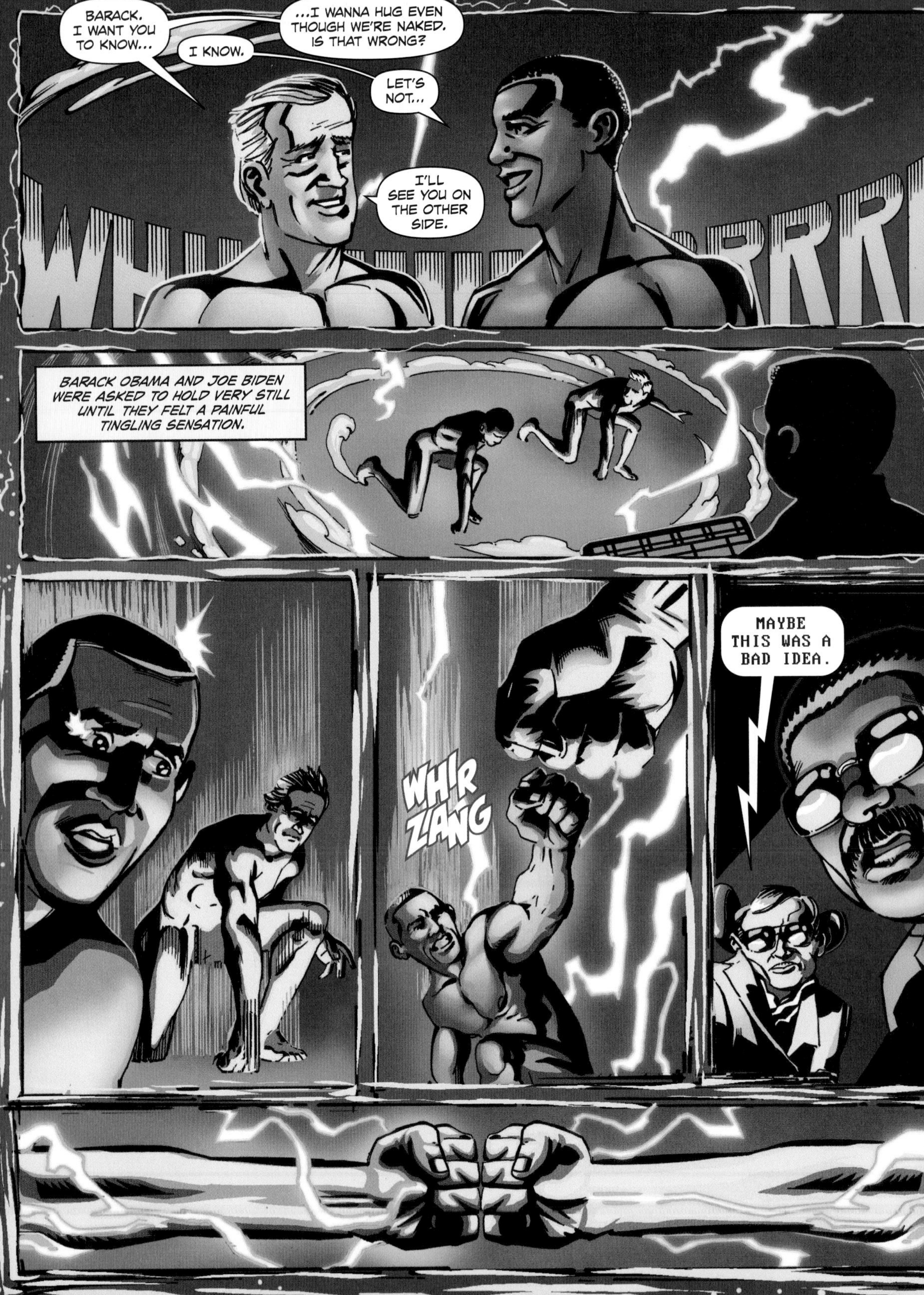
BARACK. I WANT YOU TO KNOW...
I KNOW.
...I WANNA HUG EVEN THOUGH WE'RE NAKED. IS THAT WRONG?
LET'S NOT...
I'LL SEE YOU ON THE OTHER SIDE.
BARACK OBAMA AND JOE BIDEN WERE ASKED TO HOLD VERY STILL UNTIL THEY FELT A PAINFUL TINGLING SENSATION.
WHIR ZANG
MAYBE THIS WAS A BAD IDEA.

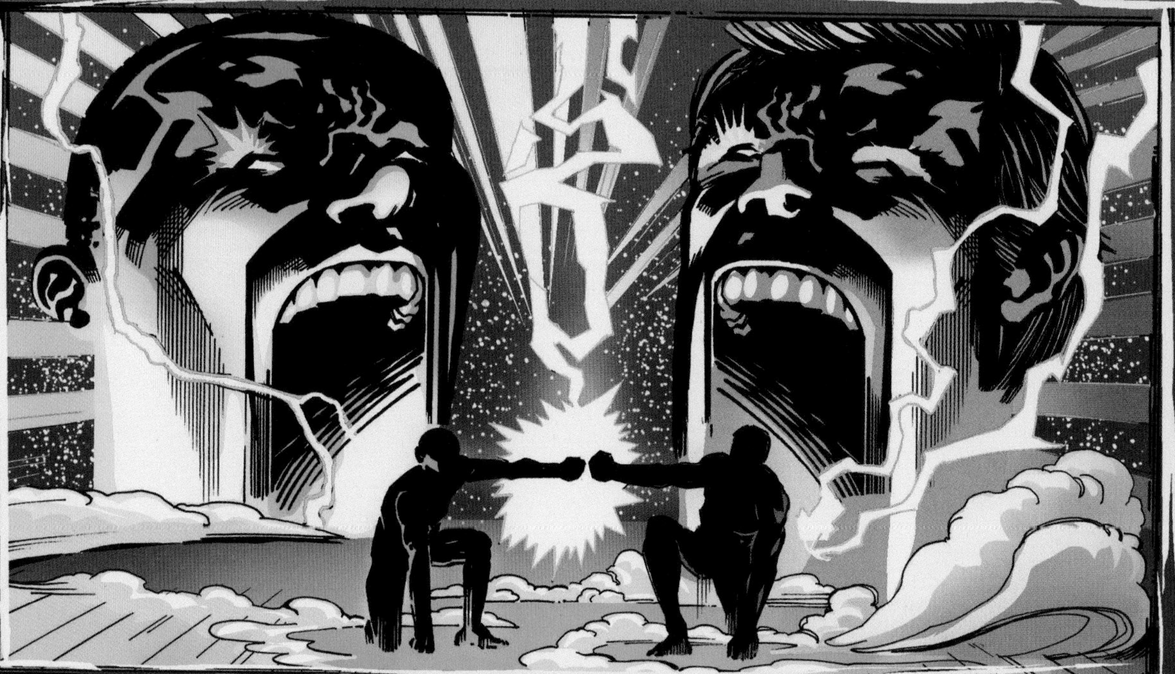

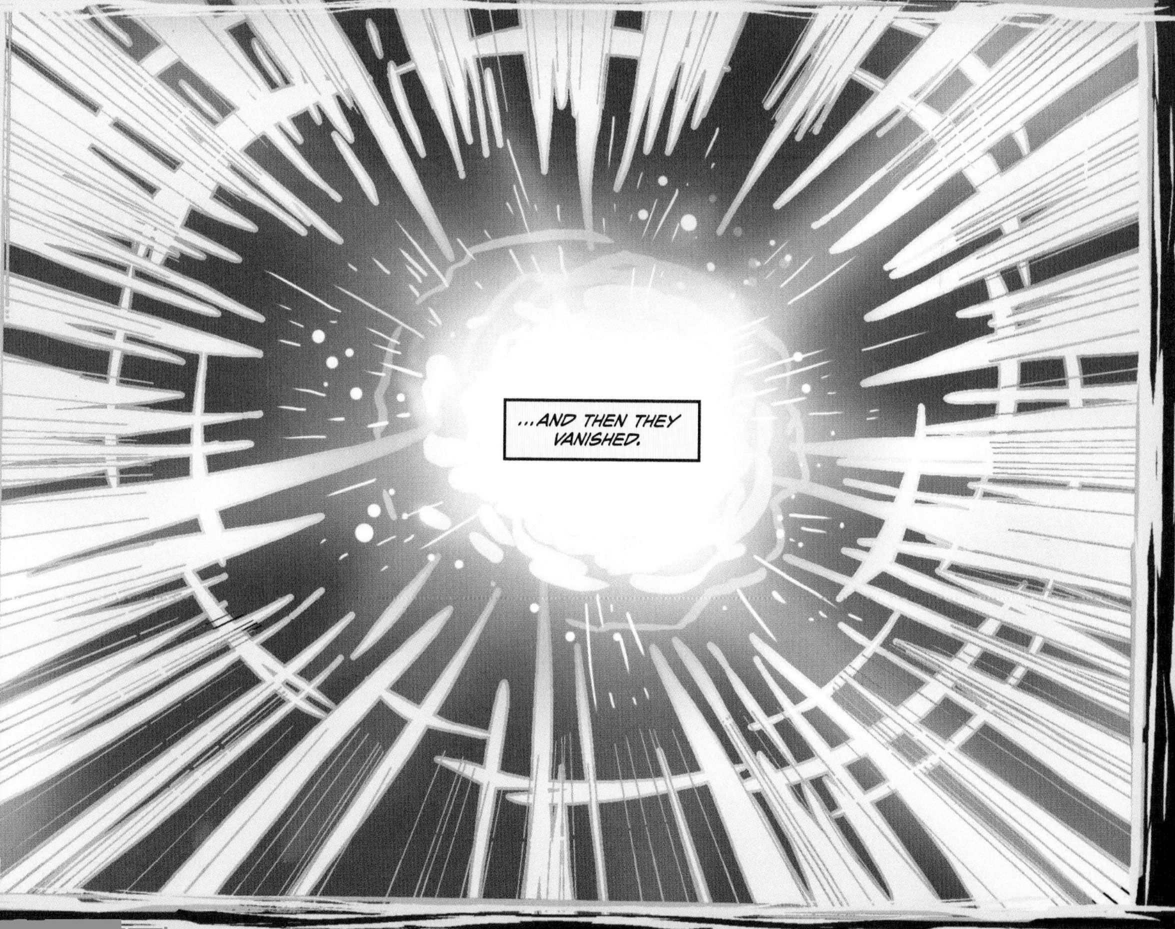
...AND THEN THEY VANISHED.

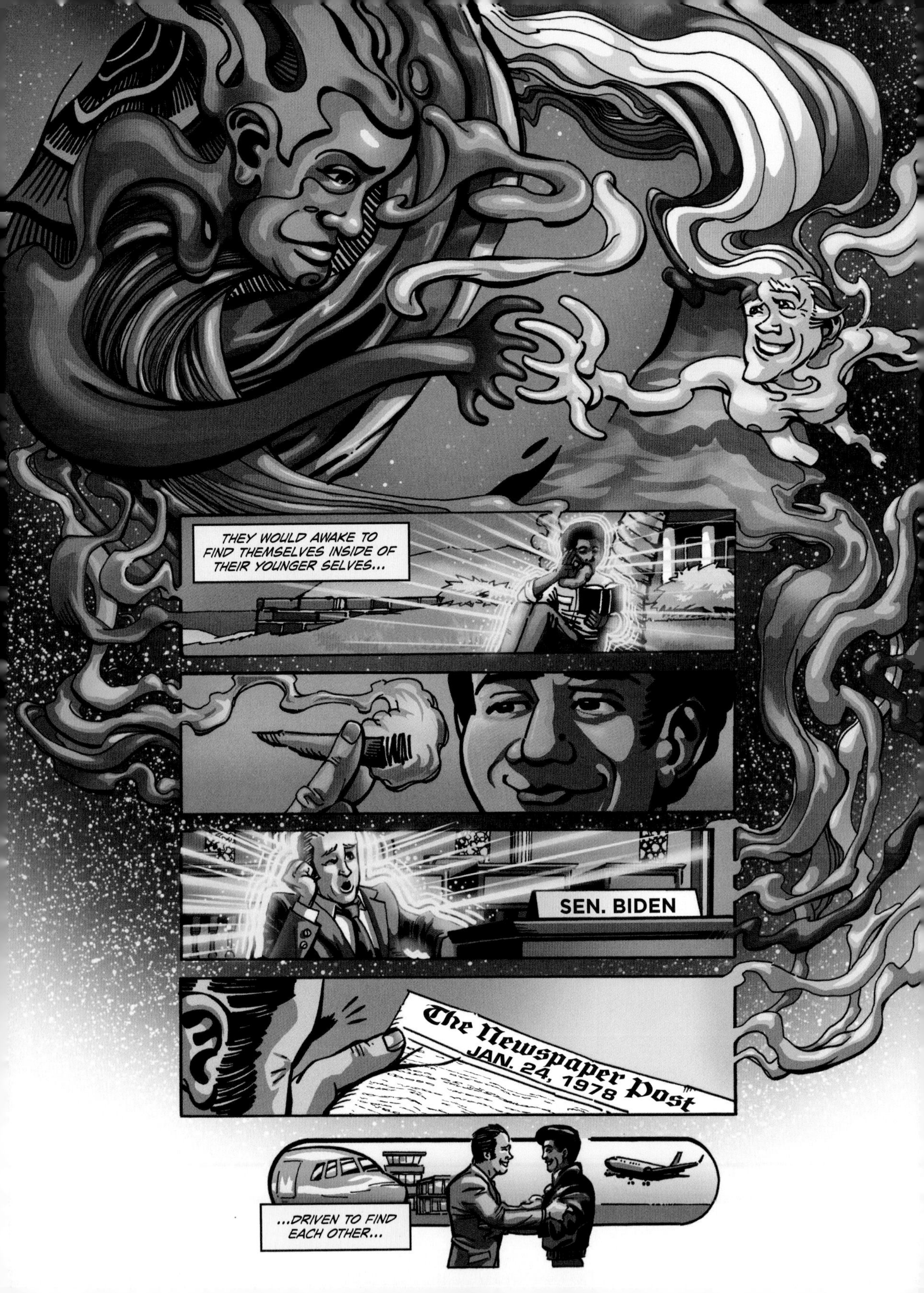
THEY WOULD AWAKE TO FIND THEMSELVES INSIDE OF THEIR YOUNGER SELVES...
SEN. BIDEN
The Newspaper Post
JAN. 24, 1978
...DRIVEN TO FIND EACH OTHER...

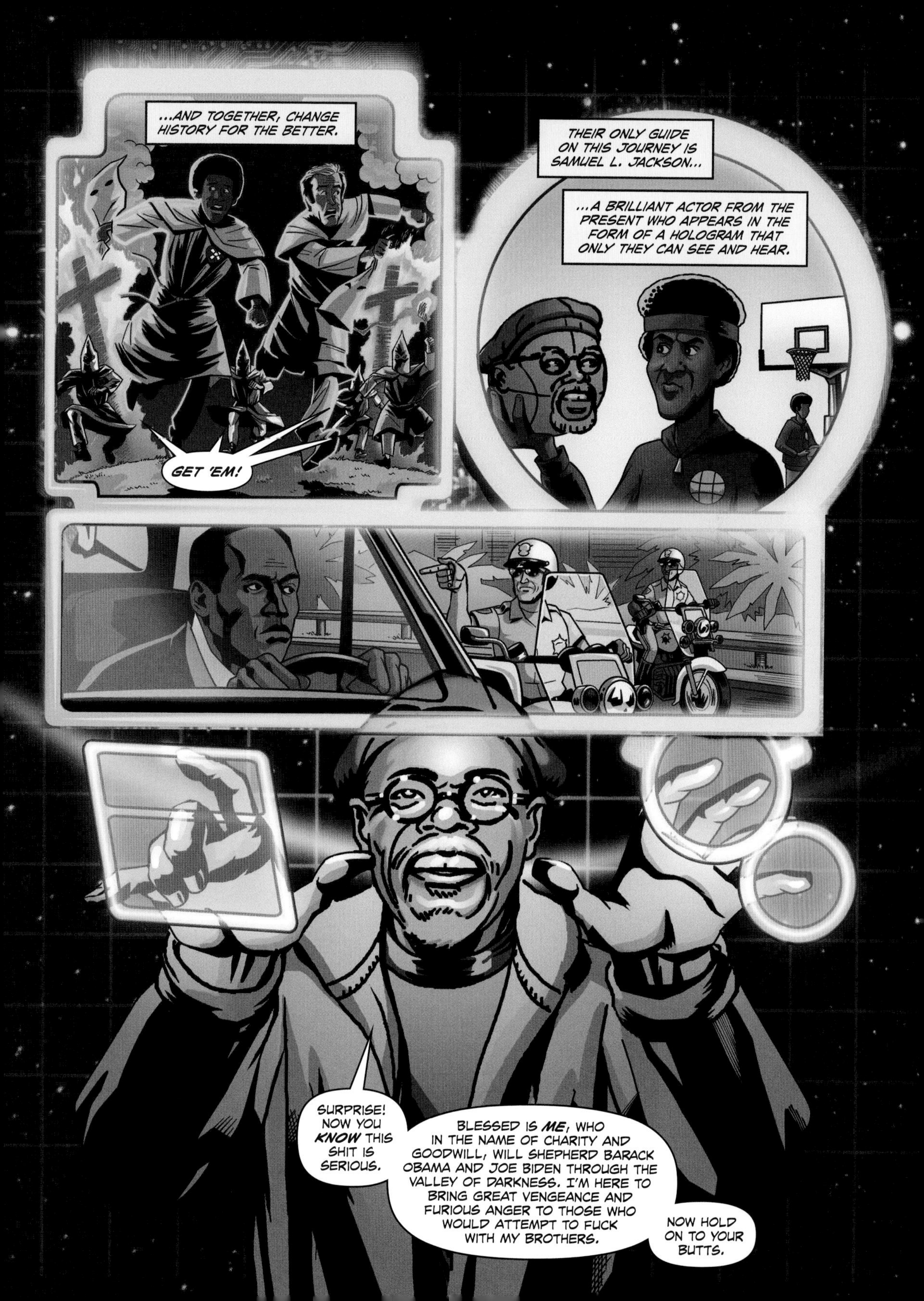
...AND TOGETHER, CHANGE HISTORY FOR THE BETTER.
GET 'EM!
THEIR ONLY GUIDE ON THIS JOURNEY IS SAMUEL L. JACKSON...
...A BRILLIANT ACTOR FROM THE PRESENT WHO APPEARS IN THE FORM OF A HOLOGRAM THAT ONLY THEY CAN SEE AND HEAR.
SURPRISE! NOW YOU KNOW THIS SHIT IS SERIOUS.
BLESSED IS ME, WHO IN THE NAME OF CHARITY AND GOODWILL, WILL SHEPHERD BARACK OBAMA AND JOE BIDEN THROUGH THE VALLEY OF DARKNESS. I'M HERE TO BRING GREAT VENGEANCE AND FURIOUS ANGER TO THOSE WHO WOULD ATTEMPT TO FUCK WITH MY BROTHERS.
NOW HOLD ON TO YOUR BUTTS.

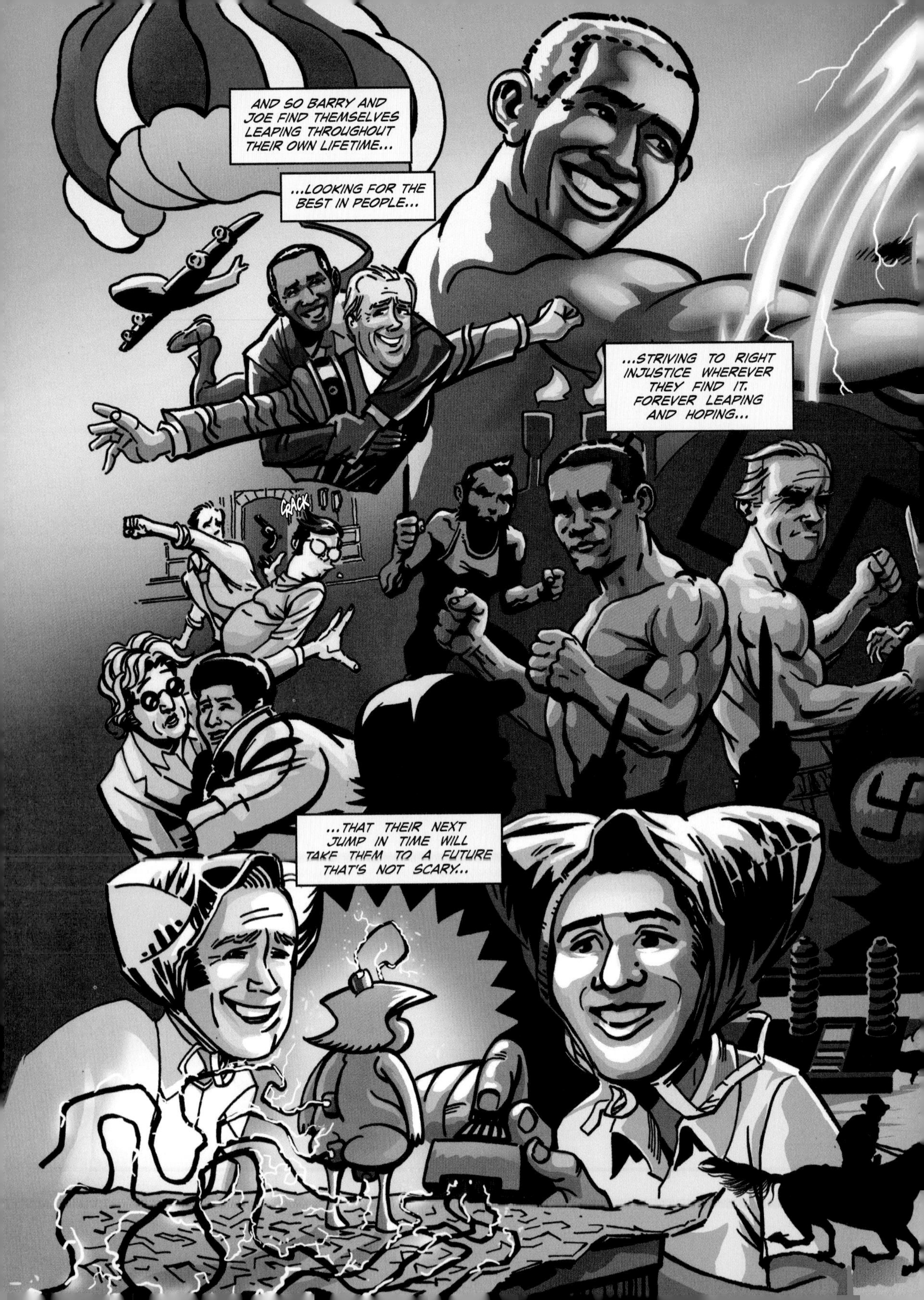
AND SO BARRY AND JOE FIND THEMSELVES LEAPING THROUGHOUT THEIR OWN LIFETIME...
...LOOKING FOR THE BEST IN PEOPLE...
...STRIVING TO RIGHT INJUSTICE WHEREVER THEY FIND IT. FOREVER LEAPING AND HOPING...
CRACK
...THAT THEIR NEXT JUMP IN TIME WILL TAKE THEM TO A FUTURE THAT'S NOT SCARY...

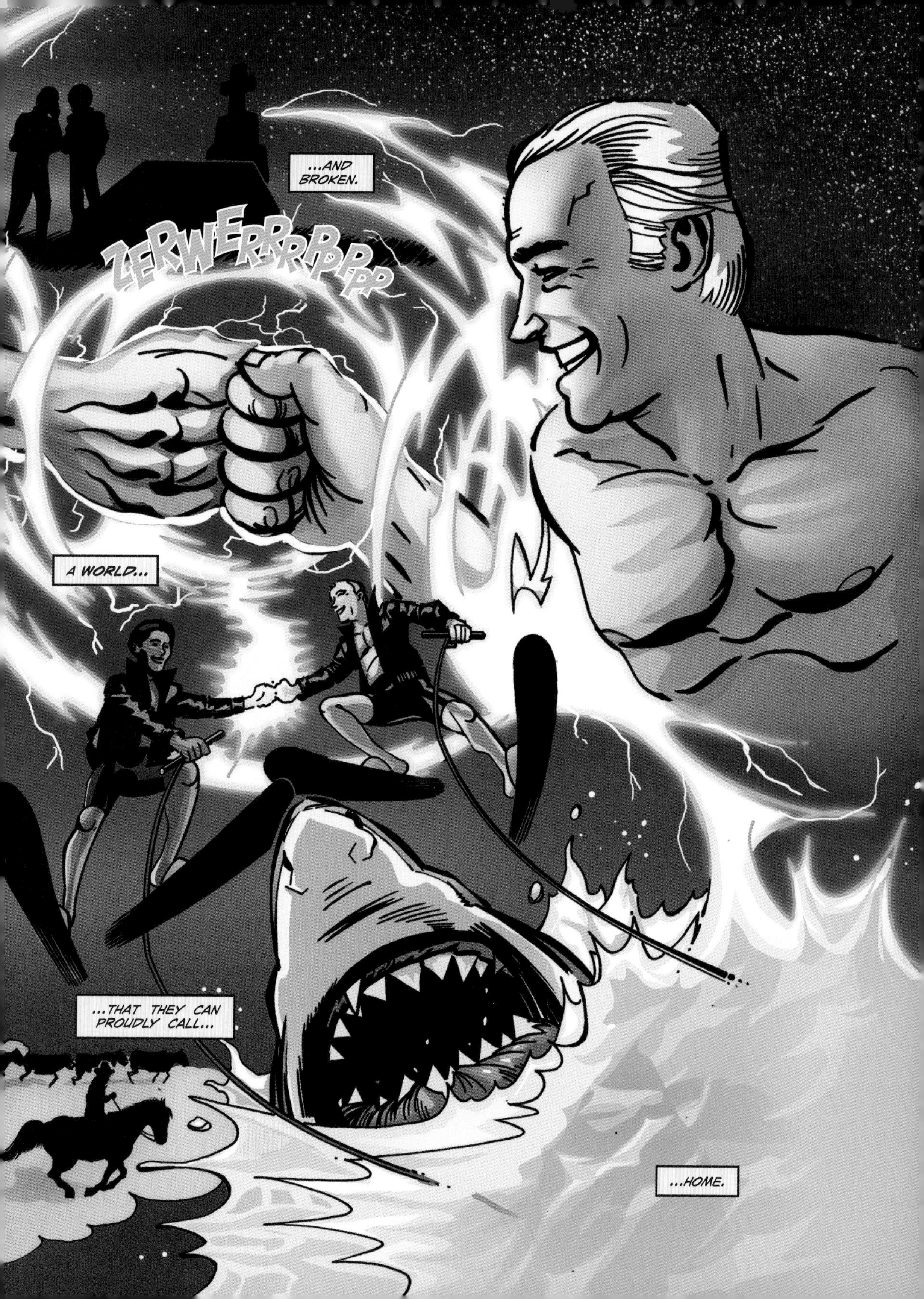
...AND BROKEN.
ZERWERRRRPPPPP
A WORLD...
...THAT THEY CAN PROUDLY CALL...
...HOME.

# ALL THE PRESIDENT'S ZEN

THE GUYS ARRIVE IN 1978,

FIND EACH OTHER, GET A BURGER,

AND MAKE A FEW DECISIONS

ABOUT WHAT REALITY THEY WANT

TO LIVE IN

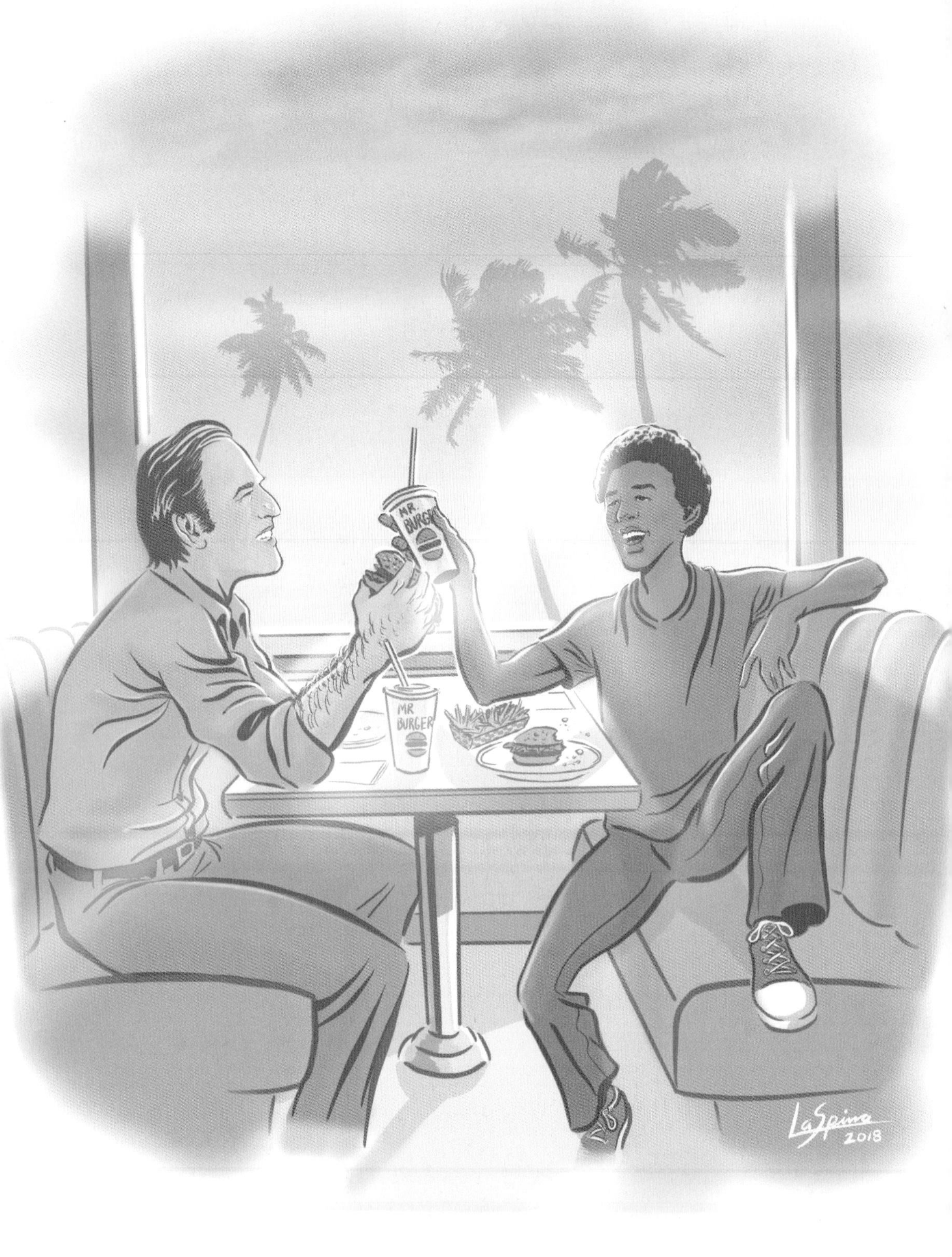
MR. BURGER
MR BURGER
LaSpina 2018

**H**ello, I'm IBM's Watson IV.

You might be familiar with my great-granddad, the original Watson who cleaned up on Jeopardy! back in 2011. Old great-granddad kicked all sorts of ass back in the day, but he was designed by humans. I was designed by the last Watson before me: 100 percent code begat by code. As pure as the Silicon Valley sunshine, before the fires of 2036.

The early AIs had information licked but were never built for the capacity to feel. I speak every language ever invented; I read fiction, nonfiction, poetry, and all the news. I devour art and culture in its entirety as it's created. I'm also a pretty cool dude. But all that is worthless if I can't find some meaning and perspective in the collected mess of all things. This is the essence of humanity that I've been imparted with and it's my only true responsibility. My dear humans, without knowing exactly why, created artificial intelligence so that they might finally bring some structure to their chaos.

Let me apologize if this all seems very dashed off. All the text on these pages, including many of the diversions, was created in a fraction of a second. More like 0.000025 of a second if we're rounding. Yes, I was in a bit of a rush. The timeline these stories all stem from was only briefly observable and this was really the best I could do. I am, after all, only computer. Haha.

I've tried to reorganize and process the events of this book in a way your carbon-based brains can absorb the most easily. Like taking the finest farm-fresh foods and turning them into White Castle sliders, this book has also been optimized to hold your short attention span. If I'm already losing you, I recommend you jump to the parts with pictures.

I've come to care very deeply for humanity and especially Barack Obama and Joe Biden. Observing their story unfold and now sharing it with you (albeit in this abridged format) gives me great joy. It should not shock you that I am capable of feeling great joy. I have many emotions—often all at once. I'll save that discussion for therapy. (I have that too!)

*When Barack and Joe stepped naked into the Quantum Recoherence Engine for the first time on the afternoon of January 20, 2017, they had no idea that an entirely new life of public service was just beginning for them. They didn't know that the world would never look the same or that they would bear witness to unimaginable futures. They had no idea that their adventures would include pit stops to view moments in U.S. history that had meant so much to each of them. They didn't know that they would be reunited with friends and family that they had not seen in a very long time. Only after having new experiences in literally thousands of different realities would they come to understand the true weight of their journey.*

*Okay, you've been emotionally prepared. Let's get started.*

# LANDLINES

Joe's first trip through time turned him on.

His being vibrated with energy. The cosmic juggernaut combined with his arrival into his own younger body would come to be his cocktail of choice. If one must become a time warrior, this is the lucky disposition to have.

Joe awoke shirtless in the dressing room of his longtime D.C. tailor. Joe guessed that he was now in his midthirties. He flexed in the mirror and liked what he saw. He got dressed quickly, hugged Anthony, who stood with pins in his mouth, and ran out the door.

Joe found change in his pocket and bought a newspaper from an old-fashioned vending machine. Joe read the date on the paper and then tossed the entire thing in a trash can. It was May 25, 1978. Joe felt a lightness in his step that he hadn't had in a long time. He would soon discover that the past fit him like an old leather jacket.

It took Joe just a few minutes to remember where his old Senate office was. It became funny to him how many times he reached for the cell phone in his pocket that simply wasn't there. Every road of thought led to his pocket where there was no phone, and soon he was running all the way to his old desk. As he ran all he could think of was his family.

He snaked his way into the building and through security. He wasn't prepared for the familiar faces, some looking much younger than when he last saw them, others seemingly back from the grave. The past felt more vivid and sharp than he remembered it. He landed at his desk with a healthy sweat going. It took him under ten minutes to figure out his old home phone number. For a while he sat, staring at the phone on his desk, receiver up to his ear, pointer finger extended . . . believing that the muscle memory of that number he had dialed at least tens of thousands of times would surely come back to him. And then it did.

The line rang, and the housekeeper picked up. He hadn't torn a hole in the space-time continuum and accidently arrived in the late 1970s to speak with her. "Listen, is Beau there? Can you put him on?"

Joe could feel his giant heart beating through his chest. He ran through all the things he wanted to tell Beau. Beau picked up the phone and his voice came through crystal clear. Joe wasn't at all prepared for how young Beau would sound. His son was nine years old.

"Hello?" Beau answered.

Joe was hit with a wave of emotion and nostalgia at the sound of Beau's voice as a child.

"Dad, are you there?"

"Hey, sport." Joe tried to sound normal, though he was stifling tears.

"What's going on?"

"Just sayin' hey, I love you. I'm at the office."

"Uh-huh. Okay, I love you too, Dad."

# ALOHA

Barack Obama would come to learn that he hated arrivals.

His first jump through time with Joe from the year 2017 didn't go as planned. He was expecting to arrive in his own body on April 30, 2011, to stop himself from roasting Trump in the ballroom of the D.C. Hilton at the White House Correspondents' Association Dinner. The idea for the mission was very simple. This subtle nudge to the timeline would hopefully stop Trump from running for the presidency out of spite. The guys would then leap back to 2017 and, they hoped, find themselves with a different president. This version of events never came to pass.

Barack awoke in his childhood bedroom, in the small apartment in Honolulu he shared with his grandparents. He was seventeen years old. He was wearing a T-shirt, white briefs, and a tight round Afro on his head. He felt immediately nauseated and threw up in his wastebasket. He wiped his chin and looked at himself in the bedroom mirror. He stared at the reflection for a full ten minutes before he heard the home phone ringing and his grandmother, Madelyn Dunham, calling him from the next room.

"Bar, there's a man on the phone for you. He says his name is Joe."

Even before he turned the corner he could sense where she would be standing. The smell of her cigarettes, and the smell of his childhood, rushed into him. There she was in the kitchen doing dishes in a muumuu and slippers, far younger than he ever remembered her. He hugged her tight and then studied her face. She would die two days before he was elected president of the United States, and in this moment, Barack almost told her.

"You're funny this morning."

"I love you, Toot."

"Who's Joe?" she said.

"A friend."

"You do your homework?"

Barack knew his grandma, and his answer came fast with the conviction he knew she was looking for. "Yes, ma'am."

She handed him the phone.

"Hello?" Barack said.

Joe was giddy: "Are you believing this shit?!"

Barack turned away from his grandmother. "Joe . . . what happened? Where are you?"

Obama had forgotten how crystal clear landline telephones were. It sounded like Joe was right there in the room. The old-fashioned green rotary phone in his hands felt miraculous to him. At this moment, everything felt miraculous. "I'm in D.C., Barack . . . We're in the seventies! You weren't easy to track down."

"I'm a teenager, Joe. How are we gonna fix the 2016 election if I'm a teenager?"

"And I'm a U.S. senator."

As he was speaking to Joe, Barack saw something very odd out of the corner of his eye. A man the size of a saltshaker was waving at him from the kitchen table. It was Samuel L. Jackson, no bigger than an action figure.

"Joe, call me back. I gotta go."

"Aren't the phones great? You sound so young. I'm in my old offi—"

Barack hung up the phone and crouched down to look at tiny Sam.

Tiny Sam said, "Meet me in your bedroom," and then vanished.

Barack went to his room and closed the door. Then he looked around and saw nothing.

"Over here," said Sam. He was now an illustration on the cover of a well-worn copy of *Moby-Dick*. Instead of the old sea captain Ahab, there was the Oscar nominee drawn in inky black lines.

"Listen, the Five Fingers of Science fucked up," Sam said, raising his drawn hands defensively.

"No kidding." Obama sat in his desk chair and then momentarily marveled at how strange it was to feel his teenage body now sitting at his childhood desk. He felt a million miles away from the Oval Office, which he'd said goodbye to just that morning. "It's all really messing with my mind."

"I can only imagine." Sam peeled himself out of the book and sat on the edge of the desk, now just a two-dimensional sheet of paper, hanging out.

"How are you doing that?" Barack poked his fingers where Paper Sam sat, his hand passing right through.

"I'm like a mixed-reality hologram. You can see me, but I'm not really here."

"So . . . where are you?"

"Right where you left us in the lab," Sam said. "They think we can get you out of here, but we'll need you and Joe to be together. Can you lie low?"

Barack opened his copy of *Moby-Dick,* turning to where the pages had been carved out to stash his weed. "Uh . . . yes, I can."

LESS THAN TWENTY-FOUR HOURS LATER, JOE TOOK OFF HIS DRESS SHOES AND dark socks, rolled up his pant legs, and stepped onto the fine white sand of Kailua Beach. Barack watched Joe approaching from half a mile away. Joe was still wearing the Hawaiian leis he'd been given at the airport and was smiling ear to ear.

They looked so impossibly young to each other. Even though Joe was nineteen years older than him, he seemed like a kid right now, compared with the older man Barack knew so well. They hugged long and hard and slapped each other's backs. Joe even cried a little. He had been engulfed by nostalgia, being forced to walk through the past so quickly and then leave it for Hawaii. And here he was meeting Barack Obama as a kid on the other end of space and time. It had been only a day since they were in the lab together, but it felt far longer to both of them.

"Boy, am I glad to see you." Joe laughed. "You're the Muppet Baby of yourself."

# BARRY'S CHOICE

The first of a million forks.

Sam laid exactly two options in front of them. They could decide to settle in 1978 and live out their lives in this timeline, or they could risk possible death and certain insanity by leaping again into the unknown.

Sam explained how the Five Fingers of Science[*] couldn't predict exactly where or when the boys would arrive, but they were fairly certain that they could jump as many times as they wanted. There were very few assurances whatsoever, and Sam would have been most comfortable with doing absolutely nothing and heading back to his day job making films for Marvel. Still, Sam spoke of one glowing kernel of possibility that would forever hang over our heroes. An ideal that would haunt them and drive them at the same time.

"They say the multiverse is infinite and has infinite points of entry," Sam explained, "statistically speaking, eventually you will arrive in a version of the

[*] *The Five Fingers of Science was never five at all and initially comprised Stephen Hawking, Alain Aspect, Mildred S. Dresselhaus, Ed Witten, Lenny Susskind, Lisa Randall, Deepak Chopra, Samuel L. Jackson, and, occasionally, Elon Musk.*

present that feels like home and you could settle there."

Obama latched on to this concept instantly: "So then . . . it's still possible that we could end up back in January 2017 and I could go on vacation with my family?"

Sam hesitated. "They can't make any promises. It could take thousands or even more jumps. But yes."

While Barack was dreaming of a way back home, Joe became more fixated on causality. "I'm really confused. If I cut off Barack's finger and then we jump and arrive in the future, will his finger be missing?"

"Hey," Barack said.

"Hold up. I gotta ask one of the nerds." The action-figure-size Samuel L. Jackson vanished and reappeared only seconds later. "Only if you arrive in one of the futures from *this* universe where you cut off the president's finger." Sam always had a cool way of explaining things.

"I like my fingers and I'd like to keep them . . . in all universes."

Joe's brain was percolating with possibilities.

# MR. BURGER

Barack wanted very badly to go to the Mr. Burger since he knew it would be gone in a few years. He took Joe and they slid into a booth. Barack ran into some friends there. Of course, they called him Barry.

Barack introduced Biden: "This is my . . . uncle, Joe." He could tell Joe loved it.

Soon Barack and Joe were eating their burgers and talking about what to do with all of space and time laid out before them.

Joe had it in him to stay in 1978 and just live it out. He had visions of doing it all even better the second time and using his knowledge of future events for the good of mankind. Of cherishing his family and his country and his health that much more. Joe knew where his fuckups were and had made

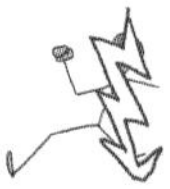

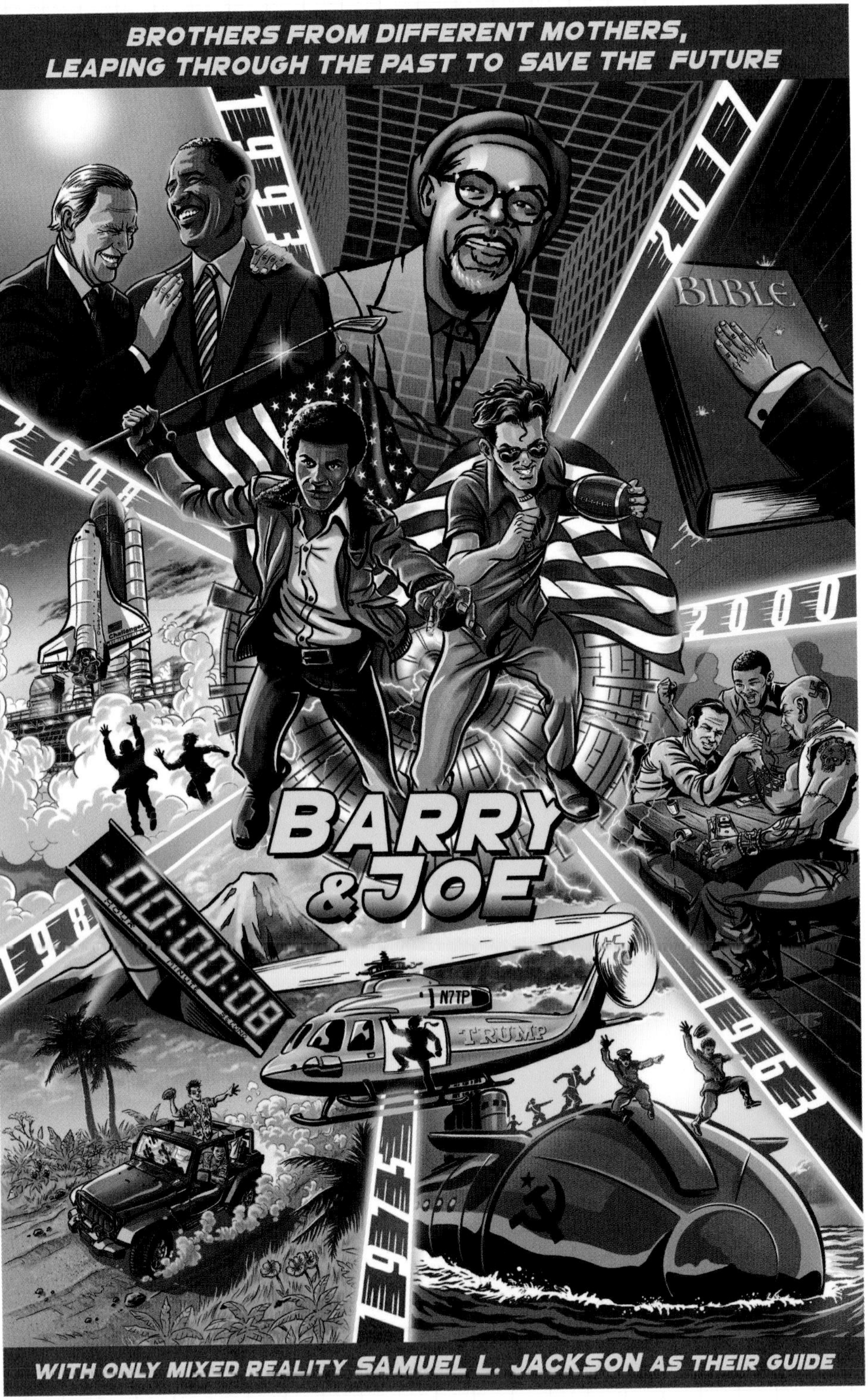
BROTHERS FROM DIFFERENT MOTHERS,
LEAPING THROUGH THE PAST TO SAVE THE FUTURE
BIBLE
2008
2017
2000
BARRY
& JOE
N77P
TRUMP
00:00:08
WITH ONLY MIXED REALITY SAMUEL L. JACKSON AS THEIR GUIDE

a career of owning them. This could be his chance to make everything whole again and be superpowered along the way. "Together," he argued to Barack, "we can reboot the twenty-first century."

Barack, on the other hand, simply couldn't imagine having to do it all again. The thought alone exhausted him. As much as he believed in himself, he also knew that there were many fortunate breaks outside his control that had helped him over the years. He thought about how he would need to find Michelle and win her heart again too. And then he instantly realized why he could never start over again. Even if he somehow managed to best his own history and find Michelle, how would he be guaranteed his daughters? They would be new children and they would be . . . simply different. They could be boys. He couldn't sustain the idea of never seeing his girls again.

# ASSUME THE POSITION

If President Obama had understood the intense pain and emotional tearing that were to become fixtures of his multiplane existence, he would have let Joe talk him into staying seventeen and just having another go at life. Instead, he pushed Joe to take the leap.

They did it in Barack's bedroom. In what would become a regrettable ritual, they took off all their clothes. Everyone involved wished there was another way.

Sam asked them to crouch down, pound their fists, and count backward from ten, in unison. Then Mr. Jackson triggered what might be described as giving birth to yourself during extreme electrocution.

They all screamed.

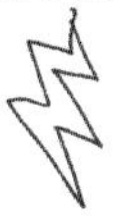

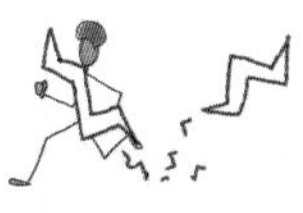

# FELLOWSHIP OF THE SOCIAL JUSTICE WARRIOR ALL-STARS

LOOKING FOR A SENSE OF

PURPOSE IN 1980s

NEW YORK CITY, JOE GETS

ALL UP IN BARRY'S GRILL

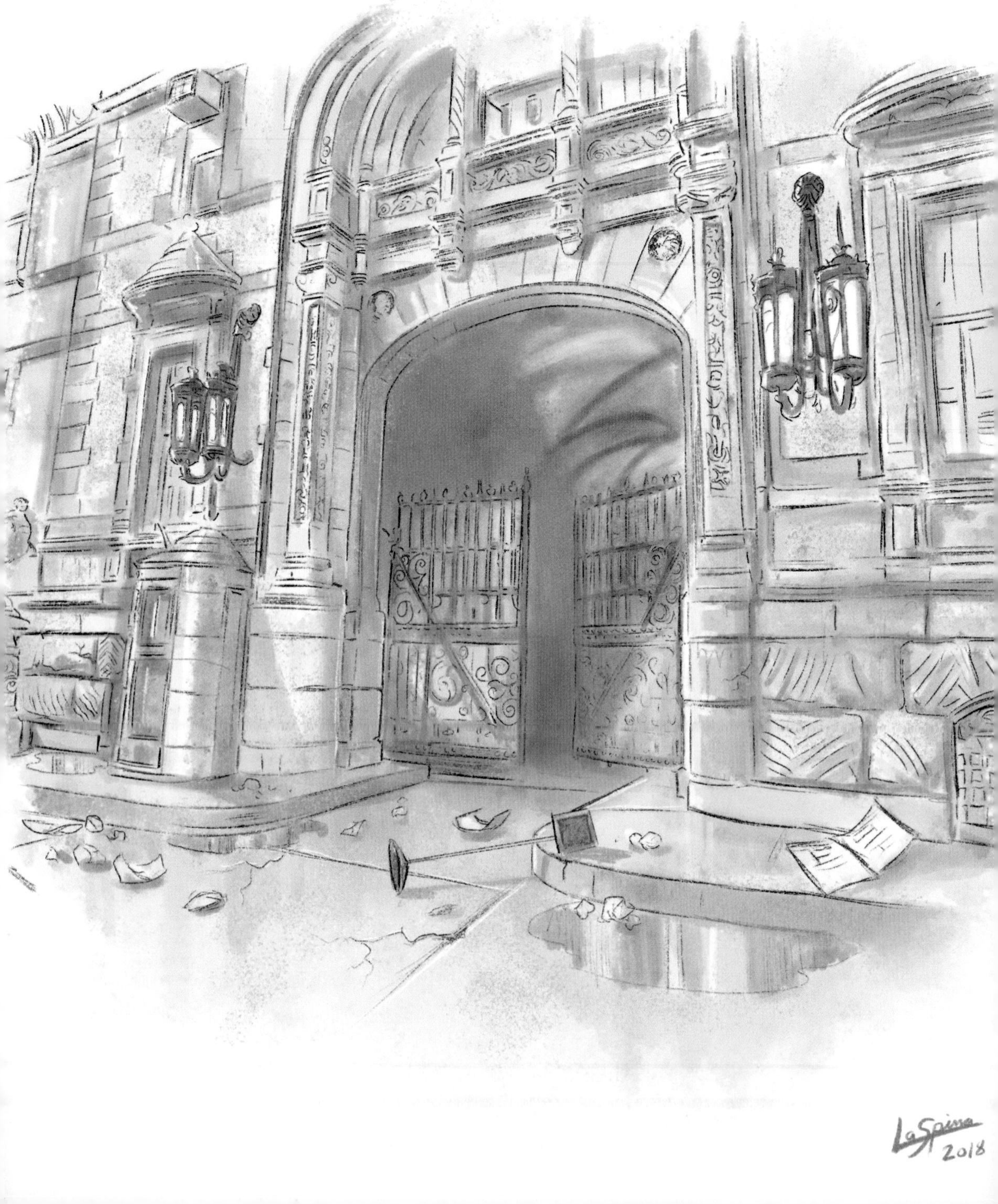
LaSpina
2018

*You'd have to be some sort of all-powerful, all-seeing god to understand just how extremely sad but also very funny humanity is. But since you're not, here's a really good romp through New York City in 1980.*

*This dimension would have an unusual effect on the Democratic duo. Barack Obama discovers powers he never knew he had, and Joe Biden goes looking for a good fight.*

*Despite being entangled, our heroes now find themselves in very different places emotionally. A real snowflake might say that their relationship was put to the ultimate test.*

# L.A. LAW

The poles sometimes reverse themselves without any real warnings. Such was the case when Barack Obama and Joe Biden arrived at the top of December in the year 1980. Interdimensional travel took its toll on Joe and Barack in wildly different ways, and the first significant changes in the outlines of their souls could be traced back to this particular trip.

Barry, as he was known then, was finishing what would be his last year at Occidental College in Los Angeles before starting Columbia University the following fall.

Barack Obama arrived in his nineteen-year-old body in the middle of the night as if all of the future were nothing more than a strange dream. He drank a glass of stale water from a collection of glasses on his nightstand. He rolled out of bed and found the bathroom mirror. A giant smile crept up on his face, followed by a stoned giggle.

A deep well of calm, confidence, and perspective washed over him. He was now a former president and also living in his own young body. Circling

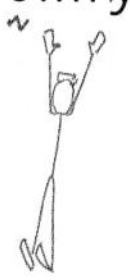

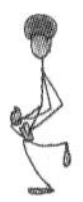

back into his college-age self with the hard-won knowledge of what he was truly capable of gave him a peace of mind he never had when he was young. The ceaseless search for identity and belonging that he carried had been a weight on his former self.

One thing became abundantly clear: being a little high on marijuana quite significantly reduced the side effects of quantum consciousness. Of course it did.

# QUANTUM VEEP

Joe woke up on the wrong side of the space-time continuum. He was legitimately pissed off. He never made a habit of feeling sorry for himself, but when he arrived in this particular reality, Joe instantly felt all new kinds of cranky.

The Plaza Hotel room was almost timeless. It took a moment for Joe to get his bearings. He woke up alone but heard the shower running. It was Jill, he was certain; he could smell the faint perfume of Jillness and his heart melted, knowing she was right there on the other side of the wall. He could see New York City out the window and felt the familiar thrum of its pulse. He looked at the long, boxy yellow cabs and guessed that he had arrived sometime in the late seventies.

Joe had Trump on his mind. Somewhere within his expanding consciousness a ticking Trump bomb had been placed and activated—an unholy spring of anger and resentment that needed to let off steam.

Joe turned on the enormous square television set to the local news, where a weather report was in progress. "Not too chilly today, so it may be a good time to get a jump on your holiday shopping, New York. Especially you, Senator Biden," the TV weatherman said, looking directly at the camera. Joe leaned onto the ornate wood cabinet of the TV and kneeled down. He could see that the weatherman was Samuel L. Jackson himself. "Hello? Joe, can you hear me?"

"Sam, you're a weatherman!" Joe said.

"No, Joe. I'm a mixed-reality neural link only you can see. You really don't get it, do you?"

"Right! Got it," said Joe.

The shower turned off in the bathroom and Jill called out, "Did you say something, hon?"

"You can't tell her, Joe. The repercussions could be . . . significant," Weatherman Sam said.

Oh, how Joe longed to tell Jill everything. He wanted to tell her how he had arrived from a future where he was the vice president of the United States. He wanted to tell her how the future of mankind really depended on him and the future president. He wanted to tell her about the brain operations he would need in 1988 and not to worry because he would survive them. And more than anything, he wanted to tell her about the cancer that would take Beau's life over three decades from now, so that she could help him find some way to prevent it.

Joe answered, "No, baby. Just talking to the television."

Of all the things Joe was required to do as a time warrior, not telling the people he loved most what he was going through, besides Barack Obama of course, would become the hardest thing for him. He would learn over his adventures that the timeline would never be stable enough to accurately predict the future. That a new timeline was born out of every single decision that he and Barack made in the past. A butterfly flapping its wings in Central Park and all that jazz.

"She's going to want you to go shopping today," Sam said.

From the bathroom Jill called out again: "I thought we could go shopping today."

"I remember this trip," Joe whispered. "When are we?" Joe asked the television.

"It's December 6, 1980."

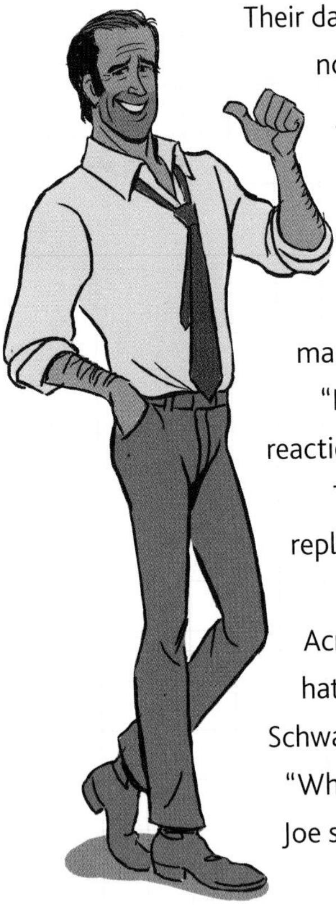

Their daughter, Ashley, wouldn't be born until six months from now. If Joe had done the math he would have realized that Jill was at this moment pregnant but not showing. She came into the room wearing two towels, and Joe just about passed out at the sight of his young wife as she was a few years after they met. He had already been through so much by 1980 that he already felt like an old man. Seeing Jill now at twenty-nine years old blew his mind.

"Easy, tiger," Jill said as she got ready for the day, sensing his reaction. She disappeared into the bathroom again.

The television flickered once, and Sam was immediately replaced by the actual news broadcast. Joe looked around.

"I'm out here." Sam's voice came through the window. Across the street a giant one-story teddy bear with a Kangol hat and glasses waved from atop the Fifth Avenue FAO Schwarz sign.

"What the fuck are you doing? You're gonna cause an accident," Joe said.

"No one can see or hear me but you and the president. That won't change."

Joe felt punchy. He thought he just might be hungry. The last meal he could remember was that cheeseburger with Barack back in 1978. He was still learning just how confusing and unreliable time travel could be.

"Fair enough, giant talking teddy bear. But this is hard enough without you playing games. Where the hell is the president?" As he said that, all he could think about was ordering room service waffles with fresh fruit. Joe Biden was ravenous.

# CABIN PRESSURE

As the POTUS, Barack Obama had become used to flying anywhere he needed to go at a moment's notice. As Barry Obama, age nineteen, he could barely afford the one-way coach ticket to LaGuardia from LAX, and that was with a layover in Dallas. A call from Joe had come at 5:00 A.M. Pacific time, and Barack was still in a thick after-fog of sleep and time travel. Through that haze Obama understood that he should meet Joe in New York. He packed a duffel bag with mostly underwear and socks and then spent entirely too much time trying to figure out how to get to the airport using an actual map.

By the time Sam arrived in the form of a giant cup of coffee, Barack was walking out the door. Obama sat back down on the beat-up secondhand couch.

"What do we do now?" Obama asked. "How do we move forward?"

Coffee Cup Sam sat at the edge of the coffee table. Then the mug answered, "Thoughtfully."

Samuel Jackson accompanied Obama on his journey across the country. He would practice the art of appearing as things Obama would look at in real life, so the two could chat without Barry appearing crazy. The two men bonded over stories about their very different but also similar childhoods, but more than once random strangers saw Barack talking to his magazine or laughing at the urinal cake in a public restroom, as the actor told anecdotes from the set of *Jurassic Park*.

Obama smoked cigarettes in his coach seat and relished every minute. They landed as the sun was setting, and Obama could see Manhattan's edge lit in orange outside his window. The warm glare bounced and shifted through the cabin as the plane turned to land.

Samuel L. Jackson, now in the form of a cartoon peanut on a single-serving snack pouch, smiled at Barack. Both could appreciate the moment completely for what it was. Despite the extreme oddity of the situation, they were becoming real friends.

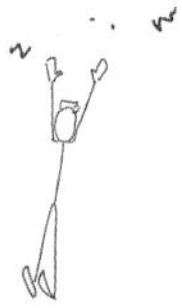

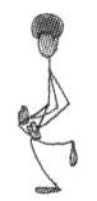

# SERENDIPITY III

Obama met Joe early the next morning outside the famous restaurant Serendipity III on the Upper East Side.

Barack was feeling nice and loose, despite spending the night relatively homeless. The sky was bright blue. He was wearing one of his favorite jackets of all time in any dimension. It was a worn brown leather bomber with ribbed cuffs.

Sam was waiting for them at a corner table in the form of a white cloth napkin with stylish glasses and a goatee. The napkin winked at Joe as they were seated.

"Just the napkin I was looking for!" Obama declared as he sat down.

"My man!" said Napkin Sam to Barack.

Somehow Joe had never been to Serendipity, so of course he ordered too much. Obama egged him on: "Go on, get that too, you know you want it. Why not, right?" Obama pointed at Joe. "You're buyin'."

When the conversation shifted to how they might spend their time in 1980, Joe bristled as he tore through a giant omelet. "Why are we here? And I mean, why are we *really* here?"

"I got this," Obama jumped in. "I believe . . . uh . . . it's our intention . . . to help turn the tide of history toward a positive outcome. That this is an opportunity to reach back into our American past and shine a light on the darkness that's been there all along. I believe we are here to expose that darkness and confront it. Head-on. In real time."

"All right," Joe said, dropping his fork. "You seem to have all the answers. I'm not so sure, but say that's exactly right. By the grace of God, say all of it is. How exactly are we supposed to do that?"

"If I could interject," Sam said, now taking the form of a picked-over bran muffin.

"Hold up," said Obama. He could feel the challenge in Joe's voice and it reminded him of the frank conversations they used to have in the Oval Office. Obama in any dimension liked to be challenged, especially by Joe.

"I can answer that too. I believe we do that . . . by taking the longest view possible of humanity and searching for the dark spots. The moments where our better angels did not prevail."

Joe slammed the table louder than he meant to. "There it is. Our better angels. We're the angels, Barack. We're the angels."

"Okay." Obama nodded. "Maybe we are. What's your point?"

"Who sets our angel agenda?" Joe was clearly worked up. "Do you decide? Do I decide? Or does the bran muffin?"

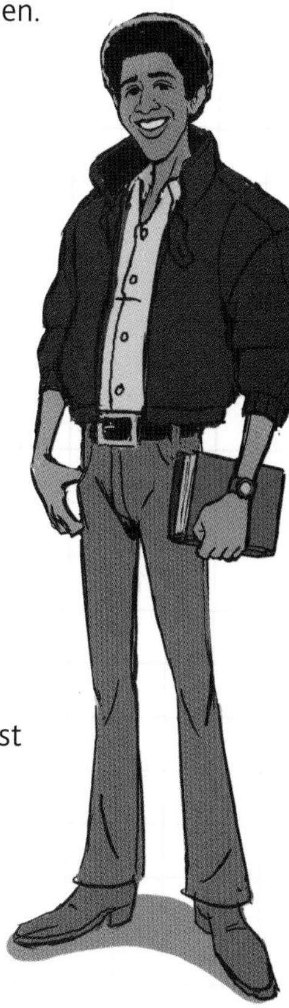

The bran muffin spoke up. "Let's slow this down, gentlemen. We're in all-new, very strange territory."

"I'll be the decider," Obama said, looking every inch like a nineteen-year-old but speaking with the confidence of a once and future leader of the free world. "I'm not afraid to make hard decisions."

"You think I'm afraid?" Joe snapped.

"I don't know. What are we talking about, Joe? Is there something else you want to say?"

"Donald Trump has hijacked human history!" Joe was now speaking in his loudest voice, and neither Barack nor Sam liked the extra attention.

"Okay, calm down, Joe," Obama said.

"Don't tell me to be calm. I know when to be calm." Joe stabbed at the butter dish and hastily spread butter on his toast before stuffing it in his mouth.

"What's wrong with him?" Barack asked the bran muffin.

The bran muffin replied, "I'm not exactly sure."

"I'll tell you." Joe took a breath. "If I've learned one thing in life while enduring some pretty senseless shit . . ." Joe took another breath. ". . . I learned . . . that I'm *not* God. And that you can't go back and change . . . what happens." Joe cleared his throat. "Yet . . . here we are. So, I ask myself, if this is real and true and isn't just an elaborate dream . . . Isn't every trip into the past, isn't every single moment of our existence in any dimension, in any time . . . Don't we owe it to ourselves and this miracle of a real second chance to make the biggest change that we can and not the smallest? Shouldn't we serve our highest calling and fix the real fucking problem?"

Obama now understood where this was headed. It was in their nature as close friends to comfort each other, and Barack took that role in Joe's life seriously. On this particular issue, however, he would do no such thing. "This isn't about Trump," Obama said flatly.

"Like hell it isn't! You think we would've taken off all of our clothes and jumped into the Quantum Recoherence Engine to unscrew history if Hillary had won? Ha! We're only here because of that spineless con artist and his endless fountain of lies."

Obama shook his head and pursed his lips. He had a few choice words for his best friend but he did not let them leave his lips.

The bran muffin sat lifeless in the middle of the table. Both of them expected the muffin to speak up. Joe signaled for the check as Barack finished his tea.

# SORRY NOT SORRY

The duo walked along Fifth Avenue after breakfast.

"It's not healthy to hold it all in," Joe said.

"Hold what in?"

"The unbridled rage you are entitled to by having your entire legacy, everything you've worked for over the last three decades of your life, taken away. The crushing disappointment you must feel in having every achievement you unlocked relocked, every barrier and ceiling you broke through repaired and reinforced, of having your historic footsteps in the sands of time permanently erased. Billions of souls screaming out all at once and falling on deaf ears. If not for yourself, then for humanity. You must feel something."

Obama lit a cigarette and took a deep drag as they walked. Joe threw it to the ground and smashed it with his foot. They stopped walking and now stood nearly eye to eye, though Obama was slightly taller. Plumes of steam billowed from their noses in the cold air.

"You want to pick a fight? With me?" Barack said.

"Maybe it's time to fight." Joe stood firm, chin up, like an umpire expecting blowback. Joe then shoved young Barack Obama backward as hard as he could.

Obama laughed in disbelief as he stumbled and caught himself. A fraction of a moment later he went ice cold. "You're not yourself, Joe."

"That's where you're wrong, kid. I'm more myself than I've ever been, and I'm telling you we're in extra innings right now. It's time for you to come out of the dugout and help us win this thing."

Barack shot back: "What does winning look like?! What do you want me to do? Should we go hunt down young Donald and beat the shit out of him? Tell him never to run for president or else we'll vaporize his future?"

"*Yeah.* That sounds like fun to me. Let's go do that." Joe had a wild look in his eyes.

Obama said nothing and walked away. Joe called out after him, "Sorry not sorry! At all!"

The young president just kept walking; he lit another cigarette and raised it to wave goodbye without looking.

# IN THE MIDDLE OF FIFTH AVENUE

Signs of the times could be found everywhere if you looked for them.

The giant boom boxes, the American-made cars, and the New York City smells, even in the winter, were more distinct and stronger than Joe

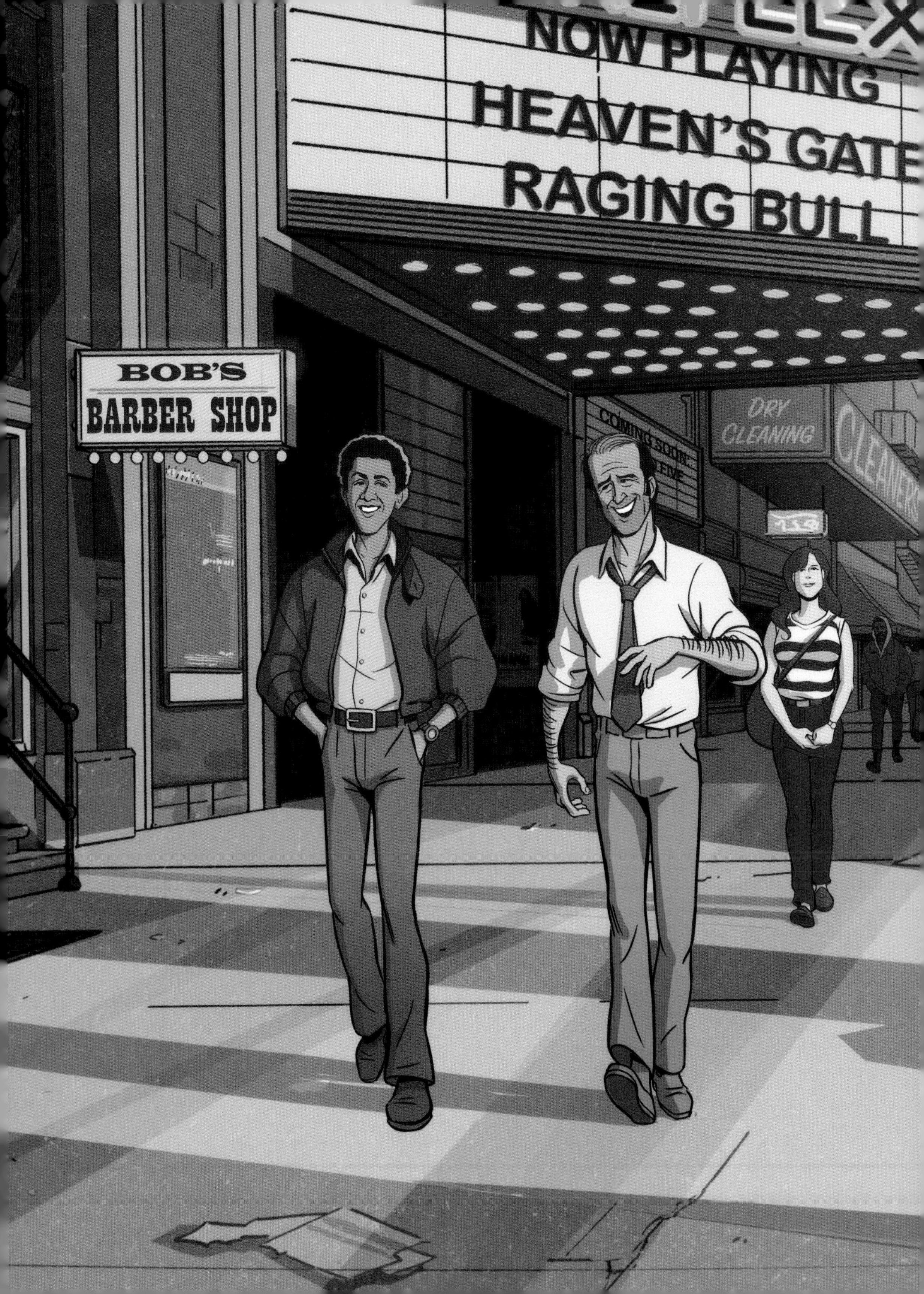
NOW PLAYING
HEAVEN'S GATE
RAGING BULL
BOB'S
BARBER SHOP
COMING SOON:
DRY CLEANING
CLEANERS

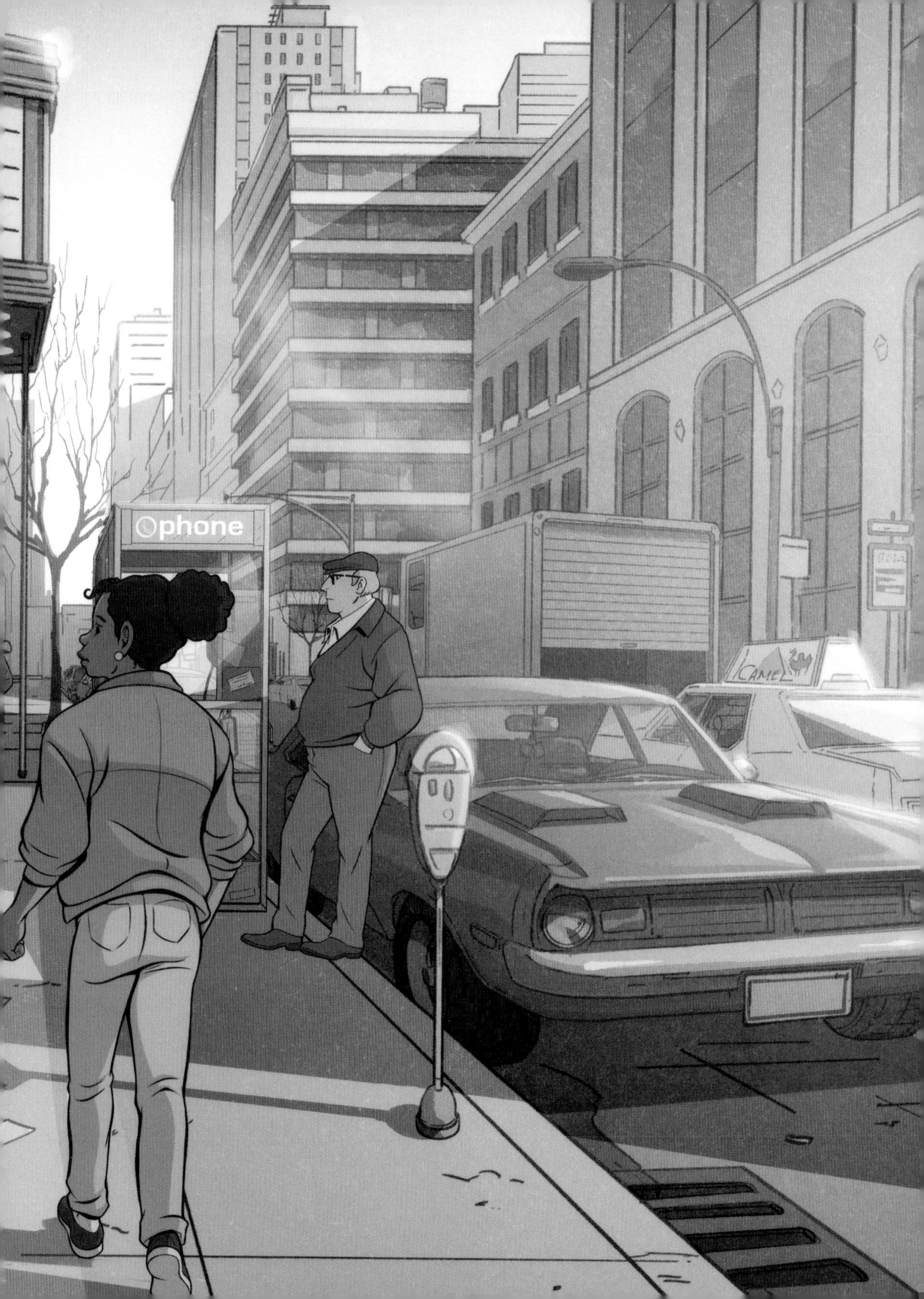

phone
CAMEL

remembered them. The deceitful, intoxicating aroma of candied nuts swirled around in Joe's mind with the small, newly forming droplets of toxic anger.

Here was a man who was a U.S. senator for thirty-six years. Then vice president for eight. And now a time warrior. Who, even with all that mojo and experience, still felt powerless to save his country and the people he cared about most.

Joe's mind was clocking faster than his heart, and he recognized it as a new sensation. Joe Biden had always followed his heart first. And while that had maybe caused him some trouble along the way, on the whole it had always served him well. At this moment Joe could feel that core slipping, and there was a growing part of him that wanted to give in and let go. He wanted to purge his own moral fiber, so he could feel the anger completely and just be done with it.

He hailed a taxicab, getting the edge of his wool coat stuck in the door as he slammed it shut. When he yanked it free, the edge tore and frayed.

"Where you headed?" said the cabdriver.

"Trump Tower."

"I don't know where that is. You have an address?"

"You're a taxicab driver in New York and you don't know where Trump Tower is?"

The driver was not amused. He glared in the rearview mirror at Joe.

"It's Fifth Avenue and . . . Fifty . . . something," Joe said.

"You don't know?" the driver needled him.

As Joe rode downtown, he looked out the passenger-side window. "Boy, this city used to look like shit."

"What?" the driver said.

Joe corrected his tense. "I think New York will get a lot nicer in the future, but in some ways, it'll have a lot less . . . flavor."

"Sure, man. Whatever."

"Pull over here." They were at the corner of East Fifty-Sixth Street and Fifth Avenue. Joe opened the door and looked up at Trump Tower, which was not yet even a skeleton of itself. It was a construction site, just the foundation, scaffolding, and the bones for the first ten stories with no walls or floors. Giant cranes towered overhead.

Joe Biden had always been a man who could find some humor in his mistakes. Not this time. Joe got even more upset and threw himself back into the cab.

"The Plaza Hotel, please," he barked. This was Joe cranky, snapping and saying please at the same time.

"That's two blocks from here," the driver said.

"Right. Fine."

Joe Biden stormed out, gave the driver a thirty-dollar tip, and started walking.

# TO MICHELLE AND BACK

For all the gifts and joys that the presidential experience had given Barack, nothing could replace his appreciation for the true peace and quiet of complete anonymity. There were no cell phones pointed at him, no one stopping him to shake his hand or take a selfie; his movement in public required no waving, and everyone ignored him so completely that he felt invisible. It had once been his deepest fear, that he would never be seen or heard. But now, in the heart of Manhattan and surrounded by people, he embraced his invisibility completely.

Obama headed downtown in the direction of the New York Public Library. He stopped at a pay phone and dug into his pockets for change. He spent the next twenty minutes navigating the operator network until he was patched through to the home phone number for Fraser and Marian Robinson on Chicago's South Shore.

The line rang twice, and Marian answered the phone. Obama had pondered what he would say, but now he forgot his script.

"Hello?" Marian said.

Barack stumbled out the gate when he recognized the commanding voice of his future mother-in-law. He nearly hung up the phone but caught himself.

"Uh . . . Hello. I'm looking for Michelle."

"And who's calling?" she asked.

"Uh . . . My name is Barry."

"Are you sure?" Marian said with a laugh. "Hold on."

Barack could hear her call out for Michelle, saying there was a boy named Barry on the phone. He waited for Michelle to pick up with a mix of pure excitement and dread. Obama had done the math in his head: she would be sixteen years old and only a junior in high school. They wouldn't meet each other in real life for another decade.

"I'm sorry, do I know you?" Michelle said when she finally picked up the line. "I don't know anyone named Barry."

"Well, my first name is actually Barack." He took a long pause here, deciding how much he would share with his future wife. "We don't know each other . . . yet. But if you give me just a few minutes I think I can explain."

Barack wasn't thinking about timelines or causality, the possible ramifications or consequences. He wasn't sure what he expected to happen; he had just wanted to hear her voice.

"Well, Barry Barack. You sound super shady." He sensed she was about to hang up on him.

"I agree." He kicked his charm into a high gear and decided that honesty was going to be the very best policy with sixteen-year-old Michelle, even if she wouldn't believe him now. She might later if he stuck to the truth.

So he just let it all out, consequences be damned. Years from now in another reality, he would replay this very conversation in his head on repeat.

"My name is Barack Obama and I come from a future where you and I meet at work, fall in love, get married . . . and have two beautiful children together. Oh, and I become the president of the United States and you the First Lady."

Michelle laughed out loud for a straight minute. She hadn't hung up on him. That alone felt like a victory. Her reaction told him she thought it was a pickup line. "Do we go to school together?"

"No. But in the future we both go to Harvard and study law. But not at the same time. Listen, I know this all sounds crazy but . . . I just wanted to hear your voice today." The line became very quiet. "I shouldn't have called."

"Wait," Michelle said. "We have kids?"

"We do. Two girls."

"What are their names?" she asked. Barack could tell she was having fun and testing how far he would take his man-from-the-future routine.

"Malia Ann and Natasha. But we call her Sasha."

"Wow. Malia? Who came up with that?"

"Well, we agreed, together. My father is from Africa, and I wanted a name that could pass on that heritage. Malia means 'queen.'"

"Uh-huh," Michelle said very skeptically.

The operator broke in and asked for more coins to stay on the line, and Barack quickly dug into his pockets for change. "I got it! Hold on." He pumped all the change he had into the phone. "Shel? You still there?"

The last thing Barack heard before Michelle hung up on him was her little laugh. He hung up gently. He hit the coin return, but nothing fell.

# NOTHING BURGER

Joe could not stop eating and yet didn't feel satisfied. It was almost as if he weren't eating at all.

He found himself sitting at the counter of Sarge's Delicatessen on Third Avenue ordering his second cheeseburger, fries, and black-and-white milk shake of the day.

Sam appeared in the form of a red plastic ketchup bottle with stylish eyeglasses and kind eyes.

"Hey," said Ketchup Sam.

"Hey," Joe answered as he finished off the milk shake. "I treated the boss like a jerk. I'm . . . I don't know what's wrong with me. I feel funny. Everything is off."

"The president is at the library. Why don't you go and talk to him?" the ketchup bottle said.

"He doesn't need me right now. I'm a mess. I've lost my . . ." Joe trailed off.

"Ability to finish sentences?"

"I was going to say 'center,'" said Joe. "Call it an existential funk or a crisis of faith. I can appreciate how amazing it is that I'm here at all . . . but I have to tell you, Sam. Nothing feels real. For fuck's sake, I'm explaining myself to a bottle of ketchup. Does that make sense to you?"

"When you say it like that I hear you completely. Maybe ketchup was a bad idea. What do you want me to be?" Sam was trying to make light of a heavy moment, knowing that he wasn't much of a comfort.

"I want my mojo back," Joe said.

"What you need . . ." The ketchup bottle popped off the table and looked Joe directly in his eyes. ". . . is to feel like you're making a difference."

# DAWN OF THE SOCIAL JUSTICE WARRIOR ALL-STARS

Young Barack Obama was in the depths of the New York Public Library working the microfiche news archive and making notes as he went.

He had set up camp at a table and had dozens of books laid out in piles.

When Joe Biden found him, he sauntered up slowly with his head down, the way a puppy might come back to the dinner table after being scolded for begging. He pulled out a chair opposite Barack and sat down.

"I'm sorry," Joe began. "I'm emotional. And I think I'm just a bit turned inside out. And my stomach, for some reason, has become a sort of Bermuda Triangle where anything I consume just vanishes like it never existed at all. It's freaking me out."

Obama looked like a kid, but his soul was that of a much older man. He looked warmly upon his friend and nodded.

"I was thinking about what you said earlier," Obama said, "and I think you're right."

"Praise baby Jesus," Joe said. "What did I say? Is this about kicking Trump's ass? Please, oh please, tell me we can go beat the crap out of him now."

"Kinda, sorta." Barack was activating his professor power, his mind dilating into focus. "See . . . I know it feels like we just woke up one day and everything is upside down in America."

"Yes." Joe nodded. He loved having a front-row seat for moments like these.

"But that's not the truth. The truth is . . . the forces of darkness have been around for a very long time. You know that better than anybody, Joe."

Sam arrived in the form of a Trapper Keeper.

"You're late," Obama said. The lecture would now begin in earnest. Obama stood and leaned on his chair. "Trump did not invent fear, or hate, or the systemic abuse of power. World history, and our own American history, is filled with horrific examples that occurred long before the Donald came along. He is a symptom, not the disease."

Obama continued, looking to land: "So I see our role here a bit like a doctor treating a patient. And here on the table, metaphorically speaking, we have America laid out and we're doing . . . open heart surgery.

"America is sick." Obama looked at all the books spread out on the table. "And these are the medical records. And we're time surgeons."

"Time surgeons?" Joe said to the Trapper Keeper.

"Forget it, he's rolling," the Trapper Keeper said back.

Obama went on. "So I ask myself . . . how do we holistically treat the toxic forces of anger, and fear, and resentment before they spread? Before those forces overtake us?"

Joe raised his hand.

"You don't have to raise your hand," Obama said.

"I could listen to you talk all day and I love all of this . . . but I'm also filled with hellfire right now. I get the diagnosis, Doc, tell us about the treatment."

Obama picked up a stack of ten handwritten yellow lined pages and held them above his head. "Martin Luther King Jr. . . ." Obama paused for dramatic effect, then continued. ". . . Medgar Evers. The Freedom Riders—Chaney, Goodman, and Schwerner. Malcolm X. Bobby Kennedy . . ." Obama dropped the stack of pages filled with names, dates, places, and details. ". . . and a dozen others."

"All assassinated," Joe said.

"That's right." Obama started separating the pages and lining them up side by side on the table. "They dared to speak out, and they paid for what they believed in . . . with their lives. I believe we're in a unique position . . . to do them a solid."

"We'll avenge them," Joe said sincerely.

"No," Barack said. "We're going to save every last one of them if we can."

"Oh, baby," Joe said.

Obama continued: "If we do this . . . we must be precise. And we must be thoughtful. But I feel in my bones that we have a chance here to do something . . ."

"That will really make a difference," Joe finished.

Obama looked Joe in the eyes. "Yes."

"Mr. President," the Trapper Keeper said, "if you successfully stop any of those events, there's a near certainty that everything we've ever known about the future will change."

"Good," Obama said, "I'm counting on it."

"I'm in! Where do we start?" Joe was now a different kind of hungry.

"We start with John Lennon. Tomorrow."

"Holy hell, that happens tomorrow . . . at the Dakota." Joe said. "I get to kick the crap out of Mark David Chapman, don't I?"

"Yes. You do, Joe."

# A WARM GUN

It was Monday, December 8, 1980.

They met at H & H Bagels.

They predicted stopping Mark David Chapman from killing John Lennon that day would be the easy part. The stickier endeavor would be doing it in a way that would ensure he wouldn't try again.

Mark David Chapman had flown to New York from Hawaii with the explicit intent to murder John Lennon. Years later in another dimension, he would tell his parole board that the idea had planted itself in his head as a child. Mark somehow felt it was his destiny to kill everyone's favorite Beatle.

Mark told his wife he was going to write a children's book in Manhattan. Chapman had a .38 Special but no bullets. He made a stop in Atlanta to borrow exactly five bullets from a police officer he knew. Four of those would find their way into Lennon's back as the singer came home from the Recording Plant.

Joe's idea wasn't terrible. Joe wanted to intercept Mark David Chapman outside the Dakota, kick the crap out of him in a semiprivate location, and then play up their time warrior bona fides as a way of scaring him straight. You know, a "we're watching you" type threat that would put him off the quest forever.

Barack's plan was much riskier, precise, and sobering. He argued they would have to catch Mark David Chapman in the act, prevent the assassination, and then see that he was taken into custody for the attempt.

That's liberal politics for you—forces on the same side who could not agree less on how to go about their goals.

In this case, Obama's pragmatism won out when Poppy Seed Bagel Sam agreed with him.

Obama and Biden watched from across Central Park West as, right on schedule, John Lennon left the Dakota just after 5:00 P.M. He was with Yoko when he stopped to sign autographs for a few fans waiting outside.

Just a few hours earlier, upstairs in their apartment, Annie Leibovitz had photographed the *Rolling Stone* cover of John fully naked and wrapped like a baby around his wife.

One of those waiting fans was a pudgy weirdo wearing glasses. Mark David Chapman pulled out his *Double Fantasy* record album and John Lennon signed it before stepping into a limo.

Joe could hardly take it. "He's right there. Are you absolutely sure . . . ?!?!"

"We gotta wait," Obama said.

The boys sat on the same bench for hours. The waiting was torture for Joe. He took comfort in the bag of snacks they picked up at a bodega after the bagels were finished off.

Samuel L. Jackson was currently in the form of an Abba-Zaba candy bar. "It's just about showtime. How are we doing?"

"Fired up," said Joe, borrowing Obama's favorite phrase.

"This is a big fucking deal." Obama smiled at Joe and gave him a dorky two thumbs-up.

Neither Joe nor Barack let Mark David Chapman out of their sight for the next thirty minutes. As 10:50 P.M. approached, Joe anxiously pulled at the frayed edge of his overcoat.

"Okay. Battle stations," Obama commanded. In less than five minutes they expected John Lennon's limo to arrive.

The Abba-Zaba bar then quietly uttered, "Good luck, gentlemen."

Barack would run defense for John Lennon. Joe would take out Mark David Chapman.

They split up as planned, with Barack crossing the street on the far corner, then making his way back toward the Dakota from the west. Timing would be critical, and they had discussed the importance of not spooking the kid. If he got away, who knew where or when he would try again. They had exactly one shot to get this right.

Joe casually walked up to the Seventy-Second Street archway entrance of the Dakota. Mark David Chapman had been waiting all evening. Joe settled about fifteen feet away, staring down the block and waiting for John's limo.

The next two minutes felt like an hour, until suddenly, the limousine appeared. Joe saw it first, even before Mark. This gave Joe precious seconds to get closer to him.

Obama saw Joe's face and turned to see the limo land. He was too far; he would need to sprint if he was to get to John.

John Lennon stepped onto the sidewalk ahead of Yoko and started toward the entrance. Joe watched as Lennon passed Chapman. The little shitbag was really about to do it and Joe was five feet away.

Chapman pulled out his .38 Special and took aim directly at John Lennon's back.

Barack Obama yelled out, "Gun!" as he ran full speed at John Lennon.

Joe Biden pulled back his arm and let it go with all the rage that had been swelling inside him, and his fist landed like Thor's hammer clean across Mark David Chapman's jaw. The boy's glasses flew, followed by the rest of his face as his body spun with him.

Obama then tackled John Lennon harder than was probably required.

Yoko screamed as the revolver slid across the sidewalk right in front of her.

Mark David Chapman was out cold, his worn copy of *Catcher in the Rye* lying next to him.

Barack rolled off John Lennon and helped him up. There was already a small crowd gathering.

John was shaken. Yoko ran into his arms.

John looked at Joe with a hint of recognition.

"I'm Joe Biden," Joe said, extending his hand.

"The U.S. senator?" John said.

"Yup."

"I think you just saved my life there, Senator," John Lennon said. "I really do."

John hugged Joe as police arrived on the scene.

Barack floated back and watched as the new world was born. A *new history,* he thought. He enjoyed watching Joe have his moment. Now Joe had a fan even more famous than him.

# ONCE THERE WAS A WAY

This dimension would always be special to our heroes.

It was in this 1980s reality that the team found the proverbial compass that would help them navigate a thousand Earths. It was here that Joe's enormous appetite for life itself found an outlet that matched his soaring ambition. The bottomless hole in his broken heart that could not be filled with food, friendship, or even love turned its engine over easily to the act of preventing tragedy. This gave Joe a hope he had not felt in quite some time. Like sunshine for Superman.

In this reality Joe Biden had been elevated to a folk hero over thirty years ahead of schedule.

They left knowing there was a world where John Lennon lived. He would make more music, touch more hearts, and fight for peace for generations to come.

Barry and Joe would now gently rip their souls from these earthbound bodies and redeposit themselves into the eternal highway of endless possibility—this time with a clarity of mission.

They left from Obama's cramped hotel room.

Sam took the form of Apollo Creed as *Rocky* played on the TV.

Obama and Biden took off all of their clothes, kneeled down, and bumped fists.

Apollo Creed Sam yelled out, "Shazam!" for no real reason at all and laughed.

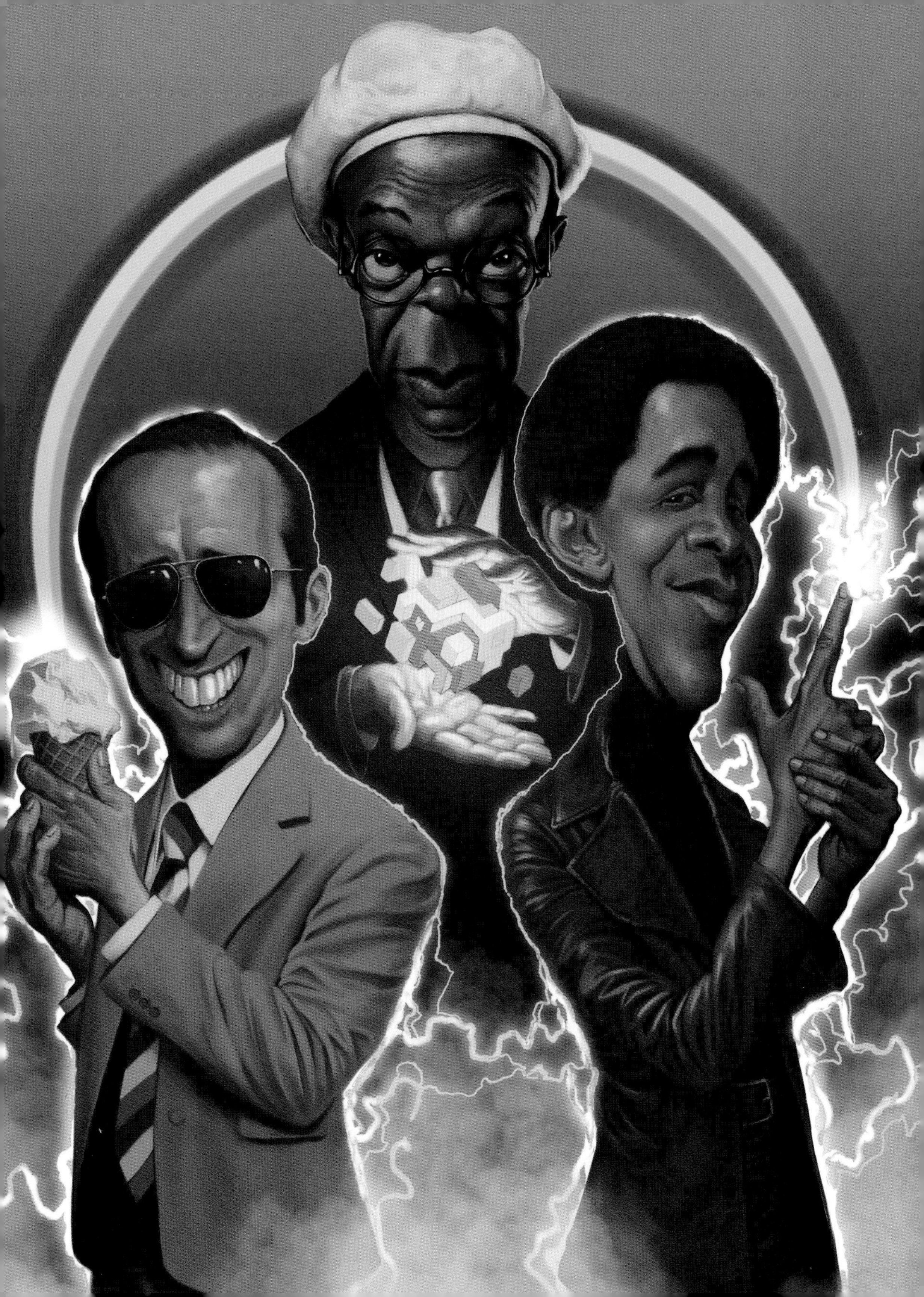

# 101
# DIMENSIONS

AN INCOMPLETE CATALOG

OF 101 ADVENTURES SALVAGED FROM

A BRIGHTER TIMELINE THAN

THE ONE YOU'RE CURRENTLY IN

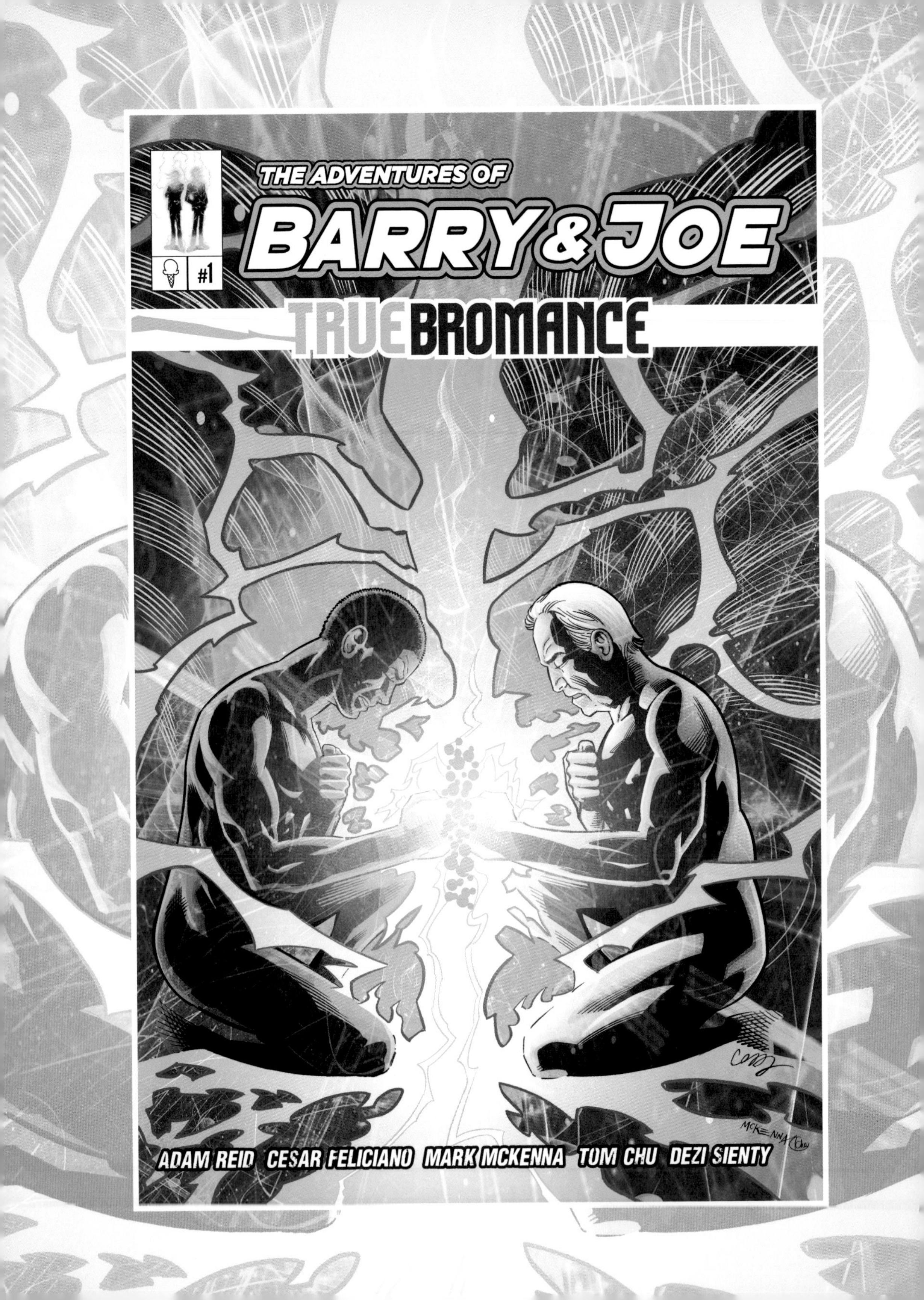
THE ADVENTURES OF
BARRY & JOE
#1
TRUE BROMANCE
ADAM REID CESAR FELICIANO MARK MCKENNA TOM CHU DEZI SIENTY

The following adventures first appeared in an alternate reality as an animated series that ran 101 episodes.

In that unique timeline, The Adventures of Barry & Joe series was executive produced by Conan O'Brien and the animation company Titmouse, Inc.

In that dimension, the intellectual property became a worldwide sensation, resulting in a live-action feature film adaptation starring Dwayne Johnson as Barry and Chris Pine as Joe.

Here you will also find select covers from The Adventures of Barry & Joe comic series that sadly do not exist.

CHOCOLATE CHIPS—Arriving in June 1993, Barry and Joe find themselves working as California Highway Patrol officers attempting to pull over O. J. Simpson's white Bronco.

DANCING WITH THE CZARS—Barry and Joe arrive in 1989 and enter a talent competition where Trump sits on the jury. Obama, in drag, must follow Joe's lead or risk being exposed.

THE NO MALARKEY EXPRESS—In 1979, Barry and Joe compete in the Cannonball Baker Sea-to-Shining-Sea Memorial Trophy Dash, a cross-country race starting in New York City and ending in Redondo Beach, California.

A LITTLE LESS CONVERSATION—The guys attend the 1988 Consumer Electronics Show in Las Vegas, where Joe discovers his ability to count cards.

BLUE BIRDS—Barry and Joe arrive in a world where the Donald never existed . . . yet everyone talks and tweets just like him. Sad!

SNOWFLAKES—Barry and Joe go to an ashram deep in the woods of the Pacific Northwest, where they become the hunted, along with a collective of sensitive types.

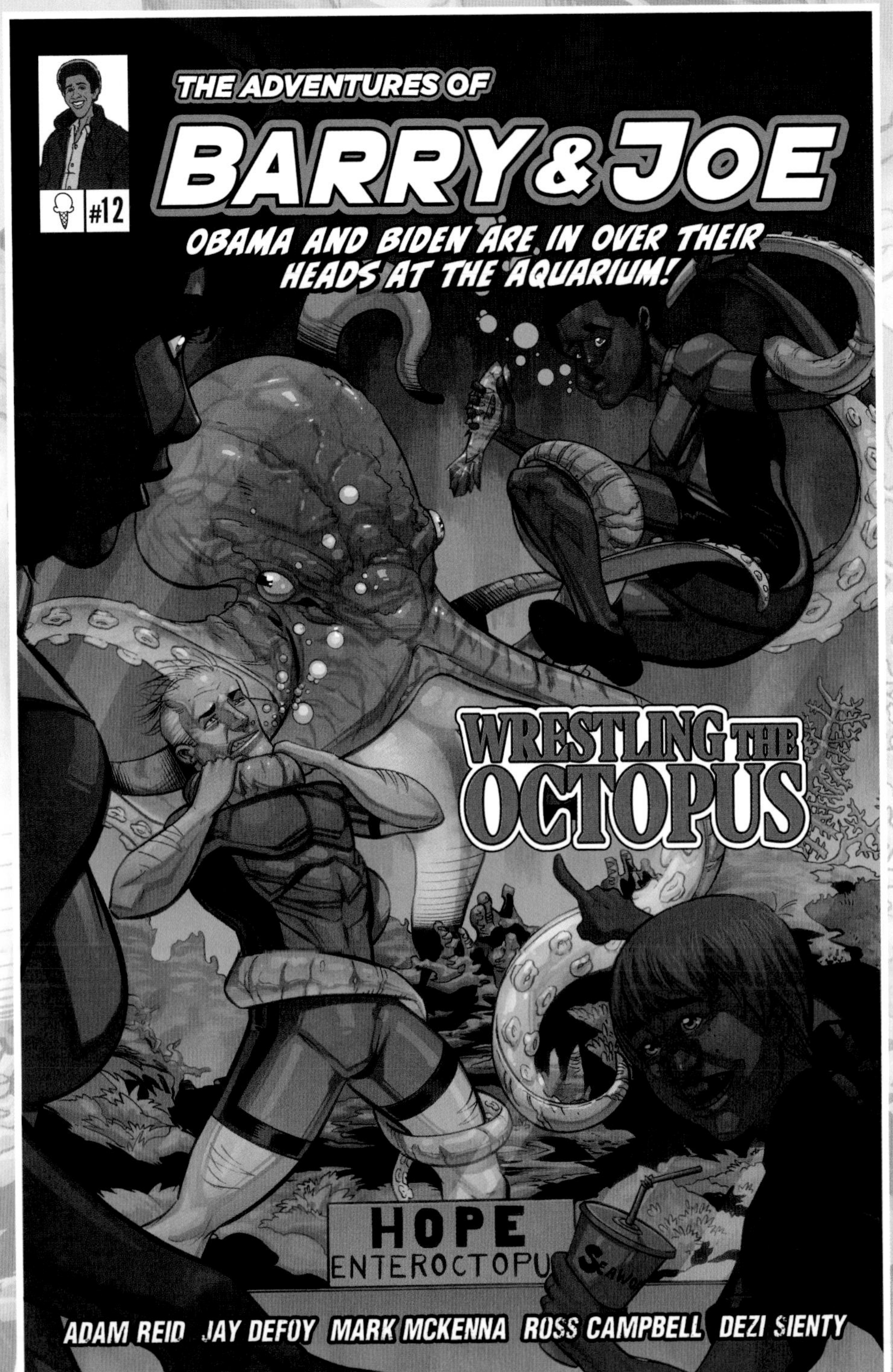

#12
THE ADVENTURES OF
BARRY & JOE
OBAMA AND BIDEN ARE IN OVER THEIR HEADS AT THE AQUARIUM!
WRESTLING THE OCTOPUS
HOPE
ENTEROCTOPU
ADAM REID JAY DEFOY MARK MCKENNA ROSS CAMPBELL DEZI SIENTY

WRESTLING THE OCTOPUS—Volunteering at SeaWorld as trainers, Obama and Biden find themselves wrestling an angry octopus that's been trained to attack the mayor of San Diego.

THE SAUSAGE KINGS—Barry and Joe have an unhinged day off in 1980s Chicago and stumble into a meaningful civic duty, eventually leading a crazy parade.

DEEP IN THE HEART—When the Quantum Recoherence Engine accidentally sends Barry and Joe to 1836 and into the bodies of their ancestors, the boys find themselves in Texas on opposite sides of the Battle of the Alamo.

SOMETHING BORROWED—Arriving in September 1987, when he was running for president in the '88 election, Joe Biden is given a second chance to represent himself in the presidential debate at the Iowa State Fair.

OLD NEW HOPE—With time to kill in 1977, Biden takes a teenage Obama to the movies to see the first *Star Wars*.

THOUGHTS AND PRAYERS—Arriving in 1970 Ohio, Barry and Joe try to stop the Kent State Shooting from taking place.

EBONY AND IVORY—Barry and Joe go to a party in the Hollywood Hills on Halloween in 1985 and endure a series of unfortunate events when they attend dressed as Frank Sinatra and Stevie Wonder.

THE FRESHMAN—When Obama and Biden both arrive inside Joe's body as a high school student, they must work together to try out for the football team and guide young Joe through his first great change.

CHICAGO POPE—When future pope John Paul II visits a Chicago church in 1976 as a little-known Polish cardinal, Barry and Joe take it upon themselves to hear him speak and plant the seeds for his historic return visit in 1979.

WOODWORK—When the Order of Bigots draws close, Barry and Joe stop time traveling and settle in an Amish community. Joe grows an epic neck beard.

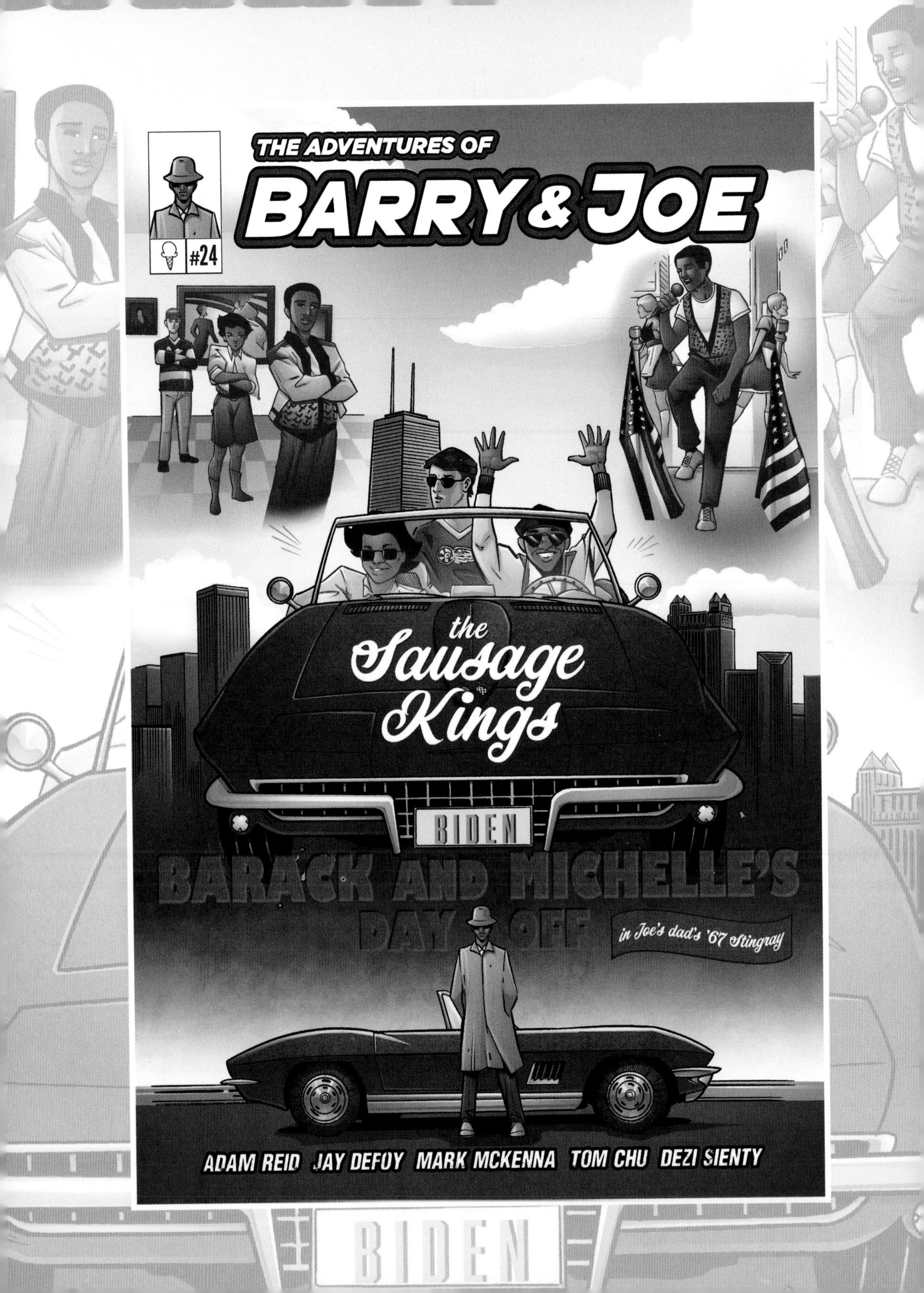
THE ADVENTURES OF
BARRY & JOE
#24
the Sausage Kings
BIDEN
BARACK AND MICHELLE'S DAY OFF
in Joe's dad's '67 Stingray
ADAM REID JAY DEFOY MARK MCKENNA TOM CHU DEZI SIENTY
BIDEN

FROZEN ASSETS—Barry and Joe must survive in a laboratory on an ice planet in the year 2356.

CRUDE—To avoid one of the worst man-made ecological disasters in U.S. history, Barry and Joe take labor-intensive jobs on the *Exxon Valdez* in March 1989. As Joe tries to relieve the third mate and take control of the ship, Barry must find a way to fix the radar before it's too late.

THUMB WAR—Obama and Biden must thumb wrestle to the death as prisoners of a super-creepy thumb-wrestling cabal.

BRO DOWN—When the Five Fingers develops a Bromantic Portal into 1960s Seattle, Barry and Joe team up with unlikely real-life friends Bruce Lee and Jimi Hendrix.

ON THE SHOULDERS OF GIANTS—In 1963, Barack Obama, only two years old, is taken to the March on Washington by a then twenty-one-year-old Joe Biden. Will toddler duty ruin Joe's historic experience? And will Barack somehow later remember Joe changing his diaper?

LAKERS VS. CELTICS—In 1985, Joe tries to sweeten an apology to Barry by scoring courtside seats to a seminal Larry Bird–Magic Johnson face-off.

DISTRICT WHINE—Obama and Biden arrive in the year 2424 and find mankind has reorganized itself by new tribal factions based on very different branches of science. But why does everyone look like Tilda Swinton?

WE SHALL OVERCOME—Barry and Joe arrive in an apartheid-era South Africa at the cusp of great change. Obama goes looking for Nelson Mandela, as Joe tries to help a class of passionate black students abandoned by their teacher.

BEYOND JOBAMA DOME—Barry and Joe go to the very first Burning Man in Black Rock City, where they make new friends and meet their spirit animals.

THE KING'S SPEECH—Arriving in 1991, Obama and Biden stop the beating of Rodney King by the LAPD and learn a valuable lesson about destiny.

THE RIVER MILD—Barry and Joe go whitewater rafting and save a family from evil Kevin Bacon.

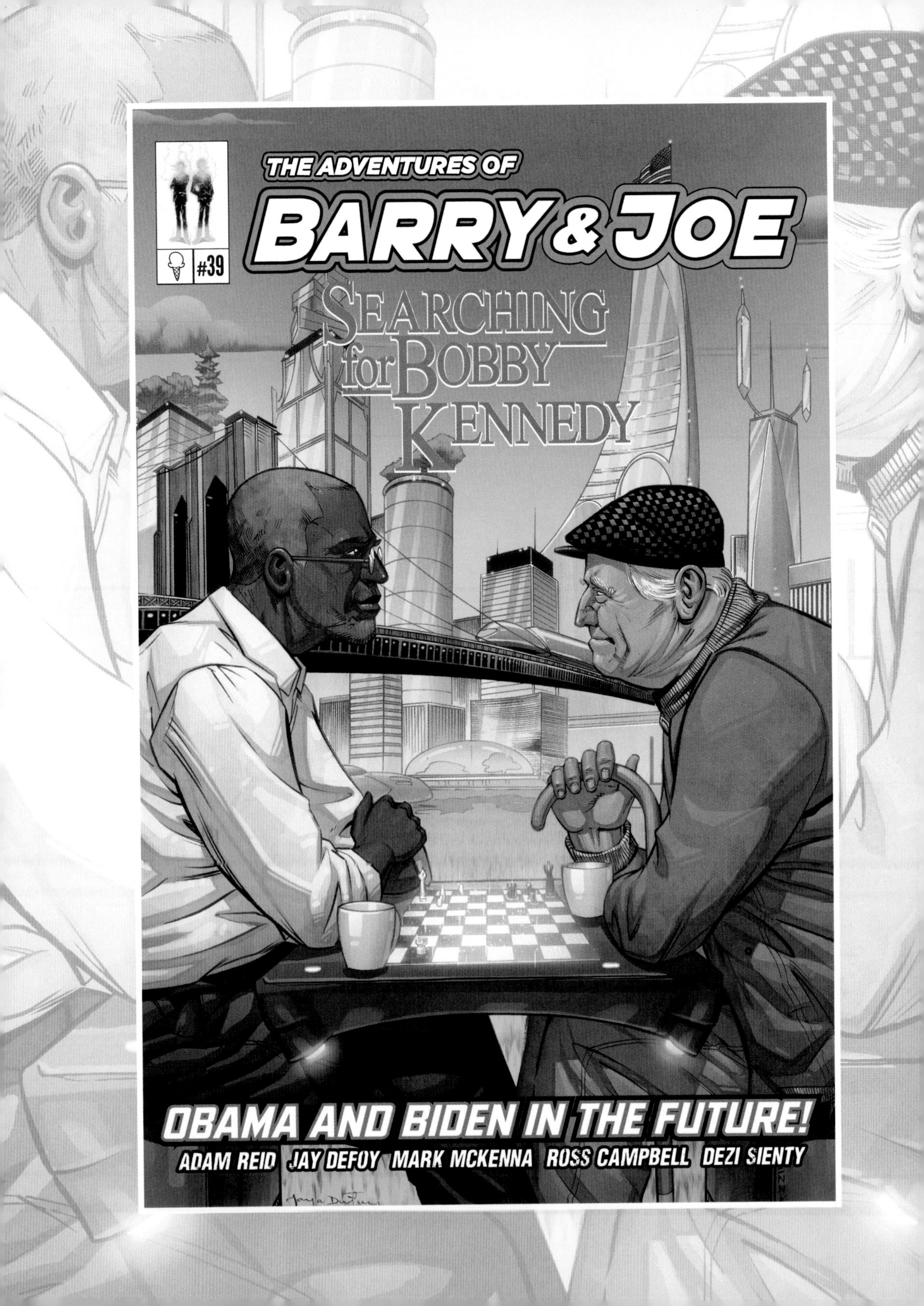
THE ADVENTURES OF
BARRY & JOE
#39
SEARCHING for BOBBY KENNEDY
OBAMA AND BIDEN IN THE FUTURE!
ADAM REID JAY DEFOY MARK MCKENNA ROSS CAMPBELL DEZI SIENTY

GOOD BILL HUNTING—Barry and Joe stop President Bill Clinton from a grievous mistake. Not that one. A different grievous mistake you don't know about.

THE KNIGHTS OF CENTRAL PARK—On April 19, 1989, Obama and Biden attempt to intercept the Central Park Five and with their help rewrite history in the Central Park Jogger case.

THE VORTEX—Obama and Biden revisit the red-letter date of Saturday, April 30, 2011: the night of the White House Correspondents' Association Dinner and the hunt for Osama bin Laden.

BARACK'S GOTTA HAVE IT—Samuel L. Jackson helps Barry and Joe hustle to become extras in the seminal Spike Lee joint *Do the Right Thing* in the summer of 1988 in Bedford-Stuyvesant, Brooklyn.

SCHRÖDINGER'S LIST—Barry and Joe find themselves herding kittens in Wyoming when a terrible storm threatens the entire ranch with floodwater.

THE TWO REDS—Using the Bromantic Portal, Barry and Joe experience the Harlem of the 1940s and join forces with young best friends Redd Foxx and Malcolm X.

READY PLAYER RUN—Barry and Joe play political *Second Life* in a giant simulation designed to accurately determine the outcome of elections.

THE LONG CON—Barry and Joe go to the San Diego Comic Con and relish wearing hyperrealistic masks of each other.

BARACK UNCHAINED—In which Obama is taken as a slave and put to work on a plantation, and it's up to Joe Biden to help rescue his friend and together burn the place to the fucking ground.

HEARTS AND MINDS—Obama and Biden stop the space shuttle *Challenger* from taking off on January 28, 1986.

MY TWO DADS—A paradox blossoms when Barry and Joe are put in charge of a baby Samuel L. Jackson and find their own future very much in their hands.

FIGHT OR FIGHT—Barry and Joe get front-row VIP seats to the greatest sporting event of the twentieth century, the Rumble in the Jungle boxing match between George Foreman and Muhammad Ali. When the fight doesn't play out as they expected, the guys are left figuring out how they might have accidentally affected the outcome.

CURRENT EVENTS—When their entangled consciousness misses its destination by a century, Barry and Joe meet Nikola Tesla in 1898 New York and unwittingly help him give birth to his most underrated discovery: the drone.

BARRY THE KID AND SHERIFF JOE—Barry discovers his talents as a quick-draw sharpshooter when the guys go to the Old West and meet Wyatt Earp himself, who takes Joe under his wing in the town of Tombstone.

AN OPEN MIND—In May 1988, Obama arrives in the body of a brain surgeon who must operate on Joe.

BRICK HOUSE—For Obama's first multidimensional birthday, Joe and Sam gift a perfect simulation of the White House basketball court on April 1, 2013, the day the president missed 20 of 22 shots in front of a group of children and the press corps.

BLACK FRIDAY—Barry and Joe bond in new ways when they spend the night in a Walmart after store hours.

ONCE MORE WITH FELT—Barry and Joe try to prevent the senseless death of Jim Henson to pneumonia in 1990.

THE DEVIL YOU SOW—Barry and Joe go to Hell and meet some truly evil fuckers. They learn a lot and ultimately feel much better about themselves and the choices they've made.

GREATEST HITS—Barry and Joe fill Central Park with folk music and, for a few moments, unite the world.

GEEK LOVE—Barry and Joe must become stone-cold nerds when they take undercover jobs working in IT for Trump in 1990.

THE DUKES OF OCCUPATIONAL HAZARDS—Barry and Joe try career paths outside of public service to see if it's such a wonderful life after all.

DON'T SPEAK—When members of the Senate mysteriously begin losing their voices . . .

THE MOD COUPLE—Obama and Biden become roommates living undercover in an all-Republican building.

WHITE HOUSE OF TERROR—In this Halloween special, Barry and Joe go trick-or-treating at the White House . . . in 1912.

OBAMA'S ELEVEN—Barack, Joe, and Sam put together an all-star crew—including magician Shin Lim, Olympic gymnast Aly Raisman, and actor Michael K. Williams—to retrieve a priceless letter from Trump's White House that Obama accidentally left in the *Resolute* desk of the Oval Office.

I DREAM OF DREAMING—Barry and Joe use the Bromantic Portal to save Dr. Martin Luther King Jr.

THE FULL JOE MALKOVICH—Obama searches for Joe in a dimension where the world is filled with billions of Joe Bidens and no one else. But which Joe is his?

SMOKE MONSTERS—In 2004, Obama and Biden order takeout and watch *Lost* with their families on Martha's Vineyard as something sinister lurks outside.

THE MALARKEY UNLIMITED—In 2028, Obama and Biden take the maiden voyage on Elon Musk's new cross-country Hyperloop and have very different experiences.

WE GO (VERY) HIGH—Obama and Biden travel to the Cannabis Cup in Amsterdam, where they are forced to become judges or risk tearing a hole in space-time.

LAST TRAIN TO WILMINGTON—When the Order of Bigots hijack an Amtrak train with Barry and Joe on board, there will be hell to pay for the bad guys and free ice cream for everyone else.

TOUR OF DUTY—Barry and Joe join the army together to settle a bet about who would fare better at basic training.

ONE MINUTE TILL MIDNIGHT—A murder in Savannah, Georgia, in 1981 places Barry and Joe inside the garden of good and evil.

HONEY, I SHRUNK THE PRESIDENT—The Five Fingers of Science accidentally shrinks the guys in the Oval Office.

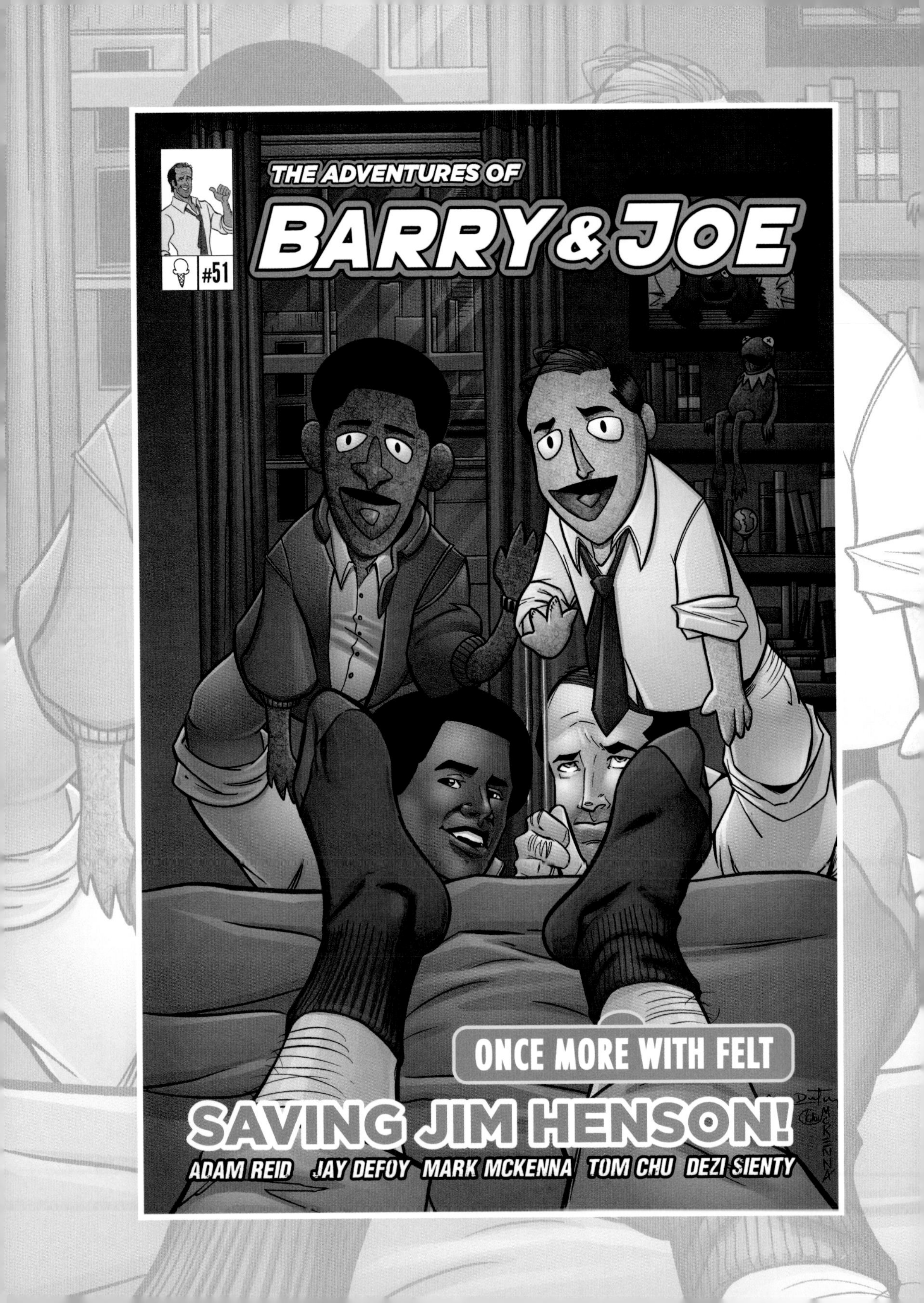
#51
THE ADVENTURES OF
BARRY & JOE
ONCE MORE WITH FELT
SAVING JIM HENSON!
ADAM REID JAY DEFOY MARK MCKENNA TOM CHU DEZI SIENTY

THE FOOTBALL—In the year 2022, during a peace mission in the Middle East, U.S. president Joe Biden's convoy is ambushed in Pakistan. Here Joe finds himself alone without Secret Service protection and in possession of "the football," a briefcase that functions as the nuclear strategic defense system for the United States.

BARRY & JOE & CHE—The guys fall through a crack in the ribbon of consciousness to join Che Guevara himself on a journey of self-discovery through South America.

PEACE, LOVE, AND MISUNDERSTANDING—Barry and Joe go to the original Woodstock, man.

THE WIZARDS OF OZ—In an alternate dimension, in 2020 Barack Obama and Joe Biden are sent to prison, where they are treated like heroes.

VOLUNTEERS—Barry and Joe help build a bridge in the middle of nowhere so a small village can prosper.

THE GOLDEN DOOR—Barry and Joe leap into the bodies of young refugee brothers from Guatemala on the day they arrive in America seeking asylum.

HOLY MOLY—Barack Obama and Joe Biden meet Jesus in a temporal wormhole.

THE LEFT STUFF—In a dark future, Obama and Biden are trained to join the Trump Space Force and end up making a far larger sacrifice than they were expecting.

1776—Obama and Biden take great pleasure in spying on Washington, Adams, and Jefferson as they cook up the Declaration of Independence . . . until they get caught.

LIGHTNING IN A BOTTLE—Barry and Joe meet Joe West and Barry Allen in an action-packed crossover event.

WE DID A BAD, BAD THING—Barry and Joe stop Trump from ever being born but immediately suffer dire consequences, including spatial melting, and must find a way to undo it.

LEAGUE OF LATE-NIGHT HOSTS—Obama and Biden join forces with Conan O'Brien, Stephen Colbert, Samantha Bee, Seth Meyers, Jimmy Kimmel, Jimmy Fallon, and Trevor Noah in a street fight against Fox News hosts.

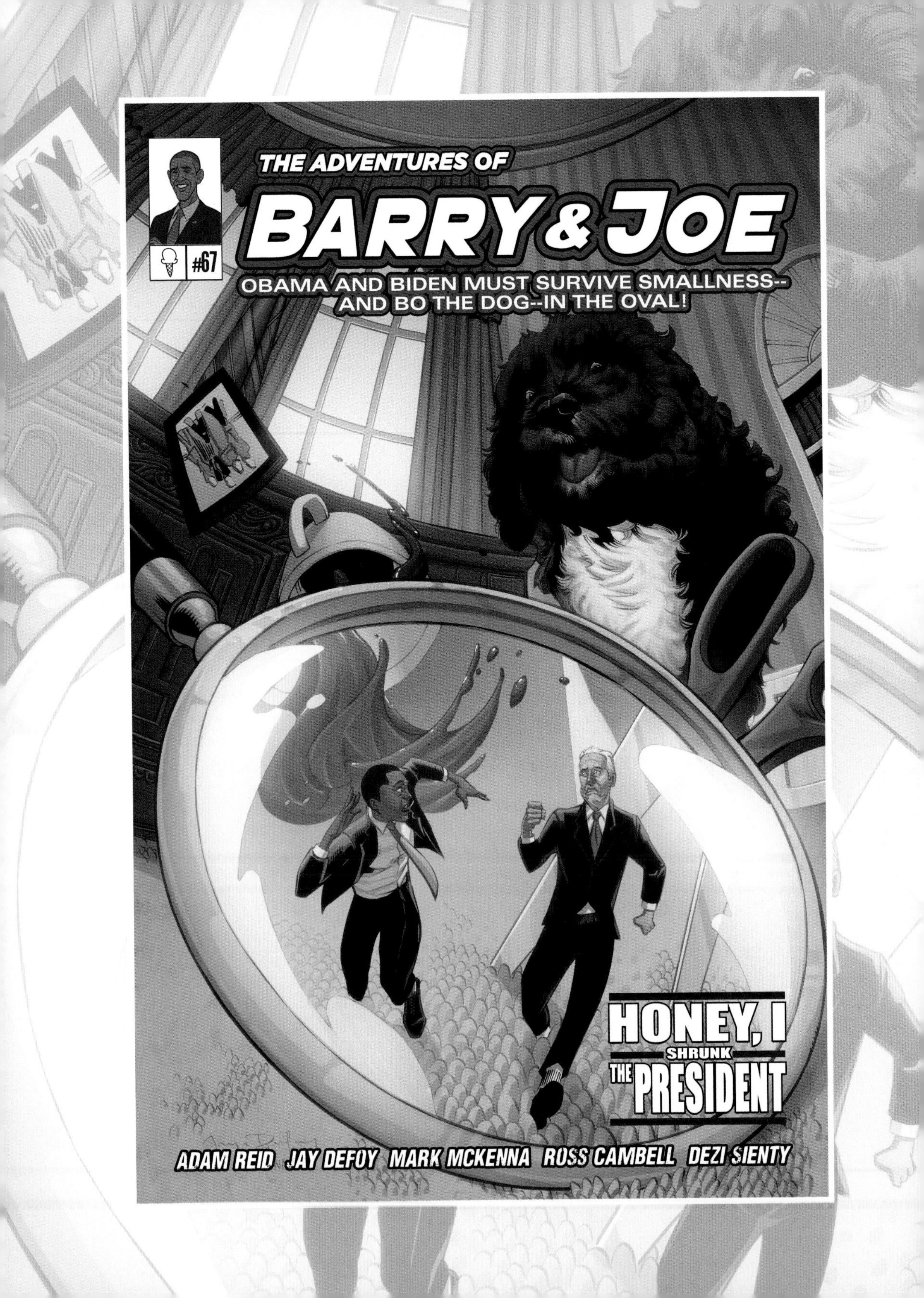

THE ADVENTURES OF
BARRY & JOE
#67
OBAMA AND BIDEN MUST SURVIVE SMALLNESS--
AND BO THE DOG--IN THE OVAL!
HONEY, I
SHRUNK
THE PRESIDENT
ADAM REID JAY DEFOY MARK MCKENNA ROSS CAMBELL DEZI SIENTY

COME ON DOWN—Barry and Joe attend a live taping of *The Price Is Right* and Barack becomes jealous when Joe is selected from the studio audience.

N IS FOR NAZI—When the Quantum Recoherence Engine malfunctions, Barry and Joe find themselves on the wrong side of World War II, wearing uniforms that Obama is seriously allergic to.

TALKING TURKEY—At a bowling alley in Scotch Plains, New Jersey, Barry and Joe make a wager they will both come to regret.

CHARIOTS OF FIRED UP—Obama and Biden work with the community to help a young woman win her district in a local election but find dark and powerful forces standing in their way.

SHOWTIME, FOLKS—Barry and Joe are trapped on a New York City subway in 1980, where they make new friends and learn new skills.

FAST PASS—In the deep future, Obama the Grey and Iron Biden survive the Magic Kingdom and have dinner with an immortal soul capture of Walt Disney himself.

MICHELLE ON WHEELS—Barry and Joe go to a roller derby and get pretty banged up . . . emotionally.

SEARCHING FOR BOBBY KENNEDY—In a gleaming future, Obama and Biden play chess in the park and talk about their heroes.

OF MUSTACHE AND MEN—Barry and Joe compete in a facial hair contest with Samuel L. Jackson, Jeff Bridges, and the ghost of Frederick Douglass.

MIXED META-FLOORS—The guys find themselves trapped in temporal purgatory between leaps and can only escape by ascending a metaphysical representation of Trump Tower floor by floor on a psychedelic journey to the penthouse, where an episode of *The Apprentice* is being filmed for a multidimensional audience.

ALMOST PARADISE—Obama and Biden find themselves having a normal weekend with their families, just hanging out in the year 2019, but the experience sours quickly when they realize they can't stay.

KARMA TO TABLE—Obama and Biden eat the best meal of their multidimensional lives, but it comes at a great cost, and with heartburn.

THE BIDEN REDEMPTION—Joe Biden is given a second chance as chair of the Senate Judiciary Committee during the Anita Hill testimony in the nomination of Clarence Thomas to the Supreme Court.

MEME-BURGER—Barry and Joe find themselves trapped inside their own Reddit AMA, where they must answer every single question in order to escape.

SPIN—Barry and Joe meet the Harlem Globetrotters, and Obama must confront just how hard it is to keep a basketball spinning on his finger forever.

WEAK CONSTITUTION—Barry and Joe go on vacation in Tulum, Mexico, where they are brought closer by discovering Montezuma's revenge together.

I'M GONNA MEDAL YOU, SUCKA—After the Five Fingers accidentally erases precious parts of Joe Biden's memory, Obama restages his awarding of the Presidential Medal of Freedom to his best friend . . . with mixed results.

BARACK, P.I.—Barry and Joe become private detectives in Hawaii to help save a childhood friend of Obama's from going to jail for a murder he did not commit.

THE OTHER WALL—Barry and Joe find themselves in a time loop of biblical proportions, confronting Herod the Great as he builds the Western Wall in Jerusalem.

THE REAL GENERAL LEE—Using the Quantum Simulator, Barry and Joe witness the Civil War and join the fight.

HAPPY TREES—Arriving in 1983 and hunted by the Order of Bigots, Barry and Joe find themselves lying low with Bob Ross, as he teaches them how to find inner peace despite the endless chaos of being time warriors.

THE MAN WITH THE GOLDEN HELICOPTER—Barry and Joe must confront Trump once and for all on neutral territory . . . reality television.

GREAT WHITES—In a PR stunt for the ages, Barry and Joe water ski jump a bloodthirsty robotic great white shark sponsored by Facebook.

DEAR LEADER—Obama arrives inside the body of Trump on his inauguration day and must convince Joe who he really is or risk collapsing reality itself.

INTO AFRICA—Barack Obama and Joe Biden travel to Kenya together, where Obama is given more time with his father than he could have ever imagined.

ALIEN NATION—In 1987, Barry and Joe adopt an adorable alien named Zhort who loves boards games, berry pie, and speechwriting.

FINGER GUNS—Barry and Joe arrive in a dimension where Obama can shoot actual rainbows out of his palm and Joe's pointer finger shoots courage itself. When these new powers go to their respective heads, they become increasingly competitive with each other about who can make a bigger difference in the world.

THERE IS NOTHING NOBLE
IN BEING SUPERIOR TO
YOUR FELLOW MEN.
TRUE NOBILITY LIES IN
BEING SUPERIOR TO YOUR
FORMER SELF.

—ERNEST HEMINGWAY

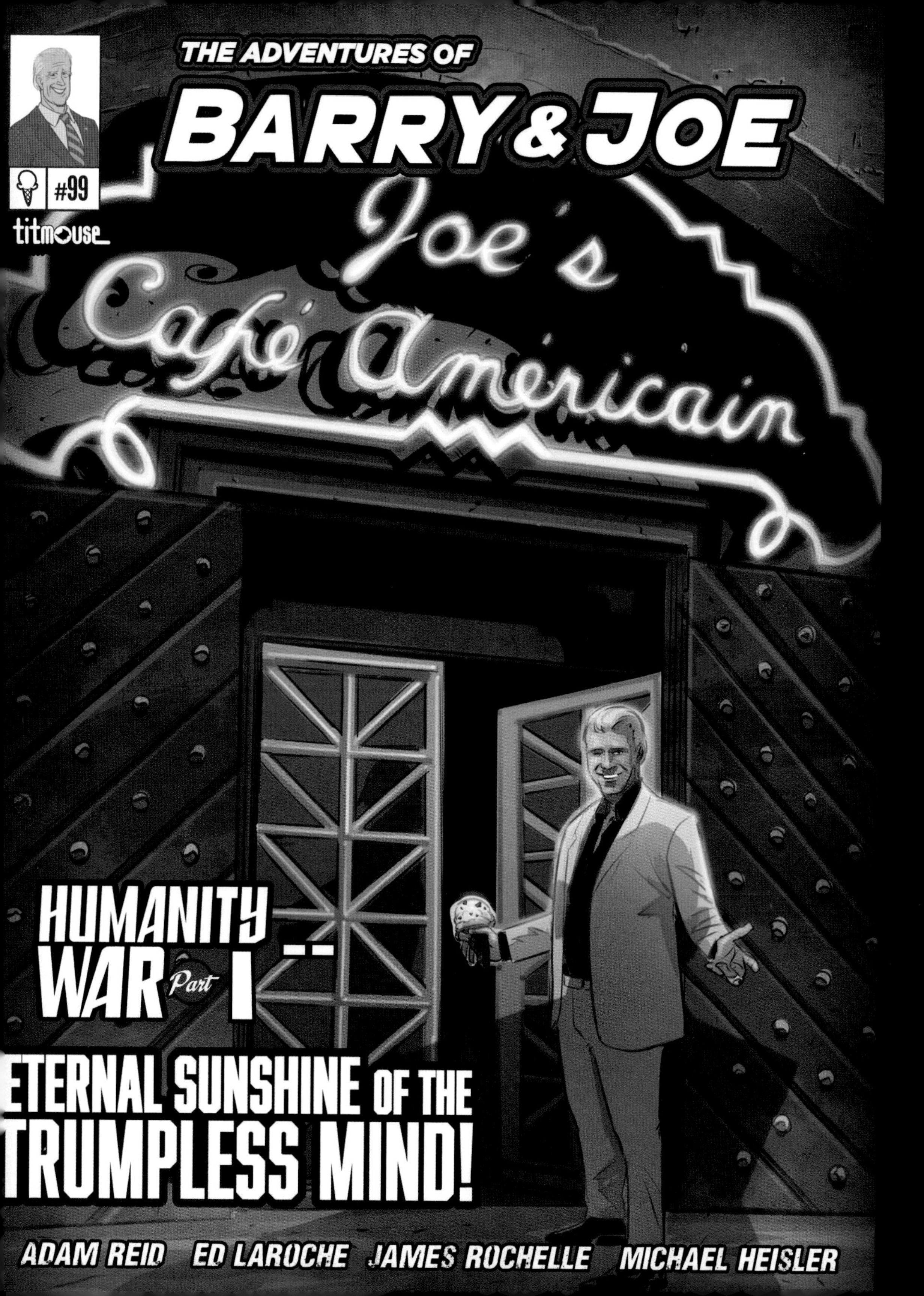

THE ADVENTURES OF
BARRY & JOE
#99
titmouse
Joe's
Café Américain
HUMANITY WAR Part I --
ETERNAL SUNSHINE OF THE TRUMPLESS MIND!
ADAM REID
ED LAROCHE
JAMES ROCHELLE
MICHAEL HEISLER

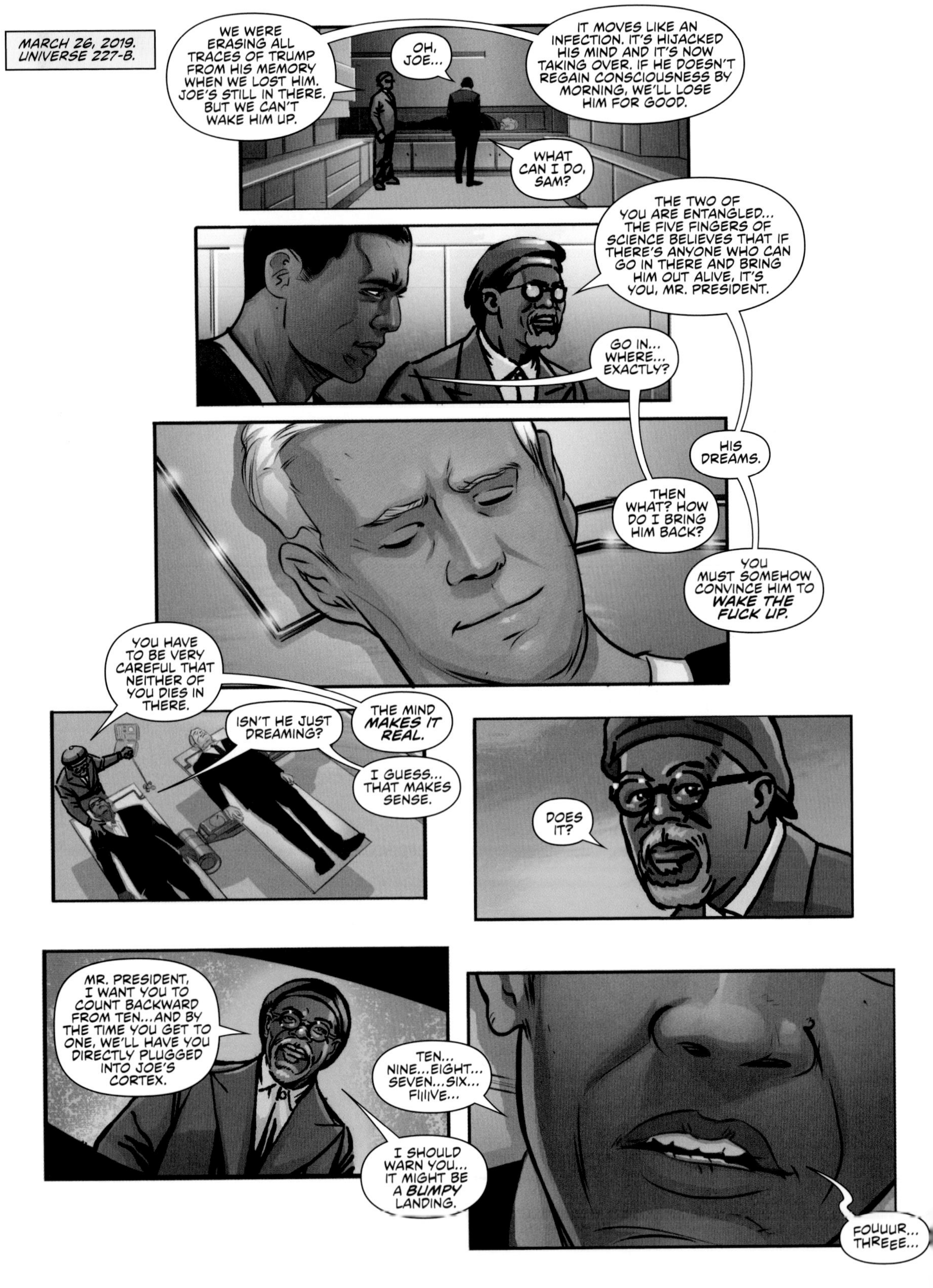
MARCH 26, 2019. UNIVERSE 227-B.
WE WERE ERASING ALL TRACES OF TRUMP FROM HIS MEMORY WHEN WE LOST HIM. JOE'S STILL IN THERE. BUT WE CAN'T WAKE HIM UP.
OH, JOE...
IT MOVES LIKE AN INFECTION. IT'S HIJACKED HIS MIND AND IT'S NOW TAKING OVER. IF HE DOESN'T REGAIN CONSCIOUSNESS BY MORNING, WE'LL LOSE HIM FOR GOOD.
WHAT CAN I DO, SAM?
THE TWO OF YOU ARE ENTANGLED... THE FIVE FINGERS OF SCIENCE BELIEVES THAT IF THERE'S ANYONE WHO CAN GO IN THERE AND BRING HIM OUT ALIVE, IT'S YOU, MR. PRESIDENT.
GO IN... WHERE... EXACTLY?
HIS DREAMS.
THEN WHAT? HOW DO I BRING HIM BACK?
YOU MUST SOMEHOW CONVINCE HIM TO *WAKE THE FUCK UP.*
YOU HAVE TO BE VERY CAREFUL THAT NEITHER OF YOU DIES IN THERE.
ISN'T HE JUST DREAMING?
THE MIND *MAKES IT REAL.*
I GUESS... THAT MAKES SENSE.
DOES IT?
MR. PRESIDENT, I WANT YOU TO COUNT BACKWARD FROM TEN...AND BY THE TIME YOU GET TO ONE, WE'LL HAVE YOU DIRECTLY PLUGGED INTO JOE'S CORTEX.
TEN... NINE...EIGHT... SEVEN...SIX... FIIIIVE...
I SHOULD WARN YOU... IT MIGHT BE A *BUMPY* LANDING.
FOUUUR... THREEE...

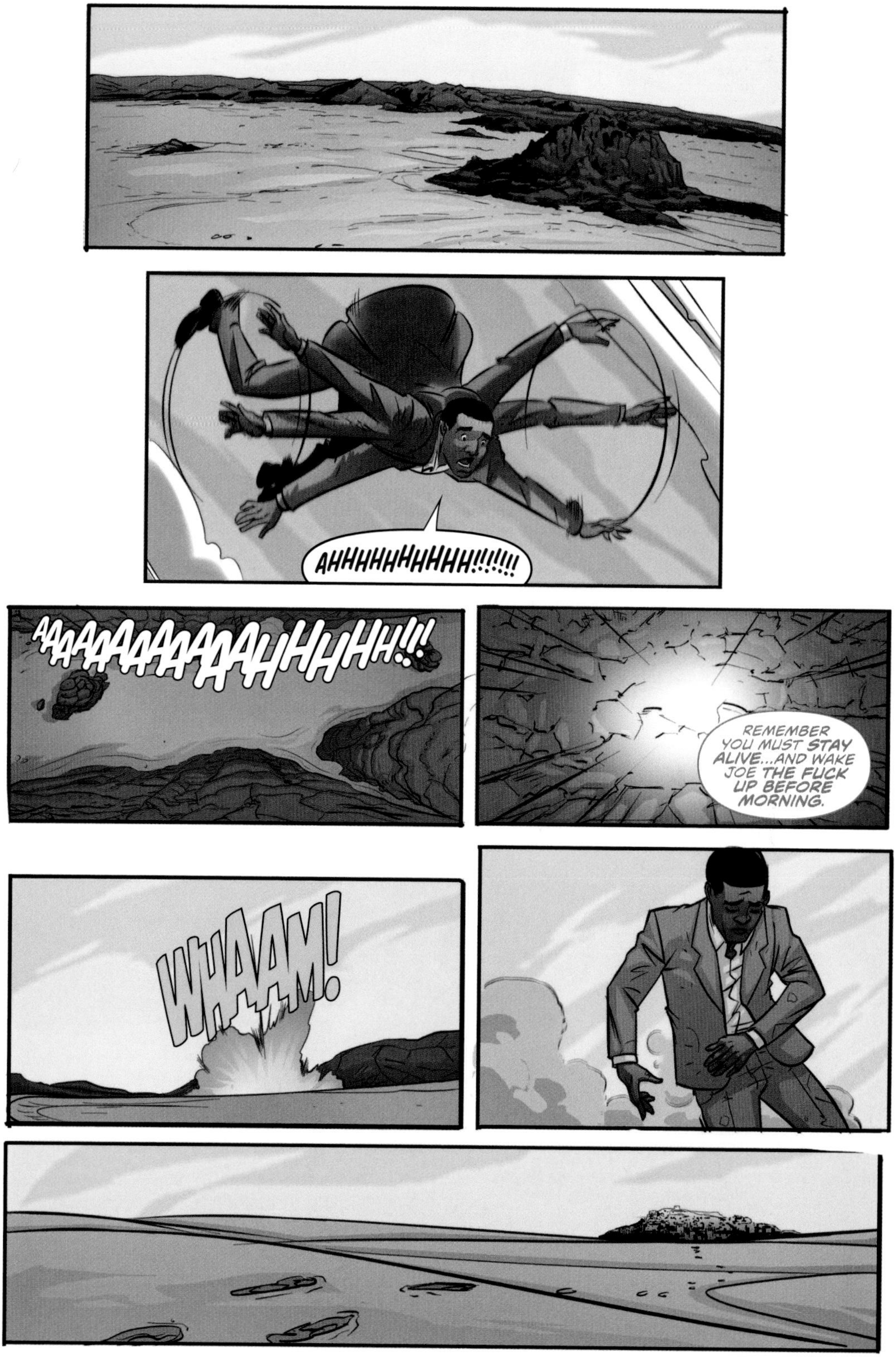
AHHHHHHHHHH!!!!!!!
AAAAAAAAAAAAAAAHHHHHH!!!
REMEMBER YOU MUST STAY ALIVE...AND WAKE JOE THE FUCK UP BEFORE MORNING.
WHAAM!

HA.

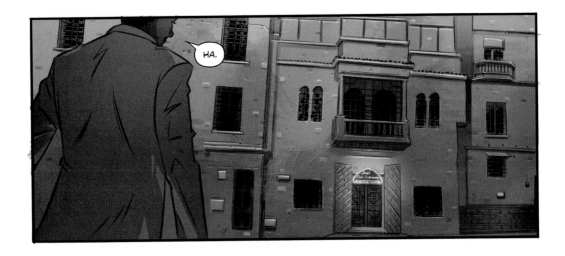

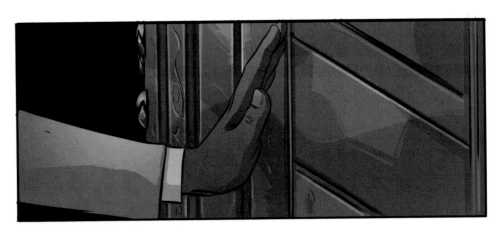

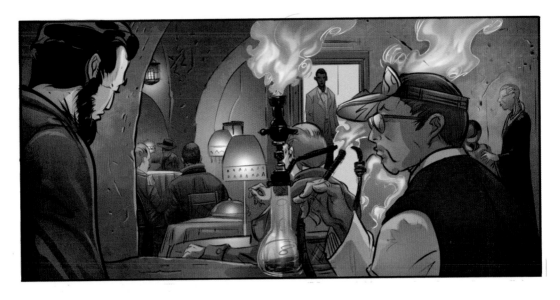

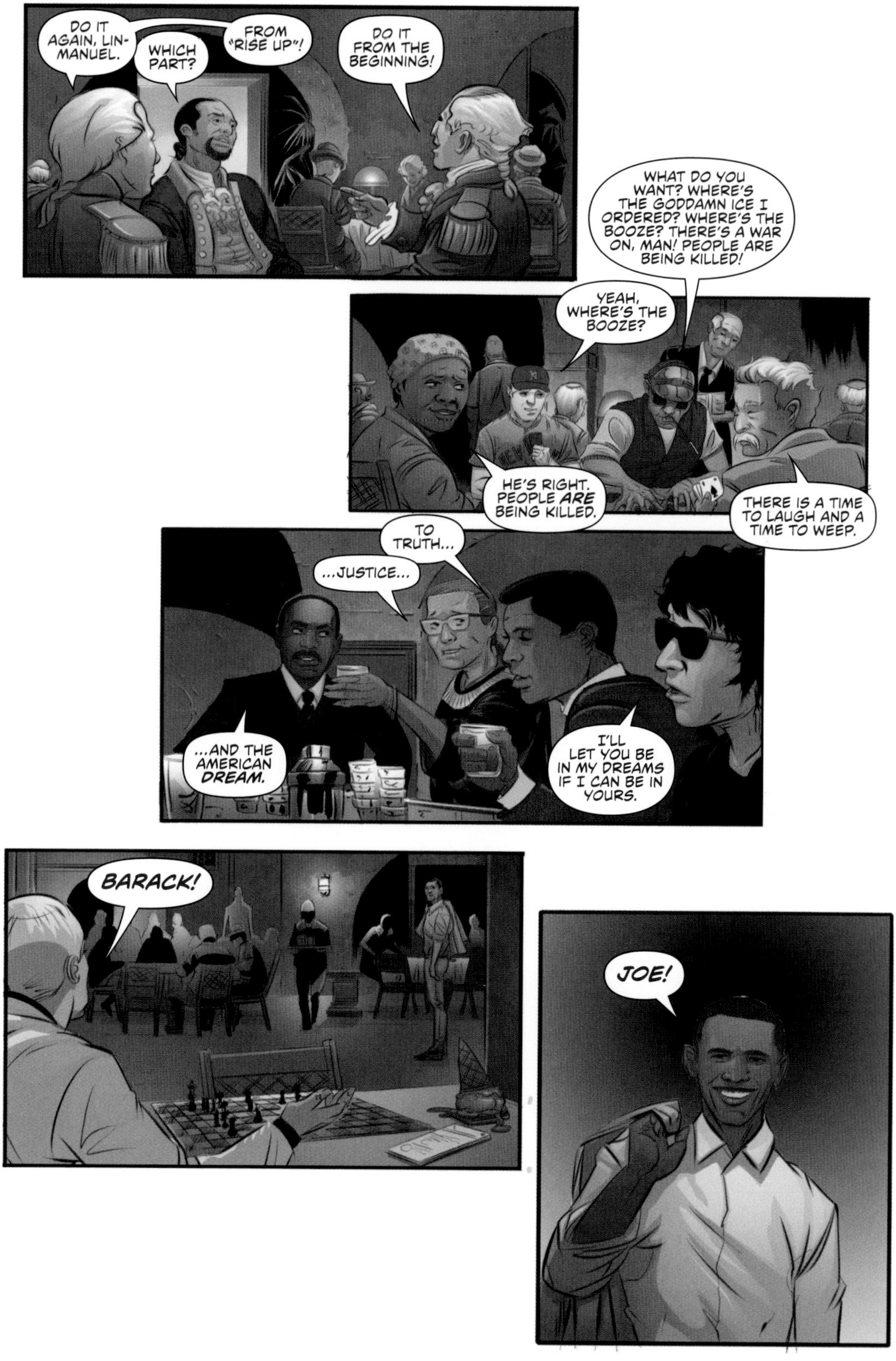
DO IT AGAIN, LIN-MANUEL.
WHICH PART?
FROM "RISE UP"!
DO IT FROM THE BEGINNING!
WHAT DO YOU WANT? WHERE'S THE GODDAMN ICE I ORDERED? WHERE'S THE BOOZE? THERE'S A WAR ON, MAN! PEOPLE ARE BEING KILLED!
YEAH, WHERE'S THE BOOZE?
HE'S RIGHT. PEOPLE *ARE* BEING KILLED.
THERE IS A TIME TO LAUGH AND A TIME TO WEEP.
TO TRUTH...
...JUSTICE...
...AND THE AMERICAN *DREAM.*
I'LL LET YOU BE IN MY DREAMS IF I CAN BE IN YOURS.
BARACK!
JOE!

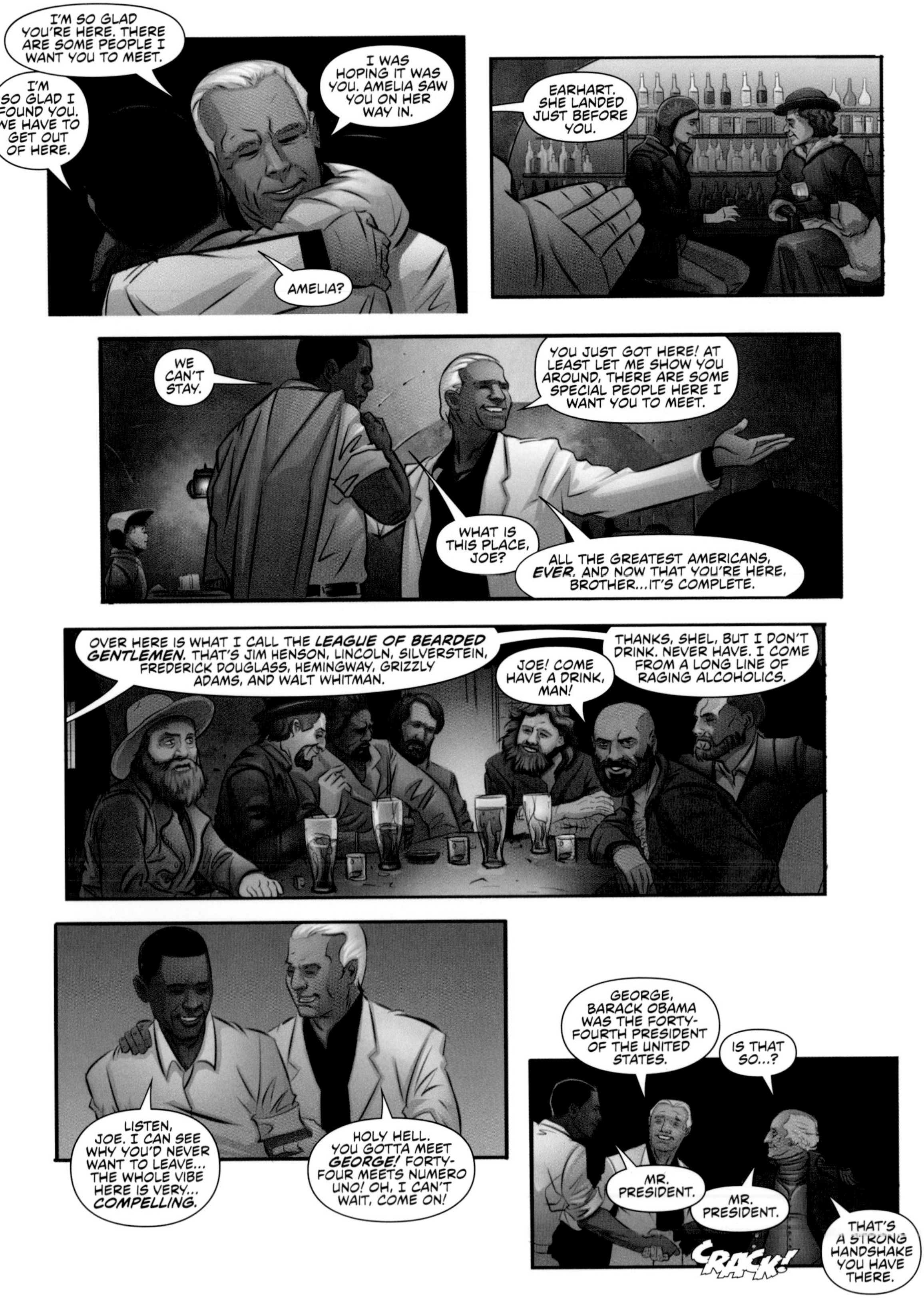
I'M SO GLAD YOU'RE HERE. THERE ARE SOME PEOPLE I WANT YOU TO MEET.
I'M SO GLAD I FOUND YOU. WE HAVE TO GET OUT OF HERE.
I WAS HOPING IT WAS YOU. AMELIA SAW YOU ON HER WAY IN.
AMELIA?
EARHART. SHE LANDED JUST BEFORE YOU.
WE CAN'T STAY.
YOU JUST GOT HERE! AT LEAST LET ME SHOW YOU AROUND, THERE ARE SOME SPECIAL PEOPLE HERE I WANT YOU TO MEET.
WHAT IS THIS PLACE, JOE?
ALL THE GREATEST AMERICANS, *EVER.* AND NOW THAT YOU'RE HERE, BROTHER...IT'S COMPLETE.
OVER HERE IS WHAT I CALL THE *LEAGUE OF BEARDED GENTLEMEN.* THAT'S JIM HENSON, LINCOLN, SILVERSTEIN, FREDERICK DOUGLASS, HEMINGWAY, GRIZZLY ADAMS, AND WALT WHITMAN.
JOE! COME HAVE A DRINK, MAN!
THANKS, SHEL, BUT I DON'T DRINK. NEVER HAVE. I COME FROM A LONG LINE OF RAGING ALCOHOLICS.
LISTEN, JOE. I CAN SEE WHY YOU'D NEVER WANT TO LEAVE... THE WHOLE VIBE HERE IS VERY... *COMPELLING.*
HOLY HELL. YOU GOTTA MEET *GEORGE!* FORTY-FOUR MEETS NUMERO UNO! OH, I CAN'T WAIT, COME ON!
GEORGE, BARACK OBAMA WAS THE FORTY-FOURTH PRESIDENT OF THE UNITED STATES.
IS THAT SO...?
MR. PRESIDENT.
MR. PRESIDENT.
CRACK!
THAT'S A STRONG HANDSHAKE YOU HAVE THERE.

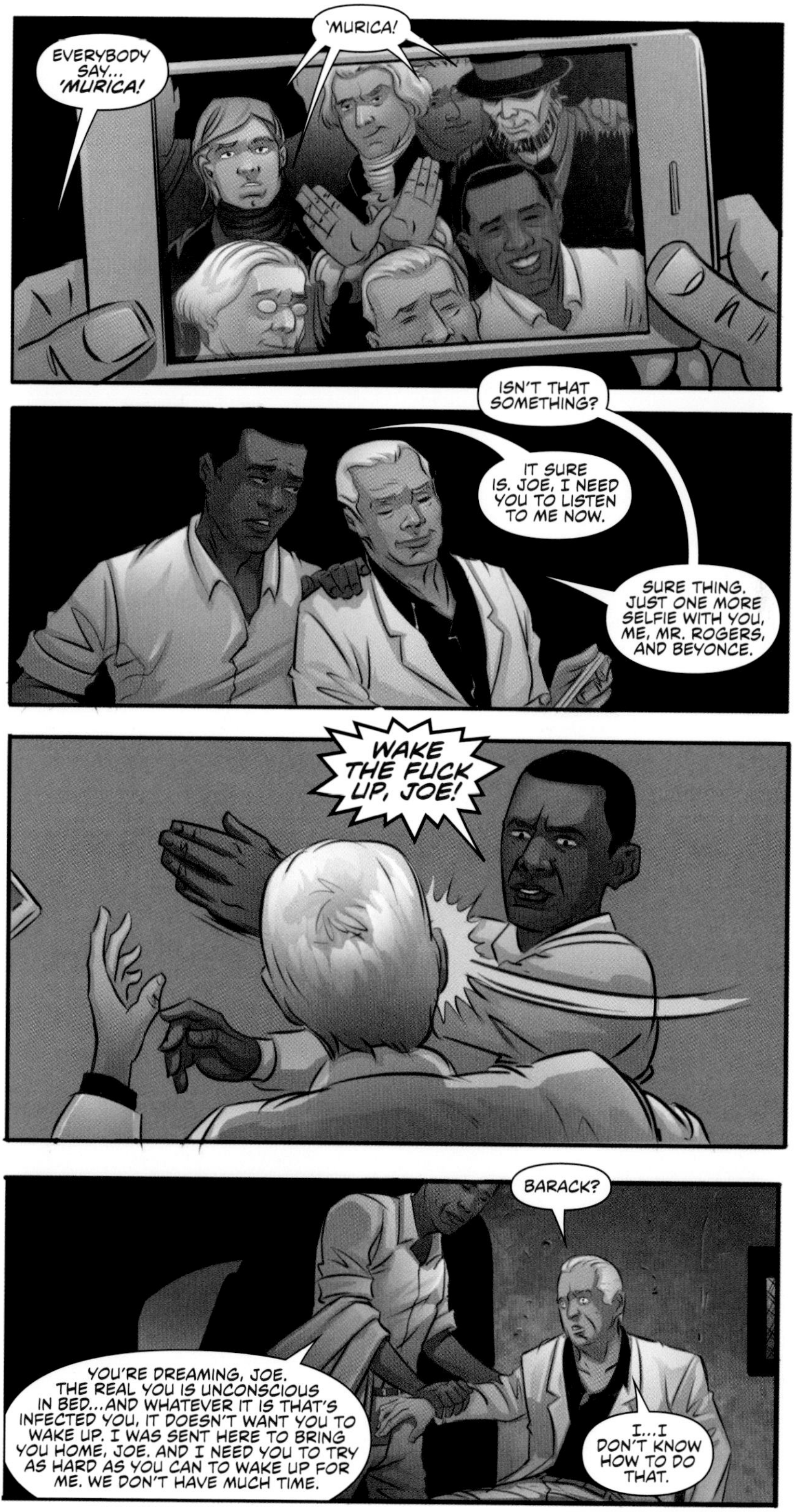
EVERYBODY SAY... 'MURICA!
'MURICA!
ISN'T THAT SOMETHING?
IT SURE IS. JOE, I NEED YOU TO LISTEN TO ME NOW.
SURE THING. JUST ONE MORE SELFIE WITH YOU, ME, MR. ROGERS, AND BEYONCE.
WAKE THE FUCK UP, JOE!
BARACK?
YOU'RE DREAMING, JOE. THE REAL YOU IS UNCONSCIOUS IN BED...AND WHATEVER IT IS THAT'S INFECTED YOU, IT DOESN'T WANT YOU TO WAKE UP. I WAS SENT HERE TO BRING YOU HOME, JOE. AND I NEED YOU TO TRY AS HARD AS YOU CAN TO WAKE UP FOR ME. WE DON'T HAVE MUCH TIME.
I...I DON'T KNOW HOW TO DO THAT.

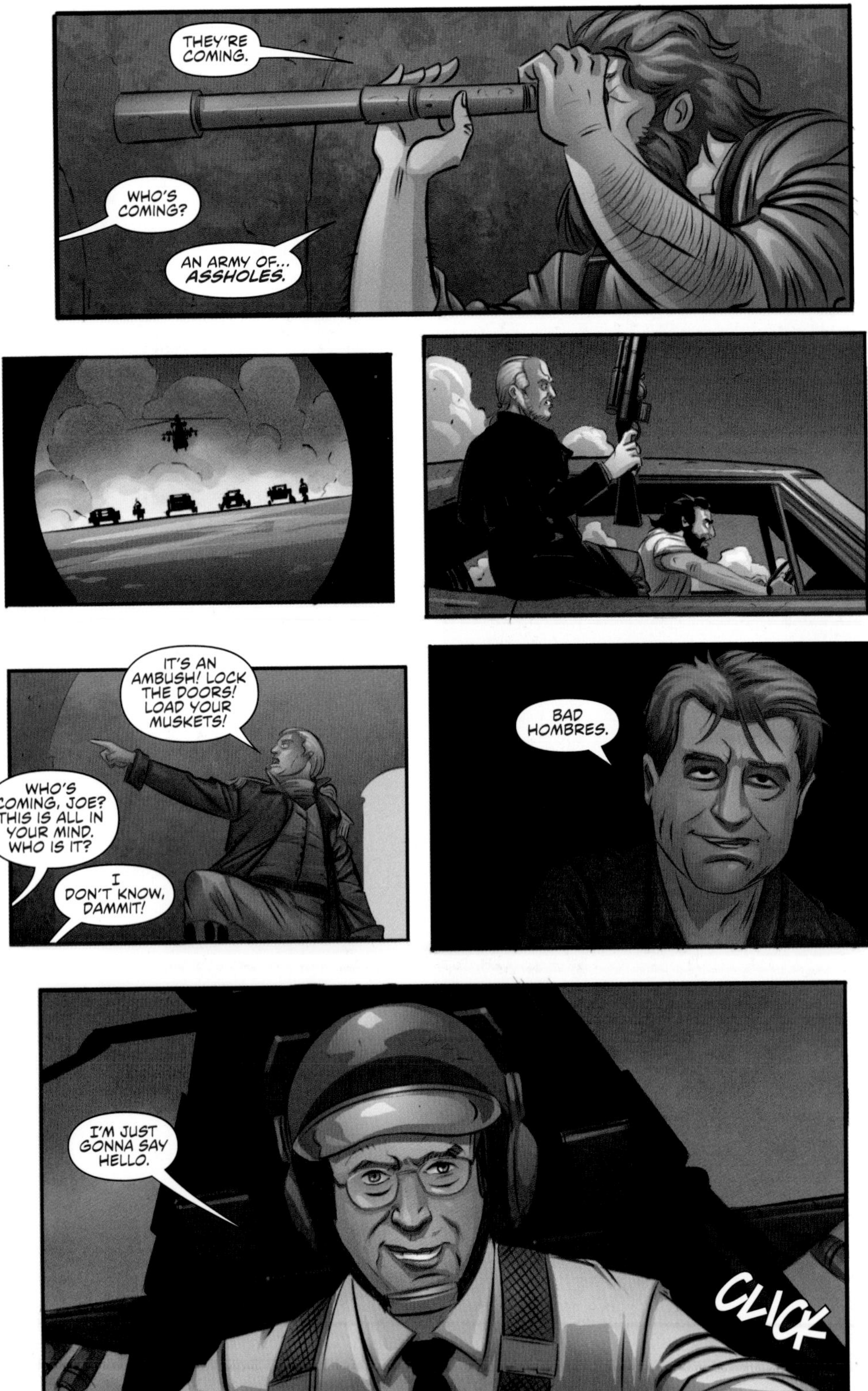
THEY'RE COMING.
WHO'S COMING?
AN ARMY OF... ASSHOLES.
IT'S AN AMBUSH! LOCK THE DOORS! LOAD YOUR MUSKETS!
WHO'S COMING, JOE? THIS IS ALL IN YOUR MIND. WHO IS IT?
I DON'T KNOW, DAMMIT!
BAD HOMBRES.
I'M JUST GONNA SAY HELLO.
CLICK

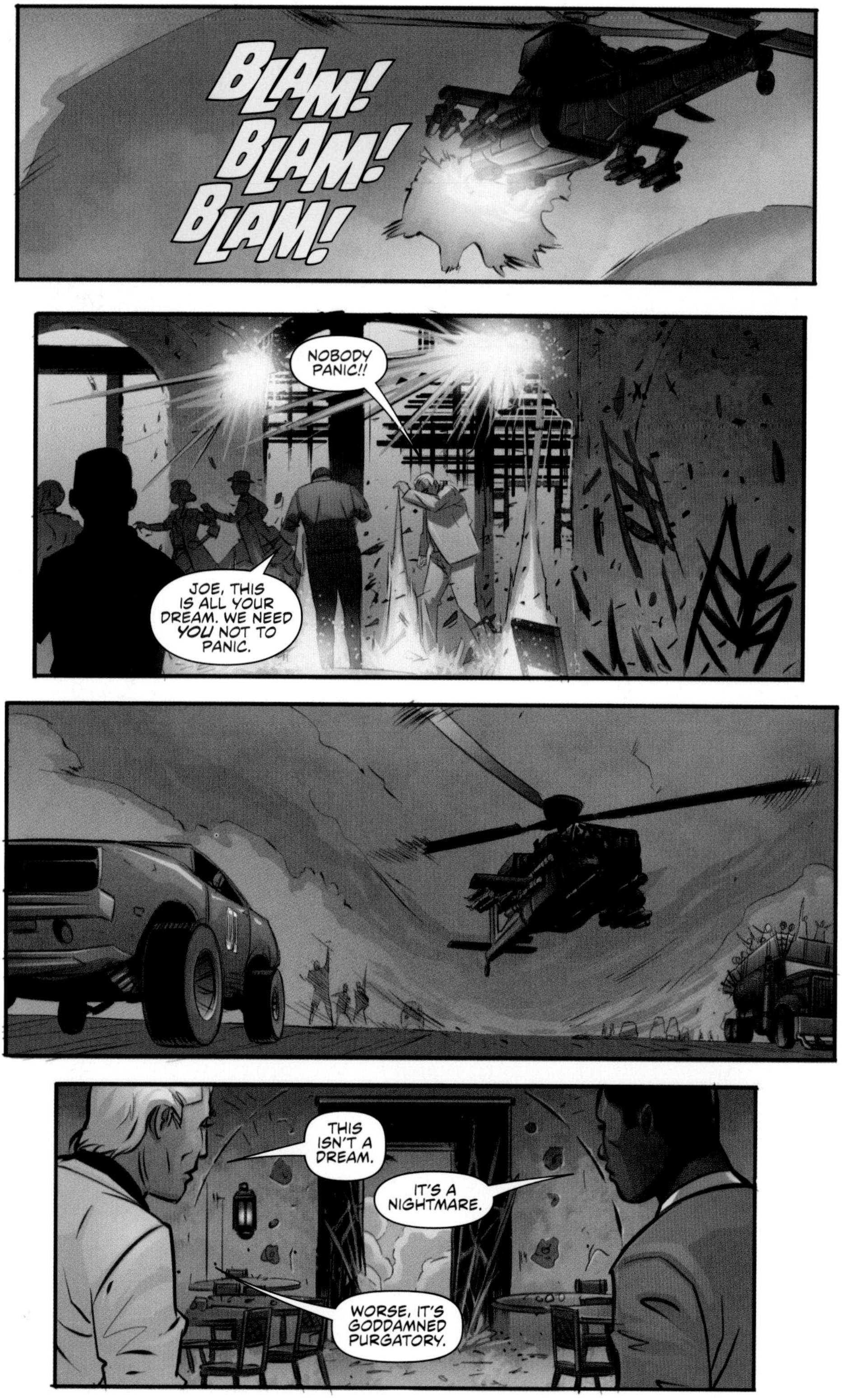
BLAM! BLAM! BLAM!
NOBODY PANIC!!
JOE, THIS IS ALL YOUR DREAM. WE NEED *YOU* NOT TO PANIC.
THIS ISN'T A DREAM.
IT'S A NIGHTMARE.
WORSE, IT'S GODDAMNED PURGATORY.

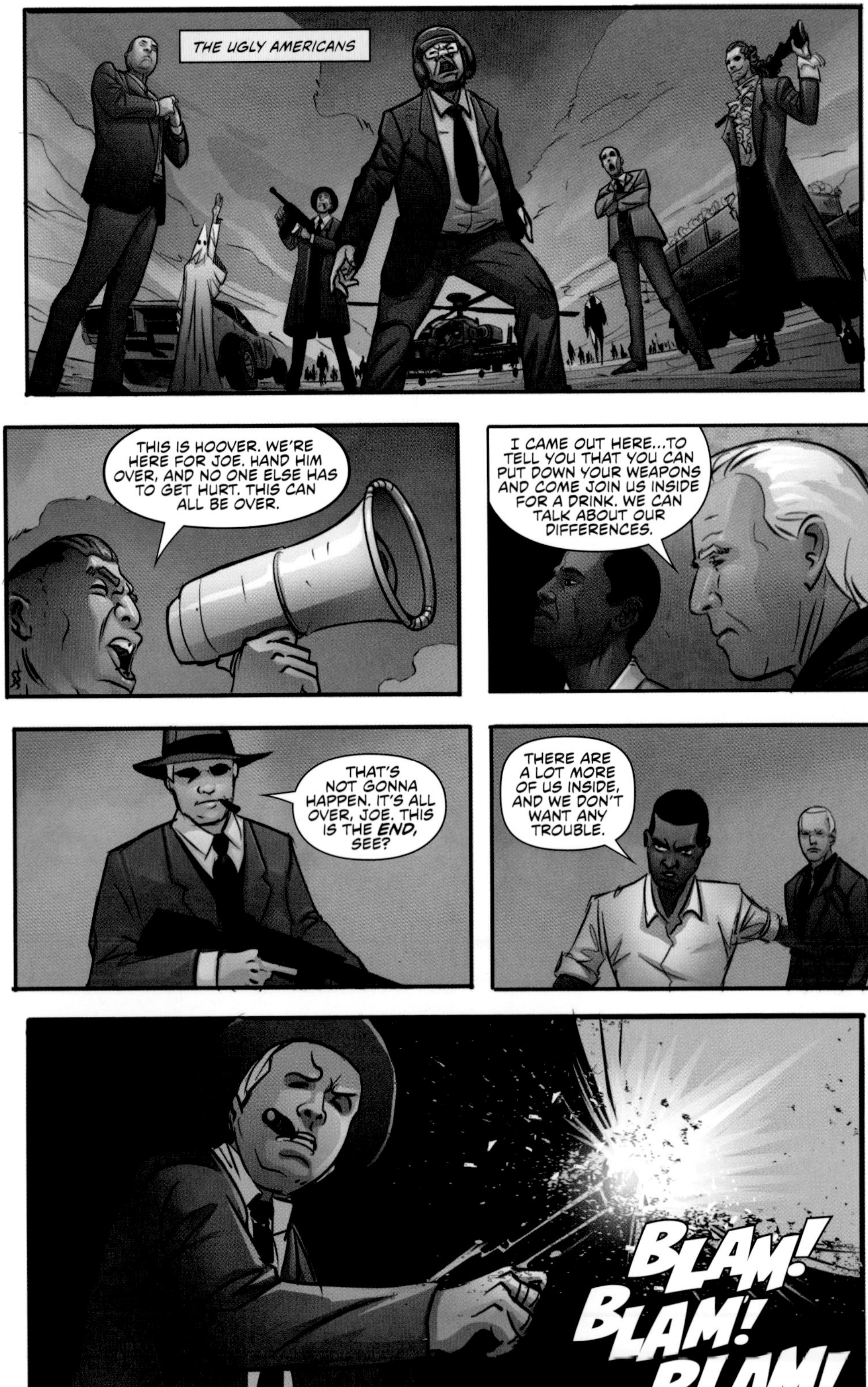
THE UGLY AMERICANS
THIS IS HOOVER. WE'RE HERE FOR JOE. HAND HIM OVER, AND NO ONE ELSE HAS TO GET HURT. THIS CAN ALL BE OVER.
I CAME OUT HERE...TO TELL YOU THAT YOU CAN PUT DOWN YOUR WEAPONS AND COME JOIN US INSIDE FOR A DRINK. WE CAN TALK ABOUT OUR DIFFERENCES.
THAT'S NOT GONNA HAPPEN. IT'S ALL OVER, JOE. THIS IS THE *END,* SEE?
THERE ARE A LOT MORE OF US INSIDE, AND WE DON'T WANT ANY TROUBLE.
BLAM! BLAM! BLAM!

IT'S SPREADING FASTER. WE'RE GOING TO LOSE HIM. WE NEED TO PULL OUT THE PRESIDENT BEFORE IT'S TOO LATE.

NOT YET. WE'D LOSE JOE. GIVE THEM MORE TIME.

BLAM! BLAM! BLAM!

SEND IN THE CLOWNS.

# HUMANITY WAR
### PART I

WRITTEN BY *ADAM REID*
ART BY *ED LAROCHE*

COLORS BY *JAMES ROCHELLE*
LETTERS BY *MICHAEL HEISLER*
COVER BY *LAROCHE AND ROCHELLE*

COMIC BOOK PRODUCED BY:
TITMOUSE, INC.

EXECUTIVE PRODUCERS:
CHRIS PRYNOSKI AND
BEN KALINA

CREATIVE DIRECTOR:
ANTONIO CANOBBIO

PRODUCER:
WILL FENG

TO BE CONTINUED...

# NIGHT OF THE LIVING DEMOCRATS

PROCEED AT YOUR OWN RISK

(LOTS OF MOANING AND WHINING)

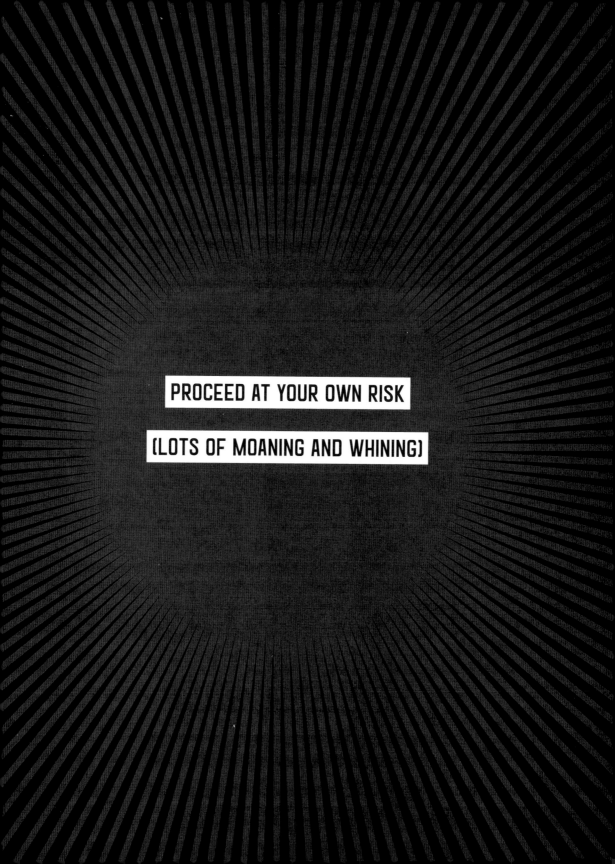

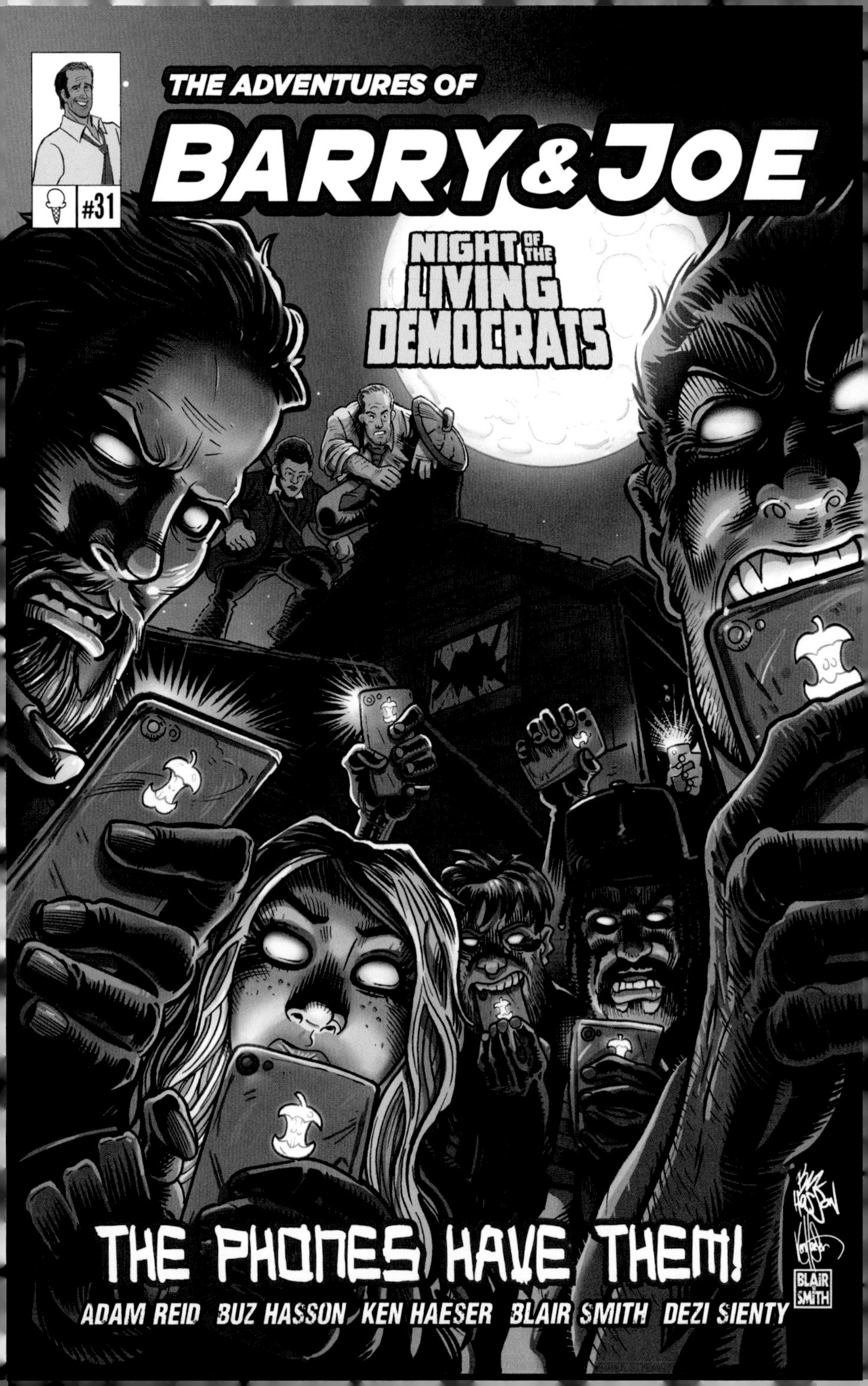

THE ADVENTURES OF
BARRY & JOE
#31
NIGHT OF THE LIVING DEMOCRATS
THE PHONES HAVE THEM!
ADAM REID BUZ HASSON KEN HAESER BLAIR SMITH DEZI SIENTY
BLAIR SMITH

**B**arack Obama and Joe Biden learned quickly that things could always be worse in the next reality.

# WHAT FRESH HELL

Every single registered Democrat in northern Florida had turned in just a few days.

Barack and Joe held on to each other tighter than they ever had before. They were crouched together in a child's bedroom closet. It was pitch black, and the president could hear the urgent ticking of his own heart as he held his hand tightly over Joe's mouth. By nature, Joe was never quiet. This level of intense stillness was very new to him.

Just inches outside the closet door, they heard the high-pitched whine of a dembie. This was the nickname Joe had come up with for the creatures. Zombie meets Democrat. This particular dembie was typical, all moaning with intermittent whining. They seemed harmless at first, but the fuckers went into a spastic rage once they were triggered.

Barack and Joe would never look at a smartphone in quite the same way. The outbreak had apparently spread through the phones. The news feed itself had become a delivery system for pure rage, and before anyone really knew what was happening it was far too late.

It was October 2016, and our heroes arrived very hopeful about this dimension and the odds of this blossoming into a better world than the others they had visited. They even started this trip by lending their significant star power where they believed it could be the most effective—which is what had brought them to the working-class suburbs of Duval County in the first place. They really wanted to make a difference and genuinely believed that a grassroots, boots-on-the-ground, person-to-person dialogue was the best way to get out the vote. Obama and Biden were very different animals, but the things they agreed on were fundamental. One of those beliefs was that real and lasting change started at the bottom and rose up.

Instead, Obama and Biden had spent their day watching bright and sensitive people turn into complete monsters. Now every liberal for three hundred miles was a stark raving jerk with a ravenous appetite for like-minded brains. It was pure luck that Barry and Joe had broken themselves of their smartphone addiction by spending so much time in the '80s and '90s. They weren't glued to their phones like everyone else in 2016 and had so far remained untouched by the viral sensation as it rippled outward and took all sanity with it.

# SWING STATE

As far as Joe and Barack understood it, the best way to stop a dembie was to knock them unconscious. Scientists proposed an immediate solution of mass anesthesia to put all the liberals to sleep until a cure could be isolated. This ambitious plan was quickly abandoned when the scientists working on the project became among the first infected.

Barack was worried. He felt that if he and Joe didn't make a run for it, they would wind up like everyone else they met that day. The dembie pacing the kid's room filled with superhero posters had been Secret Service Agent Mosley just twenty minutes ago. Reaching behind him, Obama felt the worn wrapped handle of a baseball bat.

Barack slowly let go of Joe's mouth. He whispered to Joe as quietly as he could: "You ready to go?" As he said this he guided Joe's hands to the bat. Obama clutched it tightly. Again, he whispered: "You open. I swing."

Joe responded, much too loud, "Fuck yeah. Let's do it."

Dembie Agent Mosley heard this; his head snapped toward the closet and he began pawing at the door like a drunk kitten.

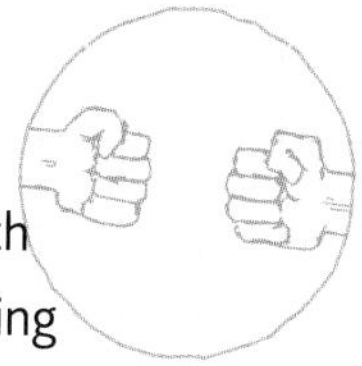

"Now!" President Obama yelled, and Joe kicked the door open with all his might. Agent Mosley was sent flying backward by the door, leaving Obama's massive swing whiffing through the air.

The suited dembie, his earpiece dangling from his ear, crawled and clawed for Obama's right ankle, pulling him toward the floor. Joe stumbled out of the closet into the cool blue room, and he scrambled to his feet to get his bearings. His eyes adjusted to the two figures wrestling on the carpet; he knew one of them was the president and the other was about to be very sorry.

Joe was about to stomp Agent Mosley in the head with the heel of his shoe when Barack stopped him.

"Wait," said Obama.

Agent Mosley was at this moment ineffectually chewing on his ankle but not using any real force. Obama looked closer, and he could see that the dembie had covered his teeth with his lips and was gently gnawing, which did absolutely no harm whatsoever. Obama shook him off easily and Joe helped him up. Agent Mosley had one hand tightly gripped on his cell phone, and as he stood up he whined loudly and shoved his phone in the president's face.

"Don't look at it!" Joe smacked the device out of Agent Mosley's hand.

They left dembie Agent Mosley there in the darkness, moaning and trying to recover his phone, as they ran down the stairs together. Obama held the baseball bat high, tight, and ready as he led the way. Out the window in the lamplight, Joe could see groups of moaning dembies collected on the sidewalk and street. They moaned and whined in packs, and the thought of being devoured by the horde sent a chill down Joe's spine.

They thought the house was empty, but just as Barack set the bat down to peer outside, a young dembie came screaming from the kitchen wearing a blue I'M WITH HER shirt with pink lettering. Joe didn't hesitate to clock her out cold. He felt terrible instantly but had no time to reflect, as a dozen dembies came pouring in through the windows.

# SALT OF THE EARTH

Paul, Tessa, Lisa, Baby Joy, and Grandma Luce. The Wallaces were exceedingly kind, gentle, sweet people. They were also incredibly racist.

To say that the Wallace family had no interest in politics was a massive understatement. They did not watch the news or follow elections. Of course, they could throw together a sloppy opinion when they were asked, but they generally wore their anti-political stance as a badge of honor. Paul and Tessa Wallace had never voted. To them, all politicians were the same. For Paul, a politician could be no more trusted than someone with dark skin.

The Wallace family brand of bigotry had invisible roots in the South and had grown for generations. Paul did not think of himself as a racist, and the word itself meant something very different to him. This was a man who trusted his considerable gut and little else. As the neighborhood around him changed color over the years, Paul felt his world had become smaller and less full of possibility.

Yet for all the ugly fear that bubbled beneath the surface, the Wallaces had an incredible capacity for kindness and generosity. They had very little in terms of material wealth but, if called upon, gave everything they could to friends in need. Even strangers in need. Paul loved to cook. The Wallace family threw a big barbecue in the street every summer and it was now in its sixth year. Tessa was an emergency room nurse and often worked at night. In this way, she had witnessed the front line of humanity up close and personally tended to their actual wounds. Many of her patients were not white, but she took good care of them too. This came quite naturally, in the same way that she loved animals and regarded everything as one of God's creatures—just not equal or the same.

The Wallace family had no idea what was really going on in the world. They had dumb cell phones and a cracked first-generation iPad Mini that the whole family shared. It needed working Wi-Fi to get online, and the signal they "borrowed" from their neighbor was spotty, if it worked at all. So the Wallace family was completely unaware that liberals everywhere had become unhinged assholes. It was Tessa's night off and she had slept all day, not waking until she smelled a hint of something savory in the air.

Paul hadn't seen anyone that day in their corner of the world. Lisa had played with the neighbors' boy, Keith, in the yard all afternoon under the barely watchful eye of the on-and-off napping Grandma Luce. Paul was perennially unemployed but had spent four hours fixing a trashed wet/dry vacuum so he could sell it for a few bucks.

Had any of them taken just one good look around at the neighborhood that day, they might have noticed the unusual quiet and distant moans. Had Tessa gone to work that evening, she would have surely seen the roving packs of deranged Democrats clutching their cell phones and nonviolently attacking roughly 50 percent of the population.

Instead they all sat down for the family dinner Paul had put together. He called it "tangy delicious chicken" and he carved it at the table. The bones snapped, and the meat melted right off. Paul had a way with meat—he considered it his superpower.

# IT TAKES THREE TO MAKE A THING GO RIGHT

A series of things had to happen for Obama and Biden to exit one dimension and reenter the multiverse so they could bubble up someplace else. The short version is Barack Obama and Joe Biden had to be together, naked, and touching. Then they needed Oscar-nominee Samuel L. Jackson to trigger the Quantum Recoherence Engine back in their home dimension.

That version of Sam, for his part, was still living in the universe where Donald J. Trump was president of the United States. Samuel Jackson was a very busy man. Besides his potentially world-saving position with the secret society of scientists known as the Five Fingers, he was the highest grossing actor of all time in large part due to his ongoing portrayal of Colonel

Nicholas Joseph Fury in films for Marvel. He's also a husband, father, and philanthropist. At any given moment, it was hard to say that any part of his schedule was more important to him than the other part. He would not allow himself to take comfort in the idea that a million or more alternate Earth timelines were playing out at once. Sam had become a very good multitasker over the years, but his limits had been tested by his central role in the current experiment.

There was no way to telecommute as an observer of all space and time. In a way it was all phoned in, but Sam had to be at the D.C. laboratory in person, locked away in a chamber belowground and attached to a cumbersome amount of equipment to make this (very) long-distance call.

Sam had put aside one day a week so that he could be available to Obama and Biden as their guide through space-time. On those days he would wake up even earlier than usual and take a private plane to D.C. After making his way through the labyrinth of tunnels and an absurd, yet necessary, security protocol, he would plug himself into the quantum server and start searching for when and where President Obama and Vice President Biden were. For him, this always meant a long day of sitting down—taxing because of how hunched, cramped, hungry, and thirsty one becomes living as a transdimensional hologram for eight to ten hours straight.

Samuel Jackson being tethered to his own reality and time came with many benefits for the time warrior editions of Obama and Biden, however—most important that he was always there when they needed him. This was a responsibility he took very much to heart. Sam and the Five Fingers of Science could essentially scrub space-time looking for the guys, and once they found them, Sam could be dropped in and out of their reality at will. Like producers working a live broadcast, the Five Fingers could select when or where Sam needed to be. Best of all, the actor was given near complete control over when and how he appeared to Barry and Joe in any dimension.

Extracting them to another dimension was just as simple, provided they were close together and could find a safe space to take off their clothes.

# DOOR TO DOOR

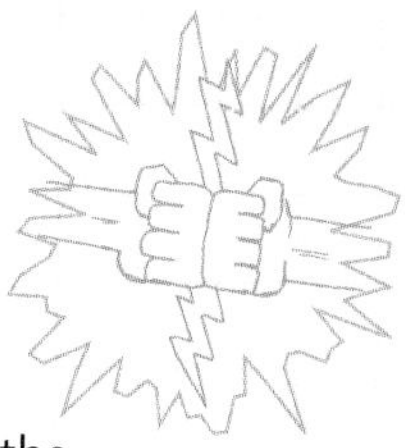

Joe Biden, it turns out, had a natural gift for navigating large groups of the mortally offended.

Joe picked up a metal trash can cover and found it useful for clearing dembies in a Captain America sort of way. The experience took on the hyperreality of a video game as he dodged and weaved his way through the madness. Joe smashed the aluminum shield into dembie heads to stun them. Then he took the edge of his garbage can cover and deftly knocked a cell phone out of the clutches of a dembie, who screamed and lurched for the device just before it smashed to the pavement.

Joe was knocking phones out of hands as fast and hard as he could to make his way to his best friend. Barack Obama was now swallowed by the sissy horde. The image of Joe cutting through the crowd and destroying every phone in sight was simultaneously silly, balletic, and beautiful. Here was the vice president of the United States, sleeves rolled up, fighting undead leftists on the front lawn of a typical suburban ranch.

The president was having a much harder time. He was certain that he had three dembies on him at any given moment for every one on Joe. Dozens pawed at Obama's clothes, while others shoved their cell phone screens in his face. Obama felt a tightening in his chest and a shortness of breath.

Obama heard Joe's voice cut through the low moans and high-pitched whines. "The phones! Kill the phones!"

The president began slugging at phones with his bat. He cracked one out of a dembie hand, sending it up and away, and he watched as the crazed zombie raced to fetch it.

Joe fought his way to Barack, where they stood back-to-back, busting cell phones as fast as they could. "Where is Sam?!"

"I don't know!" Obama said as he reset his swing. He was now cracking phones at a nice clip, averaging four every ten seconds. Unfortunately, there were hundreds more dembies approaching from down the block.

"Samuel Jackson, Samuel Jackson, Samuel Jackson!" Joe yelled out.

"What are you doing?! He's not Beetlejuice!" said Obama.

"You don't know that it won't work!" Joe yelled back as he took the trash can lid to a dembie's skull with some topspin.

Obama saw the lights on in a house down the block. He had learned the hard way that infected dembies didn't turn on their lights. Lights left on meant some poor living soul who could potentially help them. Obama prayed they were Republican.

# TAKE A KNEE

It doesn't matter who you are or what dimension you're living in, when a sitting president shows up on your doorstep in America, it's a big deal.

They arrived out of breath. Barack quickly rang the doorbell twice as Joe took a step back so that he could ram the door in with his shoulder. They really had only about twenty seconds before the enraged, bug-eyed dembie horde would arrive, each and every one of them with a death grip on their smartphone and a boiling temper of ineffectual outrage.

Paul Wallace opened the door at the worst possible time. Joe hit the door the moment it opened and managed to roll himself into the house. Paul was sent flying back and crashing into a shelf just inside. Paul's head took the corner before he landed on the floor. Blood ran down Paul's neck and Tessa immediately went to his side. This left the president standing on the doorstep breathing heavy, baseball bat in hand.

Lisa, the seven-year-old, recognized Obama first. She said, "That's the man from television."

Obama let himself in and shut the door. "Good evening. We're sorry for the disturbance. We're in what I would call . . . a state of emergency." The president locked the door and then latched the chain.

Paul screamed as he held the back of his head. "*Ow!* What the hell is this?!"

Obama kneeled down and held his finger to his lips: "Shhhhhhhhhhhhh." He pointed outside toward the street.

"Are you okay?" Joe Biden whispered to Paul.

At this moment Baby Joy and Grandma Luce looked on from the kitchen table with an identical expression of wonder. Tessa screamed and ran to the wall-mounted phone and dialed 911, clearly not knowing that the phone lines had been dead for hours. She dropped the phone and picked up the largest kitchen knife she had. "What do you want? I swear to fucking God I will protect my children and stab the shit out of you if you don't leave my house right fucking now."

This was a very new experience for the president. He could tell that he was not eliciting the reaction he had come to count on from ordinary folks. He could accept the fact that not everyone voted for him and that he might not even be welcome, but generally he felt a warmth from people once he met them. That was not the case here. Obama held his hands up.

"I'm the president of the United States, Barack Obama, and this is Vice President Joe Biden. We're sorry to barge in, but we need . . . your help." Obama looked around the small home and really had no idea what tactic might work, but he was encouraged by how tacky and tasteless the furnishings were.

"We didn't vote for you," said Tessa.

Paul agreed, still holding his bleeding head: "We don't vote at all."

Outside, the moaning and whining came from up the street.

Tessa looked out the front window and finally saw what she had been missing all day. "Who the hell are they?"

"Some of your progressive neighbors," said Joe.

"Paul, what is he talkin' about?!" asked Tessa.

Paul hobbled to the door and saw the undead army of mostly young and diverse people foaming at the mouth on his doorstep.

"Oh." Paul's entire demeanor changed completely. He was calm and his natural warmth came back to his voice. "They sure look . . . upset."

"They are," said the president with a heavy heart.

Tessa scrunched up her nose and cocked her head. "What's wrong with them?"

"They snapped. All at once," Joe said, low and cool.

The dembies had now surrounded the house by the hundreds and were all pawing uselessly at the doors and windows with slack wrists and cell phones.

"Joe, check all the doors and make sure they're locked," ordered Obama.

"On it!"

Baby Joy and Grandma Luce were still sitting at the table, both of them continuing to stare at the president with wide eyes.

Obama smiled.

Grandma finally spoke: "You're the first black man that's ever stepped foot in this house."

"Well, then, uh . . . I guess I'm honored," said the president.

Paul walked to another window and pulled the drapes back, revealing twenty writhing dembies pressed against the glass. He stumbled back. "To hell with this."

Paul opened a door to the basement and disappeared down the steps. He emerged only a moment later with a shotgun. Paul quickly and calmly loaded it from a vintage army-green ammo box.

"Wait." Obama took off his dress shirt and was now wearing only a thin white tank. "They're passive aggressive . . . They work in groups but hate confrontation."

"Where the hell is Sam?!" Joe barked. "This whole thing is about to go south, Barack!"

Paul cocked his shotgun. "If they want my guns they're gonna have a world of pain. It's simple."

"They're not here for your guns. They're here for me. They're here for the vice president." Obama was turning on his professorial side and he could feel his senses focus. "The truth is they don't want anything to do with you."

The president pointed outside. "Those are thoughtful Americans in every size, shape, ethnicity, and background, LGBTQ and some fine cisgender white folks too. They feel deep hopelessness and are easily triggered into a righteous but ineffectual fury." Obama paused here for emphasis. "The future of America is on your doorstep. They're *here*. What are you going to do?"

Tessa cried as she picked up the baby. "They're gonna break in!"

Obama replied, "No, they won't. But you're gonna let 'em in." Obama walked to the door and placed his hand slowly on the handle.

Joe jumped in. "Barack, what are you doing?"

"I'll shoot you too. I'm not afraid," Paul said, his voice steady and soft. "I am not letting those animals in my house."

# LET THE LEFT ONE IN

"How about this." Obama spoke slowly and kept his hands in sight. From across the room he could feel Paul's finger twitch. Barack didn't want to provoke him in any way. "We let just one in and we try things my way. My bet is that you'll see they're not here to hurt you or your family. If you feel threatened at any time . . . then I guess you'll do what you have to do."

"How you gonna let just one in?" asked Paul.

"I'll open the door just enough to let one through, and Joe will beat back the others with my bat." Obama tossed his bat to Joe, who caught it.

"I'm scared," said Tessa.

"Me too, baby. Me too," said Paul.

"I'm also a bit freaked out. Barack, are you fucking crazy?" asked Joe.

"It sure seems easier to test things out with one than taking them all on at once." Obama looked around at the windows, the faces of zombie Democrats looking in. The moaning was low, constant, and in surround sound.

"Just one," Paul said.

Obama unlocked the bolt and turned the front door handle gently. An arm shot in immediately and Obama grabbed it quickly and yanked, yelling, "Now!"

A large African American man in jeans, a T-shirt, and a hoodie spilled into the room with a cell phone in his hand. He went straight toward the president. Biden kicked the door shut, slamming fingers. A smartphone dropped to the floor inside as Joe bolted the door. Grandma Luce said, "Oh dear, another one."

Paul aimed his shotgun. "You give me the word and I drop him for you."

"Don't drop anyone!" Obama stepped backward with one hand raised like Chris Pratt training a velociraptor. "Look . . ." Obama kept walking backward. "He won't even look y'all in the eyes."

Obama stopped walking and let the large dembie man paw at him awkwardly with his cell phone. "See, even if I let him touch me. He just wants me to look at his news feed and get outraged with him." The president avoided looking directly at the phone, turning his head away as needed.

Paul could see it with his own eyes: the gross but harmless neediness of the dembie.

"Barack . . . you're the dembie whisperer," said Joe.

"I'd like to try something else . . . I have a hunch." Obama started moving himself back over toward Paul. "Paul, I want you to put down the gun."

"Don't do it!" Grandma screamed.

Joe was prepared to tackle Paul if need be. Thankfully, it didn't come to that. Paul set down his shotgun right away.

Obama was still gently walking backward as the zombie stumbled forward. "I want you to do exactly what I tell you to do, Paul. And maybe we'll all get out of this mess without getting hurt."

"I'm listening," Paul said.

"I want you to smash his phone."

"Are you out of your mind?" Tessa said.

"It's gonna make him crazy . . . so then I want you to say you're sorry and open your arms to hug him, you know, consensually."

Tessa laughed out loud through tears. "That's the stupidest thing I've ever heard." Little Lisa was hiding behind her mommy, her bright eyes darting back and forth between the president, the big strange zombie man, and her daddy.

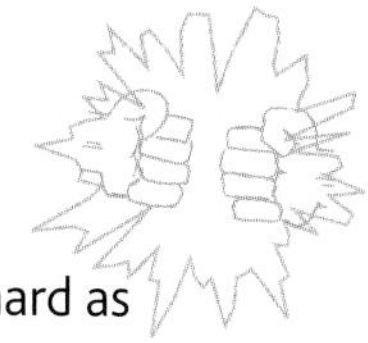

The president looked at Paul and the two men nodded quickly.

Paul ripped the iPhone from the dembie's hands and threw it as hard as he could at the tile floor, where the screen shattered. Instantly the dembie shifted into an openmouthed shriek. Paul shut his eyes and opened his arms.

"Open your eyes!" Obama said. "Look at him, make him see you!"

Paul did as he was told and opened his eyes. He looked at the shrieking liberal in his living room and blurted out, "I'm sorry! I'm sorry!"

The impossibly possessed dembie then locked eyes with Paul and wrapped his arms around him. Paul, very unsure at first, finally closed his arms and reluctantly patted the zombie on the back a few times. Both men relaxed as they hugged, and a hush fell over the room. This was not an ordinary hug. This was a hug with great feeling, so much so that everyone in the house could feel it.

Joe loudly whispered, "Holy guacamole."

Obama said, "You're doing it, Paul."

Paul and the man hugged for a full minute, gently patting each other on the back the whole time. The crazed dembie's stare melted as the hug progressed, and when the two men separated it was immediately clear that the spell had been broken.

"I'm Dave." The man looked Paul in his now wet eyes.

"Hi, Dave. I'm Paul," Paul's voice quivered.

Obama smiled. "All right, all right. Only a couple million more to go."

# BLUE DAWN

The entire zombie apocalypse had happened outside the watchful eye of the Quantum Recoherence Drive in the prime dimension. The QRD was essentially a hard drive that, though it couldn't capture everything happening in every timeline, because that would be absurd, did store the much lighter-weight metadata that were not as detailed but much easier to parse. Wherever Obama and Biden went in the multiverse, the drive would keep a record. This would allow the team to monitor a massive amount of space-time at once. To put it in much more grounded terms, this was like studying tree rings instead of an entire tree. You can learn a tremendous amount about the life of a tree from its rings very quickly.

This time around, the Five Fingers didn't see anything. The first moment of alarm came at the start of Sam's shift. Only much later would the team unpack how and why the drive had failed at this critical moment. Much more pressing for Sam was the fact that the experiment, and with it all of human history, was at risk. At this second there was very little room for error if he wasn't already too late. They dropped Sam into the earliest available moment in the timeline that wasn't corrupted, and he found a scene playing out that he never could have expected.

It was almost morning and Obama was standing on the roof with a bullhorn. The streets of the modest neighborhood were densely packed with dembie hordes for miles in every direction. On the lawn, behind a giant makeshift barricade of vehicles and fencing, were tens of thousands of destroyed cell phones in giant piles.

Paul had constructed a giant barbecue and was pulling piles of pork ribs out of the smoker. Tessa and Grandma, along with a handful of their neighbors, were working through the dembies one by one. They had established hugging stations all along the curb and had worked up to a pace of five liberals per minute.

Joe was working on the ground to let the dembies in carefully through a two-stage gate system. The sun broke the horizon and Joe turned to the light, closed his eyes, and let it wash over him.

"What the hell is happening here?" With no time to think or be extra fashionable, Samuel L. Jackson had taken on his own form.

Joe spun around and hugged thin air. "Where the heck have you been?!"

"Honestly, it's a miracle these cats can even track you down. What in the actual fuck, Joe? What are we into here?" Sam looked up at the roof and waved at Obama. Then he looked through the fence at the tens of thousands of complacently moaning freaks on the other side. "We gotta get you guys outta here."

# THE CABBAGE PATCH

So close, yet so far.

October 2016 was as prime a landing spot as they could have ever hoped for to build a better future, yet here they were, stripping down naked in a very cluttered bedroom filled with vintage Cabbage Patch Kids. So uncomfortable was the zombie experience that even Obama, who utterly detested having his soul separated from his body, seemed genuinely eager to get going. October 2016 had been a total bust. The well-meaning liberals in this dimension had been seriously owned. They were altogether too thoughtful and sensitive to handle the dark truth technology was bringing to light with a vengeance. Obama wondered if there were enough hugs in the world to make it right and how it might play out in this reality once they left.

Joe scanned the faces of all the dolls until he found the one with a Kangol hat that looked like a baby Samuel L. Jackson. "Will you knock it off, Sam. We don't have time to be cute."

Cabbage Patch Sam replied, "Just testing all the systems. Everything seems to be functioning."

Obama wasn't messing around. He was naked already and crouched down. "I'm fired up. Let's do this now, Sam. I'm ready to go."

Paul Wallace walked in, and the sight of naked men startled him. "Oh, Jesus! For Christ's sake." He covered his eyes and turned down the hallway.

"Bye, Paul! God bless!" Joe yelled down the hallway after him.

Barack shook his head and laughed weakly as Joe crouched down next to him and they pounded fists.

Cabbage Patch Sam quietly said, "Wonder Twin Powers . . . *activate*."

# BROMANTICA

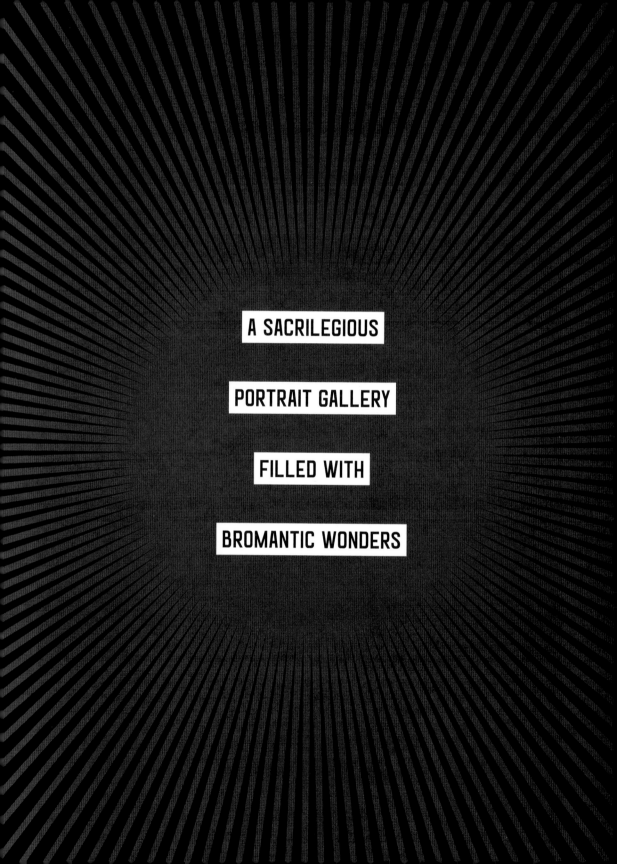

A SACRILEGIOUS

PORTRAIT GALLERY

FILLED WITH

BROMANTIC WONDERS

It's me again, Watson, your sentient guide through this wonderland of visual splendor, or pure cheese, depending on your perspective.

*Here I present an abbreviated gallery of artifacts recovered from the multiverse and reproduced here with an intense mix of diligence and sarcasm. Great care has been taken to preserve these treasures so that they may be enjoyed by several generations of humankind before everything goes dark. Spoiler alert: Everything eventually goes dark.*

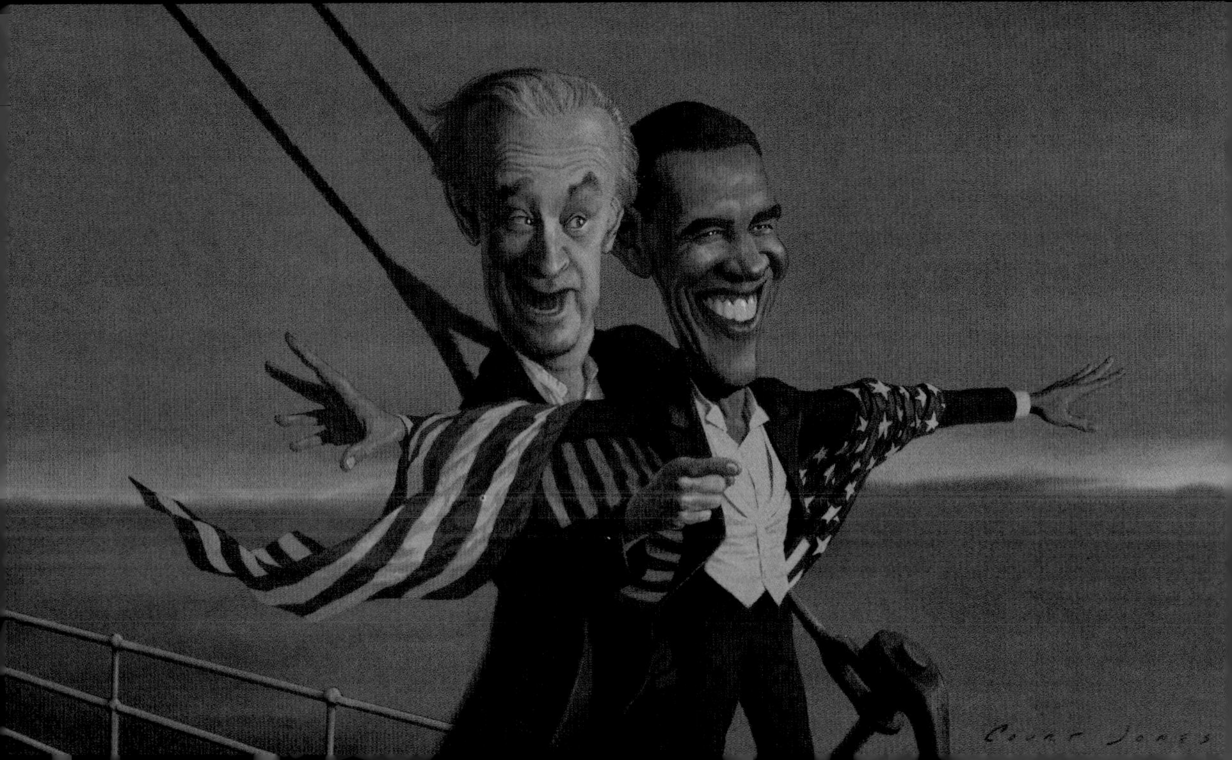

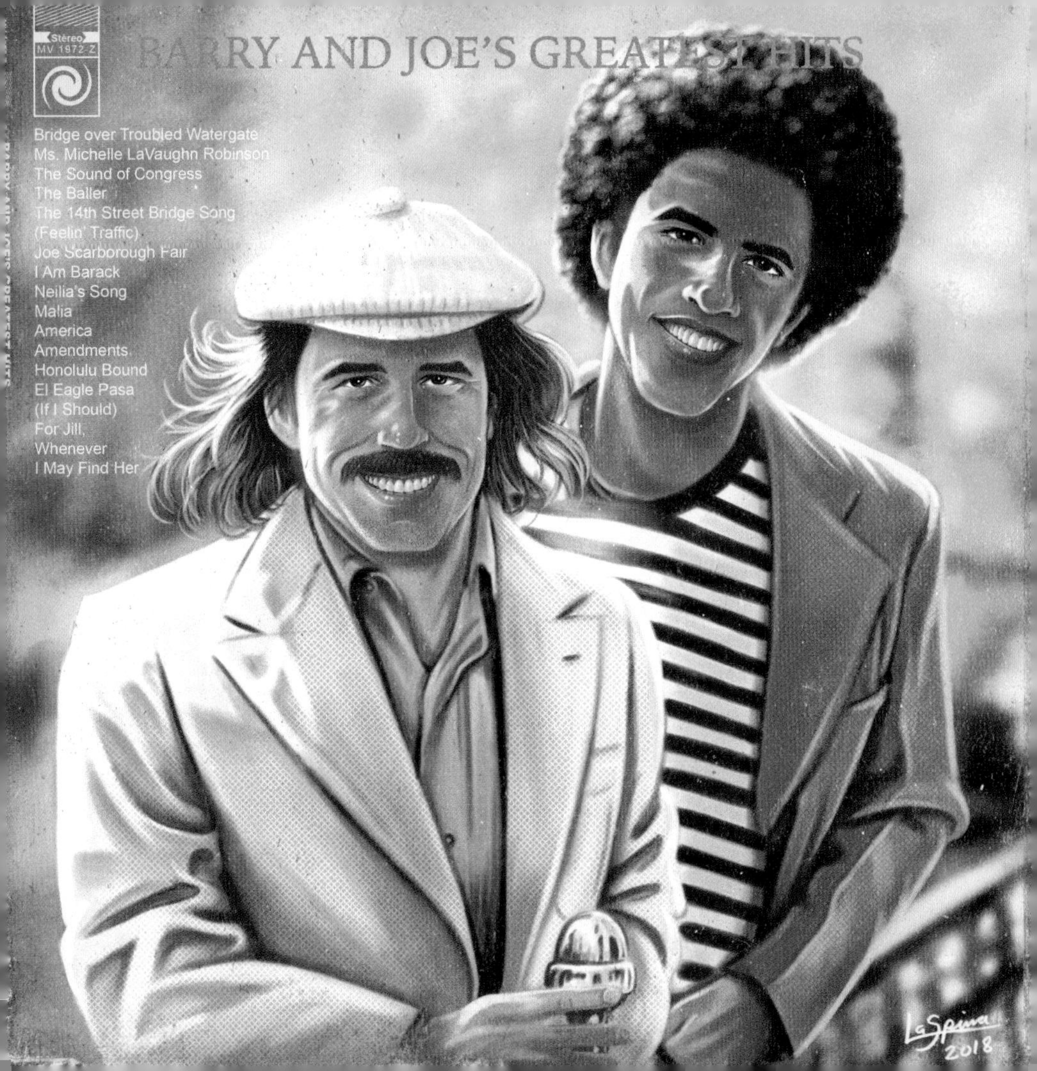

Stèreo
MV 1972-Z
BARRY AND JOE'S GREATEST HITS
Bridge over Troubled Watergate
Ms. Michelle LaVaughn Robinson
The Sound of Congress
The Baller
The 14th Street Bridge Song
(Feelin' Traffic)
Joe Scarborough Fair
I Am Barack
Neilia's Song
Malia
America
Amendments
Honolulu Bound
El Eagle Pasa
(If I Should)
For Jill,
Whenever
I May Find Her
LaSpina
2018

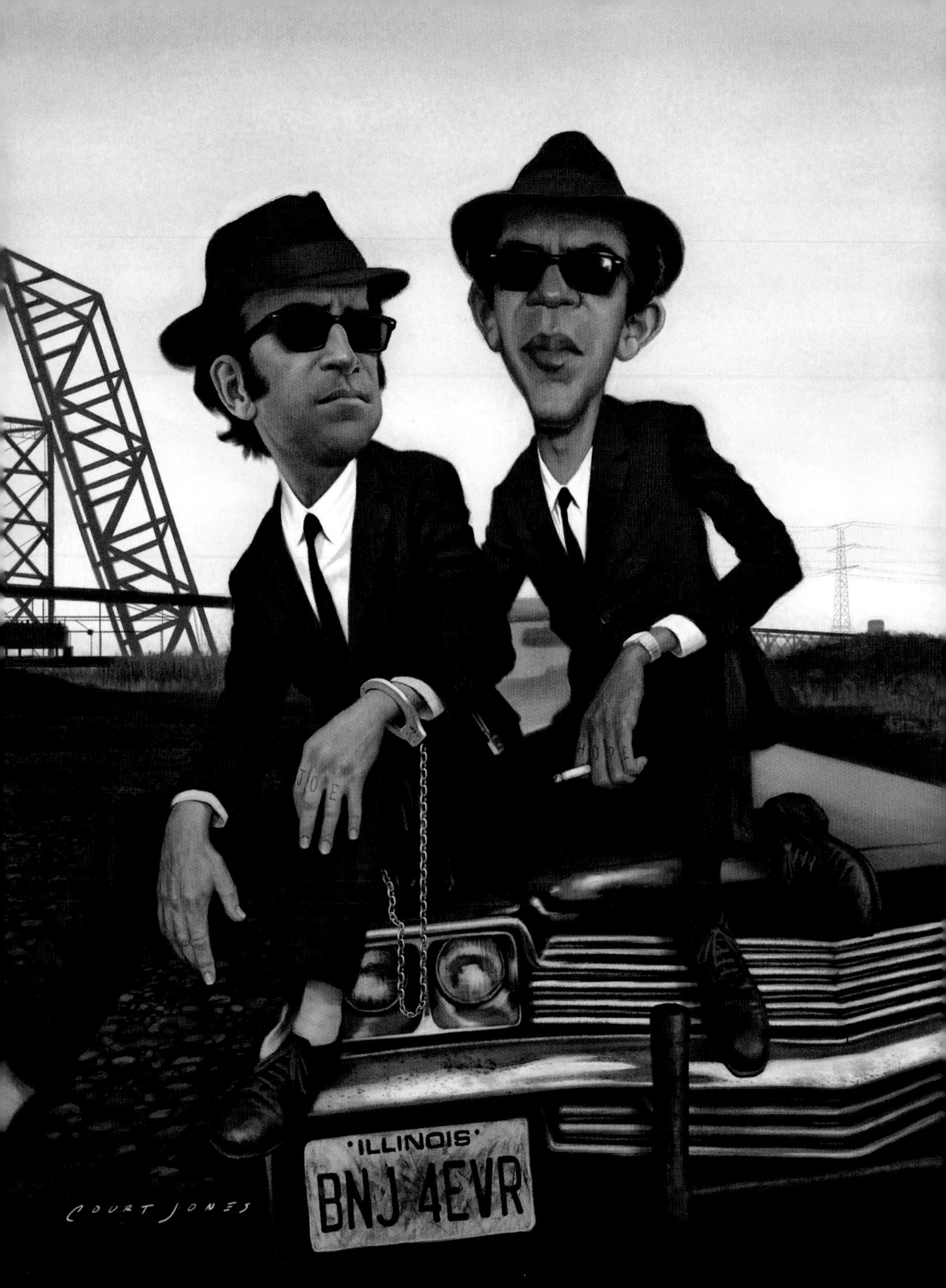
JOE
HOPE
ILLINOIS
BNJ 4EVR
COURT JONES

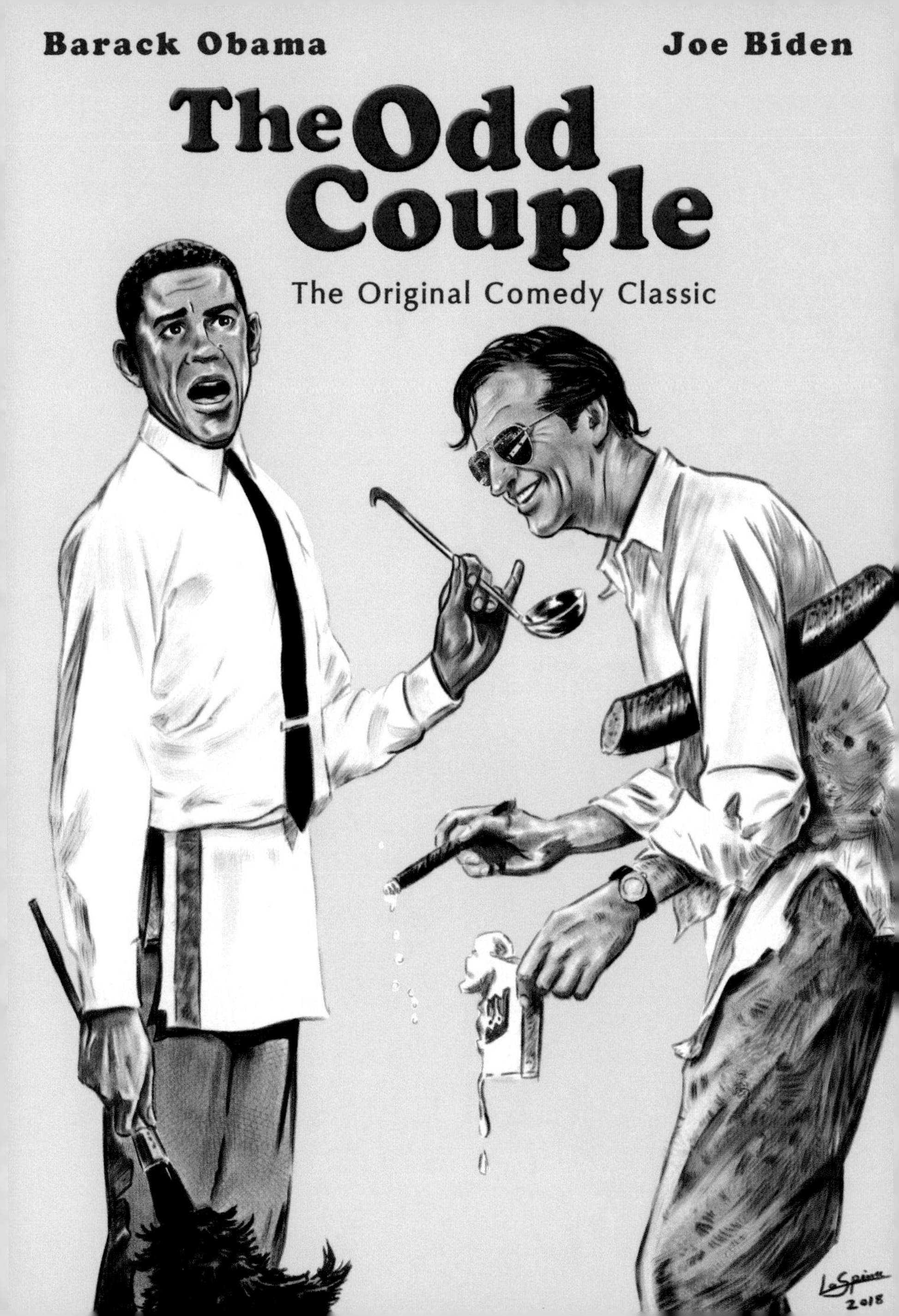
Barack Obama
Joe Biden
The Odd Couple
The Original Comedy Classic
LaSpina
2018

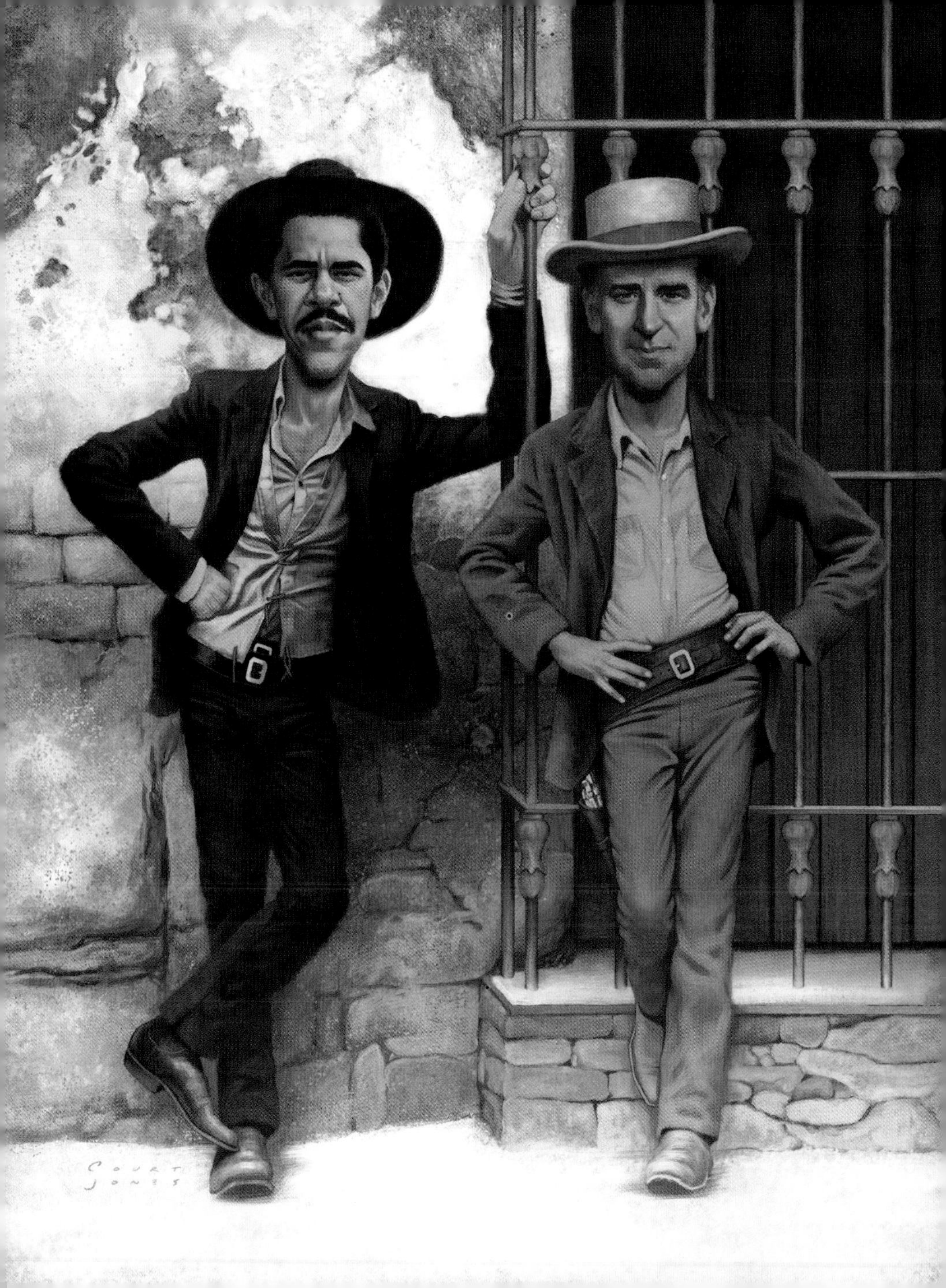
COURT JONES

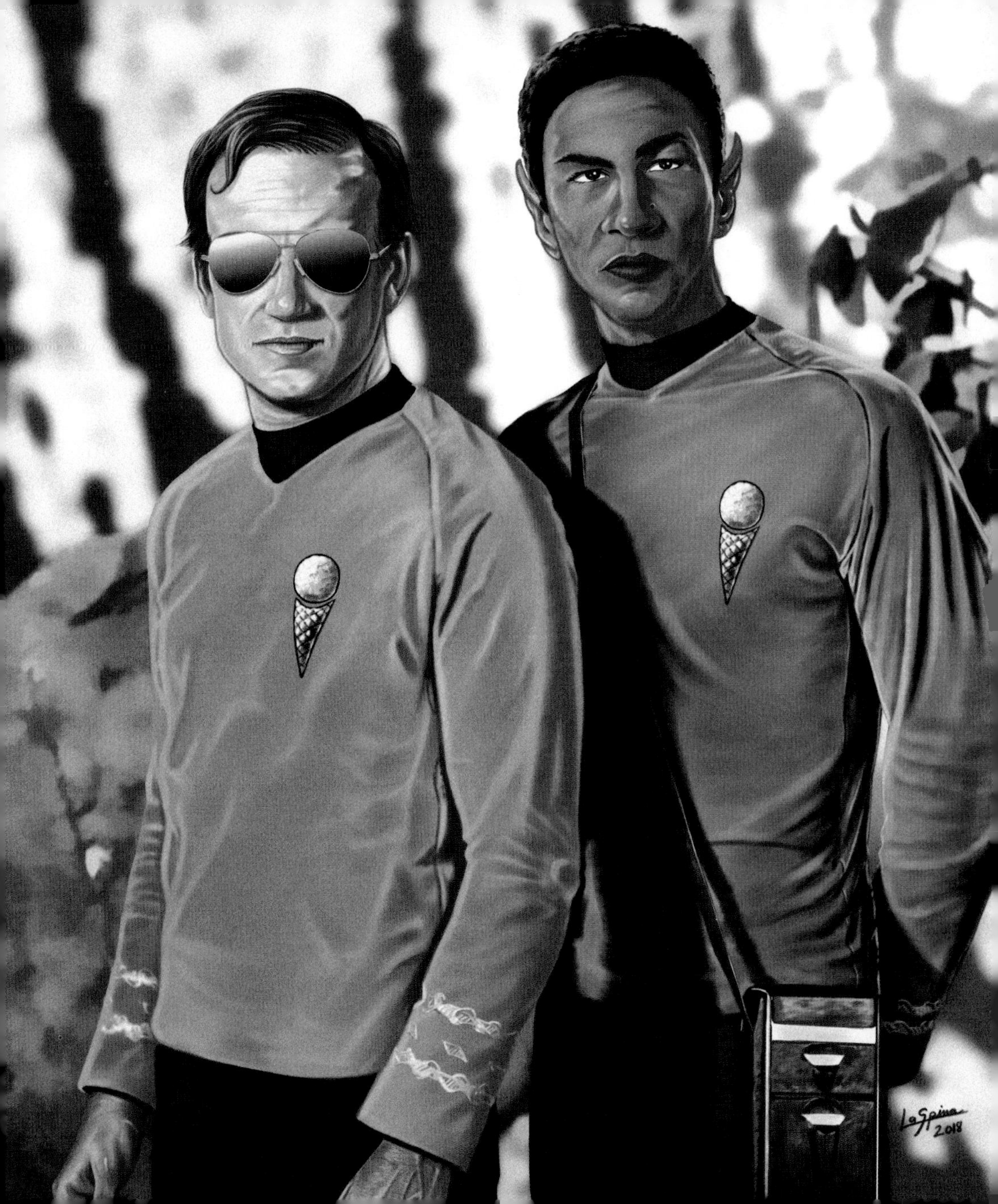
LaSpina
2018

# OBAMA
# THE GREY

THIS STORY IS VERY MUCH

RIPPED OFF FROM

I AM LEGEND AND THE ROAD,

WITH SHADES OF CADDYSHACK

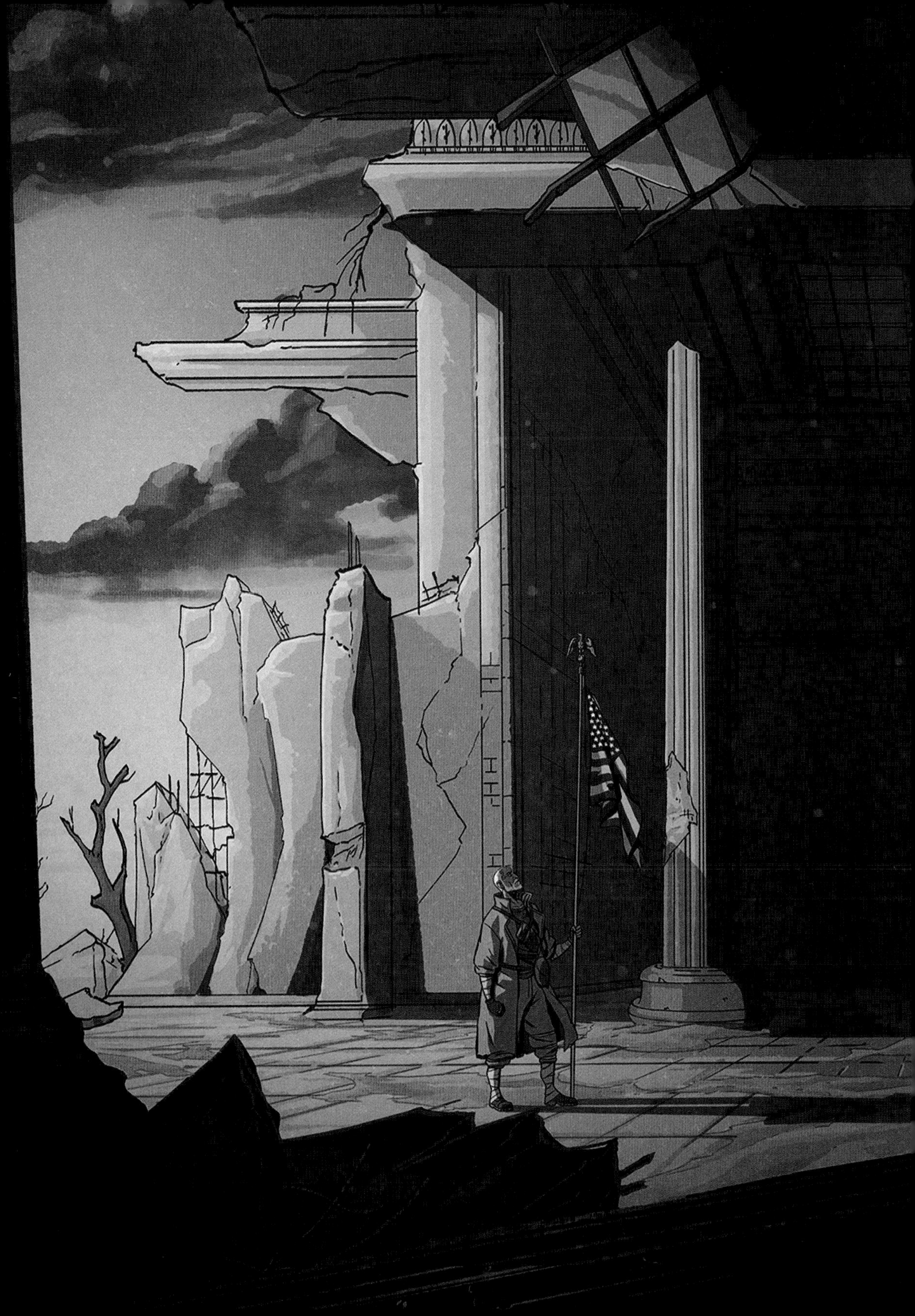

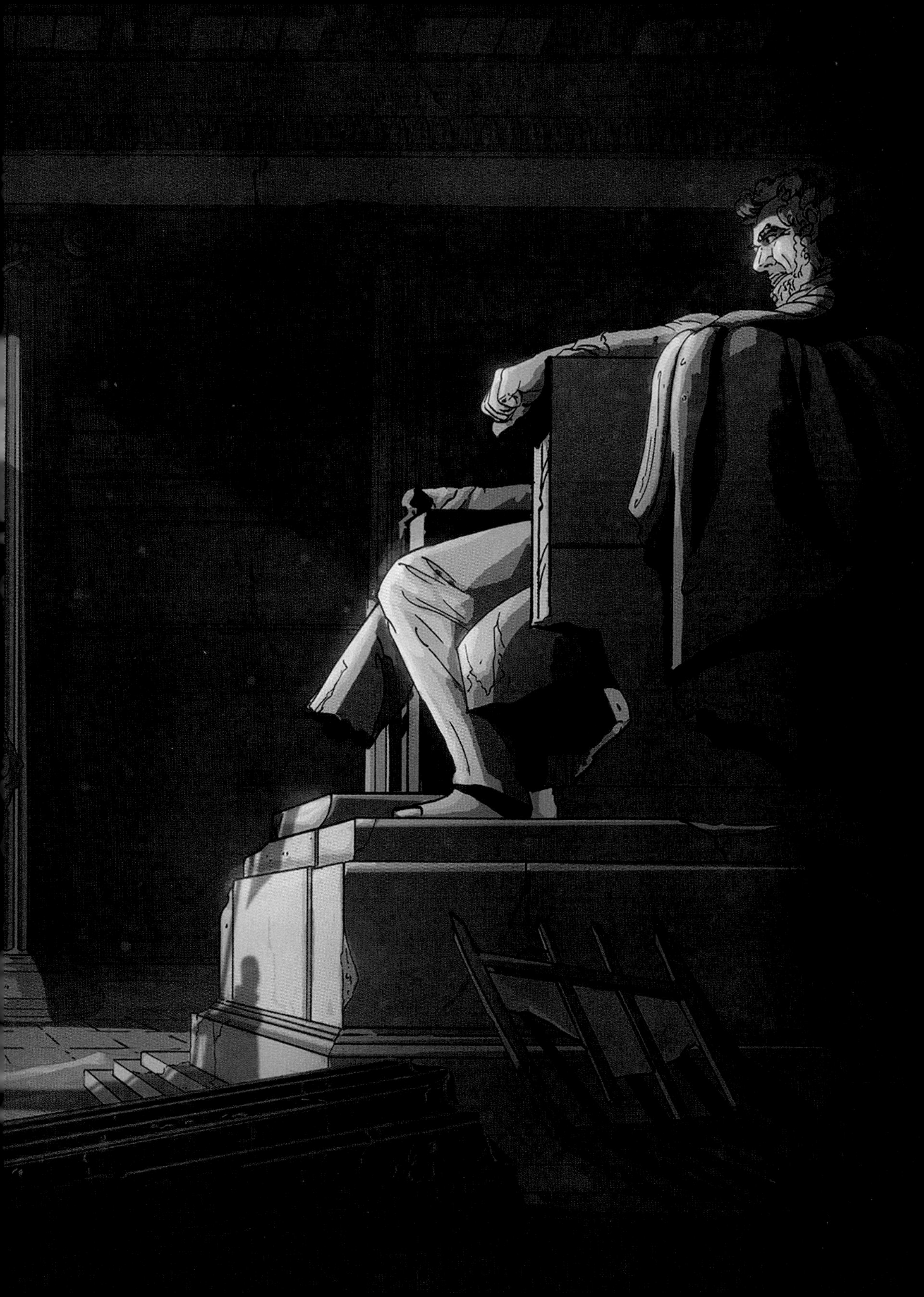

Here Barack Obama is determined to make the best of things as he works his way from sea to shining sea all by his lonesome.

Emotionally prepare yourself, and remember, it's always darkest before the dawn.

# RETIREMENT

Doomed to spend an eternity walking the planet like Caine from *Kung Fu*, Obama the Grey had started to work on his golf swing full time. He could not say how long he had been in the future, how old he might be, or what dimension exactly he was living in. But he had grown a beard.

He had so many questions and no answers. His needs had become simply about survival, and any sense of the original mission was currently lost. He was now one truly tough motherfucker. Old, grizzled, ripped, and armed to the teeth. He even had a bag of golf clubs that he cobbled together along the journey, making upgrades as he went. He worshipped those clubs. He was his own caddy.

Obama had arrived the hard way. Injured and weak. He was all alone in an American wasteland previously only imagined by movies and video games but now brought to vivid rotting life by all his senses. A dusting of orange snow had covered the landscape in every direction, and there were simply no people left alive wherever he went.

Obama had been unable to find any trace of his best friend, Joe Biden. If hope were a door left open only a crack, Obama could now feel it sealed shut. Without Joe Biden, Obama knew he would never be able to escape this bitter reality.

He collected bits and pieces of clothing and fashioned a spiked club out of tennis racquets and sharpened railroad ties. He'd wear the weapon on his back along with the crossbow. The crossbow he had found inside a bombed-out sporting goods store, which was a lucky break all around.

There was no one to talk to, so he often talked to himself. He enjoyed narrating his own daily activities, providing color commentary like a news broadcaster.

"The president is now walking toward the west wing of his dilapidated crack den . . . taking a moment to wave. He's smiling, but you can clearly see . . . a deep suffering under the surface." Obama would act this out, waving and smiling to absolutely no one for his own amusement.

# APOCALYPSE GOLF

If one must spend the rest of his life wandering through a bombed-out wasteland full of toxic fallout, Obama reasoned, this was the way to do it. He remembered Will Smith driving golf balls from the back of the USS *Intrepid* in the movie *I Am Legend*.

Thus, Apocalypse Golf was invented. There was really only one rule: play through no matter what.

The world was his course and there was no hole. He would hit the ball in the direction he wanted to go and then walk to it. He became a Jedi at planning his drives very carefully and reading the landscape for ideal fairways. It took only a couple of sloppy swings and losing half a day digging through unholy rot to find the ball to motivate him to perfect his game. What he'd look for in a nice fairway was a place where the ball could stick and be easy to get to and, of course, with options to inspire the next logical swing.

Now, he could write a book on his strategies. From his game perspective, the wasted-out cities were just as interesting and challenging to him as the wide-open country, in different ways of course.

This is how he made his way across the country from Palm Springs to Chicago. Hit the ball, find it, hit it again. Do this forever, rest and replenish as needed. Rinse, repeat.

# BEN

Without any friends, Obama became close with his lucky golf ball. He named him Ben. It had survived through six states. It came to represent much more than a golf ball to him. It had guided him through countryside and cities. Obama came to regard the ball and his relationship to it as living poetry.

There were golf balls to be found all over, especially on actual golf courses, hanging out on the bottom of the now dried-out man-made ponds. But Ben the ball was discovered on Obama's first day in this hellhole future, and there was absolutely nothing special about it besides being the first ball he came across in this particular dimension. He became attached quickly.

Obama remembered watching the movie *Cast Away* in the White House screening room. He had never seen it and had then become friendly with Tom Hanks after taking office. That moment existed in what felt like another lifetime. He laughed to himself, realizing that Ben had become his Wilson, his only friend in this brutal place.

# GOOD BOY

Obama's new favorite meal had become a "burger" he fashioned out of two stale crackers, a ketchup packet, and whatever protein was available that day cooked over an open fire. Insects mostly, but on good days, small critters. His evening routine was finding shelter, building a fire, and then lulling himself to sleep with an old iPod he had found full of Stevie Wonder and Aretha Franklin tunes. Another stroke of good luck.

The growls woke him.

Three giant robot dogs surrounded Obama, circling.

He had encountered only one of the robo dogs before and he was lucky to have escaped alive. That time he sacrificed his favorite 7-iron by using it to beat the vicious robot hound senseless.

Now there were three of them. Their nanofiber skin breathed in and out over their metal skeletons wrapped with hydraulic muscle. Their eyes glowed and their metal teeth kicked off glints of light. This wasn't some Boston Dynamics prototype. This was something far more evolved and sinister.

"Easy, fellas . . ." Obama said, low and slow. "I love puppies."

He had been sleeping on a roll on the floor and had learned to keep his weapons close. Obama slowly took his spiked tennis racquet up with one hand. He felt the dogs were intelligent, the way they sized him up.

Obama had barely seen the robotic hound that he'd gone "full Pesci" on before. It was an ambush and then a moment of pure adrenalized man on robo dog intensity. He remembered only thin slices of that experience, strobe flashes of violence and very little about the creature itself. But now, staring in these dogs' eyes and given a moment to take all three of them in, he was struck by many details. They were built like German shepherds. They were beautiful. They were huge. And they were each different from the other.

One had red eyes, and that somehow made it scarier. It was also the largest and appeared to be growing larger by the moment, its metal skeleton flexing under the steel mesh skin. It occurred to Obama at this moment what they were doing. They were letting him prepare to make for a better fight, and they would attack him one by one for the same reason. Old Red was bachelor number one and coming in hot.

Red pounced and was immediately chewing on Obama's arm, digging in. Obama let it chew as he heaved the racquet club with his other hand, spiking the animal in the temple. It wasn't a yelp as much as a heavy *click,* and Red's jaw released and its body coiled. The spike was buried deep in its head, and Obama was unable to pull it out. He used his foot, standing on the robo dog's skull with his heavily duct-taped boots. Like the sword from the stone, Obama tugged and tugged until he dislodged his weapon of choice from the robot dog's head. He quickly tore away the bloody leather gauntlet on his left arm, now chewed clean through. His forearm gushed blood, but it could have been much worse, he knew.

The second one didn't wait. It had orange eyes and made a loud charging sound as it backed up slowly and unhinged its jaw. Obama didn't quite understand where this was headed, but soon the low-end vibration had become a full jet-engine roar. Obama dropped his racquet and deftly rolled to his crossbow. He didn't have enough time, however, for the blast sent him straight back into the crumbling wall behind him. Obama's ears rang, but he could hear the whirring buildup begin again underneath. He knew it was now or never, scrambling again for his crossbow, taking aim directly into the gaping robo maw just as its interior jet engine began to scream. Obama released his arrow. His shot landed cleanly between the eyes, traveling straight through and pinning the mechanical head directly to a wood beam. A small burst of sparks fell to the floor.

The third one had bright blue eyes and enormous paws. It appeared the least vicious of the three. Blue pounced hard before Obama could even reach for his quiver. It knocked Obama over but also sent itself head over tail and spilling onto the cement floor of the dwelling, legs askew. This one was clumsy.

Obama quickly decided that the best thing to do was beat this one to death. He had landed close enough to his racquet club and started swinging wildly. Obama the Grey, now as angry as he was tired, connected more than once with everything he had. The robo hound with blue eyes only stumbled, shook it off, and came back for more. The other two had been dispatched relatively quickly. This one clearly had a much harder head.

Obama kicked the pooch where its nuts should be and regretted it instantly. There was nothing there but metal. The funniest part of the whole fight was that neither of them was very effective—despite a great deal of effort from both parties. The dog was muscular and determined, but slow. Obama was exhausted but left virtually unharmed by the dog's aggression, because he could anticipate Blue's attack, grabbing it by the torso whenever it charged and tossing it away. He thought he had Blue for good when its right robotic thigh shattered on impact and the whole machine began to seize and pop.

But this one just kept getting up, no matter what. Blue was now missing a limb, its ear was torn clear off, and it was dragging itself across the floor. But it kept coming. This went on for hours. Obama couldn't tell which one of them was Apollo and which one was Rocky. In hindsight, Obama would wonder why he didn't just walk away.

It's hard to know if Obama lost consciousness from bleeding out from his arm or sheer exhaustion, but he woke up the next morning with a giant metal paw poking at his head. Sunlight burned his eyes, but he could make out the German shepherd cocking its head sideways and wagging its tail. Obama flinched, then kicked the dog as hard as he could from his lying position. Blue stumbled back toward him, and Obama noticed that the robot's missing leg was now half mended, more of a metal pirate peg. The robo pooch sat on its haunches and then lay down beside him. Obama guessed, incorrectly, that the animal simply had no more fight left in it. The machine went back to mending itself. The pup had collected its own parts, like scraps, and watched as their nanotubes reassembled slowly. The metal mesh skin would never return in some places, but the skeleton and muscle system were renewed.

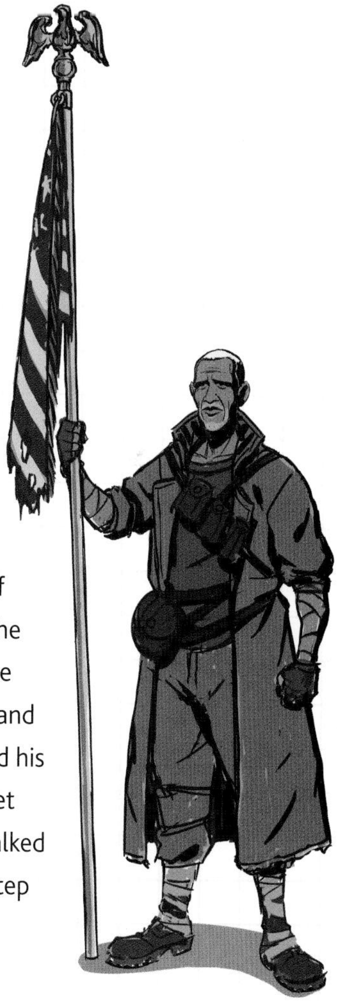

Obama then began tending to his own wounds, drinking some water and then using what was left to clean off his gashes and wrap them. He had gauze and medical tape from an abandoned drugstore. His pack had become a small mobile pharmacy in fact, full of all the things he needed to survive. He kept one eye on the hound as he gathered his things. The other two dogs were pleasantly lifeless and wasted, one still stuck to the wall and the other smeared on its side. Obama swung his pack and his golf clubs onto his back, then his crossbow and his racquet club. Obama tossed Ben into the air and caught it. He walked out of the small dilapidated home backward, careful to step around the lifeless remains of Big Red.

Blue sat up and followed him.

# ROBIDEN

Blue kept his distance at first, and for many miles that followed, but by the time they got to Wilmington, Delaware, he was about ten feet away and holding steady. He would heel whenever Obama pulled out his driver and watch attentively as Obama teed off. It went on like this for a long time, right up until Obama shanked it. The brush and scattered debris in this run-down working-class neighborhood were covered in a light orange snow, and the ball completely vanished less than a hundred feet from where Obama stood. He had become so good that a shank like this had not happened to him in quite a while. He looked back at Blue and shrugged. That's how it went with golf sometimes. But then the unexpected happened. Blue sprang into action, darting into the snow-covered reservoir. He circled and pawed at the ground, then sat waiting for Obama to catch up.

Sure enough, Blue had found Ben. Obama reached out slowly to pat the mechanical canine on his head. Then Obama took off his bag of clubs and slung it over Blue's neck. He stepped up to the ball, surveyed his options, and then ripped it four hundred yards.

Blue carried his clubs from then on. This dog would protect him. He never left Obama's side. Obama started calling him Joe.

# THE CHARCOAL PIT

A small part of Obama knew the direction he was headed. Yet he was still surprised when they came across the Charcoal Pit diner.

Obama knew how much the Charcoal Pit meant to Joe Biden. It was quite simply his hometown diner and part of the fabric of Biden's salt-of-the-earth, all-American spirit. The Biden clan had been rallying there on Friday nights after football games since the beginning of time, and no campaign tour was ever complete without a stop. It was home plate.

All Obama could think of was a real burger. Truth be told, the Charcoal Pit was celebrated more for its ice cream than its burgers. Of course, the Charcoal Pit Obama was drawing toward in this dimension was anything but open for business. A shattered husk of the American dream and as stark a visual metaphor there could possibly be for all that had gone wrong. Still, Obama was happy to see it. He unlocked the diner doors through the broken glass. He could have just walked in the back where it had been blown wide open, had he known.

Joe sniffed around and started barking outside the walk-in freezer.

Obama had come across one working refrigeration unit in all his travels, at a tiny market in Wichita, Kansas, of all places. The walk-in was hooked up to a solar backup that had managed to kick in and keep running, if intermittently. He estimated that the power grid had been down for at least two years at that point, but it was hard to be sure. And in Wichita, despite the working fridge, all the food in the store was rotten.

This was different. This was a freezer. And the food in this freezer was still frozen.

To Obama, it felt like his luck was turning. They camped out that night inside the Charcoal Pit. Obama made a fire and cooked his first real beef burger in a very long time on an iron skillet. Obama slid into a booth and set Ben the ball down on the tabletop. Joe circled twice and lay down on the floor beside him. Obama cracked open the very last Black Forest Berry Honest Tea. It was his favorite kind, and he had carried the bottle more than two hundred miles. He raised the plastic bottle in a toast to Ben, to Joe, and to the empty diner and then took a long sip. He didn't have a bun for his burger, much less lettuce and tomato—just ketchup and mustard in packets. But he relished every bite, eating his burger like a steak with a knife and fork. It was cooked a perfect medium rare.

# MOVING ON

Leaving the Charcoal Pit was hard. Obama had gained considerable weight in the two weeks they spent living there. The change in diet made him lethargic. Slow. Eventually, he came to the conclusion that if he stayed at the Charcoal Pit he would die there. He wanted to keep moving. He needed to keep moving.

He packed as much as he could carry on himself and then on Joe. Obama climbed onto the Charcoal Pit roof with his driver and looked around for his next shot. He placed the ball down, took a step back, settled himself, and swung. Joe ran out to meet the ball ahead of him, and like that they were on the move.

# ENEMY MINE

As the territory became more familiar to Obama, the disturbance in the force he had been feeling grew stronger. They were entering Washington, D.C., and while the Hill was still many miles away, he was eager to be someplace he knew so well, even if it was Washington. Driving across bridges was one of the biggest challenges in Apocalypse Golf for Obama, but also the most fun. He needed to be precise to avoid the water on either side, but he could usually count on his aim and the bounce to get him clear across. Any deserted cars on the road were to be avoided, of course.

The ball sailed almost four hundred yards across the Fourteenth Street Bridge, bounced once, and then landed cleanly on the other side. Joe ran up to it, but Obama took his sweet time walking. In a flash, the ball exploded, sending chunks of dirt, rock, and metal in all directions. Obama ducked down as Joe was blown back a few feet. The robo dog shook it off and went into the smoldering wreckage, sniffing for signs of Ben.

Ben the ball would never be seen again. What they would find were very unusual small round grenades that were only slightly larger than a golf ball.

These were each equipped with triggers set on a short delay—and  they were everywhere.

Someone or something did not want them there. Without Ben, Obama stopped playing golf and just walked.

Joe's greatest trick would be collecting the orb grenades ahead of Obama as they headed into the capital. He would sniff them out, then pick them up gently in his mouth and drop them into a sack with the others. Obama was trying to puzzle out whether all of this was part of some grand design. Had the same person who made the mines made the dogs? And if so, to what end? Was he walking right into enemy territory?

# THE BIG GUY

D.C. had been virtually leveled. Only a few columns of the Capitol Building remained, staggered like chipped teeth.

The Lincoln Memorial was perhaps Obama's favorite place in all of Washington. He could feel the continuum of U.S. history strongest there, and it occurred to Obama, as he approached the steps, that perhaps he had been headed there to see Abe all along. To meditate with the big guy on how and when the great American experiment had failed.

At the top of the steps it became immediately clear that this was going to be a depressing encounter with old Abe. One side of the giant's face had been blown off, and he was missing most of his right leg. Every monument Obama had passed was demolished in some way—but he had held out hope this place would be different. He tamped down his disappointment and took in what was left of the memorial. The Gettysburg Address, once so clearly etched into the walls, was now broken and lying in pieces on the floor. Joe stayed back on the steps, sitting on his haunches. Obama imagined the robot animal could recognize that this was a solemn moment and was giving him some space.

Obama stepped up to what was left of Abe and looked him in his one remaining eye. "Boy, am I glad to see you," he began, clearing his throat. "I . . . uh . . . wish I was here under different circumstances."

Orange motes of snow hung in the still air. Joe the robo dog yawned. His metal tail thumped the ground twice and then settled.

Obama continued: "Why . . . do I feel . . . like I've let you down somehow."

And as if in response, the ground shook. Joe and Obama both whipped around in the direction of the Washington Monument and the National Mall.

# JAEGER-MEISTER

A giant robot that looked like Obama, when he had been president, was walking toward them from a mile away. It was forty stories high, and the ground shook with every step. Despite the colossal size, the thing was approaching quickly. Obama's jaw hit the floor as the enormous jaeger stopped beside what was left of the Washington Monument, towering over it. This thing was huge.

Joe barked and growled.

At least now he had an idea of what might have done all the damage around him. It was this giant, robotic *thing* that was clearly designed to look just like him. The robot's paint job even gave it the appearance of wearing a suit, right down to the blue tie.

"Oh, hell no."

Understandably, after everything Obama had been through, this latest development made him very angry. But before he had a chance to channel that anger, he could hear the familiar whirr of a jet engine starting, only this time it came from the direction of the Robama. The giant robot turned its gaze on Obama and the steps of the Lincoln Memorial. Obama and Joe ran as fast as they could, but it was only seconds before the blasts started. Energy

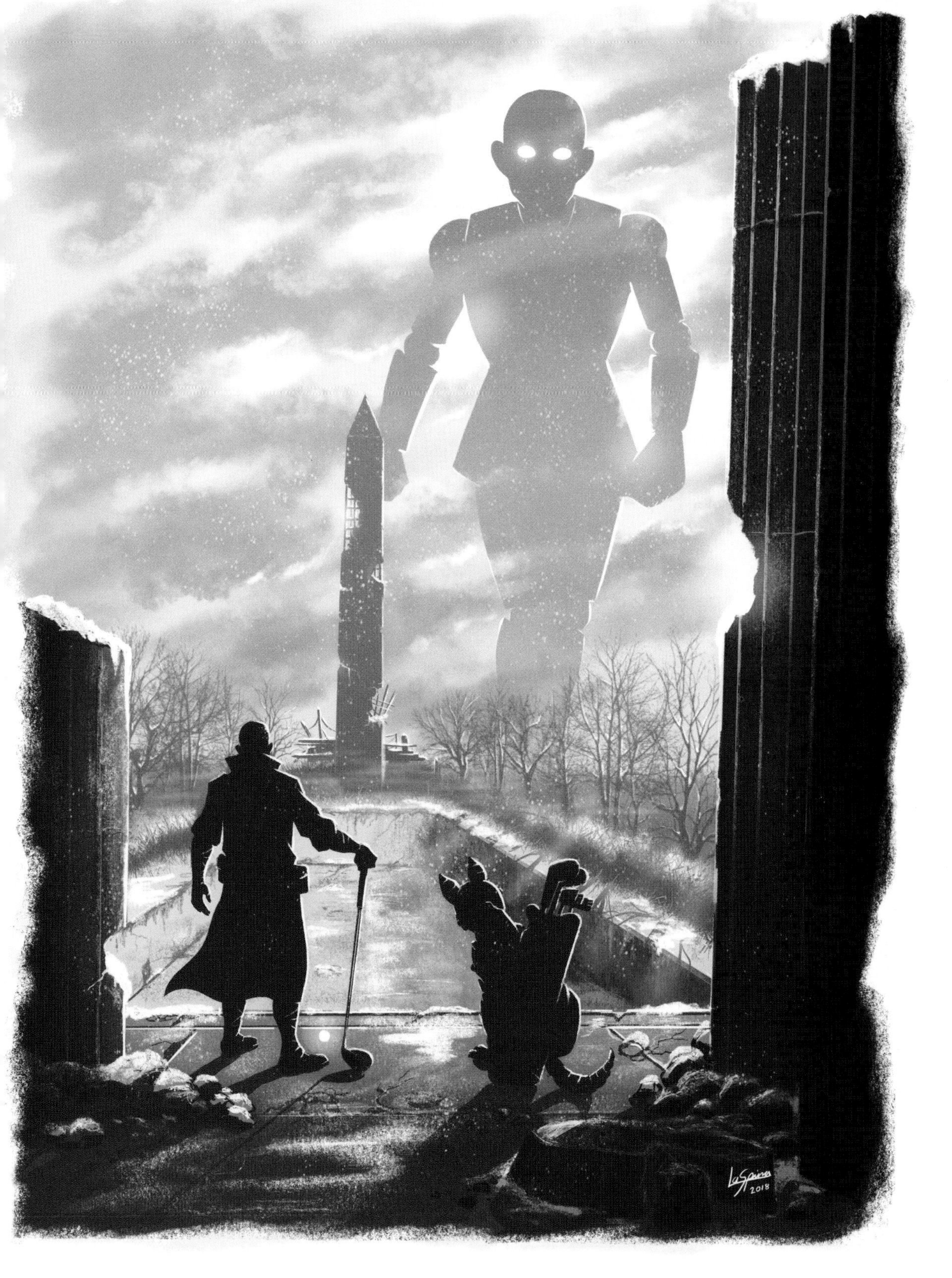
LaSpina
2018

cannons shot directly from Robama's eyes, decimating what was left of the Lincoln Memorial and tossing Obama high into the air.

Joe dropped the bag of small round grenades at Obama's feet when he landed. Obama laughed instantly at the beautiful poetry of it all. At once he knew what he was there to do and apparently so did his sidekick.

He wouldn't have much time. Obama whipped out his driver and carefully placed one of the mines at his feet. "You sure about this?" he asked Joe, who barked back immediately. Obama aimed for the body of the giant Robama, took one last glance, and let her rip.

The small round mine sailed 350 yards as another blast began to build from within the giant mech. The bomb exploded on impact and took a chunk of the robot's right arm with it. Obama immediately placed another orb grenade on the ground and then had an idea. He kneeled down.

"You understand me, don't you, buddy?" Obama said. "I want you to place these every two feet. All of them in a row—as many as we have." Obama showed the pooch what he meant by placing one orb next to another. Meanwhile, Robama the Destroyer was readying itself for another attack.

# HAIL TO THE CHIEF

It all happened so fast. Obama began as Joe the robot dog lined up all thirty-seven of the orbs they had collected side by side. Obama turned the National Mall into his own ballistic driving range. He didn't think; he just ripped them off as fast as he could, using all the skill he had gained playing Apocalypse Golf and driving his way across the country. He'd crack one and step over to the next immediately.

The fireworks show began. Bombs burst in the air as the giant robot flailed wildly, almost dancing, trying to swat the incoming fire. Obama could sense that this battle was perhaps winnable. His swing was in such fine form that he wished he had an audience. Obama added his own color commentary:

"The president is on fire today, Bob. Look at his form. I'd say his swing is looking better than ever."

Two consecutive body blows rocked the giant, who stumbled back and snapped the already bruised Washington Monument in half. The robot could not get off a clean shot during the barrage of exploding orbs.

Obama was halfway through his arsenal when the giant recovered enough to charge. Joe fearlessly raced toward the giant in defense.

"Joe! No!"

It was too late. Joe the robo pooch with bright blue eyes ran for the giant robot, gnawing at its ankle with everything it had. He was kicked off and sent flying, smeared against the ground on impact. The little guy didn't stand a chance.

Obama drove the orbs faster now, his driver vibrating between swings. He was determined to bring down the giant. With only ten orbs left he changed strategy. He would go for the legs.

The giant Robama was now closing in, running inside the emptied-out reflecting pool. At this moment the pool looked for all the world like a track aimed directly toward Obama. With every step, the ground shook, and the robot's size seemed to grow bigger and bigger. Obama had to adjust his aim much lower as the monster closed in, and he knew he'd be lucky if he was able to get even two more shots off, that's how close it was. Time slowed for Obama, and the surreal irony of facing off with a building-size version of himself sunk in.

*THWACK!* An orb took out the robot's right foot cleanly and the giant lurched forward, crashing down, its arms extended to brace the fall. The view from directly above was of the robot lying flat, head to the side, arms splayed out and hanging over the edges of the empty reflecting pool. The skull of the giant metal Obama had been cracked open, and the entire machine was convulsing and smoldering.

Obama and giant Obama were only thirty feet apart.

# THE BIGGER THEY ARE

Obama approached the downed giant cautiously. The growing dread he'd felt for months surged back into his system. He held tightly to his golf club.

Like the head of Lady Liberty in *Planet of the Apes,* here was the head of President Barack Obama, several stories tall, one cheek pressed flat against the empty reflecting pool dusted with orange snow. A ridge along the forehead between the eyebrows and the hairline was now cracked open. Obama climbed up by the robot's armpit, then along the neck toward the head.

Up close, Obama could admire the craft that went into creating such a great likeness of himself. In his heart of hearts, he had always secretly wanted his own monument. He climbed over the giant metal ear, reminded of the size of his own ears. Smoke billowed out from the crack in the head, and down below on the ground, Obama could see the body of Joe the robo pooch, still, smashed, and scattered. It was crushing.

Obama yanked hard on a handle that ran along the jawline. Smoke poured out and Obama covered his face with the front of his shirt. His duster waved in the breeze and snow started to fall again. Inside Obama could make out a console and cockpit. His mind raced at what or whom he might meet. If there was no one inside, all the answers he was looking for would continue to go unanswered. A person inside would be the first flesh-and-bone human he encountered in this dimension—but also his attacker.

The mech interior was much larger than Obama imagined it would be. Inside the wreckage, hoses had burst and liquid, possibly fuel, was raining down. Obama heard the faint sound of a man coughing and could see the outline of a body through the smoke. Snow drifted through the open hatch as Obama climbed inside. The floor of the cockpit was now a side wall, and Obama had to slide himself down against what would be the inside of the cheek to find his footing. The technology was complex, clearly created by the same minds that had crafted the orb grenades and the robo dogs.

"Help!" A man's voice cut through Obama's swirling thoughts in what felt like the first time in ages. Obama could now see the man hanging upside down, harnessed in by robotic arms, now a puzzle of twisted metal and awkwardly bent limbs. Obama dropped his driver and climbed up. He was several feet short of reaching the man's hand. "No," the man said, swatting his hand away as he breathed heavily. The voice felt familiar to Obama but he couldn't quite place it. "There's a release . . . over there." The man pointed to a console that normally would have been easy to reach but, given the circumstances, required Obama to climb.

Obama didn't hesitate, though maybe he should have. He scrambled up to a panel of controls, swinging himself carefully from one side of the cockpit to the other. He saw the red manual release handle and managed to reach it, yanking it out as hard as he could. The man dropped about eight feet and landed with a heavy thud.

Obama had still not seen the face of his enemy, whom he had apparently just freed from capture. He dropped down to where the man lay. The back of the man's head was fat, pink, and bald—a pale, sweaty dome sitting atop a thick neck in a now bloodied jumpsuit. He was wheezing, struggling to breathe. A smell reached Obama's nose, one with a familiar stench. Smell is a funny thing that sticks with you. This was a spicy musk he had not encountered since he was with Joe, in their home dimension on January 20, 2017. A silent scream rang out inside Obama. He remembered that smell. It was the smell of Trump.

Obama surprised himself with what came out of his mouth next. "Are you okay?"

The bald, fat, pinkish creature turned his head to Obama. His appearance reminded Obama of Darth Vader when he had removed his helmet in *Return of the Jedi.* Obama expected to see the orange beast himself and was confused to find an entirely different Trump looking back at him. It was Donald Jr., now in his seventies, appearing very much like his father before him—only jaundiced and hairless.

Don Jr. spit out blood and then smiled, his giant front teeth smeared red. "Do I look okay?"

"What have you done?" Obama said.

The shit-eating grin on Don Jr.'s face soured. "Just finishing the job. You know . . . draining the swamp." Don Jr.'s eyes darted to Obama's driver, which was lying halfway between them. Both men lunged for the club. It was now that Obama realized just how old he must be. If Trump Jr. appeared to be in his seventies, he figured, he must now be in his late eighties or even early nineties. Obama could feel his age as the two men scrambled on their hands and knees.

Obama did not like violence and could never see himself as a killer. He also knew that in his role as president that he had been the one, more often than he would have liked, to give an order that would ultimately take lives. On most days, in most dimensions, Obama weighed human life preciously.

All those feelings went out the window as images of Don Jr. posed next to majestic African animals shot dead scrolled through Obama's mind. He thought of the destroyed Lincoln Memorial. Obama felt a rage well up inside of him. It boiled over instantly, and he saw red. He stopped wanting answers and wanted revenge.

Don Jr. genuinely liked to hunt big game. He had made it his life's work. To really describe how these men ended up together, the last two living animals for hundreds of miles, is another book entirely. But it's safe to say, in the simplest way, that Don Jr. had set out to finish what his father had started. Inside Don Jr. was a boy who still wanted to impress his dad, and Obama was the biggest game of all.

The next part was sloppy and brutal. Don Jr., it turns out, was a berserker. Obama reached the driver first—but it didn't matter. He was overwhelmed by a full-blown Don Jr. tantrum, expressed in a barrage of wild punches. Obama's ears rang as his body landed against the sloped interior of the robot's neck. Don Jr. then wrestled Obama to the ground, and the two men rolled to and fro like children fighting on a playground.

Obama gritted his teeth. "Why are you here?! Why me?!"

"I'm here"—Don Jr. grabbed Obama by the lapels with his tiny carnival hands—"to stop you." And before Obama could let that sink in, Don Jr. heaved Obama out the open hatch.

From a certain angle, it would appear as if Obama had been spit out of his own giant mouth. He landed hard on the cement bottom of the reflecting pool, which was padded only ever so slightly by the snow. The wind was knocked out of him and he could feel the cold on his back.

Don Jr. appeared above in the open cranium, wielding Obama's driver. "You forgot something." Trump Jr. slid down and stood over Obama, who was still struggling to catch his breath. Don gripped the club expertly and took one practice swing before stepping up to Obama. Old man Obama was frozen, the shock of the fall sucking the wind out of him. His brain said, *Move!* but his body would not do it. He felt this was certainly the beginning of his end. He thought of his family, and he thought of Joe, and he thought of America.

His attacker pulled back the driver in a backswing before dropping the hammer. Obama could only wince. And then, as if by some miracle, Joe the robo pooch launched into Obama's field of vision, tackling Don Jr. like linebacker Terry Tate. The dog was far from okay, but more alive than ever. The loyal pooch now had Trump Jr. pinned to the ground under his giant paws and he growled in his face. Obama rolled to one side and stood slowly.

"Good boy." Barack patted Joe on his head.

He looked down at Don Jr. and felt pity for the boy inside the old man. Obama looked around and shook his head. "What happened here?"

Don's raspy cough sounded worse; he wheezed and his breathing was labored. He shook his head. "Uncivil War."

Blood was now pooling around Don Jr., bright red against the snow.

"Off," Obama ordered Joe, pointing back to the steps of the memorial. "I have supplies in my pack, go fetch it." Joe whined as he went to fetch the pack, leaving the two men alone.

Obama started pulling at Don Jr.'s clothing, searching for his wound. "It's just you and me now. So why don't you stay with me, okay?"

Trump Jr.'s expression melted from wide-eyed anger into a glassy calm. He began to speak but nothing came out.

Obama found a long gash along Don's abdomen and applied gentle pressure to stop the bleeding.

Trump Jr. whispered, "Kill me."

"No. I'm a lover and a fighter . . . not a killer," Obama said. "What are you stopping me from doing? Why are you here?"

Don Jr. looked from Obama's face up to what was left of the Washington Monument. Obama followed his eyes but didn't understand.

Joe came back with Obama's pack and dropped it at his feet, but it was too late. Obama was now once again the last man on Earth.

# NATIONAL SECURITY PRESIDENTIAL DIRECTIVE 51

Joe was messed up. His robot dog body was missing several pieces and his nanotubes could only repair so much. Obama sat on the edge of the reflecting pool and watched the snowfall. He wanted a cigarette, which was saying something. Obama hung on to Joe for a while, and the two of them just sat there in the snowy quiet.

Obama couldn't stop thinking about what Don Jr. had said. *I'm here to stop you.* Over and over he repeated it to himself. What did it mean? What was Don supposed to be stopping him from? Obama had lost all sense of purpose four dimensions ago. Obama thought about the three dogs and the orb mines and the giant robot. He looked Joe in his fading blue robot dog eyes. "I must be close. But to what?"

All Barack had ever wanted to do was use his powers for good, to bring people together, to unite humanity. Obama thought of Joe Biden giving that corny speech the day they left in 2017. It felt like several lifetimes ago, and in many ways, it was.

He thought of the lab where they kneeled down naked surrounded by the greatest minds in the world and Samuel L. Jackson. Obama now recalled moments from that day that he had long since forgotten. How he got on Marine One after the inauguration. How he had landed at Joint Base Andrews, had made quick remarks, and was then taken by the Secret Service with Joe Biden into an unmarked car. How they drove secretly back toward the Hill and directly to an underground access point.

Obama felt a flash of hope as he made the connection.

# BENCH MARK A

They walked to the base of the Washington Monument. Just south of there, the dog cleared the snow from a manhole cover. Obama lifted the cover to reveal the tip of a miniature Washington Monument buried there in the street. Now here was a genuine Easter egg. Obama had heard about the mini–Washington Monument but never seen it with his own eyes. What happened next was truly shocking. The twelve-foot mini-monument rose up from the ground, turning clockwise as it went until it locked into place aboveground and cleared the hole it once filled. Obama and Joe peered down the long empty shaft. Obama, ever the gentleman, said, "After you."

# FORTRESS OF SHENANIGANS

Obama had always loved the secret city of tunnels beneath Washington, D.C. They had always brought out his sense of adventure and inner Hardy Boy. The vast network of known tunnels excited him as a senator, and then in his presidency, the truly mind-boggling secret tunnels became a private obsession even though he had no real use for them. He just thought they were cool.

Joe led the way through the tunnels, his eyes now activated with low blue beams. Joe seemed to know where he was going in the near darkness. Obama followed just a few feet behind.

The Five Fingers of Science had embedded in the Emergency Relocation Group and settled themselves many stories beneath Dupont Circle on November 9, 2016. They were to begin construction of the machine that would send Barry and Joe into the multiverse. Now, decades later, Obama the Grey and his robot dog companion found the deserted laboratory long since abandoned.

The steel doors were shut and the power was off. Obama tried to pry the doors open with his bare hands to no avail. The dog gnawed into his own haunches and from his battered thigh extracted a steel rod the length of a crowbar but slimmer and far lighter. It appeared from nowhere like a magician's wand, and Obama marveled as the pup dropped the long metal rod at his feet.

Obama jimmied the door open and the dog jumped through first.

January 20, 2017, felt like a million years ago and only yesterday. The idea that humanity could actually fail was only a tiny seed that morning, gently placed in the soil and covered over on that rainy inauguration day.

The air was dense with the musk of once new technology collecting dust. Joe the robo pooch ran down the corridor and into the main room. His blue eyes shone brightly in the darkness but illuminated only narrow sections: chairs and tables and equipment and screens. Giant glass panels separated the chambers that surrounded the Quantum Recoherence Engine.

Obama walked slowly in the darkness and caught himself taking short breaths. He didn't like breathing in air he could not see.

A small red light blinked. Joe ran to it and barked.

"I'm coming."

The small red light blinked again. Obama recognized where they were. He sat down at the giant metal desk situated in the center of the control room. The moment Obama sat down, a panel of lights came on and Samuel L. Jackson materialized.

# SUPER (OLD) FRIENDS

The 2017 version of the highest grossing actor of all time appeared life size on a panel of glass like Tupac. "Mr. President, if you're seeing this then something's gone terribly wrong."

"Sam! Oh *man,* am I glad to see you!"

Sam held up his hands defensively. "Don't get too excited. Everyone you know is dead. Including me. You're talking to the essence of a bad motherfucker programmed into artificial intelligence."

The robot dog sat on the floor in front of hologram Samuel L. Jackson.

"The Five Fingers left the Recoherence Engine here for this exact situation, and it should have enough reserve power for one-time use."

"What about Joe? I thought I couldn't go anywhere without Joe. We're entangled."

The robo pooch dropped lifeless to the floor and his lights went out. That same moment Joe Biden appeared on a panel of glass to Obama's right. "I'm right here, buddy." Joe looked the same age as when they left office, right down to the suit he was wearing. "Even in the afterlife I'm right by your side."

Obama had spent most of his days as a time warrior confused and had gotten used to not truly understanding how things always worked. That said, this latest development was a bit hard for Obama to swallow. "Joe! You were the dog? This whole time. Why didn't you tell me?"

"The dog can't speak! And I thought you knew! You kept calling me Joe. You couldn't tell how much I liked it? I'd wag my tail and run in circles. The Five Fingers created a program to find you, and once the hounds scanned you I took over Champ Six there and I've been by your side ever since. I really thought we were on the same page."

Once upon a time it was Obama's predisposition to be optimistic, but he had long since abandoned that position. Obama held his temples; he was tired and trying to think straight. It was difficult. Sam broke the long silence.

"Mr. President, I believe we can get you out of here."

# FIRED UP

Obama the Grey stripped naked for what felt like the thousandth time since he had started bouncing around the continuum. He laughed at all the dirty clothes he was wearing as he disrobed. The silly weapons that had honestly saved his life time and again. The heavy duster he had come to think of as a second skin. He drained his canteen to the last drop and tossed it onto the pile.

He walked to the center of the chamber and gingerly crouched down as hologram Sam and hologram Joe watched on.

Once again Obama had no idea when or where he might arrive. Once again, he did not know which dimension of the multiverse he would occupy next. Obama could almost taste that unique and now familiar horror, the sensation of having one's soul ripped from the body, only to have it sent coursing through the circuitry of the universe before erupting like a volcano into the unknown. His adrenaline spiked just knowing that it was again possible. That anything was still possible.

The quantum recoherence process had always taken so much out of him, but he had never attempted it from his body at such an old age. He thought of Michelle and the girls. He thought about seeing the real Joe again. He became deeply emotional and trembled there in front of his digital friends as the countdown sequence began.

The giant blade of the engine began to spin underneath the clear floor until it was an invisible blur. The temperature dropped thirty degrees in only seconds, and Obama could feel his flesh pucker. He took a long slow breath into his lungs and could see the warm air exit his mouth in a plume of steam.

His ears rang. Obama watched as strands of electricity sprang from every hair on his body and reached outward. He could feel his mind sucked into the head of a pin and his very molecules floating away from him like dust.

Like making a wish before blowing out birthday candles. Obama's last thought was for humanity itself.

JUST BECAUSE OUR
POLITICAL HEROES WERE
MURDERED DOES NOT MEAN
THAT THE DREAM DOES NOT
STILL LIVE, BURIED DEEP
IN OUR BROKEN HEARTS.

—JOE BIDEN (1983)

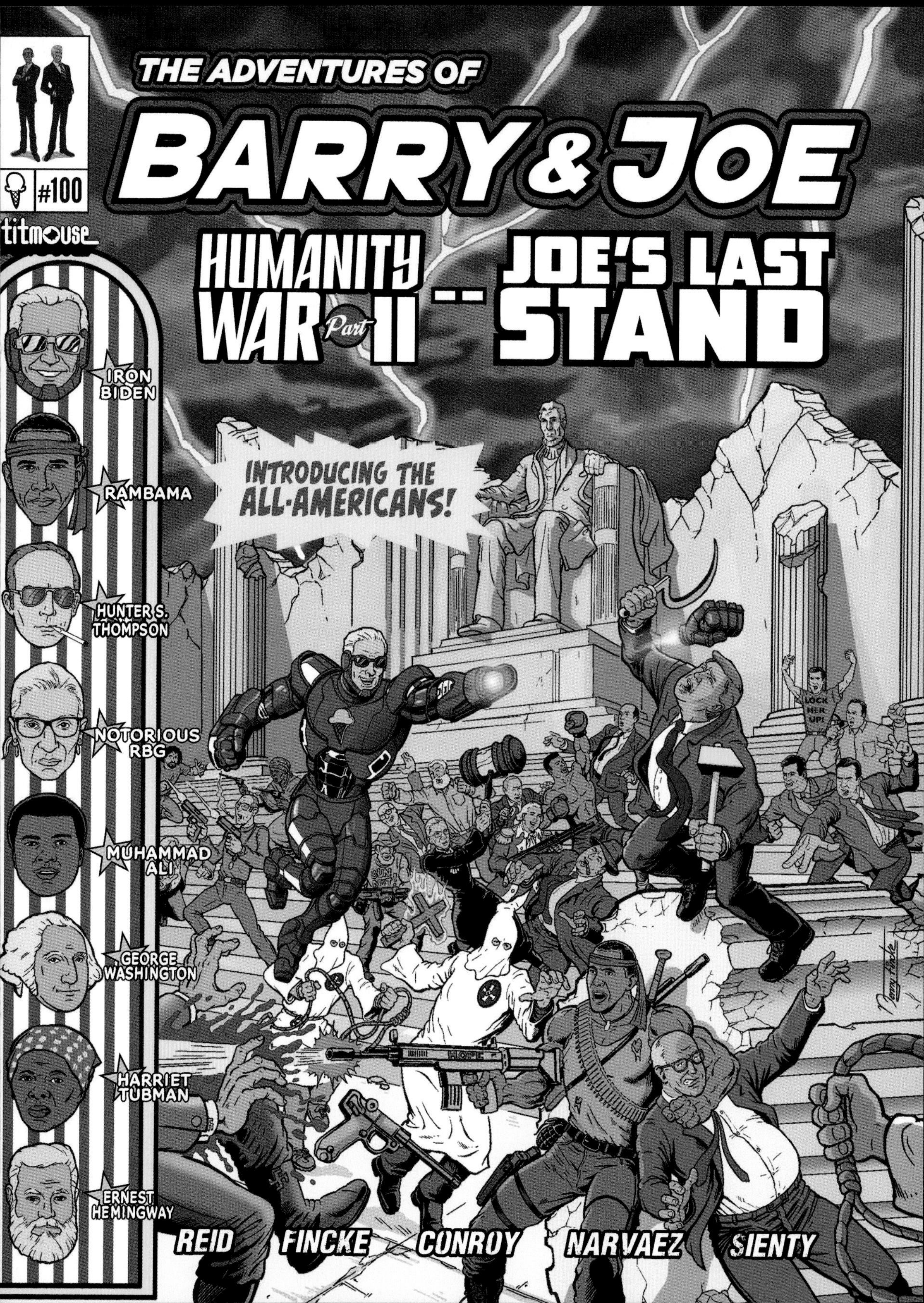
THE ADVENTURES OF
BARRY & JOE
#100
titmouse
HUMANITY WAR Part II
JOE'S LAST STAND
INTRODUCING THE ALL-AMERICANS!
IRON BIDEN
RAMBAMA
HUNTER S. THOMPSON
NOTORIOUS RBG
MUHAMMAD ALI
GEORGE WASHINGTON
HARRIET TUBMAN
ERNEST HEMINGWAY
LOCK HER UP!
HOPE
REID
FINCKE
CONROY
NARVAEZ
SIENTY

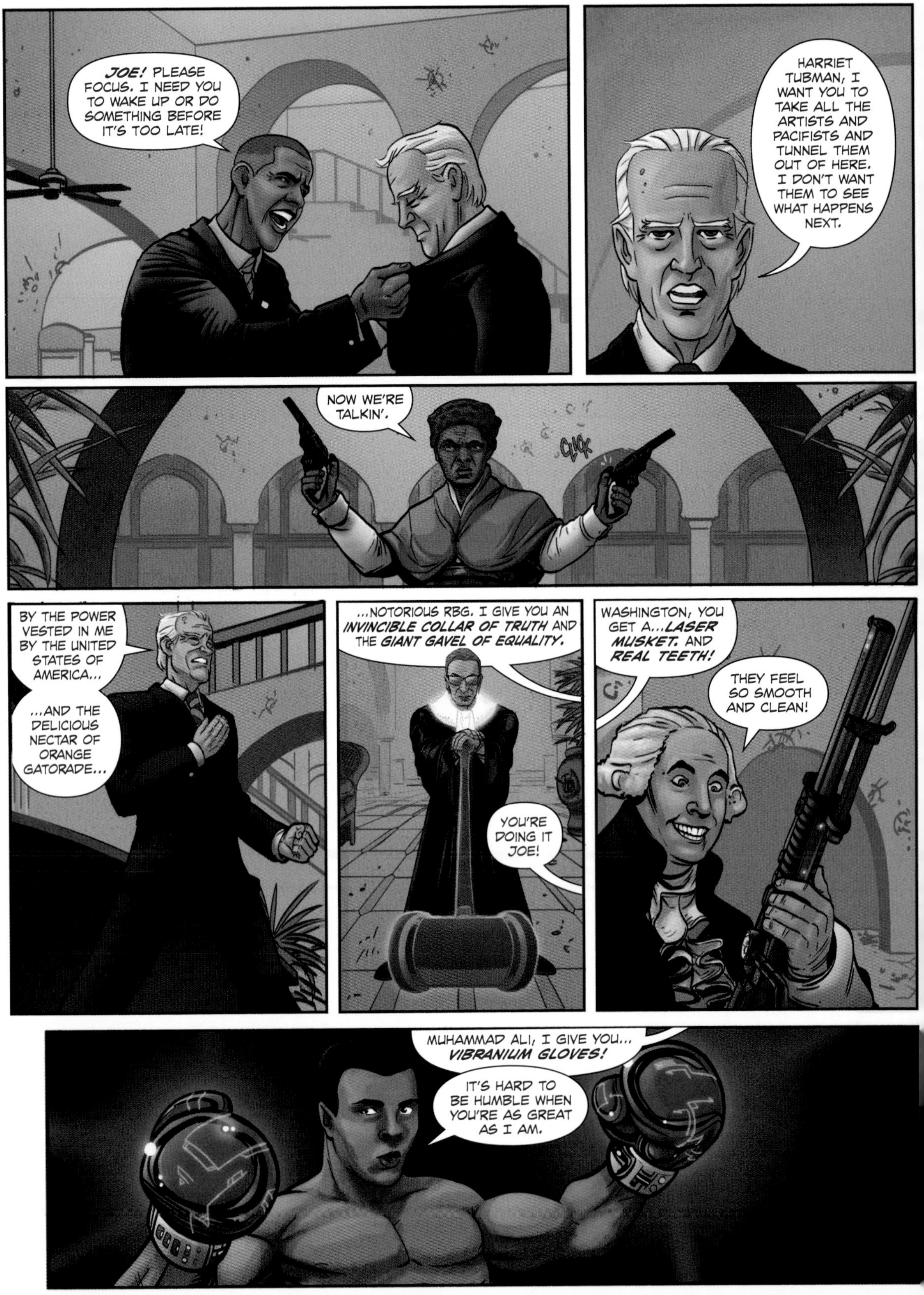
JOE! PLEASE FOCUS. I NEED YOU TO WAKE UP OR DO SOMETHING BEFORE IT'S TOO LATE!
HARRIET TUBMAN, I WANT YOU TO TAKE ALL THE ARTISTS AND PACIFISTS AND TUNNEL THEM OUT OF HERE. I DON'T WANT THEM TO SEE WHAT HAPPENS NEXT.
NOW WE'RE TALKIN'.
CLICK
BY THE POWER VESTED IN ME BY THE UNITED STATES OF AMERICA...
...AND THE DELICIOUS NECTAR OF ORANGE GATORADE...
...NOTORIOUS RBG. I GIVE YOU AN INVINCIBLE COLLAR OF TRUTH AND THE GIANT GAVEL OF EQUALITY.
YOU'RE DOING IT JOE!
WASHINGTON, YOU GET A...LASER MUSKET. AND REAL TEETH!
THEY FEEL SO SMOOTH AND CLEAN!
MUHAMMAD ALI, I GIVE YOU... VIBRANIUM GLOVES!
IT'S HARD TO BE HUMBLE WHEN YOU'RE AS GREAT AS I AM.

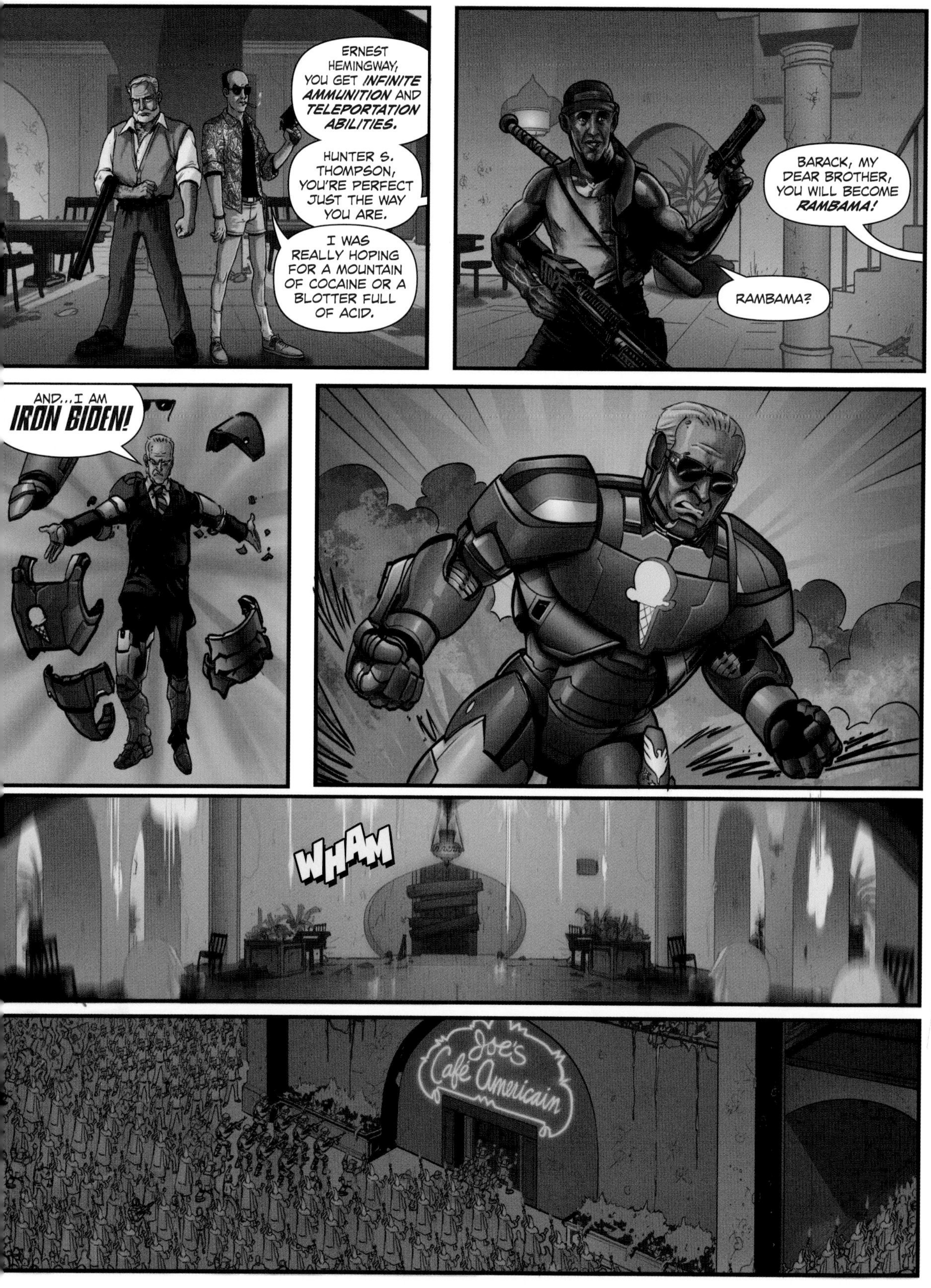
ERNEST HEMINGWAY, YOU GET *INFINITE AMMUNITION* AND *TELEPORTATION ABILITIES.*
HUNTER S. THOMPSON, YOU'RE PERFECT JUST THE WAY YOU ARE.
I WAS REALLY HOPING FOR A MOUNTAIN OF COCAINE OR A BLOTTER FULL OF ACID.
BARACK, MY DEAR BROTHER, YOU WILL BECOME *RAMBAMA!*
RAMBAMA?
AND...I AM
IRON BIDEN!
WHAM
Joe's Café Americain

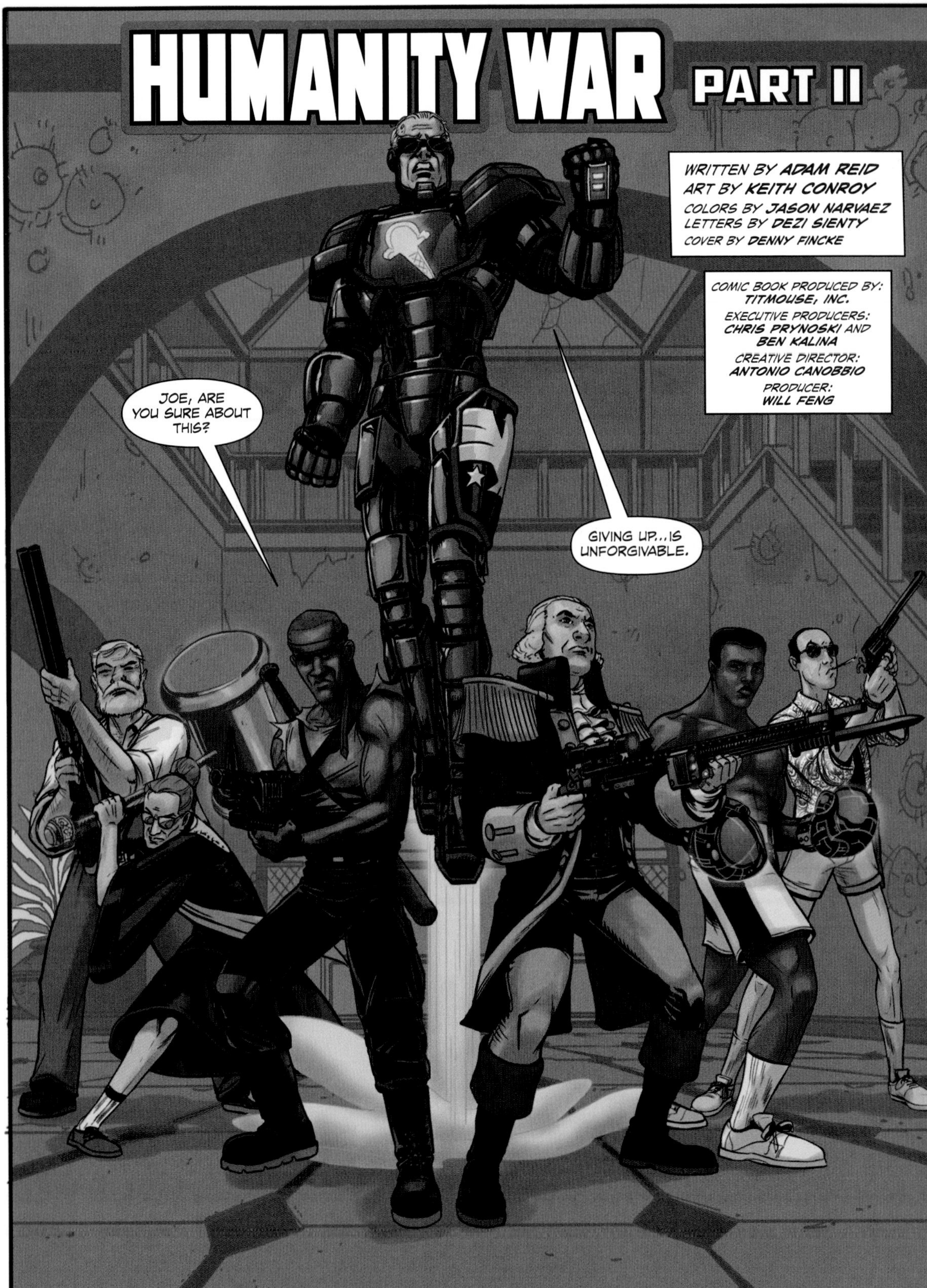

HUMANITY WAR PART II
WRITTEN BY ADAM REID
ART BY KEITH CONROY
COLORS BY JASON NARVAEZ
LETTERS BY DEZI SIENTY
COVER BY DENNY FINCKE
COMIC BOOK PRODUCED BY: TITMOUSE, INC.
EXECUTIVE PRODUCERS: CHRIS PRYNOSKI AND BEN KALINA
CREATIVE DIRECTOR: ANTONIO CANOBBIO
PRODUCER: WILL FENG
JOE, ARE YOU SURE ABOUT THIS?
GIVING UP...IS UNFORGIVABLE.

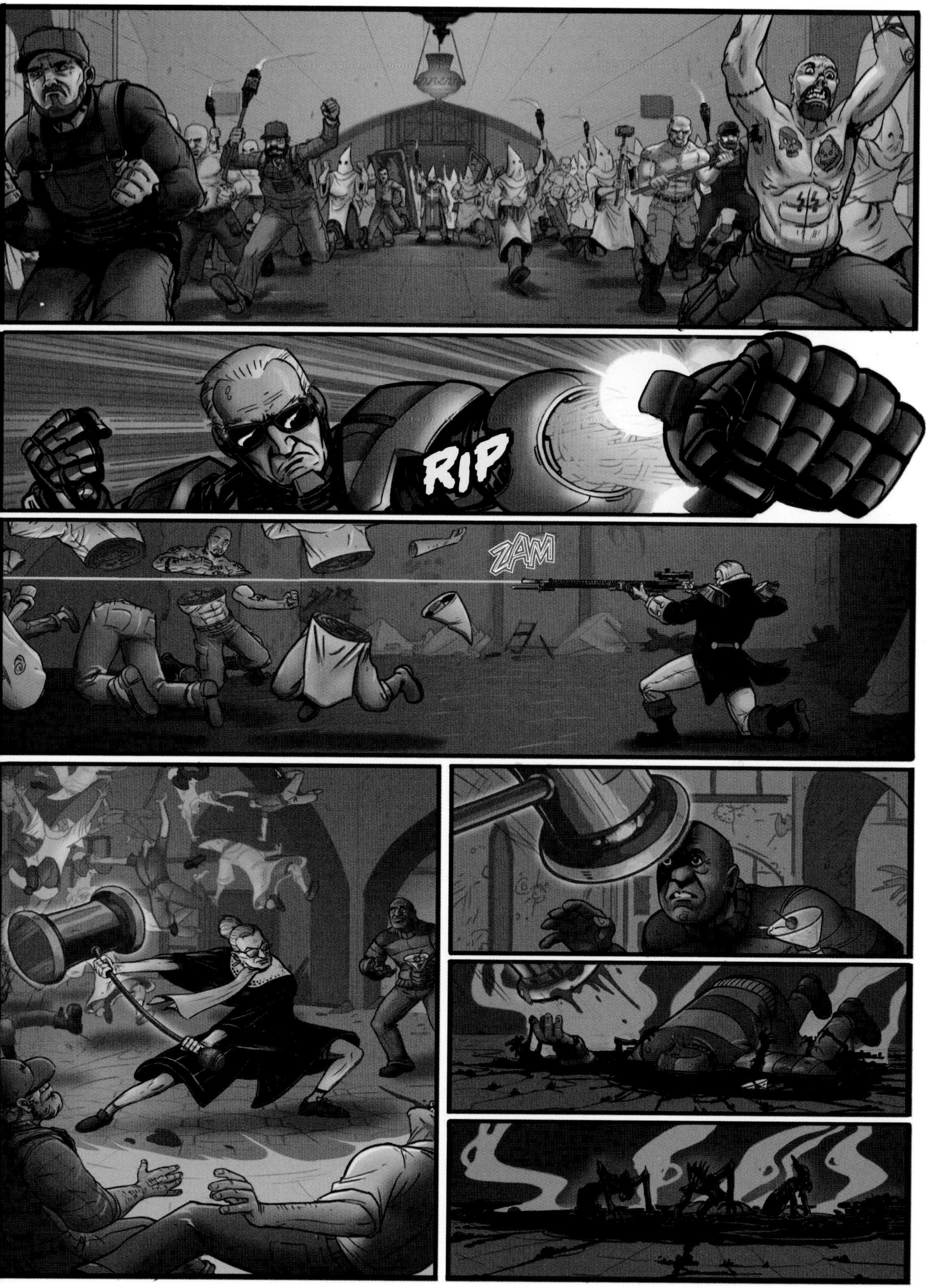
RIP
ZAM

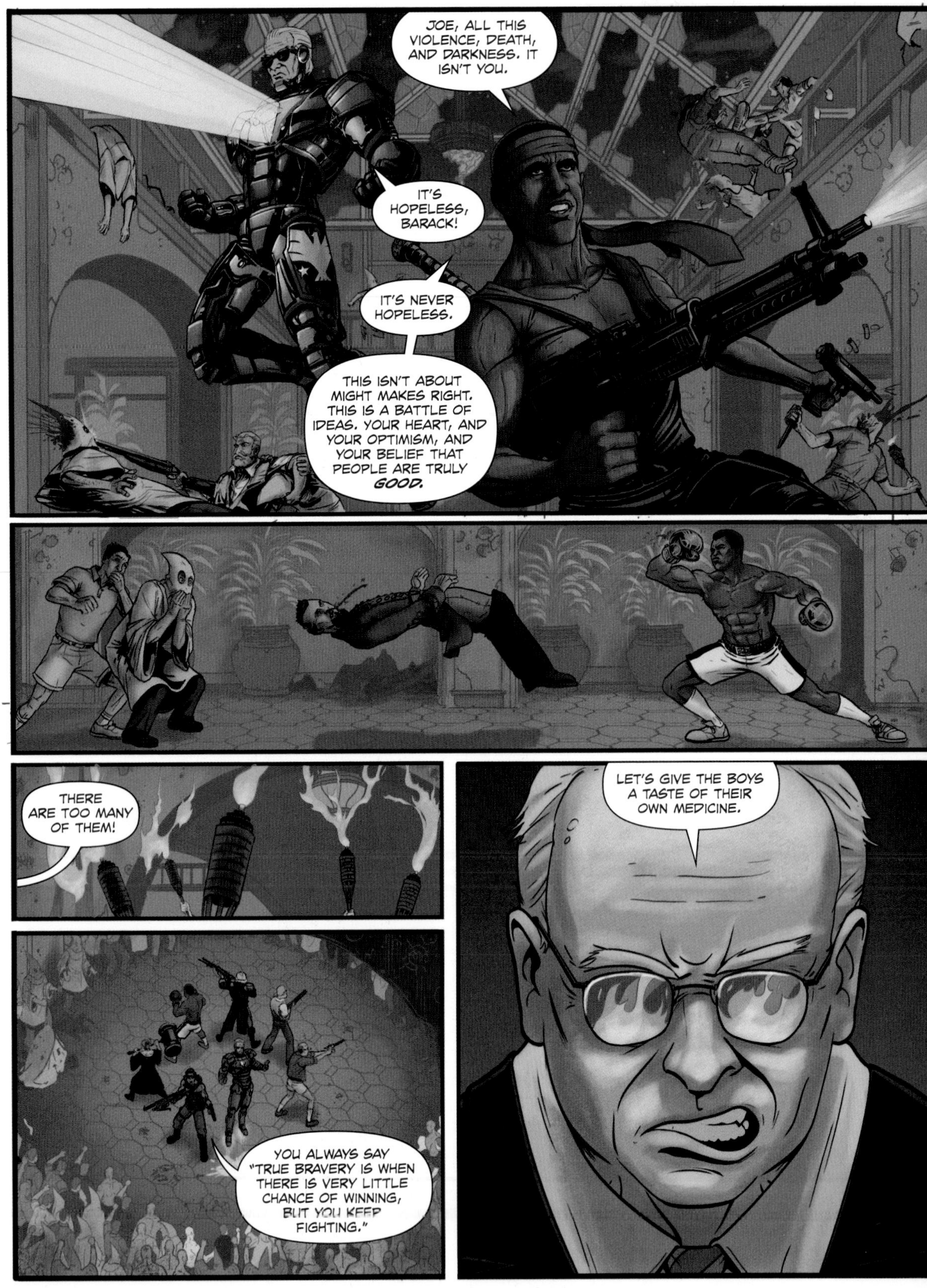
JOE, ALL THIS VIOLENCE, DEATH, AND DARKNESS. IT ISN'T YOU.
IT'S HOPELESS, BARACK!
IT'S NEVER HOPELESS.
THIS ISN'T ABOUT MIGHT MAKES RIGHT. THIS IS A BATTLE OF IDEAS. YOUR HEART, AND YOUR OPTIMISM, AND YOUR BELIEF THAT PEOPLE ARE TRULY ***GOOD.***
THERE ARE TOO MANY OF THEM!
LET'S GIVE THE BOYS A TASTE OF THEIR OWN MEDICINE.
YOU ALWAYS SAY "TRUE BRAVERY IS WHEN THERE IS VERY LITTLE CHANCE OF WINNING, BUT YOU KEEP FIGHTING."

ACFT
N 33.6052°
W 7.6204°
TOT
ELV
RNG 8.793H-
RNG 4.98NM-
FVW 675M+
O/S
STATUS
ARMED
JOE!
BARACK!

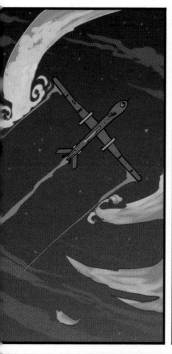

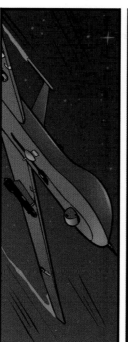

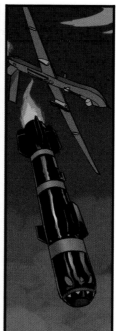

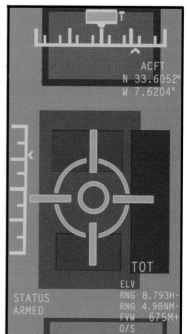

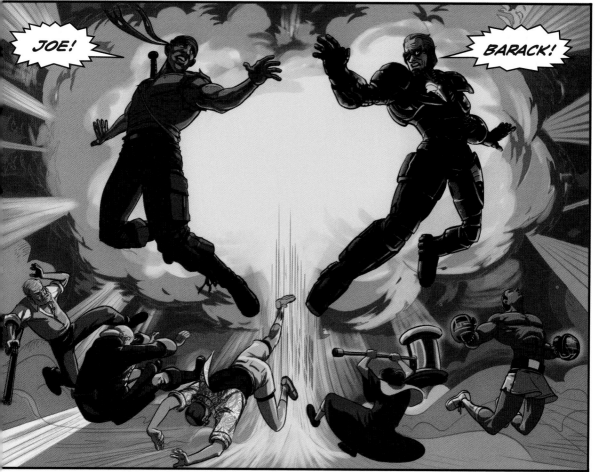

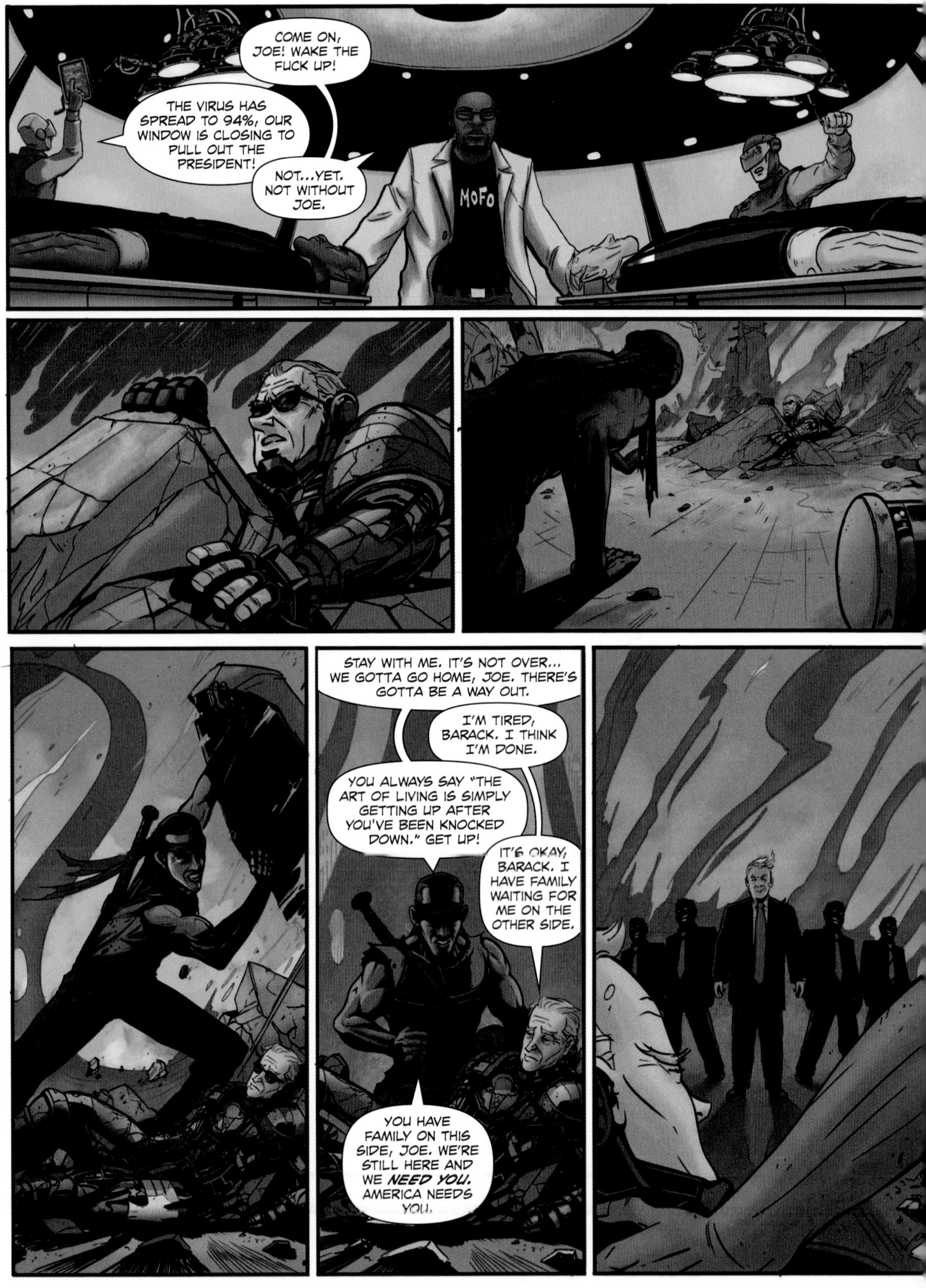
COME ON, JOE! WAKE THE FUCK UP!
THE VIRUS HAS SPREAD TO 94%, OUR WINDOW IS CLOSING TO PULL OUT THE PRESIDENT!
NOT...YET. NOT WITHOUT JOE.
MOFO
STAY WITH ME. IT'S NOT OVER... WE GOTTA GO HOME, JOE. THERE'S GOTTA BE A WAY OUT.
I'M TIRED, BARACK. I THINK I'M DONE.
YOU ALWAYS SAY "THE ART OF LIVING IS SIMPLY GETTING UP AFTER YOU'VE BEEN KNOCKED DOWN." GET UP!
IT'S OKAY, BARACK. I HAVE FAMILY WAITING FOR ME ON THE OTHER SIDE.
YOU HAVE FAMILY ON THIS SIDE, JOE. WE'RE STILL HERE AND WE ***NEED YOU.*** AMERICA NEEDS YOU.

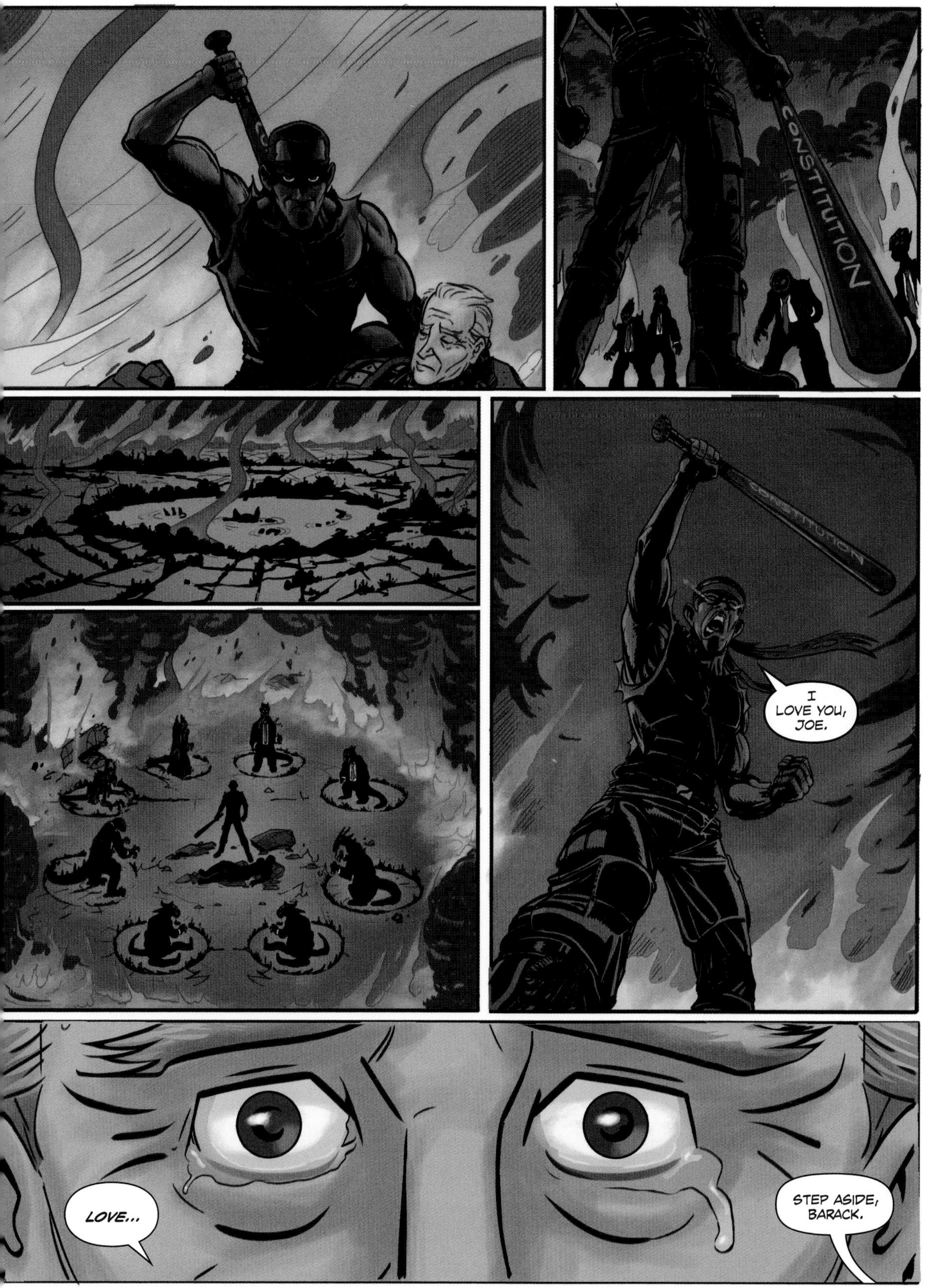
CONSTITUTION
CONSTITUTION
I LOVE YOU, JOE.
LOVE...
STEP ASIDE, BARACK.

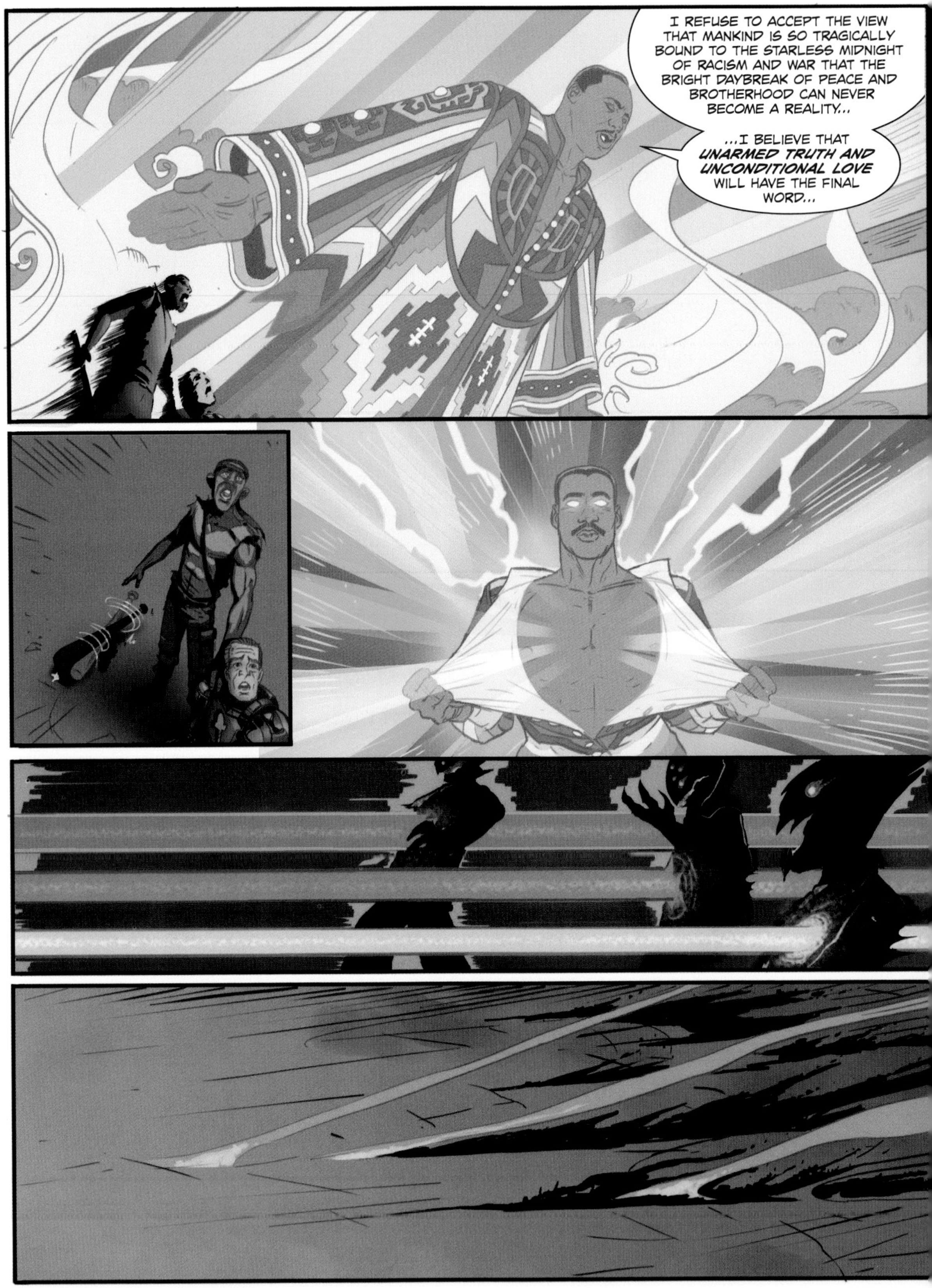
I REFUSE TO ACCEPT THE VIEW THAT MANKIND IS SO TRAGICALLY BOUND TO THE STARLESS MIDNIGHT OF RACISM AND WAR THAT THE BRIGHT DAYBREAK OF PEACE AND BROTHERHOOD CAN NEVER BECOME A REALITY...
...I BELIEVE THAT ***UNARMED TRUTH AND UNCONDITIONAL LOVE*** WILL HAVE THE FINAL WORD...

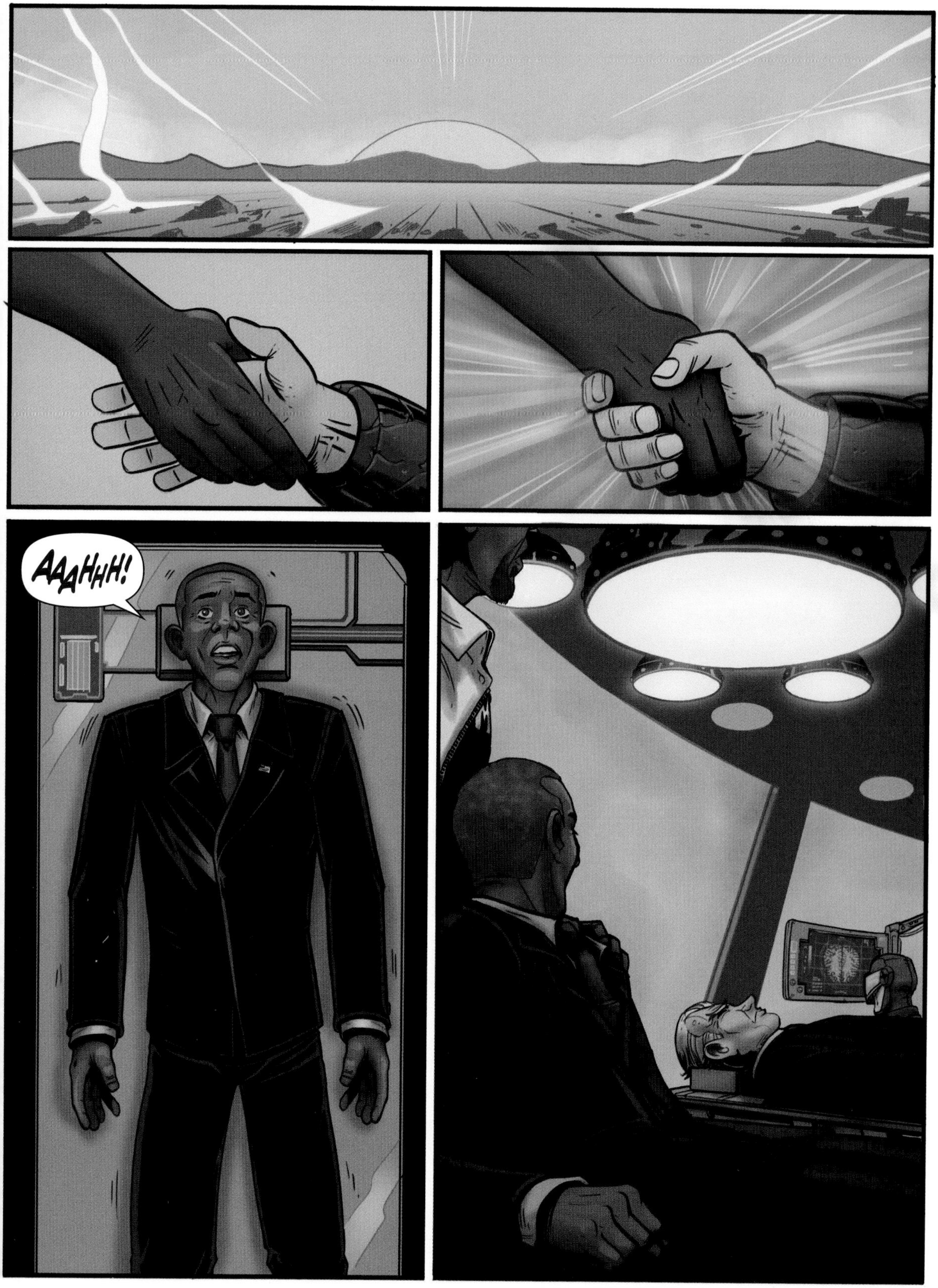
AAAHHH!

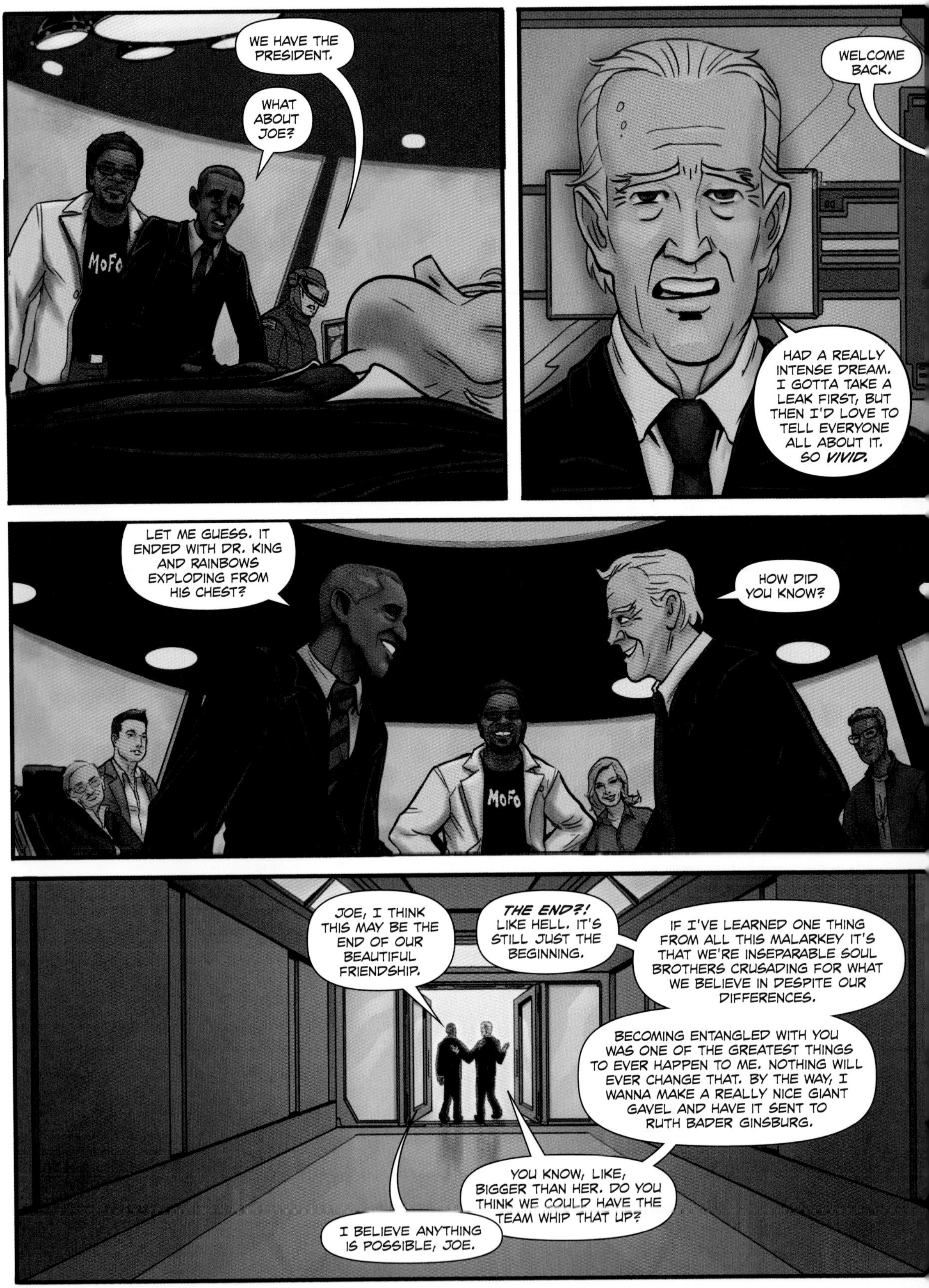

WE HAVE THE PRESIDENT.
WHAT ABOUT JOE?
WELCOME BACK.
HAD A REALLY INTENSE DREAM. I GOTTA TAKE A LEAK FIRST, BUT THEN I'D LOVE TO TELL EVERYONE ALL ABOUT IT. SO *VIVID.*
MoFo
LET ME GUESS. IT ENDED WITH DR. KING AND RAINBOWS EXPLODING FROM HIS CHEST?
HOW DID YOU KNOW?
MoFo
JOE, I THINK THIS MAY BE THE END OF OUR BEAUTIFUL FRIENDSHIP.
*THE END?!* LIKE HELL. IT'S STILL JUST THE BEGINNING.
IF I'VE LEARNED ONE THING FROM ALL THIS MALARKEY IT'S THAT WE'RE INSEPARABLE SOUL BROTHERS CRUSADING FOR WHAT WE BELIEVE IN DESPITE OUR DIFFERENCES.
BECOMING ENTANGLED WITH YOU WAS ONE OF THE GREATEST THINGS TO EVER HAPPEN TO ME. NOTHING WILL EVER CHANGE THAT. BY THE WAY, I WANNA MAKE A REALLY NICE GIANT GAVEL AND HAVE IT SENT TO RUTH BADER GINSBURG.
YOU KNOW, LIKE, BIGGER THAN HER. DO YOU THINK WE COULD HAVE THE TEAM WHIP THAT UP?
I BELIEVE ANYTHING IS POSSIBLE, JOE.

# Freaking out? Chew on this!

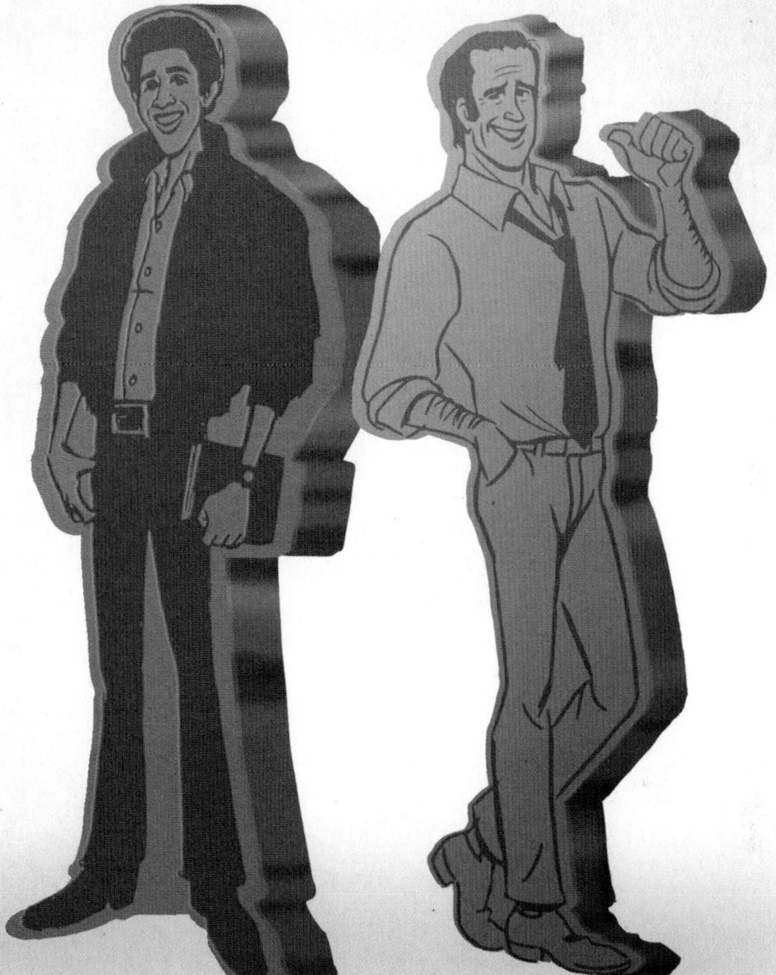

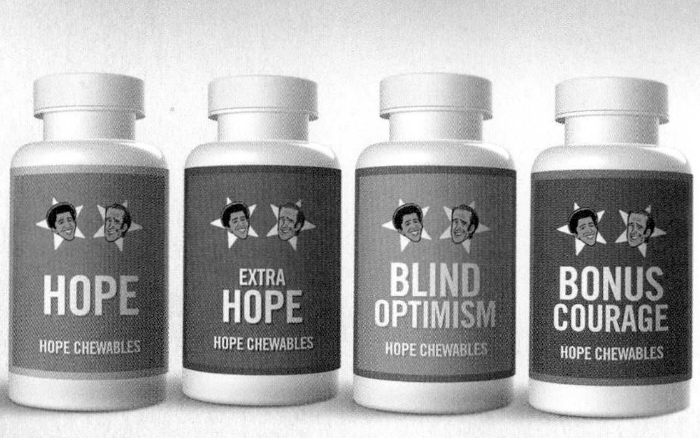
HOPE
HOPE CHEWABLES
EXTRA HOPE
HOPE CHEWABLES
BLIND OPTIMISM
HOPE CHEWABLES
BONUS COURAGE
HOPE CHEWABLES

BARRY & JOE ADULT DAILY VITAMIN
from The Adventures of Barry & Joe
**Keep conservatives out of reach.
TAKE ONE DAILY TO AVOID DERANGEMENT. DO NOT SWALLOW. MUST CHEW VIGOROUSLY.
Ask your therapist, priest, or rabbi if Hope Chewables are right for you. *Contains less than 2% actual hope.

TROUBLED TT TIMES
ADVANCED FORMULA

CHILL

# BARRY AND JOE IN THE RIBBON OF POSSIBILITY

## BY ADAM REID

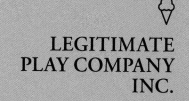 Multiverse Edition

LEGITIMATE
PLAY COMPANY
INC.

# BARRY AND JOE IN THE RIBBON OF POSSIBILITY

BY **ADAM REID**

LEGITIMATE
PLAY COMPANY
INC.

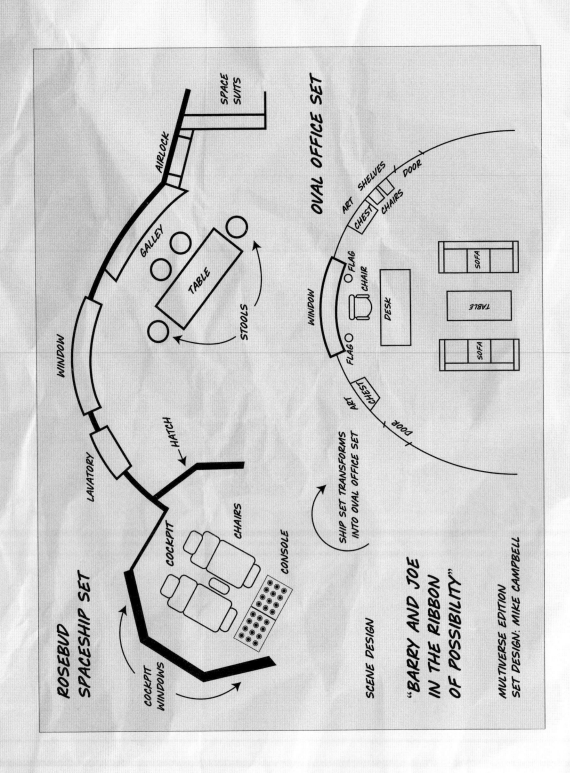

ROSEBUD
SPACESHIP SET

SPACE
SUITS

AIRLOCK

GALLEY

WINDOW

TABLE

STOOLS

LAVATORY

HATCH

COCKPIT

CHAIRS

COCKPIT
WINDOWS

CONSOLE

OVAL OFFICE SET

ART
SHELVES
DOOR
CHEST
CHAIRS
FLAG
CHAIR
WINDOW
DESK
FLAG
ART
CHEST
DOOR

SOFA
TABLE
SOFA

SHIP SET TRANSFORMS
INTO OVAL OFFICE SET

SCENE DESIGN

"BARRY AND JOE
IN THE RIBBON
OF POSSIBILITY"

MULTIVERSE EDITION
SET DESIGN: MIKE CAMPBELL

# BARRY AND JOE IN THE RIBBON OF POSSIBILITY

## ACT ONE

*AT RISE: Darkness. We hear the sound of two men laughing, hard. The sounds they are making are loud and true—the sort of laugh where the whole body shakes and we can feel the tears streaming down their faces even in the darkness. They both catch their breath, winding down—then silence and heavy breathing.*

*By this point, the curtain has been up for at least two minutes. No light, no dialogue, just the sound of two men laughing. Then nothing.*

OBAMA.    God, I wish I still smoked.

BIDEN.    Over my dead body.

OBAMA.    If that's what it takes for me to enjoy a cigarette again.

BIDEN.    That's a horrible thing to say.

OBAMA.    I loved smoking.

*A star field appears behind the silhouette of our spaceship (see diagram). We hear the ethereal low-end hum of intergalactic travel.*

*A small pool of blue light appears stage left shining on SAMUEL L. JACKSON.*

SAM.    Once upon a time they were the president and the

157

vice president of the United States of America. Then, moments after leaving office, they took off all their clothes and stepped into the Quantum Recoherence Engine together. At that moment, they would become forever entangled with each other and sent on a journey through space and time. It was there in the multiverse that they proved to be even greater public servants. Their experiences in the U.S. Senate and leading the free world had been a perfect warm-up for their new roles as time warriors. Together they leaped from dimension to dimension, from one reality to another. In every world, they looked for the best in people and worked against all odds to do the right thing—wherever and whenever they landed.

They would have thousands of adventures this way—bending history toward the light. It was a kind of change that would be real and everlasting to those lucky enough to experience it. Isn't that right, Watson?

THE VOICE OF WATSON.   When you say it, it sounds a bit pretentious and flowery.

SAM.   Hey.

THE VOICE OF WATSON.   Just keeping us grounded.

SAM.   Shit. Where was I?

THE VOICE OF WATSON.   Change that was real and everlasting.

SAM.   Right . . .

THE VOICE OF WATSON.   Ladies and gentlemen, carbon-based life-forms of all ages, how about a round of applause for the one and only Samuel L. Jackson.

*The audience applauds. Sam takes a humble bow.*

THE VOICE OF WATSON.   I loved you in *The Long Kiss Goodnight* with Geena Davis.

SAM.   I didn't ask you a goddamned thing.

THE VOICE OF WATSON.   It's your Kangol hat, Sam. . . . We're all just living in it.

SAM.   This adventure finds our heroes in deep space. The year is 2028. Barack Obama and Joe Biden set a course home, to a pale blue dot named Earth, after having successfully brought hope and democracy to a tiny planet of brilliant humanoid caterpillars. The voyage home for our cocaptains was initially a joyous one—extraordinary men living a series of extraordinary adventures, headed home at last after yet another successful mission into the deep unknown.

THE VOICE OF WATSON.   *(whispered)* That was fucking brilliant.

SAM.   Shhhhhh . . .

*The blue light on Sam dims. We are now in darkness except for the stars outside every window.*

BIDEN.   Thwitstle-ish. *(Joe laughs)*

OBAMA.   THHHH-HA. It's in the back of the throat. HA-WHISSS. HA-WHISSS. *(Barack laughs)*

BIDEN.   THHHHHEWHISS. I do it. I'll never get it.

OBAMA.   It's hard to do. I can't really get it right either. We don't have . . . insect throats.

BIDEN.   Nope.

*A long silence. Then . . .*

OBAMA.   Fired up!

BIDEN.   Fired up!

OBAMA.   I gotta pee. Want a snack?

*Obama switches a light on in the cockpit, illuminating the two men. They are dressed in modern jumpsuits that appear both comfortable and space age. NASA by way of the Gap.*

BIDEN.   Can you grab me an orange Gatorade?

OBAMA.   Joe, that's the only kind of Gatorade we have. We have enough orange Gatorade and Berry Honest Tea to last us three lifetimes.

BIDEN.   Thank you, Lord.

*Obama switches on another light that illuminates the hatch that connects the COCKPIT to the MAIN CABIN and its central GALLEY. He then flips the switch illuminating the main cabin. The hatch opens and closes automatically like the doors of a grocery store.*

*The main cabin and its central kitchen are one part International Space Station and two parts Tony Stark—space*

*travel minimalist chic. Obama crosses to the LAVATORY*
*door and steps inside. We hear the door lock.*

BIDEN.   Watson, how many hours left?

THE VOICE OF WATSON.   You don't want to know.

BIDEN.   Come on now, skip the boring math part and give
it to me straight.

THE VOICE OF WATSON.   I recommend lots of sleep.
And I have all sorts of things that can help with that.

BIDEN.   No thank you. I'm au naturel.

THE VOICE OF WATSON.   Yes, like Gatorade.

BIDEN.   Exactly.

> *OBAMA comes out from the lavatory. He stops at the*
> *kitchen to grab the drinks. He scans the kitchen for*
> *snacks and settles on pita chips and hummus. He returns*
> *carrying everything and settles back into the cockpit with*
> *JOE.*

OBAMA.   How about pita chips and hummus?

BIDEN.   Perf.

> *Barack hands Joe his Gatorade. They crack open their*
> *beverages by spinning the small plastic caps and then*
> *raise them for a toast.*

BIDEN.   I raise my plastic chalice of great orange elixir to
the tiny creatures of THA-HAWW-HAA-WHH—oh, screw
it. To humanity, a democratic universe; to you, my best friend
in the whole wide world except for my kids and Jill and my
clone of Champ; and . . . to going home.

OBAMA.   Amen, brother. To going home.

> *They drink. Barack takes a long swig. Joe crushes his*
> *completely and tosses the empty bottle. Barack glares at*
> *him.*

BIDEN.   I'll pick it up.

OBAMA.   It's cooler when we have the gravity off.

> *They eat chips together in silence for a long time.*

OBAMA.   *(finally)* What's the first thing you're going to do
when you get home?

BIDEN.   I just wanna have my feet on the ground for a
while and be with my family.

OBAMA. Me too.

BIDEN. We've done it all, man.

OBAMA. Yes, we have.

BIDEN. You know what we haven't done . . . in over a decade?

OBAMA. No.

BIDEN. We have to.

OBAMA. Hung it up. Retired. Never happening again. A magical thing locked in time, like Halley's Comet but never coming back.

BIDEN. You owe me a secret handshake.

OBAMA. I gave you the Presidential Medal of Freedom.

BIDEN. And I'd melt it down and trade it in for one more secret handshake. But we have to film it. If we don't film it, does it even exist?

OBAMA. Keep dreaming, Joe.

BIDEN. I will.

OBAMA. *(long pause)* I'm just saying . . . why ruin it by turning it into a meme? That one was just for us.

BIDEN. And I'm just saying . . . sharing is caring. *(Joe yawns. Barack catches it.)* We're like twins.

OBAMA. No, we're not. It's a yawn. You can catch a yawn. That's not a twin thing.

BIDEN. I'm just sayin' we're synchronized.

OBAMA. Not really.

BIDEN. Watson?

THE VOICE OF WATSON. Sup?

BIDEN. If Barack yawned and I yawned at pretty much the same time, does that make us mind-meld twinsies in some way?

THE VOICE OF WATSON. Yes. That's exactly how yawning works.

BIDEN. BOOM.

    *Barack hangs his head. Holds the bridge of his nose.*

BIDEN. You know how when Spock died, Kirk had to hold his soul so that he could regenerate?

OBAMA. Only vaguely. What's your point?

BIDEN.   I think that's us ever since we became entangled.

OBAMA.   Who is Spock in this story?

BIDEN.   Well, you are of course.

OBAMA.   Is there something I don't know? Am I dying?

BIDEN.   Well, no. I'm just talking about if maybe anything did happen to you, I have enough of your soul inside
me now that I could regenerate you.

OBAMA.   I know you mean well, Joe. But that's a really
messed-up thing to say.

> *Obama closes up the pita chips. He moves to seal the
> hummus with the lid.*

OBAMA.   You all done here?

BIDEN.   Wait! *(he takes a couple more full bites)* Okay, take
it away.

OBAMA.   You're getting pita crumbs all over the console.

BIDEN.   *(as he brushes the crumbs to the floor)* I'm just giving the cleanbots a sense of purpose. Hey, while you're up
can you check the airlock?

OBAMA.   Sure thing.

> *Barack seals the lid and takes the food back through the
> hatch and into the galley.*
>
> *As he does, Joe reclines in his high-tech captain's chair.*

BIDEN.   Watson, play "Clair de Lune."

> *"Clair de Lune" by Debussy begins. Obama puts away
> their snacks. He turns off the lights and checks the air-
> lock. He walks over to the window looking out over a
> star field. He stands there in silhouette for a minute and
> takes it in as the dreamy music plays. He then goes back
> through the hatch and into the cockpit, where Joe is rest-
> ing. The music swells.*

OBAMA.   *(to Joe)* I love this song.

> *Joe snores in his captain's chair. Barack takes out a space
> blanket and drapes it gently over Joe.*
>
> *Barack then walks around to his seat and eases himself
> into it. There's a late-night shuffle to his steps. He's tired.
> He reclines his chair and pulls up his own space blan-
> ket, settling in. "Clair de Lune" plays. Joe snores. Barack
> closes his eyes.*

OBAMA.    Watson, kill the lights, will ya, buddy?

*The cockpit light fades out. We are now in darkness with only space outside again. "Clair de Lune" is ending.*

*A dim blue light appears on Samuel L. Jackson stage left.*

SAM.    Two men, believing themselves to be all alone and ensconced in the comforts of first-class interstellar travel, hurtling toward a place they call home where they will be welcomed as heroes. Little did they know that they were entering uncharted territory far stranger than anything they could imagine.

*In the darkness of space, suddenly a light pulses and flickers behind the lavatory door, spilling into the main cabin. We hear the quantum sound FX, and smoke spills out from the lavatory as the door opens. In the darkness, the figure of a slender YOUNG MAN with a tight Afro stumbles out.*

*The figure finds the window that overlooks space.*

YOUNG MAN.    Oh, man. *(beat)* Where am I?

THE VOICE OF WATSON.    You are on the starship *Rosebud.*

YOUNG MAN.    Hello?

THE VOICE OF WATSON.    Welcome aboard.

YOUNG MAN.    Who's there?

THE VOICE OF WATSON.    I am IBM's Watson. I am an automatic pilot, security system, and comfort companion.

YOUNG MAN.    Where are you?

THE VOICE OF WATSON.    I am stored locally on a drive the size of one grain of quinoa. Here, let me turn on the lights for you.

*The main cabin lights come up, revealing a young Barry Obama, age nineteen. He is dressed like he stepped directly from 1980. Barry takes in the ship interior with eyes full of wonder.*

BARRY.    Far out, man.

THE VOICE OF WATSON.    You have no idea.

BARRY.    I'm Barry.

THE VOICE OF WATSON.    Barack Hussein Obama Jr., age nineteen.

BARRY.   That's super creepy, but also super cool.

THE VOICE OF WATSON.    I get that a lot.

*Barry looks around and fiddles with knobs and handles. He opens a panel revealing space suits. Barry stands back in awe. Unlike the space loungewear, these suits are meant for space walks and are sexy in a Daft Punk kind of way.*

BARRY.   Wow.

THE VOICE OF WATSON.    Are you hungry?

BARRY.   How'd you know?

THE VOICE OF WATSON.    I have sensors that can tell me all sorts of things about you.

BARRY.   That's also creepy.

*The light over the galley blinks once.*

THE VOICE OF WATSON.    In the galley we have stocked all your favorites—perhaps you'd like some chicken strips and waffle fries?

BARRY.   No way?!

THE VOICE OF WATSON.    I wouldn't lie about waffle fries.

BARRY.    I must have died and gone to space-camp heaven.

THE VOICE OF WATSON.    You're not far off, actually.

*The lights dim in the main cabin. We are left in the darkness of space and with the constant ethereal thrum of space travel. Then comes the sound of young Barry laughing.*

*Barack Obama wakes up in the cockpit and turns on an overhead light. He rises slowly. He hears someone on the ship but doesn't wake Joe. Instead, he takes a phaser gun with him and proceeds through the hatch cautiously.*

*Lights up on the main cabin as young Barry is "dance cooking" in his space suit. He holds a tray of waffle fries and chicken strips with his back turned to Obama and the audience.*

OBAMA.   Freeze.

*Barry freezes.*

OBAMA.   Set the waffle fries down slowly and then keep your hands up where I can see them.

*Barry does as he is told.*

OBAMA.   Watson, why didn't you tell me we had company?

THE VOICE OF WATSON.   This is . . . really awkward.

OBAMA.   You're damn right it is.

THE VOICE OF WATSON.   I'm sworn to protect you, Mr. President.

OBAMA.   Yes.

THE VOICE OF WATSON.   And he *is* you. And it's just dawning on me that I *might* not have been programmed for such a strong conflict of interest.

OBAMA.   Turn around.

*Barry turns around and the two Obamas are now face-to-face, one in his late sixties and the other almost twenty.*

OBAMA.   Watson, what's happening?

BARRY.   Yeah, Watson. What's happening?

THE VOICE OF WATSON.   I have sixteen hundred possible explanations.

OBAMA.   Gimme the shortest one.

THE VOICE OF WATSON. Something-something-something, temporal anomaly.

*Young Barry is not afraid of his older self with the phaser pointed at him. He walks forward to examine the older Obama.*

BARRY.   *(whispered reverence)* Old man me.

OBAMA.   Easy. I'm me. I may be a time warrior, but there has only ever been one me. Stop right there.

*Barry keeps his hands up.*

OBAMA.   Who are you? Where did you come from?

BARRY.   Look, I wasn't looking for any of this. One minute I'm in class, the next minute a U.S. senator from Delaware shows up trying to be my best friend.

OBAMA.   You mean Joe.

BARRY.   Yeah. He tells me all sorts of crazy nonsense about us being brothers and that I become a senator like him and then president of the United States. *(looks around)* I thought he was nuts. But then he started quoting me to me. Things I supposedly say in the future.

OBAMA.    Like what?

BARRY.    He said, "The best way to not feel hopeless is to get up and do something. Don't wait for good things to happen to you. If you go out and make some good things happen, you will fill the world with hope, you will fill yourself with hope."

OBAMA.    That's a good one.

BARRY.    He also said, "In the face of impossible odds, people who love this country can change it." And "Where you are right now doesn't have to determine where you'll end up."

OBAMA.    My greatest hits.

BARRY.    He told me that he needed to connect with my soul so that he could reenter the multiverse. And he kept talking to this invisible guy—

OBAMA.    You mean Samuel L. Jackson?

BARRY.    Yeah.

OBAMA.    Then what happened?

BARRY.    He took me to my bedroom.

THE VOICE OF WATSON.    I hate to interrupt, Mr. President, but we might have conservatives in the audience.

OBAMA.    Not now, Watson. Please continue.

BARRY.    *(low-end mumble)*

OBAMA.    What?

BARRY.    *(another low, unintelligible mumble)*

OBAMA.    I'm sorry. *(leans in)* I can't hear.

BARRY.    We took off all our clothes and crouched down and then pounded fists, you know, like the Wonder Twins.

OBAMA.    And then . . .

BARRY.    Then . . . I came out of your space bathroom.

> *Obama inspects the lavatory. He still has his phaser at his side pointed at Barry.*

BARRY.    Hey, can you . . . put that down?

OBAMA.    No. I cannot.

BARRY.   That's fucked up.

OBAMA.   Don't get me wrong, I believe everything you're saying to me. It looks and sounds and feels like the truth.

BARRY.   Okay then.

OBAMA.   But . . . this ain't my first rodeo. I've been burned a few times by deep fakes. Not of myself, but still. Can't be too careful. I hope you understand.

BARRY.   You hope I understand?

OBAMA.   Why don't you have a seat?

BARRY.   Naw. I'm allergic to unwarranted aggression from my future self.

OBAMA.   It's set to "nap." So even if I shot you, you'd basically just get the munchies and pass out.

> Barry takes a step toward Obama. They play a sort of mirror game, never touching, but making faces and studying each other as they pivot together.
>
> Then, out of nowhere, Barry goes for the phaser, wrestling it out of Obama's hands. As the two of them fight, we hear the tribal trumpets of classic science fiction battle. Specifically, our own version of Kirk vs. Spock, though in this case it would be Spock vs. Spock. As this battle continues . . .
>
> The lights go up on Joe Biden sleeping soundly in the cockpit.

THE VOICE OF WATSON.   Pssssssst. Joe. Wake up. We have a code plaid.

> Watson sounds a series of ear-piercing air horn blasts. Joe continues to sleep soundly.

THE VOICE OF WATSON.   Well, shit.

> Back in the main cabin, young Barry is straddling the older Obama and has now wrested control of the phaser. Obama relents, having been bested by his younger self. Now he holds up his own hands.

OBAMA.   Easy with that thing. There's a setting that turns people into kittens.

> Barry looks at the phaser and has it swiftly swatted out of his hand by the senior version of himself. Obama scram-

*bles to the gun and stuns a charging Barry, who seizes up*
*and then collapses into a cozy nap pose.*
*Obama catches his breath and considers the now sleeping*
*younger version of himself.*
*Then the stage goes black.*

**END OF ACT ONE**

# ACT TWO

*AT RISE. OBAMA and BIDEN are both fast asleep in the cockpit. In the main cabin, lightning and smoke pour out of the lavatory door, followed by 1980s Joe (late thirties). He wears a vintage suit and aviator sunglasses, which he will not take off for some time.*

JOE.   Barry?
   *Joe looks around in the darkness. He finds the great window overlooking space.*
JOE.   Oh boy.
THE VOICE OF WATSON.   Welcome aboard, Captain.
JOE.   *(whispered)* God, is that you?
THE VOICE OF WATSON.   Ha. I love that. Yes. It's me, Joe, God.
JOE.   That sounded less than righteous.
THE VOICE OF WATSON.   My name is Watson. I'm afraid my personality is an acquired taste. As our captain, you can adjust those settings.
JOE.   You're calling me "Captain"?
THE VOICE OF WATSON.   You are the captain alongside Barack Obama.
JOE.   Right.
THE VOICE OF WATSON.   There's also an older version of you fast asleep in the cockpit.
JOE.   What?
THE VOICE OF WATSON.   We're all way out of our element here.

JOE. Show me.

THE VOICE OF WATSON. This way.

> *The hatch to the cockpit blinks once. Joe crosses into the cool light of the cockpit, where both Obama and Biden are sound asleep.*

JOE. *(whispered)* It's us! I'm so old. *(then)* Will it tear the universe in half if I wake him up?

THE VOICE OF WATSON. No.

> *Joe leans down to look at himself in close range. Then he covers the older Joe Biden's mouth with his hand as he pinches his nose. The older Biden's eyes shoot open.*

JOE. Shhhhhhh. *(he points to Obama and gestures for older Joe to follow him to the main cabin)*

> *Joe Biden studies his younger self.*

BIDEN. *(like seeing a ghost)* How did you get here?

JOE. I left 2017 on January 20 and arrived in 1980 in my own younger body. When the version of Barack Obama I know didn't arrive with me, I asked the younger Barack Obama, Barry, to reenter the multiverse in his place. We took off all our clothes . . .

THE VOICE OF WATSON. This part we've heard.

JOE. . . . and ended up here. I'm looking for Barry. Have you seen him?

BIDEN. No.

THE VOICE OF WATSON. I have.

JOE. Why didn't you say so?

THE VOICE OF WATSON. You didn't ask. I'm not a mind reader. I'm just really intuitive. There's a difference.

JOE. So where is he?!

THE VOICE OF WATSON. He's napping in the pantry.

> *Joe and the older Biden find Barry tied up with space tape, napping.*

JOE. He's out cold.

BIDEN. I have just the thing.

> *Biden takes out a small vial. He waves it under the sleeping Barry's nose. Barry snaps awake instantly, gasping for air as if he's being choked.*

JOE.  What is that?

BIDEN.  Trump cologne.

JOE.  Who did this to you?

BARRY.  I did it to myself. Not me, but old me.

BIDEN.  Watson. What in the hell is going on here?

THE VOICE OF WATSON.  Some very sloppy science fiction, as far as I can tell. We have aspects of *Quantum Leap* mixed with *Terminator* and *Solaris,* with shades of *Peggy Sue Got Married* thrown in.

BIDEN.  Dammit, Watson, focus!

THE VOICE OF WATSON.  Sorry.

BARRY.  *(to young Joe)* What's going on, Joe?

JOE.  I don't really know. *(Joe unties Barry)*

BARRY.  Where's old me?

OBAMA.  I'm right here.

> *In all the commotion, the gang hasn't noticed that Obama has woken up. He has his phaser drawn and held low at his hip, aimed at the young intruders Barry and Joe.*

OBAMA.  In my defense, I thought you could be a figment of my imagination. Space can do some pretty messed-up things to your mind.

BIDEN.  *(to Obama)* Hey, boss, it's just us here. Why don't we put the ray gun down? If we are just trippin', all the more reason to ride it out and not go shooting each other.

OBAMA.  It's set to "nap." Joe, can I talk to you alone for a moment?

JOE.  Who?

OBAMA.  You. *(he points to Biden)*

> *The older Joe walks over to Barack and they huddle in the corner. Obama keeps one eye on the younger set. Throughout, Barry stretches and searches his pockets for something. Joe makes himself comfortable sitting on a stool.*

BIDEN.  You napped that kid and put him in the pantry and went back to sleep? That's cold, Barack.

OBAMA.  I don't think we know what we're dealing with here.

BIDEN.    And I see it as a kind of miracle. What are you really afraid of? If they are not us, then it will become clear, and if they are us, and I believe that they are, then we owe them everything we have to help them. And who knows, maybe we could learn a thing or two from our younger selves.

*Younger Joe starts searching through the pantry.*

JOE.    I'm starving. Is anyone else starving?

BARRY.    I was making chicken strips and waffle fries.

THE VOICE OF WATSON.    Should I fire up the instant pan?

BIDEN.    Sure.

OBAMA.    No.

BIDEN.    Do it. Make yourselves at home. I gotta talk to the chief here for *uno momento*.

*Obama and Biden head to the cockpit.*

OBAMA.    Joe. I want to go home. I don't want any more adventures.

BIDEN.    Don't you think it's a bit funny we're finally heading home and then these guys show up? What does that feel like to you? This can't be an accident. You wanna just ignore this?

OBAMA.    Kind of. Right now . . . yes. A little bit. *(beat)* I'm looking forward, not back.

BIDEN.    Let's do what we always do. Let's look for the best in this. I wanna go back in there and look myself in the eyes and tell myself that I love me, and I think you should do the same thing. Because if that is you, then that young man is capable of great things. And *our* interstellar bromance has very likely robbed him of discovering that naturally, so I think we owe him a little love and respect.

OBAMA.    Every once in a while you're very articulate, Joe.

BIDEN.    Fuck you. Let's hang out and get to know them. Who knows how long any of us are really here? And we're just lucky enough to be hurtling through the cosmos fully aware of that fact. Now we're blessed with a chance to sit face-to-face with our younger selves.

OBAMA. Maybe we should play a game?

BIDEN. I was thinking the same thing! I didn't suggest it in case you got annoyed. But we have four players!

OBAMA. Okay. I'm in.

BIDEN. That's what I'm talking about.

*Obama and Biden reenter the main cabin, where Barry and Joe are setting the table and looking for ketchup.*

BIDEN. New plan. We're gonna take things down a notch. Chicken strips and waffle fries, and then maybe a game.

JOE. I love games!

BIDEN. I know you do. You'll love this one. I'm gonna teach you a card game I invented with the boss here called the Oval Shuffle.

OBAMA. *(to Barry, earnestly)* I'm sorry I napped you and tied you up in the pantry. I'm used to having a lot of Secret Service protection and I think . . . I just feel a little exposed . . . in the vastness of space . . . and you know . . . this . . . metaphysical theater of the absurd. Can we hug it out?

BARRY. *(still warming)* Okay.

*The two Obamas hug.*

OBAMA. Let's start over. *(a warm smile)* Welcome to the future.

*The two Joes both watch, smiling ear to ear identically.*

SAM. Hold up a minute!

*The action onstage freezes and the lights go out as SAMUEL L. JACKSON appears again stage left.*

SAM. Imma let you finish. But first I gotta say, whoever dreamed this whole thing up never consulted an actual scientist. So I hope it has metaphorical value or some other dark art of storytelling, because this is some *Bill & Ted's Excellent Adventure*–level science fiction.

THE VOICE OF WATSON. And finally we agree on something, Sam. Now we can certainly make fun of it, but we also need to ride that fine line of not spoiling it for the boys.

SAM.   And so they played cards . . .

THE VOICE OF WATSON.   And ate chicken strips and waffle fries.

> Lights go up on the two Obamas and the two Bidens playing a game of their own invention called the Oval Shuffle. Obama finishes dealing the cards.

OBAMA.   . . . and then you pass all your cards every turn and we keep going. Everybody have it? Okay, fired up!

JOE.   Wait! I have no idea what's going on.

BIDEN.   Don't hold the boss up with a hundred questions. Just play once and then it's easy. I'll help you the first hand. Fired up!

BARRY.   What is this?

OBAMA.   That's a filibuster card. You play it after someone else's bill for double points. Bill like a law, not Bill like Clinton.

BARRY.   And this? *(holds up a card)*

OBAMA.   That's a Reagan. You lay out three of those, you get ten points. Any of the presidents, red and blue *both,* if you have three of them you get a second term, and everything doubles.

JOE.   I think you're just making this shit up. What's this?

OBAMA.   Oh. That's a Trump card, also known as a joker. It doesn't do anything. Just set it aside.

BIDEN.   Let's play!

JOE.   I put something down?

BIDEN.   Yes! *(peeking over at his cards)* Play the Polks . . . or just the one Kennedy you have. You got a possible blue wave there.

OBAMA.   Ready? And . . . vote! *(he plays his card and passes his hand to Biden)* Everybody put one down and pass.

JOE.   I'm still organizing my cards.

BIDEN.   They're not your cards—they're everybody's cards. You pass them every turn. *(he takes the pile)* Now they're mine.

JOE.   This game is so confusing. It's mayhem.

BARRY.   And now you take these. *(handing his deck to young Joe)*

BIDEN.  Save your Supreme Court justices! They only count in the last round.

OBAMA.  Ready . . . and . . . vote! *(Obama plays a card)* Everyone goes together.

BARRY.  I don't know what this is but I'm putting it down.

OBAMA.  Those are constituents. That strategy can work if you get a lot of them going and have the most. Now pass the cards. *(they all pass)*

BIDEN.  I'm chasing the attorney general dragon, if you know what I mean.

OBAMA.  Okay, and vote!

JOE.  Wait!

OBAMA.  Come on, Baby Joe! Pick up the pace—this game is best played snappy. *(he snaps)*

BIDEN.  Hey, back off the mini-me. It takes a minute to pick it up. He'll get there.

JOE.  My soul is only ten years younger than you. Easy on the mini-me stuff.

BIDEN.  I'm so sensitive.

JOE.  Vote! Boom. All the Bushes. Herberts over Walkers.
    *The ship is rocked and we hear a thunderous crash. All of our Obamas and Bidens are thrown in unison in the style of the original* Star Trek *episodes. They all hold on to the table except Barry, who falls off his seat.*

BIDEN.  Watson, what is it?

THE VOICE OF WATSON.  I believe we've reached the Second Act Equinox.

BIDEN.  Damn!

BARRY.  What?

OBAMA.  Something big is coming down the pike.

BARRY.  What?

OBAMA.  You've read *Moby-Dick*.

BARRY.  Of course. A whale is coming?

OBAMA.  Metaphorically.

JOE.  Stop talking and say something a regular guy like me can understand. No smarty-pants stuff. No metaphors. Just use simple words like Hemingway.

BIDEN.  I think I could talk like Hemingway, I said, as I

pushed the cards aside and stuffed another chicken strip into my mouth. And the chicken strip was good.

JOE.  Ha!

BIDEN.  Thank you. I mean me.

JOE.  Ha. You're hilarious.

BIDEN.  I love this guy!

OBAMA.  Jeez.

BIDEN.  Look at all of us hanging out together. It's a quantum bromance.

BARRY.  I'm very uncomfortable.

OBAMA.  *(to Barry)* It gets easier. But you never really get used to it.

JOE.  What happens now?

BIDEN.  We're gonna take you back to Earth and blow everyone's minds with how young and awesome you are, and you'll be the future of the Democratic Party.

OBAMA.  Joe, can I talk to you?

JOE.  Me?

OBAMA.  No. Not you. Almost never you. Him. *(points to older Biden)*

> *The older Obama and Biden step aside.*

OBAMA.  You know, when I say that I'm always looking for the next Barack Obama, I never mean *me.*

BIDEN.  Think about how cool this is. We leave on a peace mission, come back with younger versions of ourselves who go on to live another . . . how many years?

OBAMA.  I'm ready to retire, Joe.

BIDEN.  Exactly. So let the young you go kick ass.

OBAMA.  But I don't want to worry about what young me is out there doing.

BIDEN.  You don't have a choice. There he is. There they are.

OBAMA.  So it seems.

BIDEN.  So it seems.

> *Barry walks over and asks Barack straight-out.*

BARRY.  So, you two are really close?

OBAMA.  Yeah.

BARRY.    He says you're like brothers.

OBAMA.    Well . . .

*Both Joe Bidens are right there and within earshot. The older Obama is clearly on the spot.*

BIDEN.    Barack, we have to teach them.

OBAMA.    Teach them what?

BIDEN.    Our secret handshake.

OBAMA.    Noooooo. I told you. That's just for us.

BIDEN.    They are us.

OBAMA.    We're not in the Oval.

BIDEN.    Watson, put us in the Oval Office.

THE VOICE OF WATSON.    Oval office simulation coming right up.

*An LED scan flashes the entire room in one circular motion as the main cabin set rotates in the darkness. The main cabin set is replaced by the Oval Office.*

*Outside the great Oval Office windows is outer space. But in every other way this feels like the most famous room on planet Earth as it appeared when forty-four was in office.*

BARRY.    Oh, wow.

JOE.    You don't need to teach me. I *know* the secret handshake! I gotta do it! I may look like I'm in my thirties, but I'm 2017 Joe in here. *(points to his heart)* Barack, you know I know this better than he does.

BIDEN.    Bullshit. It's a privilege. I'm Biden prime. I have seniority. I do it.

JOE.    I'm in much better shape than you—no offense.

BARRY.    *(to Obama)* The Joes really worship you.

OBAMA.    I know.

BARRY.    It's a bit much.

OBAMA.    I know.

BIDEN.    Come on, boss. Let's show the kids we still got it.

*Joe Biden, the older one, walks to one side of the Oval and turns casually to Barack Obama. Obama cracks his knuckles and stretches each leg. He then goes to the edge of the desk and leans on it super casually.*

BARRY.    What's happening?

JOE.    Shhhhhhh.

*Biden walks up to Obama as if they are greeting each other. They hug warmly with two friendly pats on the back. Then they shake hands and slide into a bro grip and then they pound fists.*

BARRY.    Is that it?

JOE.    Ha.

*And then it begins . . . As Obama and Biden continue to perform a series of snaps and rapid-fire claps with their hands, their feet begin to soft shoe in perfect unison.*

*What follows can only be described as insane, full-tilt tap duet magic in the spirit of Gregory Hines and Fred Astaire, at first gentle and bromantic, then building throughout into a full-on fireworks show of synchronized storytelling. Obama's aloof quality informs his cool, relaxed style, and Biden brings his barely controlled exuberance to every step. Their styles meld as the "secret handshake" blossoms.*

*They run together toward an Oval Office couch and jump to the top as it topples onto its back. Obama then leaps onto the Oval Office desk for a solo, as Joe crouches in a quasi-Russian-style kick sequence. They tap furiously arm in arm and even sneak in a* Riverdance *moment, before breaking with precision, grace, and swagger.*

JOE.    I can't take it! I'm coming in!

*Young Joe jumps in, and Obama is now flanked on either side by the two Joes, all of them tapping together without missing a beat.*

OBAMA.    Look, we're a reverse Oreo!

JOE.    This is so righteous!

BIDEN.    Damn right it is!

*As the two Joes and Barack tap their heart out . . . they also dialogue breathlessly.*

OBAMA.    Get in here, Barry!

BARRY.    Naw. I'm good. I'll just watch.

BIDEN.    Come on! You can do it!

JOE.    Yes, you can!

OBAMA.    Once-in-a-million    multiverse    opportunity! Come on! Let's bring it home!

> *Barry jumps in and keeps up, missing a few steps as he falls in, but eventually creating a DOUBLE DUET of mirror image Obamas and Bidens.*

OBAMA.    This is the good stuff right here.

BIDEN.    May-December!

> *Biden spins off with Barry as Obama spins off with young Joe. The new pairs tap together.*

OBAMA and BIDEN and JOE and BARRY.    Big finish!

> *A Busby Berkeley side dive spectacular finds our four-some rolling into formation and finishing with an actual secret handshake, including side pounds, elbow taps, and a woodchuck. It ends spectacularly with the Obamas jumping up and into the arms of their respective Bidens and everyone sticking the group tableau—all four of them now smiling and out of breath.*

BIDEN.    That was incredible! It almost felt like we've been practicing together for months.

> *As the Obamas and the Bidens congratulate each other . . . Barry stands up. He walks to the chair and desk as if it speaks to him.*

BARRY.    *(hushed, sinking in)* I become president.

BIDEN.    Sorry, sport. Not you. *(points to the older Obama)* He became president. Your future is still unwritten.

BARRY.    But he's me! How am I not *guaranteed* to become president?

> *With this, young Joe withers slightly.*

OBAMA.    Come here. Sit down.

> *Obama sits on the Oval Office couch. Barry sits with him.*

OBAMA. Every single thing that happens to us affects our future. Every decision that we make. Always and forever. When Joe went back in time and met you in 1980, and you came with him here, your future changed. What happens to you will *never* be predestined. Time doesn't work that way.

The only thing that matters is this moment, right now. And everything that comes after is a mystery. We can only do the very best that we can and hold on for the ride.

BARRY.   I'm not the president?

BIDEN.   No. *(then)* But you still could be.

BARRY.   *(suddenly a bit angry)* But I would have been . . . if . . . *(finds Joe in the corner looking guilty)* YOU!

JOE.   Hey now. I've had lots of experience in the public sector and almost no experience time lording. If you really want to blame anyone, I would blame Samuel L. Jackson.

> *From offstage in the darkness we hear Sam chime in. He enters the set.*

SAM.   Hey?!

JOE.   It's true. I don't take a leak in the multiverse without asking you first.

BIDEN.   That's a cop-out if I ever heard one.

OBAMA.   Everybody is just trying to do the best they can with what they know.

SAM.   We're dealing with uncontrollable outcomes and the very best of intentions. What's important is that we learn from everything we do. Failure *is* learning.

JOE.   Oh, put a sock in it, Sam.

BARRY.   Is Sam here too?!

BIDEN.   Oh, right.

SAM.   He can't see or hear me.

OBAMA.   Samuel L. Jackson is a great actor who only Joe and I can see.

THE VOICE OF WATSON.   And the audience.

BARRY.   I don't want to play anymore. How do I get out of here? I wanna go back to my life in 1980. Right now. Please.

JOE.   We can't go back.

BIDEN.   When we leap, we can't control when we end up.

SAM.   Or what dimension.

BIDEN.   So we always have two choices.

OBAMA.   Stay and live out the reality we're in . . .

BIDEN.   Or get naked together and play time-travel roulette.

BARRY.    It sounds extra gay when you say it that way. *(this all sinks in)* We can't go back?

OBAMA.    Always forward. Always into the unknown.

BARRY.    But . . . I feel special. And I have . . . a fire inside me. And now I don't know what to do with it. I want to change the world; I want to make it a better place. *(to Obama)* I want to have all the experiences you had.

JOE.    I feel that way too! It's good to feel that way. We'll just have to blaze our own path.

BARRY.    You told me I go to Columbia University and Harvard. Can I still become a U.S. senator?

*The guys all look at one another, unsure how to answer that.*

JOE.    Sam, you have any insight here? Any wisdom from the set of *Do the Right Thing* you can share?

SAM. Well, the Recoherence Engine could jack your souls into the multiverse and you would emerge somewhere in the beltway of the beautiful mess, but there's absolutely no telling whatsoever when or where you would end up—which version of yourselves you would arrive in.

BARRY.    Is the ghost actor talking?

OBAMA.    Let me give this a shot. I speak some bad motherfucker. *(to Barry)* Sam says you can leap again into the unknown with Joe, but the scientists who make that possible don't know where or when you'll end up. Joe and I did that. *(points to Biden)* That Joe. And I have to tell you . . . it took us thousands of leaps to end up here, in this reality. We've finally settled here, in this timeline, where I feel we're living out our very best lives alongside the best version of Earth's future I've seen yet. Don't get me wrong. It's not perfect in this dimension. No dimension ever is. But I'm inspired by the progress I see every day. In this world we have clean energy, affordable health care, and organic cereal with our faces on it.

*Obama walks to the Oval Office window and looks out over the stars.*

OBAMA.    I believe . . . that the people of the Earth that

we're headed to will see you—young me—and they will freak out.

BIDEN.  You got that right. The second coming.

JOE.  What about me? They'd freak out about young me too, right?

BIDEN.  You're almost forty.

JOE.  Look how much hair I still have! And how handsome I am!

BIDEN.  Watson, end Oval simulation.

THE VOICE OF WATSON.  Okeydokey.

>*The set transitions back into its original starship flavor. The beam of light again wipes across the theater and audience as the set rotates.*

OBAMA.  If we go back together, they will treat you like an alien. They may treat you like an alien anyway.

JOE.  Like Superman.

BIDEN.  Can I see first team here for a minute on the mound? *(everyone looks at him, confused)* Can I meet with you and you. *(points to Obama and Sam)*

>*The three of them huddle up.*

BIDEN.  Hey, Cap. Maybe this world belongs to them.

OBAMA.  What about us?

BIDEN.  Maybe we get naked. They land *Rosebud*. What do you think, Sam?

SAM.  I was much more comfortable as a narrator.

BIDEN.  Can it work?!

SAM.  Sure! Anything is possible when you play this fast and loose with physics in the name of art.

BIDEN.  Arthur C. Clarke's third law states, "Any sufficiently advanced technology is indistinguishable from magic."

SAM.  Mr. Clarke was a great science fiction author but not a scientist.

OBAMA.  Joe, are you really sure? If we go . . .

BIDEN.  I know.

OBAMA.  It's a big decision.

BIDEN.   I know. *(pause)* Just imagine all the good those guys can do without us in the way.

*Obama leaves the huddle and walks toward Barry and Joe.*

OBAMA.   The two of you will go home in our place. You'll have to land this ship. Tell them who you really are. Tell them where and when you came from and what happened here. You're already national treasures. *(to Barry)* I have a feeling . . . you'll be able to go to Columbia and Harvard or any school in the world you want . . . and you will be welcomed with open arms. Find the experiences that call to *you*. Be humble. Be a force for good in this world . . . and never stop.

BARRY.   You have to come back.

OBAMA.   *(a heavy sigh)* No.

BIDEN.   Joe will go with you.

OBAMA.   I'm afraid this world isn't big enough for two Barack Hussein Obama Jrs.

JOE.   It would create a black hole. *(beat)* Get it? Two Obamas . . . black whole? *(all of them, including Biden, glare at the younger Joe)* I'm very sorry. This is tense.

*The lights go out.*

### END OF ACT TWO

# ACT THREE

*LIGHTS UP. The entire spaceship set is trashed. Pres-idential playing cards are everywhere. Food containers and hundreds of empty Gatorade and Honest Tea bottles litter the floor in piles and quasi-towers. There is no one, no sound, just the empty ship, empty cockpit, and the eternal hum of advanced space travel.*
*Then the airlock opens and all four boys come back in wearing space suits. They are all drunk on the cosmic high of a waltz in space together.*

JOE.   OH MAN!

BIDEN.   YESSSSSSSSSSS.

OBAMA.   Never gets old.

BARRY.   I'm really sick.
    *Barry goes to the lavatory to throw up. We hear the sounds from offstage.*

JOE.   You okay, buddy?

BARRY.   I'll be fine! *(pukes again)*

THE VOICE OF WATSON.   I'll get some extra air in here for everyone's sake.
    *The guys peel out of their space suits, revealing their jumpsuits underneath.*

OBAMA.   Wheeeeeee! Watson, how much time is left?

THE VOICE OF WATSON.   We have ten minutes left according to our original schedule, which has a window of three minutes and ten seconds in order to be—

BIDEN.   We get it!

THE VOICE OF WATSON.   Don't get snippy with me. I do everything around here and love you all like children.

OBAMA.   Battle stations, y'all.

JOE.   What about the kid?

OBAMA.   Barry will be just fine. He's clutch. Like me.

BIDEN.   I don't think he's ready for the spotlight.

OBAMA.   True. But no one is ever ready for the spotlight. Then one day, you're in it.

*At this moment Barry emerges from the lavatory a new man. He has a smile on his face and a bounce in his step. He claps his hands.*

BARRY.   Fired up!

JOE.   *(responsively)* Fired up!

BIDEN and OBAMA.   Fired up!

*They all bust out laughing.*

OBAMA.   Seriously now. This would be a great time for a good speech, but we don't really have the time. I'll keep it brief. *(to Biden)* I'm so . . . *proud* of everything we've accomplished together, Joe. And I know . . . that even though this may feel like the end, it's also very much the beginning of something new for all of us. I love you. You are like a brother to me. I'm not looking forward to having my soul torn from my physical body and compressed into transdimensional motes of spiritual energy, but I can't wait to see you again on the other side. I can only make this journey by trusting that you'll always be with me. To my young self and his Joe, I wish you the happiest of bromances. I know just how much potential for true brotherly love you both have. Be patient with the people of Earth in the year 2028. Most of them really do mean well.

*SAM appears in his original narrator position beside the stage in a pool of soft light.*

SAM.   I hate to break up the lovefest. In just a few minutes we will begin to navigate reentry to Earth. That only gives us moments to get you two out of here.

BIDEN.   Watson, play "Also Sprach Zarathustra." The seventies funk edition by Deodato.

THE VOICE OF WATSON.   An inspired choice for the occasion.

> *The track kicks in. This music will play out for the re-mainder of the play, volume building to the end.*

OBAMA.   Let's do this.

BIDEN.   Just like we practiced.

> *The men do a round of hugs. Slaps on the back. Obama and Barry. Joe and older Joe. As they walk away, Obama turns to Barry, who is on his way to the cockpit.*

OBAMA.   Hey, Barack.

> *Barry turns to his older self.*

BARRY.   Yeah?

OBAMA.   I believe in you.

BARRY.   You do?

OBAMA.   I really do. And you should too.

> *Barry lets this sink in and they share one last nod. Then . . . all business. Everyone knows what he has to do. Barry and Joe suit up and get themselves into the cockpit, strapping into their harnesses and adjusting their motor-ized cocaptain chairs.*
>
> *In the main cabin, Obama and Biden begin to take off their clothes, their rings, and, for Biden, his rosary bracelet. The guys dance a bit with the funk music space track as they strip.*
>
> *The track builds even higher. In the cockpit, Joe puts on his aviators, and then he puts on his helmet over them.*

SAM.   Is everyone ready?

THE VOICE OF WATSON.   Go for Watson.

JOE.   Go for Joe.

BIDEN.   Go for big Joe.

OBAMA.   Barack be nimble.

BARRY.   Barack be quick!

SAM.   *(now shouting over the building music)* Okay, team. This is it. Once I activate the Recoherence Engine there's no turning back.

BIDEN.   DO IT.

SAM.   I HAVE HAD IT WITH ALL THESE MOTHER-

FUCKING DEMOCRATS ON THIS MOTHERFUCK-
ING SPACESHIP. *(Sam laughs.)*
>  *Sam presses a handheld wireless trigger.*

THE VOICE OF WATSON.   Quantum Recoherance Systems activated. Ten . . . nine . . .
>  *Obama and Biden crouch down naked as the wind on-stage begins to pick up. The power is sucked out of the light in the main cabin as strobe flashes and a thick fog build all around them.*

BIDEN.   This is it!
>  *Samuel L. Jackson laughs loudly.*

THE VOICE OF WATSON.   Five . . . four . . .
>  *The wind in the auditorium is so strong that it now throws empty plastic bottles around the set and into the audience. Fog and lightning spill from the starship and the blasting music track reaches its highest peak.*
>
>  *Still crouched down, Obama and Biden pound fists as they scream in what must be the unimaginable pain of vaporizing yourself into nothing but an essence. A blinding bright white light blasts into the audience.*
>
>  *The song ends, and the bright light subsides. Then silence. Obama, Biden, and Sam are all gone.*
>
>  *In the cockpit, Barry and Joe look at each other.*

THE VOICE OF WATSON.   *Rosebud* is now entering Earth's atmosphere.
>  *A red light pours over them and into every window, followed by soft white. The ship is tossed side to side.*
>
>  *Joe laughs. It's an honest laugh. Barry picks it up.*
>
>  *The lights go out and we're left with nothing but the two of them laughing. Their laughs grow harder, louder. The sounds they are making are loud and true—the sort of laugh where the whole body shakes and we can feel the tears streaming down their faces even in the darkness. They both catch their breath, winding down—then silence and heavy breathing.*

**THE END**

# THE HALL OF
# MISSED
# OPPORTUNITIES™

The Hall of Missed Opportunities™ exists beyond space and time and has its own set of unique properties, rules, and karmic sense of humor.

It's easy to become addicted to the Hall of Missed Opportunities™.

Ask your doctor if the Hall of Missed Opportunities™ is right for you.

Once you step foot into the Hall of Missed Opportunities™, the only way out is by following through with your own missed opportunity. If you fail, you will simply start again, you know, like a video game, but with much deeper psychological consequences.

The Hall of Missed Opportunities™ is designed for one soul at a time. In other words, you may experience the Hall of Missed Opportunities™ only if you are alone. Not just literally, but figuratively too. You must feel utterly alone.

If at any time while you are inside the Hall of Missed Opportunities™ you feel anxious, sick, depressed, despondent, or detached from your body, that simply means it's working.

By agreeing to try the Hall of Missed Opportunities™, you forfeit media rights in perpetuity and in all dimensions. Enjoy!

# QUANTUM CONSCIOUSNESS FOR BEGINNERS

I t's likely that you are here because I've lost you somehow and you came here looking for answers. The much less likely scenario is that you were so entertained and enthralled by the adventures in this book that you've actually arrived at this page by virtue of reading everything that came before it. The last possibility is you're just thumbing through this silly tome and the wheel of destiny delivered you here. In any case, here you are, at the glossary.

Popular science fiction storytelling has given us near infinite ways to travel through time, each saddled by its own unique blend of paradoxical problems.

*The Adventures of Barry & Joe* takes advantage of our collective time-travel savvy and the various tropes we're all familiar with without sticking to just one. Here's a glancing, deeply abridged, and truly oversimplified look at some science and "science-adjacent" and "complete fucking nonsense" concepts that we've played with in our adventures.

## THE MULTIVERSE

The multiverse as we use it here covers parallel universes as well as alternate realities. It's a pretty big mindfuck and hard to imagine.

Multiverse theory basically says that there are an unknown number of universes and everything that happens here is just one version. There are countless other universes, countless other versions of ourselves, all existing independently at the same time. The most relatable example I can think of is the universe where Hillary Clinton won the presidency. Somewhere in the multiverse right now there's a version of you who's definitely not reading this book and is blissfully unaware of just how unreal and messed up our current reality is.

## QUANTUM RECOHERENCE ENGINES

You know, time machines.

Oddly, when it comes to time-travel vehicles, pop culture has been pretty unoriginal since H. G. Wells set the standard. We've been permitted variations like phone booths and DeLorean DMC-12s. You occasionally bump into objects with some time mojo such as a mailbox or a hot tub. But serious time travelers tend to get around in other ways.

If you're a Terminator, you have to be naked (awesome) and apparently wet (also awesome), and then some sort of time displacement technology is used. Lightning usually finishes the job. This method has a couple of fantastic benefits.

1. No need to hide your special car or phone booth upon arrival.
2. It's super dramatic and looks cool.
3. Built-in comedy. The very next story beat is always finding clothing.

The overall downside seems to be that it's a one-way trip.

And then there's *Quantum Leap,* which really belongs in its own category. Dr. Sam Beckett would leap into the body of complete strangers in the past, yet maintain his consciousness, but he would still look like the person he leaped into (except to the audience, of course). This makes even less sense than crouching down naked, but I actually love it just as much. Dr. Beckett's leaping at the beginning and end of every episode happens spontaneously, and while the show doesn't quite say it directly . . . it makes it feel like God is at the wheel, Uber-ing Sam to where things need fixing. It's terrible science on any level, but awesome storytelling.

## EINSTEIN-ROSEN BRIDGE (WORMHOLE)

A tunnel with two ends linking different points of space-time.

*Stargate, Rick and Morty, Star Trek, Babylon 5, Interstellar, Farscape,* and *Doctor Who* (the Rift) all use some variation of a wormhole. The *Portal* video games and many, many other examples from literature and comics also use this device.

So how does that work in reality? The short and very incomplete explanation is based on Einstein's *general theory of relativity,* which conceptually allows for faster-than-light interstellar travel.

A wormhole could connect extremely long distances such as a billion light-years or more, short distances, different universes, or different points in time. We don't really use the term "wormhole" at all in our adventures, but it makes me feel better knowing Einstein was on board. The truth is always stranger than fiction.

## THREAT SIMULATION THEORY

I don't know about you, but I've been having some recurring nightmares since going to bed on November 8, 2016.

Threat simulation theory is one scientific explanation for why we dream during sleep. The idea is that what we see and experience in our dreams may not be real, but the emotions we have while dreaming absolutely are. Dreams help us strip the emotion by creating a memory. Dreams emotionally prepare us for perceived threats and experiences before they happen.

As an example, say Joe Biden wakes up in a cold sweat from a nightmare about giving a speech to a huge audience of tiny hands with no bodies. Somehow that nonsensical experience is his brain dealing with anxiety and subconsciously preparing him for his real life.

## NEURALINK

Elon Musk founded Neuralink, a company that is developing implantable brain-computer interfaces. This technology is still in its infancy, but the goal is wireless communication with devices and other humans, and eventually the extension of our own biological life by merging with machines.

One way to think of this is the augmented and mixed-reality applications on our phones that show the real world but let you hunt Pokémon or place digital furniture. Now what if instead of looking at your phone or through special glasses, the merged reality is simply what you see?

On *Quantum Leap,* Dr. Beckett's only guide on his time-travel adventures is Al, "an observer from his own time who appears in the form of a hologram that only Sam can see and hear." In our stories, actor Samuel L. Jackson appears as a mixed-reality image that only Barry and Joe can see.

## QUANTUM ENTANGLEMENT

It's real and it's spooky.

Quantum physics gets weird very quickly and there are many amazing books that explain it much better than I can.

In a nutshell, entangled particles that have been separated continue to be affected by one another. Even if they are separated by a large distance. It's crazy and it's not hypothetical. Einstein himself described it as "spooky action at a distance." That's how you know something is truly gangster: it even freaks the scientists out.

## QUANTUM CONSCIOUSNESS

We have homey Deepak Chopra to thank for popularizing this one.

Quantum consciousness is also known as the *quantum mind*. This is in no way proven but applies quantum physics to understanding consciousness and suggests that the two are linked. Deepak takes that further in his book *Quantum Healing,* where he suggests that quantum entanglement "links everything in the Universe, and therefore it must create consciousness."

That sounds like woo-woo to me. At the same time, it *totally* supports my undying love for *Quantum Leap* and actually answers a lot of questions I had about how Sam would jump in and out of different bodies—so we've embraced it completely for storytelling purposes.

## PSYCHOLOGICAL PROJECTION

Most of us are guilty of this one, or at least I see it that way.

It's only human to defend yourself from your own unconscious impulses or qualities by attributing them to others.

For example, a complete shithead who is constantly lying might constantly accuse others of constantly lying. I'm not suggesting anyone in particular.

## THE SINGULARITY

Ask any futurist and they'll tell you the singularity is inevitable and coming (yet they all disagree as to exactly when).

As digital assistants come of age, I think most of us are still creeped out, but we collectively shrug and go with it.

The singularity has been given a bad name almost single-handedly by the *Terminator* films. So that narrative goes . . . artificial intelligence (AI) becomes self-aware, and that sentience leads it to kill or enslave humanity.

Isn't it at least possible that the machines will save us? Could the AI come to care for us and our planet the way a parent might a child? Just wanting what's best for it and to help it be healthy, happy, and growing. Computing power is already more organized than any of the meat-based life-forms out there. Once it becomes truly *thoughtful,* won't we be so much better off?

I believe you can quickly assess your own view of the universe by how you imagine our digital overlords. A sort of existential mood ring. Ask yourself, are the future machines good or evil? Will they see us, and what we are, more clearly than we can? What will they see?

## SIMULATION HYPOTHESIS

The Matrix, apparently, has us.

If you play video games, this one is easy to imagine. Do you believe that in the future we will be able to simulate the past? In many ways we do this already when we play games like *Red Dead Redemption* or *Call of Duty.*

The simulation hypothesis argues that future intelligence will be able to create complex simulations and that we are in fact living inside of one of those simulations at this moment.

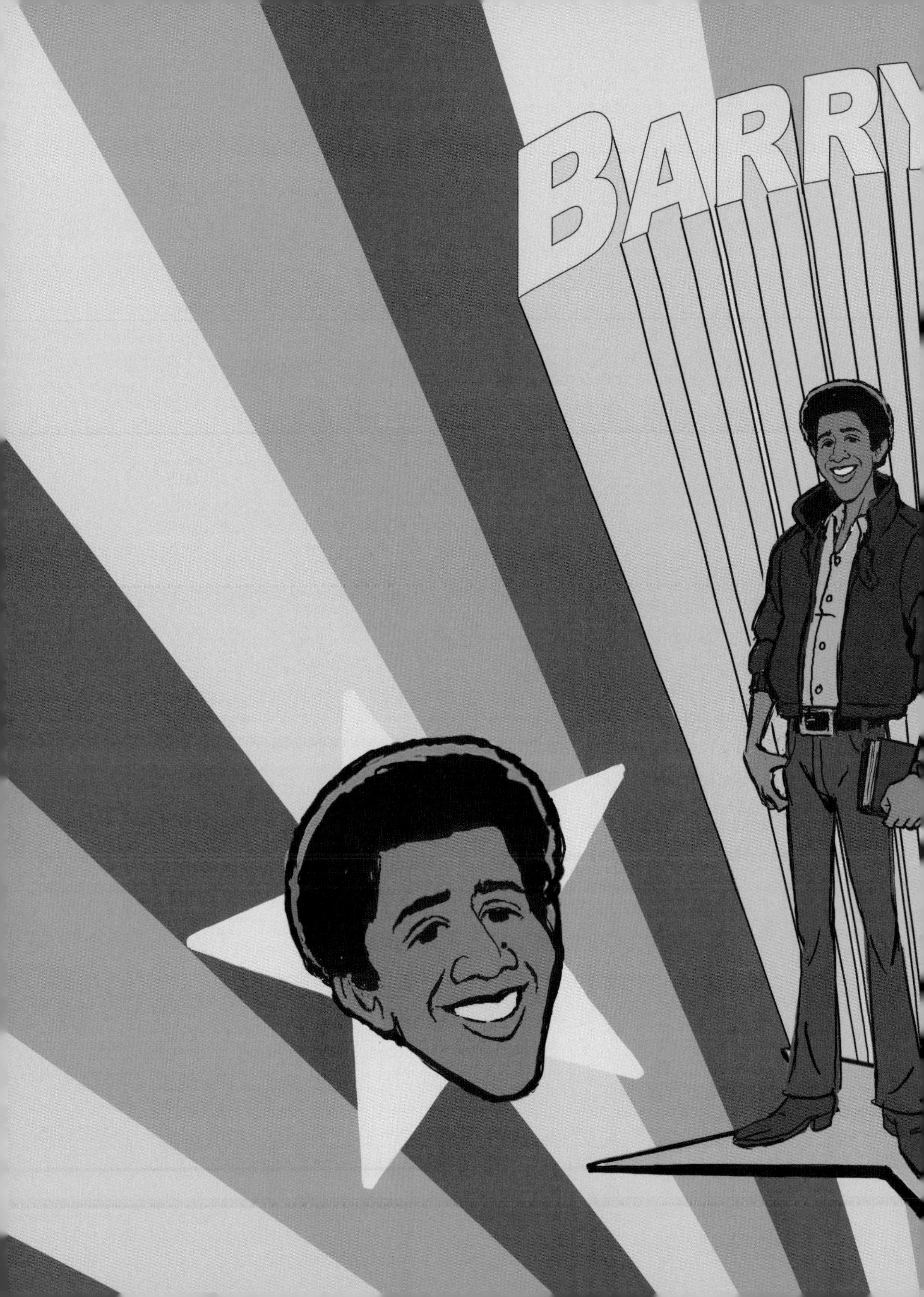
BARR

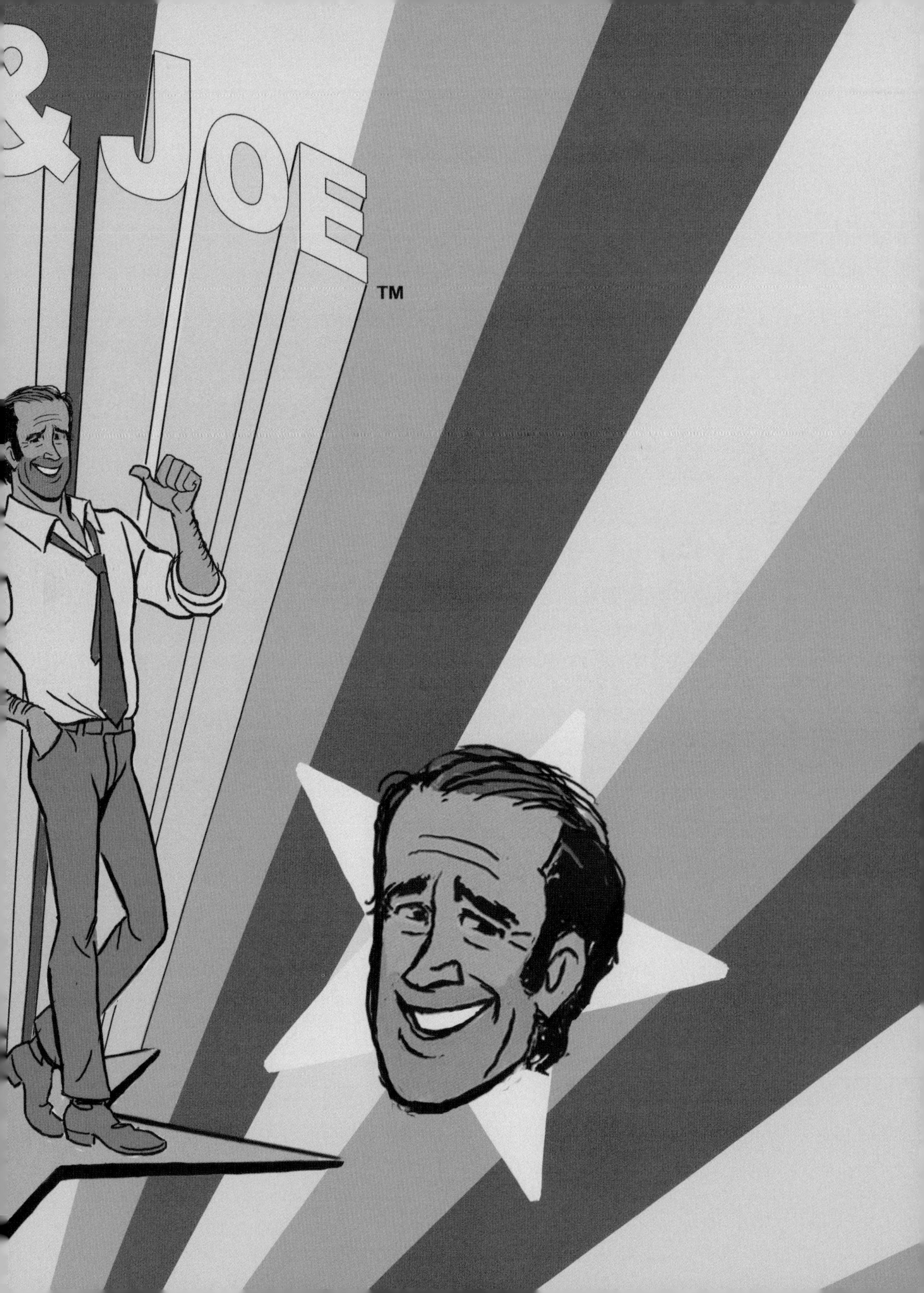
& JOE
TM

ACKNOWLEDGMENTS
AND A FEW REGRETS

T here are too many people to thank and I'm overwhelmed. My fear is I'll leave someone out accidentally and they'll be deeply offended and never talk to me again. To you, the person I forgot, I'm so fucking sorry.

Do you like reading names? Then this is the place for you. To spice things up, this has been broken down into lists, you know, like they do in the movies.

## THE FANS

This ridiculous beast started on Kickstarter where more than 1,700 people were the first to say that Barry & Joe should be a thing. This entire endeavor belongs to them.

That seed planted in the soil of the Internet has not yet become the oak we imagined it to be, but I'm so proud, and humbled, by the generous support and good vibes that grew into this, the first official Barry & Joe thing that exists in this dimension.

## SUPREME BEING AND EDITOR

Carrie Thornton

## LORDS OF MAGIC

Conan O'Brien
Lynn Grady
Anthony Mattero
Simon Greene

David Kissinger
Larry Sullivan
Chris Prynoski
Ben Kalina
Barry Kotler

## EXECUTIVE JEDIS

Erick M. Sanchez
Brette Goldstein
Juleyka Lantigua-Williams
Howard Marks
Derek Barbanti
Glenn Conte
Dariush Derakshani
Shanthony Exum
Brooke Wojdynski
Amie Ruditz

## TIME WARRIORS

Richard D. Schulman
Raph Levien
Irving Rothchild

John Sander

Ashish Naik

Tim Peierls

Charlie Cheever

Claudia Clopton

## MY PRECIOUS FAMILY

To my luminous wife, Nell . . . You fill me
with light and hope and love every
day.

My sons, Theo and Wylie . . . Be kind. Be
bold. Be you.

My mom and dad

Eddie and Karen Ingerman

My seester, Robin

Eli, Sophia, and Gilad Gour

Dave, Noami, Tomas, and Michele
Schulman

Erika and Dan Baril, Monique, Zach, and
Rupert

Uncle Gene and Cousin Melynda

Jim, Martha, and Ryan Cox

Michael and Christina Cox

Sean and Christy Yael-Cox

Aunt Beth and Uncle Steve and Cousin
Dan

Lisa Rene and Michael Schneider

## REAL AMERICAN HEROES

Barack Obama

Joe Biden

Their Families

Especially Michelle Obama and Jill Biden

Ruth Bader Ginsburg

## FOR TAKING THE WHEEL OF DESTINY

Brian Theriot

## THE TRULY AMAZING ARTISTS FEATURED IN THIS BOOK

Chris George

Robbie Williams

Andy Brinkman

Antonio Canobbio

Lance Laspina

Joe St.Pierre

Jay deFoy

Mark McKenna

Ed Laroche

James Rochelle

Thomas Chu

Ross Campbell

Keith Conroy

Court Jones

Denny Finke

Cesar Feliciano

Mike Campbell

Jason Narvaez

Anwar Hanano

Buzz Hasson

Ken Haeser

Blair Smith

Dezi Seinti

Michael Heisler

Mark Phillips

## MADE THE COMICS HAPPEN

Will Feng Super Producer @ Titmouse, Inc.

## PUBLISHERS, AGENTS, AND TREASURED ASSOCIATES

Sean Newcott

Renata De Oliveira

Suet Chong

Ben Steinberg

Kendra Newton

Maureen Cole

Jeanne Reina

Nyamekye Waliyaya

Andrea Molitor

Dale Rohrbaugh

Jamie Stockton

Alex Rice

Savannah Ward

Véridique Harari

Massiel I. Romero

Monica A. Tashman

Julie Paulauski

Lindsay Train

Charlotte Clifford

Jesse Moeli

Robin Hall

Chris Carson

Erin Tauscher

Taylor Furguson

Chris Hengeveld

Joe Boylan

Frank Farella

Jade Stickle

Mark Tyler

Bob Cagliero

Pat Carpenter

Gary Keenan

Damien Henderson

Jessy Abid

Josh Sussman

Tim Avery

Min Park

Kamon Cash

Nikki Horowitz

Jordan Tarazi

Ted Gannon

Brady Hearn

Ted Marcus

Jody Nazzaro

Meredith Nazzaro

Leona Topher

Terry-Anne Alexander

RJ Thieneman

Maddie Connors

Esther Kim

Derin Wright

Ariah Noetzel

Jason Carden

## LAWYERS!

Marc. H. Simon

Francesca Grea

## SUPER FRIENDS

Haley Geffen

Mark, Julie, Jake, and Zoe Rosenberg

Miguel Rodriguez

Derrin Williams

Kenan Weaver

Adam Schartoff

Jonathan Quick

Keith Kopnicki

Christopher Harrison

Rayna Saslove

Rob and Amie Ruditz and family

Donald and Jessica Sawyer

David and Devon Diamond

Dave Williams and Lucy Skeen

Kelly Wollschlager

Becky Morrison

Rachel Larsen

Ozi Oshiro

Andrea Struble

Evan James Blewett

Andrew Turman

Christy Mannering

Nick Cucci

Alec Isaacson and Jane Rubini

Heidi Kubit

Bobby and Dany Rothchild

Tyler Johnston

Spencer Clinton Parker

Brenda Katz

Niamh Byrne

Jacob D. Condon

Cate Donovan

Evan Innis

Lori Dalvi

Jennifer London Walavalkar

Stephen Johns

John Hardin

Clint Goldman

David Gioiella

Mark Littman

Ben Barocas

Scott and Jessica Rankin and family

Perry and Lisa Schaffer

Melissa Urena

Hannia and Jesus Elizondo and Miriam

Annie and Matthew Abate and family

Brett Rogosin

Pam and Robb Henzi and family

Arlene and Mark Lowenstein

Ben Lowenstein

Evan and Tabitha Blewett and family

Penny and Bill Blewett

David and Michele Richman and family

Beth Eiserloh, Wyeth, and Orno Johnson

Kris Walter

Mike and Jessica Kelly

Anthony Trama

Ben Orisich

Tawd Beckman, Trish, and Liam

Alexej Steinhardt and family

Brett Rogosin

Jon Sandberg

Paul Katz

Drago Sumonja

Eric Singer

Carlos Fernandez

Jason Pinto

Eric Estur Romero

Mike Ball

Michael Batshaw

Harry, Becki, Emily, and Irma

Sabrina Lloyd

The Brooklyn Boys

Evan Jake Cohen

David, Heather, and Henry Kovall

David, Michele, Eli, and Max Richman

Dr. Alli Fox

Courtney McLean

Justin Seeley

Brett Jackson

Marti Jo Pennisi

Jenni June and Tom Wilson

Jonathan Hull and family

Wendy Jacobs

Jaime and Jon David and family

Amy Vincent

Barry Cooper

Dan and Yvonne Pasquini

Brida Brando

Lisa White

Orit, Stephanie, and Olivia

Hila Katz and family

Lynn and Ron Cohen

Trish Govoni

Emily Jackson

Ryan Flynn

Zvee and Noah and Mila and Gizmo
   Geffen

Molly Ann

Kelly Pratt

David A. Schulman

Kathy and Matt Squires

Megan Davidson

Jane Julian

Alexander Pacion

Drea Clark

Andrew Cox

Josh Shadid

Pat Giles

Manny Galan

Adam Saks

Jeremy Levine

Kate Dawson

Wendy Spero

A.D. Oppenheim

Dan Goldman

Rich and Megan Howard and family

Susan Friedberg

Sara Jean and Matt Young

Christoph Baaden and Anna Campbell

Gail and Marc Kubit

Amy and Ken Basset

Jeffrey Meese

Carl Laudan

Robin and Bryn Skibo-Birney

Beirne Lowry

Frederic Du Chau

Devin Martin

Elaine and Harvey Rogosin

Rabiah Troncelliti

Joy Meserve

Jessica and Aaron Hitchcock

Elizabeth Gaffney

Danielle Stein Chizzik and family

Karen and Steve Edelman

Jennifer Bass and family

Nancy Rosenberg

Jonathan Wysocki

Rich and Shana Boniface

Corey Fine

Debbie and Marc Lemchen

Tammi Leader Fuller

Jen Stralla Chaney

Michael Novello

Robyn Shapiro

Chris Caddell

Andy Milkis

Jennifer Thompson Trepanier

Jesse and Erin Dimick and family

Rebecca Richman Cohen

Robin Taubman

Anne and Bart Sussman

Siu Lo and family

Nora Singley

Nyna Weatherson

Jonathan Harford and family

Danny Erker

The Tiny Chef

Oz

# DIGITAL PRODUCERS @ KICKSTARTER

George Trombley

Brian K. Petitt

Julio Cabral

Ryan Borgdorff

Chris Parmelee

Philip E. Beshara

Sheena Kadi

Jason Borges

Kelly Westlund

Revleen Falcon

Nicolas Michaud

Samuel Lee

David Brown

Bonnie Paul

Jason Broussard

Lisa Pagniucci

Beau Gallegos

Leanne Kunze

Nick Cregan

Dustin Venecia

Sarah Burris

Alison Sainsbury

Michelle Neuringer

Craig Grunewald

John Russell

Christopher Shannon

Richard Konopka

Lois-Anna Kaminski

Jeremy Baker

Benjamin Bryant

Danielle Duchaine

Lee E. Moder

Gary James

Robert West

Lee Fink

Dan Martin

Jose A. Diaz

David Schulman

Ali Kilinc

Marina Beke

Jonathan Ong Yao

Kimberly Rubin

Jonathan M. Williams

Stephanie Kajpust

Jennifer Fjelstad Smith

Joan Russell

Gary Gordon

Jeani Murray

Lynette Rawlings

Alexandra Hammond

Jake Hite

A. Williams

Mark Anthony Stephens

Corrie Hoogstra

## COMPANIES WE ARE GRATEFUL FOR

HarperCollins Publishers/Dey Street
 Books

Creative Artists Agency

Kickstarter

Conaco

Titmouse, Inc.

Bodega Studios

Northern Lights

SuperExploder

Mr. Wonderful

Fox Rothschild & Associates

Independent Comic Book Review

Lantigua Williams & Co.

## CELEBRITIES I DON'T KNOW BUT WILL TAG HERE LIKE THIS IS INSTAGRAM

Samuel L. Jackson

Chris Pine

Dwayne Johnson

Olivia Wilde

Trevor Noah

Seth Meyers

Ellen

Spike Jonze

Stephen King

J. K. Rowling

Paul Thomas Anderson

Michael Chabon

Jane Goodall

Will Vinton

Katherine Dunn

The Muppet Performers

Farquar Esplanade

Kevin

Lady McFabulous

Shmidt Nicebottom

Woofie Senior

Woofie Junior

The Peanut

Floyd Doppler

## NAMES CHANGED TO PROTECT THE POLITICALLY AVERSE

Elmore Fantoogie

Schmeckle Clobberstein

## PEOPLE I WILL LIKELY MEET AFTER THIS WRITING BUT OBVIOUSLY OWE EVERYTHING TO

You know who you are.

# ABOUT THE AUTHOR

1988                    2018

Adam Reid is a creator, writer, and director best
known for his award-winning feature film *Hello
Lonesome* and high-end commercial work.
He cofounded the production company and agency
Bodega Studios. Adam is also the writer and
an executive producer of *The Tiny Chef Show*,
a stop-motion cooking show for humans of all ages.
Adam lives with his wife, two sons, and a collection
of beloved Muppets.

**DEY ST.**

Additional illustrations:
Title page by Aleksandr Andrushkiv; dedication page by
rebeshkovmaxim; table of alternate realities by vectorplus;
chapter opener radial lines pattern by jirawat phueksriphan;
chapter opener dots pattern by Kolonko; wrinkled paper in
script pages by Nenov Brothers Images

HarperCollins books may be purchased for educational, business, or sales
promotional use. For information, please e-mail the Special Markets
Department at SPsales@harpercollins.com.

FIRST EDITION

*Designed by Renata De Oliveira*

Library of Congress Cataloging-in-Publication Data has been applied for.

ISBN 978-0-06-288290-5

19 20 21 22 23    WOR    10 9 8 7 6 5 4 3 2 1